'As compulsive as it is shocking . . . a brilliant debut – the best
Irish one in a strong year'

Irish Examiner, Books of the Year

'Remarkable . . . the book's great achievement is to demonstrate
how, in the face of death, atrocity and extraordinary dysfunction,
the normal activities of life proceed'

Irish Times

'Captivating characters and stunning storytelling'   Jan Carson

'Exceptional . . . Fitzsimons is an incredibly skilful writer who
infuses every scene with depth of feeling and authenticity'

Irish Sunday Independent

'A beautifully structured, compulsive, sensual, and sometimes
raw read . . . a huge achievement'

Niamh Boyce

'Sexy, outrageous, yet heartbreakingly tender'   Michelle Gallen

'Alive with teenage desire, frustration and anger turned inward'

Irish Independent

'Dazzling . . . [Fitzsimons is] a writer of immense talent'
Danielle McLaughlin

'An uncompromising, lyrical tour-de-force that marks the arrival of an extraordinary new voice in Irish fiction'
Ulster Gazette & Armagh Standard

'A brave, essential book . . . beautiful'   Luke Cassidy

'Brilliantly observed, smart, bold, funny mad and devastating'
Elaine Feeney

'Lyrical and explosive in equal measure, this book pulses with love and loss'   Sheila Armstrong

'Arresting'   *RTE Guide*

'Olivia Fitzsimons writes about things that most of us are not able to think about. It is almost as if she has excavated this story from one of the most inaccessible parts of the Irish psyche'
Louise Nealon

'A courageous and openhearted testimony to an unsung generation'
Alan McMonagle

'An enchanting, coming-of-age debut'   *Image*

The Quiet Whispers Never Stop

Olivia Fitzsimons

JM ORIGINALS

First published in Great Britain in 2022 by John Murray (Publishers)
An Hachette UK company

This paperback edition published in 2023

1

A CIP catalogue record for this title is available from the British Library

Paperback ISBN 9781529373592
eBook ISBN 9781529373608

Typeset in Sabon MT by Manipal Technologies Limited

Printed and bound in Great Britain by Clays Ltd, Elcograf S.p.A.

John Murray policy is to use papers that are natural, renewable and recyclable products and
made from wood grown in sustainable forests. The logging and manufacturing processes are
expected to conform to the environmental regulations of the country of origin.

John Murray (Publishers)
Carmelite House
50 Victoria Embankment
London EC4Y 0DZ

www.johnmurraypress.co.uk

Daughters, stay difficult

'Do I want any of this? The heartbreak of this place?
Love it and hate it like no place else on earth.'

Beth Winters,
Death and Nightingales by Eugene McCabe

'She's been everybody else's girl
Maybe one day she'll be her own'

'Girl', *Little Earthquakes*, Tori Amos

A Seven Day Week, the Sun and the Moon

Sam, 1994

Difficult. She is fed up hearing her da say it. Such a difficult girl. He never asked for such a difficult girl. All the bloody time, all she gets told, is that she's spoilt rotten. That Patsy indulges her too much.

It didn't matter if it was true or not.

Like her mother, she supposed.

She considers if the good-looking fella that watches her is difficult too. He looks like he might be.

He's older, much older than the other boys, schoolboys she knows fairly well, who swing alongside her talking about gigs, or discos, or some other shite. He just sits outside the library in the centre of Downpatrick holding court over a pathetic kingdom of dole-heads, but still, he is king. His eyes hold the movement of cats, liquid, shimmering pools of darkness, his hair jet-black, jaw a pencil stroke against his neck. There is something so jagged about him it makes her laugh nervously to think about it. She knows of his friend Murph, who has all the sharpness but none of the swagger, not solid enough yet; he is just another lanky man-boy whose ambition outgrows his image of himself daily. It must be strange, she thinks, to imagine yourself one way and find yourself another.

Her school is always going on about knowing yourselves. Like any of them do. She changes her hair colour with cheap dyes every few months. Just to pretend. She knows less than most who she is. Lacking in something.

This guy knows himself, that much is obvious. He is certain, like the days of the week. You have a name for those twenty-four hours but the shape, the form they might take, those hours, minutes, seconds, you never know, they constantly surprise you. They arrive each week, like it or not, and you have to live them, over and over again.

Patsy's Side of the Mountain

Patsy, 1982

Everybody knew Fionnuala was a highly strung woman but Patsy loved her. Always did, always would. Maybe he should have told her more often, but he was not one for much talking. Not much for a drink either, and that made him what, odd? Because he was a Pioneer and went to Mass every Sunday and could still outrun a man twenty years his junior. The papers said he was a karate champion. Karate. What kind of stupid ignoramus printed that? Couldn't get their facts right. Judo. It was the judo that he had the black belt in.

That morning he'd gone out to bring the cows in as usual and taken the wee lad with him. Patsy John loved the cows. He could see the gentleness in his son's hand, steady, measured even as a toddler. He'd be a good farmer one day. Take over the place, not that there was much left to manage. Most of it had been frittered away before he bought if off his soused brother. He carried the wee lad down on his shoulders in the early light, one hand on the boy, the other held tea. Patsy threw out the drop of cold tea from his tin cup as they arrived in the shed, wooden slats barely visible against the upcoming sky, darkness spread thick, still refusing to give way to morning. He sat the wee fella down on the corner of the pillar. Usually it barely took a call for the cows to arrive in, driven by routine and the smell of their masters, but that morning, there was a desperate lowing. The cow in calf stayed in the corner of the field, a few others gathered round her. He knew rightly she must a needed help, knew from the sound of her, but he got the rest in first and sorted them for milking as quick as he could.

3

Patsy thought about going up to the house and getting his wife but then the daughter would come and she was so skittish, nothing would settle around her. So instead he tucked the wee boy under his arm against him, his hip flask of a child, and marched down towards the cow thinking his son would remember this, the smell of birth and the feeling of easing a living thing into this world. That was something, really something that. The real cut of that. They would always have this together, even if his son didn't remember and even if Patsy eventually forgot.

Except the cow did not look so good when he got there, lying on her side, low low breaths. Dangerously low. He placed his son tenderly on the ground beside her head and the child instinctively put his small hands on her face, rubbed their length down her nose, like a little prayer, and he smiled at how right he was about the boy. As he did so he felt the warm ooze along her belly, slick on his hands. She was roughly sliced, not wide open, but enough. Patsy reached down and found the water bag but nothing else, no calf. He felt the boy beside him then. The little impatient kick of his wellies on Patsy's shin. He looked down and saw they were both standing in a thick pool of blood, his son's too-long pyjama bottoms soaking it up like a paper towel on a kitchen spill. The child reached down to touch the redness, Patsy snatched him up too late, felt his son's wet fingertips around his neck.

The light was coming up and around now as Patsy searched the field for her newborn calf. In the half-light he saw a broken outline, a heap of deformed flesh. The animal's limbs contorted into an unnatural mess. Destroyed. He backed away. Headed towards the shed. All the time holding his son rope-tight.

When they got there, Patsy fished a sweet from his coat pocket and bribed the boy to stop the onslaught of tears. He took him to the tap outside. There was a nub of soap hanging on mangled blue binder twine by the wall but not enough to get the blood from the cracks of both their hands. He focused on washing his son's soft, tiny palms. Checked the animals again. He figured

4

whoever did this was long gone. He went to the locked cupboard, his fingers scrabbling for the hidden key, relieved as he felt its dusty edges, nothing disturbed, fetched down the shotgun and loaded it carefully. The boy watched him religiously. Every click and lever made his eyes pop.

It was never the right time for this but he took his son's hand and they strode back across the field, lit by a sun rising so bright it made his eyes water. That's what he told himself. He had never enjoyed this part. Putting something out of its misery. He was glad his daughter was in her bed asleep. Sam would have made a scene. She'd be five soon enough but that girl would have been curled up inside her mother still, absorbing all the love Nuala had to give, if PJ hadn't needed the space in his mother's belly. Sam was soft. His son too, but that would be gone now. Two was young but he'd been about the same age when they'd put down his father's horse. It was his father had done it. His da cried after and Patsy never saw him shed a tear for another living thing.

He reached the cow, felt her breath almost gone now. Seemed a shame to waste a cartridge but still, she could go on for another hour like this. The boy was talking to her, singing something soft and low. 'Old MacDonald', he thought.

Say goodbye now, son, he said. The boy's puzzled face shot up, holding all the innocence he would ever have in that moment. Patsy swept him up with one hand, shoved the boy between his legs, trapped him, the child squirming, then without pause cocked the shotgun and fired.

The echo of the shot mingled with his son's shocked cries, fear giving way to sobs, but it was done.

Away on a'that. There's not a thing wrong with you. You're alright.

Only his mother would do now. Only his mother would stop the bawling. The wailing of his children was a thing Patsy could not abide.

*

5

As Patsy approached the house he started to swear blindly. There were no lights on: normally there would be, with Radio Ulster blaring in the background. The last few days bulletins had all been about devolution, whatever that meant, and DeLorean laying fellas off. Maggie preaching war at home and abroad. The Falklands. The country was going to hell in a hand cart. Reporters always topped and tailed with bloody headlines: Belfast, Derry, some wee townland that had suffered, the usual Troubles litany of shootings, bombs, obituaries. The latest Catholic or Protestant person to die. Local traffic. He hated listening to them city people and their lazy tongues, ready to give away all their secrets to whoever asked. Spilling their guts while you tried to eat. Patsy wanted breakfast waiting on him, some tea and bread at the very least, the house warmed up and Nuala to take the boy away and soothe him, return him settled. He didn't want to have to see to these things, these woman's things, himself.

He noticed the back door slightly ajar then; he knew he had not left it that way. He was a man certain in his way of doing things. He had not left the door open.

He whistled for the dog to come. She was old and so he let her lie in with the wife in the mornings and only took her down to the fields on the second run. An indulgence to be sure, but a new pup meant the end for her and he wasn't ready for that yet. She did not come and he left the bawling boy on the step and went to her box, and that's when he felt his heart stutter. The dog wasn't there but he could see blood glistening on the grass.

He hadn't checked on his wife and daughter before he went out. Fionnuala slept too often in the spare room for his liking. That morning her side of their bed had been cold again.

She must be in with the girl. They must be okay.

He picked up the boy and walked into the kitchen shouting, Fionnuala. Fionnuala! Trying to tie up the concern in his voice with well-worn irritation. He saw it then, a letter lying flat on the kitchen table, an envelope beside it, ripped open.

He picked them both up. The envelope, pale and white and addressed to him. Patrick. His wife's dainty penwork, cursive letters in black ink. Her trademark slash underneath his name, cutting open an unsayable worry in him. He hadn't had time to even sit down this morning when he took PJ out with him. He hadn't noticed it.

He began to read, couldn't stop, his body crumpling into a seat as he started to understand.

Loowit/Fionnuala

Nuala, 1981

Patsy has started getting the paper delivered as a treat. It is sweet really, he knows I love to read, and I suppose it is his way of keeping me satisfied, in touch with the outside world – while my inner life leaks out of me like excess breastmilk.

I know he thinks I should stop. That I'm too attached. To the children. What he means is that I'm not attached enough to him. Men. They love the idea of things. The dream of a thing. Not the mess; not the lived-in, insomniac chant, the stink of raising their *want*. They want children and then they don't. They want you to open your mouth, then they don't. They long for offspring, mini versions of themselves, little men to take over, little girls to give away. They long for the future, they ignore the now, the present, the need, the lack. They just keep moving forward, while we are expected to stand still. Wait. Never catch up.

I want more.

I am not expecting a visitor when I answer the knock on the door with PJ attached to me. Patsy, the dope, has forgotten as usual to tell me anyone was calling.

An hour earlier I'd been sitting in a shallow bath with my children, trying to ease the relentless wave of tiredness, while Sam's hair fanned out like sea grass and suddy droplets ran off PJ's plump little stomach when he kicked his legs. Sam protested as I got out with her brother, the water gone cold like my coffee. Afterwards she fought sleep, her damp face defiant. Her grizzly cries ate at me, she wanted me all to herself. I waited to check on her. Dressed her little brother, let her self-soothe, like the book said, even if it felt wrong. I was so tired. I put PJ in the bouncer, went into her, felt her little hot breaths on my fingertips, settled at last.

Will I put clothes on today for a change? What do you say, baba? PJ sucked his fingers and watched me with big eyes as I pulled out an expensive flowery dress I loved. The coloured material seemed inadequate held against a body bowed to motherhood and all its scars, but when I slipped it on I fitted into a younger, brighter, carefree version of myself. He cooed at me. My easy baby. I hate that term but it's true. I lay on the floor beside his giddy, moving chair. Suddenly I didn't look as bad as I'd felt in months but then he reached for me, his cry demanding, and I was a mother again, the feeling I had for myself lost. I fell asleep nursing PJ on the floor.

The knock wakes me up. When I open the door the baby moves off me to look at our visitor: a youth, who sees my nipple, hard dark open, a trickle of milk rolling down my breast. His eyes sweep down to take me in, but he isn't embarrassed, gazes at me, openly curious. It feels like being seen again. The timid redness barely touches his sallow skin, but those eyes – brown and endless, as he steps closer, reaches up and motions to pull the dress around me.

I instinctively catch his fingers. Grasp them just for a moment. He doesn't pull his hand away. The gentleness of his touch, it strikes me as so perfect; beguiling tenderness from a breeze of a boy.

There is only the breadth of the baby between us. He comes in kissing close, then hands me the paper, eyes firmly on mine. It is all there then. All of what might become; right there in that moment, we both decide what is going to happen. That sun-speckled morning is the start.

My Pet Lamb at the Rock Garden

Sam, 1994

I need to pee, Sam says.

Can't you hold it? Gav replies.

For three more hours? All the way to Dublin?

Why don't you just piss in a bottle or something? I heard you're dead bendy in places. Gav laughs and clocks James in the rear-view mirror. James waves his bottle and the boys crack up, laughing so hard the spots on their teenage jawlines might burst.

Becca, you wanna tell your boyfriend to shut up or I'll take a piss in his ma's car?

Dirty minger.

Stop the car, Gav, Becca says. Look, there's a gate.

Gav does a ridiculous swerve off the road, stones flying up.

Sam rolls her eyes as Becca lets her out of the car. You're comin' with, she says, grabbing Becca's arm.

They climb over a farm gate into a huge barren field and make their way up along the top, in the gap between the stubble and the hedges. It's already dark. The ground is rock hard, solid. January cold.

Sam just stands there, pulls her huge red scarf around her face.

I'm not going with James. Can't believe you dragged me along for this.

Keep sketch, Becca says as she hunkers down. It's a free ticket. He's not *that* bad. He's pretty nice. And, he really likes you. Becca fixes herself quickly, shivering with the cold. Plus, Pet Lamb are class.

He's like a fuckin pet lamb, Sam says back. Nice. Boring. Baa, baa, baa—

Becca laughs. Look, I'm not saying if you meet someone you have to stick around but just be nice. For me.

You mean for Gav?

Sam, come on. Just this once.

I'm not snoggin his friend. Okay?

Okay. Fine. Do you know they call it shifting down here?

Shifting?

Yeah. Like you're furniture.

Gross.

You going or what?

Piss. Off! That travel prefect badge is gone to your head. Sam makes a face as she pulls her knickers down and pisses onto the cold ground.

You don't need to watch me.

Hurry up, I'm freezin!

Go on then. I'll catch up.

Lift it and shift it! Becca says as she picks her way over the stubby field. Sam catches her up as they approach the car.

What were you doing? Building a toilet? Gav says as they climb in.

No, your mausoleum, Sam says smiling, and opens a bottle.

Wha?

Grave. Your grave. We were digging your grave.

Ha ha, watch yourself, Malin. You say that shit to the wrong person and it won't be my grave you're worried about.

Christ almighty, chill out, you two, Becca says.

They drive in silence for a bit.

Sam necks two beers in quick succession, then reaches across James and into the front between Becca and Gav. She changes the station until she finds something she likes, blasts Björk's 'Big Time Sensuality' as loud as she can.

Dublin is excited. Like it's on a permanent night out. Tall, showy and bright. Buildings bullying each other for room, people thronged together, spaces swelling with noise and dirt. Everything so different from the North.

11

At this time of night on Saturday, Belfast city centre would be dead. Everyone stays in their patch. Living late-night legacy of the Troubles bullshit, but it's not really a legacy – the Troubles haven't ended – more like a bad hangover. The kind that starts you drinking again, just to get over it. Putting it on the long finger, you still have to deal with it but just not yet. Troubles haven't gone anywhere even if peace hangs around like a bad smell on the tongues of politicians, mouth washed of the unpalatable aftertaste till they start talking again.

Dublin is different. You can go anywhere you want. Still, Gav takes a few wrong turns as they make their way along busy streets, Becca giving the finger to taxi drivers beeping at their Northern reg. They park near Whelan's, in a warren of posh streets with perfect little redbrick houses one minute and concrete-cradled flats the next, the city changing mood as they walk down George's Street towards Temple Bar to the Rock Garden.

Not a chance, boys, the bouncer says, before they even get to the door. Sam has hung back slightly, notices a skinny fella looking over, dissecting. He looks familiar. She watches him nudge his mate, but Becca pulls her away before his dark-haired friend turns around.

Gav and James wave their fake IDs and the bouncer laughs. Not tonight. And I don't want to hear a sob story. You're not getting in. End of.

Girls, how's it going? The skinny fella comes over, arms around Sam's and Becca's shoulders as if he knows them. Derek, he says to the bouncer, what's the story?

Chiz. You know these chancers?

Aye. Course I do. Rest of the lads inside?

Upstairs bar.

Cheers, mate, Chiz says.

Derek looks the girls up and down, finally says, Come on, then.

Sam goes to open her bag for the bouncer but then remembers they don't check bags for bombs across the border. Only at home. She closes it again. Doesn't want to look like a dick. Chiz has slipped his arm around her and she sees Becca whisper something to Gav, then Becca takes Sam's hand and they head in, under Chiz's steam, leaving James and Gav behind, heads bent, staring angrily at the wet cobbles shining on the street.

It's darker inside but when they get down the stairs the girl on the ticket desk is lit up like a Madonna. She has tattoos inching from her skull around her face, twisted petals on a pretty flower, black-lined cat eyes, the rest of her jet hair slicked back into a high pony.

Sam can see Chiz is pleased with himself even in the smoky gloom of the basement bar.

Thanks might be in order, he says, leering at her as she unwinds her scarf from around her neck and stuffs it in her bag.

Thanks . . . Chiz . . . is it? Becca says warily. Where's the bathroom?

Over there. Chiz points past Becca. You wanna drink . . .?

Sam. It's Sam. Sure. Vodka tonic.

I'm gonna go out and let the boys in, Becca whispers. Gav's waiting on me. You okay here?

Sure. Don't be too long though, will ya?

Ten minutes. Tops. Becca is already gone.

The place is buzzing. What does your friend want? Chiz says, turning from the bar.

Same for her. Please. Don't I know you? You from the town?

Yeah. Small world. You're at The Sisters of Suck Em and See, right? Chiz says straight-faced.

For my sins, yeah.

Chiz grins and lets out a small chuckle.

You work down here?

Taking some time off at the moment. Sabbatical, you could call it. I'll get these, your money's no good here.

She insists on paying for the next round but Chiz blatantly refuses so she downs Becca's vodka in one. He hands her another. The support act come on. Becca still hasn't come back.

Chiz's mates arrive. She knows them all to see but has never spoken to any of them. He takes her over and introductions are

13

made: Murphy, and a few older girls whose names she doesn't bother to remember. Murphy goes to the tech across the road from the bus station in Downpatrick. He's a regular fixture. Cousin of one of the girls in her year. Good few years older than them and always stoned.

Where's Naoise? she hears Murph ask. She likes the sound of this name. Nee-sha.

Chiz shrugs. Upstairs. Some bird. Says he'll be down later.

Then the band comes on. The lead singer like a trainee Michael Hutchence. They're good. Everyone surges forward. She drinks another vodka. Accepts Becca isn't coming back. Figures she'll meet them back at the car. The usual back-up plan for when they get split up. She has another vodka. And another. He's buying. Or one of his friends. They seem to know everyone. Time swells.

And then he sticks his tongue in her mouth.

What the fuck? she says.

You think those drinks were free?

What?

Tease.

What?

Can't you take a joke?

Fuck you.

She shoves Chiz hard and he lands on his friend Murphy, who looks so surprised she starts to laugh even though she's raging. She forces her way through the pit, easy when you're as tiny as she is to melt into the smallest spaces.

At the top of the stairs she bumps straight into someone.

Hey, he says, his accent a mirror of hers.

Hey yourself, she slurs, barely looking at him as she dodges on past and up the steps and is out on the street in seconds. The air is cold, fresh, wide. She pulls her scarf out of her bag, twists it around her neck and head, a cocoon, and starts to walk up the cobbled road to Dame Street.

Ten minutes later, she walks into Roma for chips. Hopes Becca might be there. She isn't but it's still early. Eleven thirty.

Nurses some warmth into her body from the proximity of the fryers, luxuriates against the silver hoods and chats to the chipper woman. The woman gets Sam a cuppa while she waits. Sam loosens her scarf and sips the tea while they listen to the fish batter singing with the fat.

Later she leans against the wall at the side of Whelan's, eating her chips, the harsh hot vinegar finally destroying the bad taste Chiz left in her mouth. There are a few other stragglers about. Strangers. Pissheads. A girl fighting with her boyfriend.

Hey.

She straightens when she hears the accent. Hey yourself, she thinks.

A dark-haired man approaches. The guy who sits outside the library. The guy who seems so certain of himself. Up close he is handsome in a way that you can't miss.

Becca's friend, right? Sam?

Yeah. And?

He holds out her scarf in his hand. This yours?

Shit – Sam reaches to her neck – yes. Where'd you find it?

Just outside the chipper.

He hands it to her. She winds it around her neck one-handed.

I'm Naoise. He reaches out his hand. The sound of his name, Nee-sha, unbalances her. He smiles as he says it.

Were you following me?

How about thanks very much? I saw you wearing it earlier. When you legged it outside.

Sam pulls the scarf closer, eats another chip. Sneaks looks at him. He is *so* beautiful.

Surely that gets me a chip? he says, watching her eat.

Piss off. Get your own chips.

Why don't we do a swap? Naoise holds up a small bag of green, and quickly puts it away as two Garda stroll past the end of the lane. He moves closer to her.

Sam smiles and pops another chip in her mouth. Nah, I'm fine.

There's a secret park in the city, two streets over. Iveagh Gardens. Have you been?

Nope.

He laughs. Wanna see it?

Err, no.

Ah you do wanna see it, come on, he says, leaning a little closer. Or you can stand here in the street and watch that.

Just up from Sam a drunk middle-aged man has his dick out and is pissing on the ground. He sees Sam and waves, nearly falls over. All righhht, goood lookin'?

Naoise smirks.

The man steadies himself with a chuckle and continues pissing like a horse while grinning at Sam.

Sam eats the last chip and scrunches up the paper in her hands. Well, the alternative's not great.

Naoise holds out his hand again.

I've vinegar fingers, Sam says, refusing to shake. So where's this magic fucking park then?

Iveagh Gardens

Sam, 1994

He vaults his body over the high black gate easily. She follows suit. In the garden they are on their own. The noise of the city recedes. It is beautiful, the damp quiet intoxicating. They walk around in silence for a bit. He grins, the lamp light magnifying the outline of his body. Something like the feeling of heat hits her whenever she looks at him.

The statues in the park are elegant bystanders. She runs her fingers along their smooth feet, their stone skin shimmering against the slivers of light that move across the gardens. She is sure that in the daylight the stonework must appear mottled, discoloured by years of keeping watch over this hidden paradise in the middle of the city; not unblemished like their kin in museums, only on show for the lucky few.

They sit on steps near the fountain and he rolls a joint, lights it, takes a drag and brings it to her mouth, his fingers touching her lips. She hesitates momentarily before taking a long deep inhale. Naoise keeps looking at her as he smokes; his coffee-coloured eyes, set with a black ink iris, swell and diminish against the splayed light every time he stares at her. She stares right back. His features seem too perfectly measured somehow. His is a beauty that would let you get away with things.

Why have we never met before? he says.

Don't ask me, she says.

He smiles. That smile.

It's beautiful here.

It's Baltic, he says, moving closer.

You go to lots of gigs down here?

I do a bit of backstage stuff, like the odd time. He takes a huge drag and exhales, then hands her the joint.

I can probably get you into Nirvana at the RDS in April.

Are you *serious*? I saw them in King's Hall. Unreal—

Epic gig.

They were amazing, though, weren't they? Tori Amos song at the start and everything. Sam can still feel the music throbbing through her body, melodies like memory. Kurt.

What d'you think of Pet Lamb? he asks, bringing her back to him.

Good. Pretty good, she says, unsure. Gav loves them. Becca not so much.

Who's Gav?

Becca's fella.

Right.

He goes to the High School.

Those two wee skinny lads outside who looked about twelve?

He's seventeen, same age as me. She stands up.

He joins her, tucks his arm into hers without asking. The other guy?

James. Gav's mate. Nothin' to do with me.

Naoise smiles. You'd never have got in without Chiz. Not a chance.

His friend Chiz's sneering face appears, she can almost smell his breath, hot, sour, wanting. It makes her feel sick.

We never had a problem before. She wrestles her arm back from Naoise, sticks her hands in her pockets and starts to move ahead. She doesn't know where she is going, stays on the gravel path.

He catches up, walks in step with her, leaning too close, trying to get her to slow down.

You fancy another smoke? he says.

Sam keeps walking. No, thanks. I'm fine. We should head.

Listen. Don't mind Chiz, he's a headless fuck. Totally harmless.

She missteps then, moving out of time, just a fragment.

Right. Dead on. Better go, don't want Becca to leave without me.

You can get home with us.

I'm not sitting beside Chiz.

Naoise laughs. He's driving. Sit beside me. There's room.

What time is it? Becca's gonna kill me.

Ah, she'll be alright.

You don't know her.

Ah she must be well used to you disappearing with handsome strangers. He smirks, stops walking and so does she.

Sorry, are you calling yourself handsome? Sam laughs. Who does that?

Hah, he laughs back. Okay, *plain* stranger. Better?

Much. And no, I don't make a habit of bunking off with randomers.

So I'm a randomer now?

No. Just—

Not your type?

I don't have a— you don't know a thing about me.

Okay. Gimme a sec. He stands back. Circles her, then swoops in close, his answer ready.

You like … boys in bands … and drugs and … and … what else floats a girl like youse boat? He smiles, buying time. Poetry. Lots a pretty words.

Oh, yeah? What do you know about poetry?

I love poetry.

Yeah?

Yeah.

Go on then. What's your favourite?

He doesn't miss a beat and says, Breaking Wood.

> I was breaking wood in the shed
> As dark fell. The wind gusted
> And slammed the door, pitching
> Me into such blackness that I
> Missed my stroke and struck
> A spark from the floor.
>
> It brought back my father . . .

She watches him perform. Perfect, easy. Delicious.

When he is finished, she is on the cusp of laughing: such a shock, his borrowed words still rolling over her.

. . . Will take my feeling to the night, he says, finishing.

Heaney, she says.

Deane, he says.

Two Seamuses. Smart, she thinks, trying to dust off the impact those words delivered from that mouth are having on her. He's moved closer to her the whole time he's been speaking, inched nearer and nearer and the last lines have been given dream-like to her mouth, like a kiss waiting.

Will take my feeling to the night, she repeats. They are standing looking at each other, oak and ash trees bent over eavesdropping on either side. The gardens are spider-webbed with moonlight, dispensed through the branches. He smells of all kinds of smoke. Even though these old trees have seen this a thousand times before, the kindling, igniting, they whisper to each other to lean closer, steal what they can.

He's a beautiful writer, she says.

You're beautiful, he says.

Her whole body creases at the word beautiful.

Fuck off. You're *so* full of yourself, she says, sharp, short, trying to hide the reaction, straighten herself out, but he sees it. Notes it. Knows his way in. The trees snap and straighten out in the wind and they walk on.

She almost forgets that there is anyone else in the whole city but the two of them when suddenly Northern voices carry across the shadowy hollows of the park.

It's Becca. Arguing. With Chiz.

Sam runs to the entrance, towards her voice.

Naoise is behind her.

He gives her a boost and she is on the other side.

Go on, he says and she turns up the road towards Harcourt Street.

Sam sees Becca and the others. Gav sits in the driver's seat with a face on him. Chiz is sitting on the bonnet of Gav's car, holding court.

Where the fuck have you been? Becca shouts as Sam arrives out of breath. *He* wouldn't tell me where you were. Prick.

Chiz snots out a contemptuous laugh.

Let's go, Becca says, shoving Chiz off-balance as she walks around the front of Gav's car.

Oh, I like you, Chiz says to Becca's back. I like you a *lot*.

Becca ignores him, opens the door and pulls her seat forward so Sam can get in.

Bye, Sam says.

See ya, Naoise says.

Naoise, Chiz and the others walk off up the street. Chiz shoves Naoise playfully as they stroll away, mucking about. They seem to duck out of sight about halfway up.

One sec, Sam says to Becca, and she is running up the street after him.

For fuck sake! Becca says.

Hey, Sam calls down the gap she saw him disappear into, a lane underneath pale brick buildings, lights at either end but in the centre only darkness. A figure emerges from the gloom.

Hey you, Naoise says. Thought you had to go?

I ... we're going to Lavery's, next Saturday ... if you're around? Sam blurts out.

Might be, might be, might definitely be there next Saturday. You think Becca will still hate my guts by then? He's moving towards her.

No. No way. She's actually really sound, it's my fault.

Three blasts of a car horn stop her motion towards him. Better go before they really do leave me behind. Saturday? she repeats.

See you round, Sam, Naoise says. Saturday.

She smiles, unable to hide it. Surprised at herself. And he is gone, into the shadows of the lane, into the body of Dublin.

Neon Loneliness

Nuala, 1981

Every day he appears is a special occasion.

I don't pretend to myself that it is anything other than what it is. I want him to think about me. I am blatant, like red lips on Sunday faces. Shiny patent shoes with a short skirt. Coyness is not going to be part of my armoury. Teenage girls have that in spades and I couldn't hope to pry him away from their endless innocence, despite the finite surety of that one fleeting special thing. I am old. I am experience. I am living, breathing, lust. I am not playing games and that is new to him. It is not my newness he wants. He wants to know my stretched skin, and I want his youth, devotion. Fall in love with me just a little. The ticking need of all that. I want to succumb to it all, be whispered about, the dirty beating heat of gossip. I want people to stare and turn their heads away, smile and wince. I want everyone to remember me. I want to feel something. Anything real.

I just don't realise soon enough that is not what he wants. He wants silence and secrets and some sort of respectability that I have missed. In all that rush I have missed it. Missed his camouflaged cruelty until it is too late and I become the tiniest Matryoshka doll locked inside all the other painted versions of me he has created, glazed with a shiny and improbable lustre that only a teenage boy can conjure, ready to be destroyed with all the rage his broken heart can bleed into my world. I'm careless with myself.

In the end it is loneliness that blinds me. Long silent days of broken sleep and washing and peek-a-boo and nappies and weekday dinners that kill me. Dull my senses so much I could just walk into oncoming traffic and no one would even notice me. I wouldn't notice me. I've forgotten myself in petty little increments. The shaky feeling of knowing who you are but not wanting to admit it to yourself, pretending to be someone else for so long that you forget yourself. The first time you see a reflection and think you are beautiful and the last time someone makes you feel ugly. And you believe them. It's all and more of those things. As simple and as complicated as breathing. As life itself.

Little Earthquakes in Lavery's Limelight

Sam, 1994

Everyone throngs to Lavery's in Belfast. There's a floor for every kind of muso. The ratty brick thrums with the sound of escape, the old building becoming young as darkness gives way to dancing. Drinking. Getting lost. There is no science to it. No explanation that Sam knows as to why the song playing makes her move the way she does. Why the way she moves, and not the way her friend moves, makes other people move. Makes other people want to move towards her, and still other people watch, because she's lost in it.

Sweat trickles down her back and thighs, her forehead glitters, starbright with it.

Not everyone can give in to it, but she can.

She does.

Pulse herself, contort, twist

fall

and still not stop.

Because the more she moves, the more she craves it.

The crash of bodies, the smell of letting go, the high of not giving a shit. Dancing is like that magic bit just before you come, it makes sense and it doesn't. She can't resist it, this feeling buzzing all over. Her body colluding with alcohol and drugs and anything she can get her hands on to make her feel out of it; she wants terrible beauty, demands anything that leaves her shimmering with delight.

Becca has said Sam's mother was beautiful, would have stayed beautiful, but how could Becca know what time and sadness and the day-to-day shit of life might have done to her mother? How could anyone know what they would become? There is only now and nothing more, nothing easy, nothing certain. Life *has* to be now or what's the point; today is all they have. Becca talks endlessly about her plans, university or what she will do this summer, next, at college. The future is in everything she does, but Sam doesn't feel like that. She doesn't think she will make it out of this town alive.

She tries not to think about that.

She tunes into the music. Suede. Brett Anderson sounds like a god.

Naoise finds her in the dark corner dancing, and watches. Doesn't move towards her. It's sort of shocking to her. People move around him but he remains transfixed.

It's like she's a kid again, playing hold-onto-the-electric-fence, the one that's meant to keep cattle in the field, shaking her body till it gives out a flick, a burn of electricity, so sweet and tender that it radiates from her, covers every bit where skin kisses bones and skims nerves, surrounds her, she can feel each vibration, the hum of him with the music set against the throb of the heavy dark.

Becca tries to talk to her but she can't make out the words, just feels her friend's rushed breath on her ear like a warning, while she watches him watching her. Becca finally gives up. Walks away.

Nothing is stopping this. Naoise picks Sam up as he kisses her, twisted explosion written between their mouths, her arms around his neck, his hands connecting firm around her waist as he slams her against the wall. He is hard, she feels it through his clothes. Breathless. Violent. Like he wants to fuck her right there, in front of everyone, and she feels every single bit of it.

It's Becca who breaks the spell, drags her out, and Sam is laughing, high, buzzing, freer than she's ever been.

Her fingertips search for traces of him left on her mouth. They journey home, teenagers shoved sardine-like, unsafe, into Gav's car. Out through the city, receding lights of Belfast behind them as they speed past Carryduff, grateful there are no police checkpoints tonight. The long sweeping belt of road to Saintfield, soft and dark and almost green-black like the wide fields and towering trees that keep watch above them. They see the glitter of small towns and villages set out in front of them, rising and disappearing in the drumlins, blurry with drunken speed, as Gav picks the winding back roads.

He drops James off at a long drivewayed, low-set bungalow. Sam's whitewashed farmhouse is next.

So that's a thing now? Becca says, as she lets Sam out of the car.

What?

Gav said he's bad news, nearly killed someone last year.

Who?

I dunno.

Gav says. Christ, Becca, you sound like your ma. I'll take my chances.

You know everyone gets their drugs from him? Becca says.

Sam shrugs her shoulders. So we'll get free drugs? Never known you to have a problem with that. Besides, he's not my boyfriend.

Yet. He's an oul man. Becca laughs. Sam doesn't join her. He used to go with my sister Lucy's friend, Leah. Really fucked her up too.

Leah's not exactly a pushover, Bec.

Yeah, she's totally mental, but still. He's twenty-eight, Sam. You're seventeen.

Twenty-eight. Eighteen in two months.

I can do the maths.

He doesn't look twenty-eight.

No, he doesn't. That's the problem.

God, Becca, relax, will ya? You look at someone funny round here and that's it. Guilty.

Fuck off.

Becca, c'mon. Gav revs up the car. I'm starving.

Dick, both girls say in unison. They hug goodnight and Becca gets in the car. Sam sits on the wall, lights up a ciggie, watches the tail lights of the car disappear up the lane. Petrol-burn smoke escapes as Gav runs through his gears on the steep hill out of the gap onto the main road.

Sam goes inside, falls asleep saying his name. Naoise. The sound of it, hearing his voice. His words in her head. You are mine. You belong to me.

Special Occasion

Nuala, 1981

Children both asleep that morning, miraculous really. Sullen little faces snoring gently, rain their relentless lullaby. Patsy out for the day at the sales, looking to bring back some or other helping of new heifer to the farm. I figure the paper will not be delivered. When he appears I surprise myself, shove my bare feet into old battered boots that I wear winter and summer, the leather repaired and repaired and repaired rather than find another pair that wouldn't suit my feet as perfectly. There are some things in life you shouldn't need to replace.

He has already dropped the paper on the doorstep and is retreating in his red Adidas jacket down the driveway but he swings back around as he hears me step out, his gaze open, curly hair matted to his forehead with sweat and drizzle. I don't bring him in, instead lead him back around the farmhouse, out past the barn to the edge of the field, where the banged-up Rover sits on top of concrete blocks, waiting to be fixed.

My children would play in that burgundy car eventually, laugh and cry out and never know that I break myself open in that car, am remade in that car, scream in that car. I haven't considered that his lips would do anything other than bruise mine that day. I am not prepared for the crack in my bones under the solidness of him. I thought he'd be supple and air but he is determined, tastes every part of me, fluttering mouth moving with jarring damning tenderness so that when he goes down on me, pauses to look up, I think I will come before he has even touched me.

And then I do the same for him.

His flesh is baby-sweet and I want to bite him, draw blood and mark him, and I do, above his jutting hip bone, a precious little nip. I have no idea how long we have been in that car when I remember who I am and gather myself up, pulling on my dress. He slides his hand up between my thighs, his thumb pushes into my sex, still buzzing with pleasure, setting my desire out, like child's prints in clay.

My son is screaming when I get back to the house, my daughter playing quietly with bricks beside his cot. I take the baby, shush him, tread steady steps in ever-growing circles around the kitchen, then stand in front of the rain-washed window.

I do not see him for another week and touch myself every chance I get. My children's naps. Early morning. I crawl into the bathroom in the middle of the night and silently push myself to orgasm again and again thinking of his swollen mouth around me. It never fails. It seems to grow into something more powerful in my mind, takes over my imagination, remakes me in a giddy image of myself that feels uncontrollable, dangerously wanting, demanding that intensity again and again.

I even have sex with my husband to try and bridge the gap. It only makes it worse.

Mocks

Sam's kidding herself, pretending that these are the real-thing-exams that dictate her life. They are only mocks. She should be fine with that, used to that. Her whole life is a mock. A cock-up. A practice run.

Like Faux Gerry Adams on the telly. Everyone and their ma knew Gerry was dubbed when he came on the BBC – the slight delay as he spoke, his mouth and words in minor disagreement. Unreal. Dubbed Gerry sounded just like the other actor on the telly, telling you not to join the Provos. Were there really so few thespians in Northern Ireland that they have to have the same one saying completely opposite things concurrently? Clearly people on the *mainland* gave so few shits about us over here that they probably thought, Who the fuck would notice? Because, well, don't all those *Paddies* sound the same, like. So one minute he's on talking about 'the peace process', and a few moments later, during the ad break, he's saying 'See something. Say something'. Faux Gerry. Not real Gerry. Good-for-TV Gerry. Not I-was-never-in-the-IRA type Gerry. There's a difference, you know. As if anyone from here would miss that.

She misses Naoise. All the time. Has tried to focus on studying. Not on him.

Not on his perfect face. His gaze as he takes her in. His mouth on hers.

He is a movie star left behind to shine in a small town. She is his audience.

Girls from the year below, the lower sixth, walk past. She gets up, follows them past the statue of Our Blessed Virgin, Mary, who judges them all benignly. Those girls have another year to wait. Another year of this shit in a shit place, with a shit life in a shithole.

Soon the pretend exams will become real. Results will loom. She does not apply herself, her English teacher wrote on her last report – she is highly intelligent but her grades do not reflect that. Reflect. On reflection they're all kidding themselves, kidding everyone, kidding life. There's no kidding the system.

Just a few weeks ago, RTÉ let Gerry Adams and the others speak in their own voices on the telly, voiceovers a thing of the past. Some poor fucking actor out of a job, Sam's English teacher Miss Denvir says, laughing, harsh.

She meets Becca. Who chats incessantly about what might be on the mock paper. She loves her but she has to zone out.

At least all Becca talks about is exams and boys. Everything is starting to change. All the bad guys get to sell their particular murdering brand of shite to the masses, their killing manifesto. Our lovely accent tucked in with death forever more: when they hear our voice in England it sounds out trouble. Marked as dangerous as soon as you open your mouth. Say nothin.

They trudge into the exam hall. Find their places, sit down. She reads the questions three times. Like she's been told to do. Tries not to focus on everyone else furiously scribbling around her. Knows that she is in trouble.

Last year in school they announced a march for peace and everyone was giddy about the day off. The girls were told to be on their best behaviour and present themselves in a manner that would uphold the reputation of The Sisters Of Perpetual Succour Grammar School, Newcastle. They got in the papers. Not the *Guardian* or the *Sun*. Just Belfast papers. A bunch of schoolchildren and their teachers simply *walking* did not make headline news across the water. English people didn't give a fuck and neither did the Irish, and they are only down the road. Dundalk, Drogheda, Dublin. They do not give a rat's ass about the North. Unless a guard gets shot or something blows up down south. Then they pay attention. Then they talk. Then they sit up. Northern Ireland learned to be the problem child, attention for bad behaviour, because that's the only thing that worked. Being good as gold simply did not endear. Bombs worked. Guns worked. Semtex worked. Good-looking fellas starving themselves worked. American presidents doing a John Wayne impression, with big smiles and bigger wallets, worked.

These things work. These things always worked for a while. Until they didn't.

It was on the news. The peace march.

Practice makes perfect pretend paramilitaries. Say it again, Sam.

Since RTÉ lifted their ban Sam can just change the channel and hear Gerry talk in his *actual* voice whenever she wants. Sometimes they do switch, but even Margaret agrees Gerry sounds better when the actor does his voice: smoother, more gravitas, like a fine wine. I don't think Gerry drinks wine himself, Margaret says. Margaret Caher says you have to be careful of wild boys, twinkle-eyed terrorists she calls them, because Gerry was a quare looker in his youth, and a lot of freedom fighters are very handsome. Like Che Guevara. Sam had to look him up. Margaret actually pointed at Naoise one day in the town and said, Like that fella there, he has that swagger, that ragged edge about him that could snag you, unravel all your sense like thread. He's up to no good, that one. No good at all. Sam pretended not to know him.

When she was younger Sam used to wonder would Saint Margaret ever get with her da, realised that everyone round here had thought it at one point: two sort-of widowers, four kids between them, but she'd understood as she got older they just sort of rubbed along together. A chaste support system, not an addled love affair. A freedom with each other they couldn't get from other people.

No one could really do what they liked here. Naoise tried but freedom was a fantasy. There were rules, unwritten, unspoken, to keep you in check. To keep you safe. To keep you apart. Questions asked when they already knew the answer. Waiting to trip you up, watch you fall.

She's tired of it all. The questions. Where abouts you from? Where do you go to school? Hates it. Hates being told she is one thing or another. Them or us. Everyone is getting tired. Ordinary people would like a break. Even the unnamed voiceover actor might like to be in a Hollywood movie, playing a good guy not a bad guy for a change. Bit of regular Shakespeare.

She thinks about writing this all down in English paper two. Comparing Gerry to Romeo. Paisley could be Juliet. Or they could both be Romeos, Gerry and Ian star-crossed peace lovers whose feuding political families get in the way. She laughs out loud in the pen-scratching silence of the exam hall and attracts the unwanted glare of the supervising teacher. Becca looks at Sam with a what-the-fuck's-so-funny face. Then goes back to her paper, keeps writing like everyone else. Sam still hasn't written a word. People are all the same underneath. In the end. Different but the same. It's what makes people interesting. Free speech even when you don't like what's being said. She doesn't understand why they have to fight. She has too many gaps, so little knowledge. She leaves the question blank, turns the page.

You have to think about your future, Mr Malone says, looking at her results in the days that follow. If you need extra help we can provide that. You're falling behind. What's going on, Samantha? I'm here if you want to talk. Anytime. Anytime at all.

She knows Malone means well but she can't match his expectations. His face – *you've-let-me-down* – is a killer. No one has ever looked at her like that and she fucking hates it.

Patsy's face says it all as he reads the report at the kitchen table. He points his finger at her; the other hand fetches up the paper.

What the fuck are you playing at? he says, low menace hunting his words, his delivery settling on righteous disapproval. She knows the script from here. Word for word.

She doesn't hang around to be given out to.

Skittles with Loowit

Nuala, 1981

I want to say we're not going, I want to protest, but I don't. Instead I pitch up with baby asleep in the buggy, his fat legs curling like overstuffed sausages on the grill, almost too much meat to be contained under that fine milky skin, sticking out from a knitted blanket, toes wriggling against a breeze that can't get started properly under all this sun. He's almost two but he's still my baby. My last one. Patsy tries to take Sam ahead. She pulls like a terrier, throws every pound of knackered muscle into sticking herself solid and unmoving, a dead weight, against the grassy green hump of the one-car lane. You can't call it a road, it's a by-way for horses, two of which peer at us from the tops of the busy green and white thicket as we saunter past. A big white mare leans, crushes the thick hedge to nibble at my stubborn daughter, a friendly prodding of those huge pink and grey dappled lips. Sam reaches a tiny hand up to pet the animal's nose like they are regular neighbours and not different species altogether, and I am frozen by the wonder in me at her, her tiny little hand extending, unafraid to touch this great grey maiden a warm hello. My child. Fearless. Magnetic.

Patsy, as he does so often these days, breaks the spell.

Ah, for fuck sake, child, he says, but when he scoops her up the tears and screaming for mummy start and he turns away, red-faced, from the gathering crowd.

Skittles on a Sunday evening, young fellas and oul boys and too-young-to-be-so-old ones – my category I think – congregate to watch this game of paupers. The heat is causing the road to pulse and bend, the tar seems to bloom but still they play. It won't defeat them. The pub sends up cool pints and a bucket of stout and lemonade for the kids. Younger lads drink and laugh loudly, too loudly, unsure of themselves. I have the girl wrapped around me now, pushing the buggy with the one-handed expertise of the dominant, the only parent who matters really. Patsy only seems to get involved with the children when it suits him. He argued with me for months before PJ was christened. Had his heart set on calling the child John Paul – JP. Might as well have named him Pope. A name that would tell every person my son ever met everything about him before he even opened his mouth. Patsy had fallen for the smiley supreme pontiff just like the rest of the country. Eager to be conned by the show-bizziest Catholic on earth. A converted white van and a day out in Phoenix Park. The doctor told Patsy it was too far, too risky for me to travel at this stage. I'd lost my last baby. He said lost like I'd misplaced something. Like I – my body – was amiss. Miscarriage. The shame of a woman's body doing just one of the things it was meant for. There shouldn't be shame, another thing for us to carry. Patsy relented when our GP hinted that it might be a son this time, went on the shabby smelly bus himself, one of the faithful devoted, waiting for hours to listen to pious prayers that he barely remembers. I stayed home with all the Protestants and enjoyed a curious quiet that suited the place. I gave in to the christening in the end. I pretended for him. Had to give ground, compromise. Every other boy around here is called John or Paul or John Paul or JP. My boy had a lucky escape.

I lift a cold black pint from the tray and sit near the cool shade of the makeshift seats at the side of the road. I sip and watch. Watch and sip. See the sneer of the plain local lassies. Know what they say about me. *A blow-in. Not one of us. Not local reared and raised like Patsy*. I realise I should not be here. Don't belong. Or fit. I tame my mongrel vowels in an accent that could still shift back when I needed it to, try to sound like my mother. Clip the past. Thought this place would fix the shifting inside me. Patsy, could be home.

These people. The madness coming out here, taking on this. They don't even understand themselves. My little dream of

34

stability. A rural idyll. I am a fucking eejit on a weird experiment that has turned into a life, children, domesticated animals. I set up my sad existence like the lesson-laden fairy tales I read to my children.

No one will rescue me but I need to be free, to leave, to go. I neck my pint and grab the girl from the ground and hoist her onto my back. I can hear Patsy talking and chattering, joining in; these men are his real communion and I know he hasn't even noticed me leave. We are at that place now, the place with no love left in it. It should never have gotten here, we shouldn't be in this mess. I feel responsible: he had no idea what he was getting with me, I tricked him into thinking I was just like every other girl and I accept that now. He was a fool for me, sure, but I let him be a fool. That was my part. I played this little game and let it overtake me, those perfect pink feet we created, the energy of those children that flinted, sparked up out of our love – if it was that – perhaps the chaos of electricity that happened every time our bodies met in the beginning was the secret to their wild, bitter beauty. That is gone now, and no amount of oxygen, no paper held up to the fireplace, will coax that flame into being again. I know that. I'm already knee-deep in ashes but he is there, still trying to shut off the draught, to make it work, slow down the death of us.

Wind Yer Neck In

My mum loved to travel, must get it from her.

She waits for Naoise to ask about her mother. He's flipping through the *Rough Guide to Europe* that she's borrowed from the library. He ignores this comment, turns the corner on the page and reads on.

That's a library book.

I am aware.

Don't damage it, she says, and tries to take it off him but he holds it high above her head, then carefully folds out the crease and gives it to her for inspection.

Better?

Someone else has to read this. I can't afford to pay for a new one.

I do know how libraries work. He clicks his lighter and teases the flame across the pages, just for a second, before she slams the book closed.

Not funny. She wants to check it but shoves it in her battered bag. Feels the cold when she didn't before.

He smiles at her. The warmth in him. Where are you going again?

She is irritated by his surety, he seems so satisfied with himself.

In the summer? I don't know. Paris first, I think. If I save up enough money.

He lights up, offers her one. They are at the appropriately named Mound of Down, huddled in the inner ditch, lying against the thickly planted bank that runs to the top of the mound, under a few trees. The cathedral hangs back in the distance, keeping watch over the teenagers who have replaced the long-dead Irish kings who supposedly hung out there once. The young people of Dún

Pádraig come here to get off with each other, drink, take drugs and have sex but there is no one else mitching today. Just Sam.

His coat is spread wide underneath them, her legs draped over his lap; below them, the ground is damp, still holding winter in it. They are hidden from view, have crossed the outer ditch to the hidden part – this wild overgrown space so close to the town was meant for making secrets. He kisses her again.

We should go to Paris, he says.

Paris?

You'd like Paris.

I thought you hadn't been?

I didn't say that.

So where else have you been?

Ah, you know, around. Amsterdam. Bruges. Cannes. Morocco.

Morocco? Why'ja come back here?

Aren't you lucky I did? he says and kisses her full on the mouth his answer.

I have something for you. He searches his coat pockets, his hands slipping under her arse to access them, his smile solid as he does so, their bodies awkwardly posed. He eventually hands her a small brown envelope, lies back, his eyes closed, not needing to watch her reaction.

She opens it carefully, her unvarnished nails tearing the thin brown paper. Inside are two tickets for Nirvana at the RDS, April 8th. She squeals. Jumps on top of him. He opens his eyes.

Oh my god. *Oh my god, Naoise!*

I can give them to someone else if you're not that fussed, maybe whoever borrows that book next? He studies her, serious for a moment, and then dissolves into laughter as she faux-punches him and kisses him, long and hard. We can stay with a mate in Dublin. For the weekend. Just us.

Sam feels his hand lower against the fabric of her skirt, searching.

Naoise, she breathes. Stop.

I don't want to and you don't want me to. She breathes hard, into him. He kisses her again. His kisses are a gateway drug.

37

Teenage girl perfect kisses. He knows how to draw her in, kiss her until she forgets herself, would do anything for his mouth on hers.

He touches her like no one else has.

I can't.

Are you a virgin?

She can't have sex. With her luck, she'll be the Next Virgin Mary, and just the *idea* of telling Mags that she'd got herself into trouble made Sam close her legs. What her getting up the duff might do to Margaret.

Sam? He stares at her, demanding an answer. Are. You. A. Virgin?

No.

On the pill?

I'm not gonna have sex with you, if that's what you're asking.

I didn't say I wanted to fuck you, did I?

She blushes everywhere as his words land, excruciating red scalds her cheeks, neck, chest. It seemed that was all he was saying, everything about him was sex.

Fine. Cool. She feels neither of those things.

I didn't mean it like that, he says, looking at her, then kisses her cheek, her neck, her chest, his lips slowly touching everywhere the redness has, as if the blush will come away on his mouth like paint. Like he wants to relieve her of any embarrassment, accept her just as she is. He's on top of her, his weight a pleasant crush. Just enough force to make her feel real. Sometimes when she's with him she wants to dissolve into him. She doesn't feel real at all. She feels light, unburdened, free. He kisses her again, his breath on her neck, the weight of him bringing her back to her senses.

Well, I'm not a virgin, just in case you're wondering, he says, staring at her.

They both laugh at that.

It's no big deal if you are.

Should I take the sticker off my vagina?

Hah, you *know* what I mean. I'm not blind. Everybody watches you.

Sometimes I think we live in different places. She taps on her forehead and rolls her eyes.

He pulls her back to him.

So no one's ever tried it on? His hands squeeze her waist tight. The pressure of his grip intense, strong, holding her like it might elicit some hidden truth. It hurts a little, and she likes that she can't wriggle out of it.

Of course they bloody have. I'm female, aren't I?

Who?

Boys.

Names.

No one you know.

Tell me. His hands tighten enough to make her gasp a little, she tries to laugh but her breath is caught.

Chiz.

He wouldn't dare. He laughs and releases her momentarily just to bring his mouth against her skin again. It feels like he is claiming her in a way. Marking her as his. It gives her a strange sensation of being in control. Powerful. Sometimes he makes her feel like she could do anything.

Tell me when you want me to stop, he repeats again and again.

Later, much later, she tells him, sighs out the word. Stop.

Sure, I need to be somewhere. I'm late. He nudges her off him.

She takes a beat to feel the loss of him, her heart hammering in her chest. Tries to gather her stuff up without looking needy, and all the power is gone.

Okay. Have to study with Becca tonight anyway. Where you off to?

Never you mind.

Naoise?

Paris.

In your dreams. I'd love to go to Paris but I'm busy—

Exams?

Exams.

Then Paris, he says.

With you, she almost says back. Catches herself just in time, tries to be distant when all she wants to do is fling herself at him. She can imagine Paris with him, living there together. Café noir and a tiny apartment and cigarettes and everything cinematic black 'n' white. Like *Jules et Jim* or *À Bout de Souffle*. She'd thought of getting her hair cut like Jean Seberg once. She and Becca thinking it would look cool on them but they chickened out. Only a trim in the end. Sam hadn't understood everything in the films at all – no one on screen ever seemed to have a proper job – who could live in Paris selling papers – but she liked the way the actors looked, the images that replayed in her head, the way the whole thing made her feel. The way it made her feel about herself. The way Naoise made her feel. She wants to be that feeling for him.

You cold? He puts his coat around her shoulders. Let's go to my place first.

They walk back to the town, wrapped around each other. Twenty minutes later they saunter past the side of Down Museum and the courts, down to his flat. Everything is ancient in this part of the town. Tall buildings echo grandeur even in decay with their elegant stonework costumes, dressed in their past glory as an important market town; imposing structures housing an architectural tendency towards judgement. They always make her feel like she has done something wrong. She has. Skipping out of school early to see him has become routine.

The only other people around are some barristers and their devils carting hefty files, collecting themselves as they get into their cars outside the courthouse, raising eyebrows as Sam and Naoise pass. Sam laughs nervously at their open displeasure. Jealous, Naoise whispers into her ear.

He refuses to be judged. He lives above all that. She doesn't even know how to defend herself from those punishing gazes and she has no one to help her figure out why she is so deserving of this verdict. She could ask Margaret but she doesn't think Margaret would understand. Margaret would tell her she is guilty, guilty, guilty. Margaret would be right too. She is.

Anno Domini

PJ, 1994

Margaret is the only sort of mother PJ's ever known and he's never seen her this angry before. Sam sends her over the edge. Who else could make a saint lose their rag? His sister has that special gift.

Sam has been giving out about their da. Margaret normally lets it go. Lets Sam wind herself up and burn herself out. His sister is more like a bloke than any girl he knows. She is tough, harsh, takes no shit from no one.

Well, she was before Naoise. There is A.N., and B.N. now. Like he is Christ.

Naoise has sort of remade his sister. Since he noticed her, everyone notices her. PJ's mates have started to bring her up in conversation – or shut it down, when PJ approaches. It's fucking gross and now he feels bad for perving over his mate Brian's older sister the week before. Well, not bad, but like, bad for Brian. It isn't nice. You can't help what your sisters like.

His sister takes in heat like a cat, and stays as close to the stove as possible. PJ is reading the local paper, scowling at the sports pages. The fecker who takes the photos always manages to leave him out of the shots, no matter how well he plays.

He doesn't give a shit about me, Sam keeps whining, lounging in Margaret's kitchen.

Sam's rant is familiar, like the smell of slurry on a hot day – unpleasant but after a while you get used to it and it doesn't really bother you anymore.

But today, Margaret's shoulders tighten as he watches her pause. She has been kneading bread.

He feels the change before she blows her top. Neither of them has ever seen Margaret lose her cool. She lets fly. Bellows. Her sons say when she loses it you wouldn't want to be anywhere near her, they called her a right oul bitch, but neither him nor Sam believed them, before today. Margaret is soft. She is embarrassing hugs, and fivers slipped into pockets and a lift home when you really need one but don't wanna ask.

Sam! I never want to hear another word against that man. Do you hear me? Do. You. Hear. Me? Young. Lady?

PJ thinks Sam will answer back. She is the queen of that, normally, but she just sits up, mouth open, gaping at this new version of Margaret.

He fell apart when your mother left, and God help me I loved her but to leave like that. Without a … without … your father did the best he could. Two wee weans in tow. *You* never forgave him. He made mistakes. God help me he did, but, but, but …

Margaret can't finish the sentence.

She's been untying her apron the whole time she speaks, like a surgeon discarding scrubs after an operation gone wrong. PJ puts a hand out to her as she barges past; she catches his palm briefly as she rushes from the kitchen. Drops her flour-dusted apron on the sill before she pulls the door behind her.

Fuck sakes, Sam, what'd ya do that for? PJ says.

I didn't fuckin do anything, Sam says.

Just give it a rest for a while, will ye?

PJ, don't you lecture me. You don't remember anything about that.

PJ sighs and starts to read the paper again. Sam gets up and turns off a pot that has started to boil over. Floury potatoes ruined, the water spilling over the top, a milky sop. She flings herself down on the tiny two-seater sofa. They don't say anything, just sit waiting in the quiet ticking of the kitchen. Five minutes pass with PJ pretending to read. Sam lies still, eyes closed, her head tilted as far back as possible. Her hair trails on the floor. PJ wants to pull it, drag her into reality.

Then he remembers what day it is.

It's her and John-Jo's anniversary, PJ says. Fuck. That's what's up. Would have been, I mean.

Crap, Sam says. They would've been married what, like, twenty-five years? *Merde*. How do you remember that shit anyway?

He pushes his chair out, rocking up on the two back legs like a question. Twins told me.

Where are they?

Out getting her flowers.

I'll go. Make some tea, will ya?

She slopes out of the kitchen, looking contrite. He rests the four legs of the seat back on the ground in answer as she passes him. PJ knows Sam and Margaret will have one of their *big* chats because Margaret treats her like the daughter she never had, so they can never stay mad at each other long. He wishes Sam could see their da the way she sees Margaret, reserve something kind for him, but wishing for things doesn't make them real.

Snap Shot

Nuala, 1981

I wait with Margaret outside the photo booth in the far corner of Boots for what seems an age. Margaret is restless, tired, the heather rose lipstick she always wears has hardened at the corner of her mouth and she's started to tut. I want to laugh at the tangled feet just visible under the curtain. At Margaret's lack of patience with anyone who isn't me. The machine spits out a photo in the little metal slot but the feet remain giggling inside the booth.

They're just kids, I mouth, but she replies loud enough for the entire shop to hear, Have they no homes to go to? Emphasis all on her country twang but it doesn't work. Everyone goes back to smelling perfume, buying cold cream, lipstick. The feet recede then appear. So we wait.

I shouldn't but I can't help stealing a look at the strip, smile at the four images caught like seasons: shy, laughing, pouting, kissing, all in rapid succession. When the curtain yanks back I quickly replace the photos. A lanky couple emerges, teenagers not kids, still tangled up in the other, hopelessly besotted. The girl catches sight of us, blushes. She snatches up the strip of pictures. Walks away.

Lemme see? The boy grabs them from her. Ah, here, you're gorgeous.

Am not.

Stop, he says and kisses her.

We are both a bit lost watching them when I nudge Margaret, who just shakes her head and hands me her shopping.

Nuala? How does it work again? Margaret says, head sticking out of the curtained metal box a moment later. I don't – why they can't just take the picture—?

44

Look, if it doesn't work we'll go back in the queue, I reply, as she pulls the curtain back, studies the buttons.

Nice to be off my feet though all the same. Margaret yawned. Those wee fellas. Never stop.

Sorry— I have to lean past her to show her how it works. Okay, you push this, then wait. And no smiling. Passport. Remember?

What are you trying to say? I've a face on me like a wet week?

You're all sunshine, now hurry up. I draw the curtain across. Right, I hear Margaret say to herself. Telling herself to get ready. We always seem to be talking to ourselves, telling ourselves off.

The shutter snaps and I glance at the watch Patsy gave me last Christmas. Butter-brown strap. Fancy. He must have sent away for it.

Oh, Christ, I'm not ready, Nuala! Margaret roars and in an instant I jump in, squished beside her, bags dropped at our feet. Smile! and Margaret laughs, the last photo spent.

Other shoppers eye us as we emerge still laughing. Like any kind of happiness was contagious around here, they'd pick it up on their way past. The unearned silliness of two country women up for the day. That's what I was now. A blow-in there and a misfit here. But I still loved Belfast. Loved it.

Ah, Nuala, they're awful. Look at the state of me. I'll have to go back into Anderson McAuleys.

Except this one – we look alright, Mags! We look good.

We look like eejits! Here, you keep it! Sure, you're a big child yourself.

I put it into my bag, figure there's no point closing it now as we step into the street.

Will we get a bite to eat after? Margaret says.

At the end of the street is a bottleneck of people waiting to get through the barriers. Big metal barricades, like teeth or traps. Cogs of people passing through. A chorus of bags open for the security checks searching for an unidentified device. A homemade bomb. A switch. The terrorist twitch off someone. Any excuse to put them up against the wall and search them. Bundle them off in the back of a van. Everyone a suspect. Everybody a target. Even housewives. British soldiers khaki-clad, guns ready, look on, forced blank faces part of their uniform.

It's raining. Umbrellas pop up and down, flashes of round colour appearing and disappearing. So many black, plain canvasses. Some women take small see-through plastic head coverings out of their bags to keep their do's perfect. Knot the white ties under their chins. Faces held high. Margaret covers her head with her hand while I let the rain come.

Will we just treat ourselves and go to The Upper Crust?

Are you made of money? I'm not too flush.

I'm buying.

No, no, you can't.

Margaret shushes me. Get me again. Next time we're up.

We stand in line, waiting for the security guard to check our bags on the way in. Obedient creatures.

Busy day, ladies, he says, smiling at me. Weren't you just in here, love?

Forgot something, didn't we? I smile back.

Ah, buy something nice for me, he says over his shoulder as he lets us go.

Margaret looks at me. There was something in that look. Not just that I always get male attention. It never left me. I could see soldiers forget themselves and want to talk, chat me up, see a glimmer of who they were out of uniforms sometimes. See the hardness shift in their eyes despite the fear of what me, Margaret, any of them, might be capable of. Biology interrupting politics. Sometimes I could feel rough hands linger during body searches and longed to slap them. I wasn't stupid, though. We just endured it. The good, bad and indifferent. The way this place was eating itself alive.

I wonder can she sense the tiniest ruined part of me that is jealous of her. Her menopausal body. A body that is hers and hers alone. I know that's not strictly true, we don't just belong to us, *ever*, but I dream it. A time after hot flushes and lost sleep and aching joints – all the ailments she's complained to me about – when we are just like men. When we are free from our biology. I know she has suffered through it. She searches for words in the fog, frustration sweated out on her top lip, the excess hairs bleached blonde with Jolene. Early menopause. Going through *the change* as she called it. All of our bodily functions reduced to a throwaway line, as if we become other, grotesque, strange, not women anymore but the old hags of fairy tales, a curse placed on our useless carcasses. And I can see how she's changed but I see, too, a freedom in it. A magnificence. I see it as better, not worse. I'm not sure she sees that yet. Possibility is gone. She mourns it, but I crave it.

The café was around the corner, off Cornmarket. Inside, rose-gold wallpaper and heavy floral brocade curtains hung from giant pelmets above chic cuisine served with tiny gold forks and delicate china; Belfast masquerading as Budapest. It was always busy despite the prices. Margaret caught me looking at my watch as we sat down. Time was ticking away.

They'll be alright. Sure, we haven't left the country.

Chance would be a fine thing.

We laugh. Order. I have Quiche Lorraine, coleslaw and rice salad. Margaret the same.

No dessert for me. Just a black coffee, I tell the waitress.

That's why she's so skinny, not a pick on her, Margaret says.

A pot of tea – she hesitates, wants dessert, but doesn't want to embarrass herself. Be judged by some glitter-slicked teenager for her small indulgence. I'd seen old photographs of Margaret's mother and grandmother, the same thick red mane of hair, strong handsome features, broad hips, indefatigable expressions on their lips. Hips that were passed down, hips that carried them through and on. Formidable in their measure, bones of survival and solidness. And having apple tart or not having apple tart wouldn't change that. My mother was thin, flighty, always looking ready to run from something. She was built for that. So was I.

Sure, will we both have tart? It looks great, I say.

47

The waitress notes it down.

Bring plenty of cream, Margaret adds as she walks off.

You should bring Sam here, Margaret says, as we watch a little girl and her mother eat a high, Chantilly-filled chiffon cake, raspberries tumbling over ballet-pink icing on top, the girl's mother gently wiping her daughter's dimpled chin.

I don't think she'd like it, she doesn't really get dolls. Or sweet things. She's such a tomboy. But maybe it's just my baking.

Margaret frowns. God, do you remember that first birthday cake, the one that was meant to be a hedgehog?

That looked like road kill? There is a pause and we both laugh, thinking of the blood-red insides, the shocking contrast to the dark brown cake, studded with chocolate fingers, meant to look like spikes. Oh, Christ, Margaret, the child was traumatised, inconsolable.

Ah, it looked fine once we'd mixed it up with a bitta ice cream.

It looked like the mouldy insides of a dead cat.

Can't believe she'll be five next year. Where does the time go, eh?

PJ is different.

Boys. Boys are easier. Margaret nods. I would have loved a wee girl all the same. Spoilt her rotten.

I sigh. I want to emphasise different – not better, not worse, just different, but I don't contradict her, because it's unfair, because in the years I've known her only her childlessness has made her vulnerable to criticism, because those boys she adopted are thriving, because she'll never have a daughter to chastise.

Dress Rehearsal

It is Margaret's idea to go to Belfast to get the material for her formal dress. They are standing knee-deep in a rainbow-soaked fabric shop, the sort that normally has one of those *hilarious* names like 'Kurl up and Dye' or 'Mad to Measure', except this is called 'Donegal Fashions' and it's not trendy or cool or any of the things you might associate with *Vogue*. This is Belfast, a place where fashion trends go to die or appear fifteen years later as part of the city's particular fetish for reinvention. Balaclavas will never be cool. Still, for once Mags says Sam can have whatever she wants, so Sam is flipping through pattern books like records. They're similar in some ways: paper sheaths all laid out in order of potential popularity – here it is all housecoats and wee girls' frilly dresses. And then, as if by some high-end miracle, a vintage section tumbles out with a Ralph Lauren classic. Black, high neck, backless; cut on the bias, silk or crêpe de chine. Sam hungrily devours these details. Simple, classy, sexy. Shite, she thought she was immune to all that glossy fashion-mag bullshit, but Sam realises she wants the fancy frock. Mags will never go for it. Sam envisions herself in some horrendous mauve toilet-holder creation, all pouffe and shout, but as she pushes the envelope back in, Mags's washed-out fingers gently lift it back out, hold it up to the light for a better look.

Turn around, Margaret says. Stop. Stand up straight. By this time she has a tape measure in her hand, starts to put figures down in pencil on the back of the paper envelope. Arms, Margaret says, her voice muffled by the other end of the tape wedged in her mouth. She sighs as she jots down Sam's measurements. I used to be as skinny as you, child, Margaret says wistfully, catching her own reflection in the mirrors that hang everywhere.

When she finishes, Sam can barely contain herself. She never, ever, gets what she wants.

She wants to ask Naoise to go with her. He won't. She won't even ask him. Becca's been pointing out various replacements. Boys. You could have any one you want. Just ask someone, Becca says. She'd rather go alone. She only wants him.

Becca, of course, is getting a dress from the fanciest boutique in Belfast, 'The Belle of Belfast City'. Daddy's little princess. Money no object. It costs an absolute fortune, three hundred quid, and she's getting a make-up artist and going to the hairdresser, too. None of this is even a possibility for Sam. Becca has been trying to persuade her to get ready at hers and then probably her da would just foot the bill for the two of them, but Sam couldn't bear this sort of handout. Becca means well but it is too much to take sometimes. The kindness. Sometimes you just have to accept where you are and let things be.

Black, I suppose? Margaret asks and answers. The sales lady, a Belfast version of a *Dynasty* character – loud make-up, loud heels, loud attitude – tries to push silk on Margaret, but the look Margaret gives her makes Sam think she is going to carry the head off her.

Is Michael not here? she says. I normally deal with him. He gives me ten per cent off everything. I'm a regular. Coming here years.

Dynasty lady wrinkles her heavily made-up nose.

Michael's on a minibreak.

Anywhere nice?

North coast with the wife and kids.

Isn't it well for some? Margaret says. Sure, with all this holidaying he can well afford to give me fifteen per cent off.

When the price has been agreed, Margaret backtracks and asks for crêpe de chine. Sam is impressed: once lining and the pattern and thread are all included, she saves them a tidy amount.

That'll be lovely on you, the saleswoman says to Sam, making small talk.

We won't go that low, though. I'll fix that neckline to make her dacent, Margaret says, cheery against Sam's frowns.

Gordons has lovely make-up in, if you need some. I'm sure your mother will let you pick whatever you want. The saleswoman smiles at Sam and Margaret, as she rings up the material.

Margaret pats Sam's arm.

They stand at the till in silence as Margaret pays, all the brightness gone from Sam's face. We can spend the rest on some make-up and shoes, Margaret announces, semi-triumphant, on her way out of the shop, and maybe a wee cup of tea somewhere and a bun.

Sam moves slowly but Margaret motors on. Keeping moving is the only thing she can think to do. Keep going.

Margaret can sew up anything; she's been trying to mend Sam for years. All her work has never quite taken, though. She watches her knock-off child, patterned with buttoned-up emotions, barely holding it together. These days are hard on Sam. Sam is different from the other girls. No point trying to make her fit in now. Too late for that. Sam will arrive with sleek, flat hair, her pale features bold against the birds' nests piled high on her friends' heads, their jangly, expensive earrings swinging in the wind at the start of the night. Some will tumble from their owners' lobes into pools of vomit by the end, the cheap bronze wantonness covered by cheesy regurgitated garlic chips and vodka. Margaret knows what they get up to. She was a young one, once, herself. Fashions might change, but you don't forget.

Choose Life

Naoise, 1994

Naoise sees an old girlfriend struggling with a child, bags of groceries, harried. He doesn't recognise her at first, her body embracing middle age early, eyes drawn, face like an elasticated waistband. They are the same age, though. The majority of people he grew up with are doing what they should be: coupling up, getting married, having kids, steady jobs, buying houses. Fulfilling society's expectations of them. Proletariat sheep. Worn down by the boring day-to-day routine.

He catches her looking at him, the recognition; what he does not expect is her response, the disgust that travels across her features, her disapproval as she takes in Sam, so he pulls his teenage girlfriend closer, the way he used to do with her, and kisses Sam, deep, taunting, caught up in him.

He can't even remember the woman's name.

Deirdre, maybe. One of many.

He watches maybe Deirdre the whole time he is kissing Sam. She can't look away, it's almost like he's with both of them. His kiss makes so-called Deirdre flush. He grins at her as she gets into her car, flustered, stuttering, awkward movements as she tries to manoeuvre her child and her shopping. She was almost sneering to herself moments earlier, now she is desperate to get away, return to the safe nest of her boring existence. He sees her smile reassuringly at the child in the car seated behind her and she pauses to stare at him. Sam is chattering on about her formal as they walk in the other direction. He turns to wave at Deirdre, then winks at her, and she starts the car, her features hardening as she engages the steering wheel.

He can't have that.

He lets go of Sam's hand and runs up to the front of her car and bangs the hood with both hands. She jumps, startled, and in the back her child starts to fuss as the engine stalls. He laughs as Sam catches up with him, pulls him away.

What's all that about? Do you know her? Sam asks.

No. Thought I did.

She knows you. That face.

No, she doesn't. Just thinks she does. Easy mistake to make. Car was gonna hit the kerb. I did her a favour. Good Samaritan, me.

Yeah, right, genuine saint, Sam says.

They walk away and Naoise doesn't look back.

Educational Attainment of Mother and Child

Sam, 1994

Assembly is always a production. There are prayers, pronouncements, provocation. The Sisters of Perpetual Succour love a good show. And they really love singing.

There seems to be a hymn for everything. Today is chastity. Last week there was a discussion on why the girls should not use tampons – forget toxic shock syndrome, the nuns seemed more worried about them getting used to sticking things up inside them. Like their fingers. Or a banana. Or some massive sized cock. Because obviously using a tampon might make you want sex. From the podium the nuns plough straight into a morning hymn from a morning prayer to diffuse impure thoughts. So they sing about how morning has broken, like the first morning, and all Sam can think about is sex. Having sex for the first time. Breaking. There are a lot of virgins in her year still. Proper ones, not like Mary, mother of God. No one is being visited by the Angel Gabriel; at least, Sam hopes not. The girls' voices rise and fall as Sam watches Sister-Principal-Eudoria-Regina-chief-God-botherer-whatever-her-title-is – Sister PE is what the girls call her behind her back, PE for short – spit out the words in her direction. The first nun. PE would like to be the First Nun. She's the nun that breaks everybody.

After, PE runs through the usual school notices. There is a new geography teacher, Mr Travers, covering Mrs Walsh's maternity leave for her sixth form classes. PE asks him to say a few words. He comes across as slimy as a politician. Sam watches him perform from the audience. He seems to gaze at her when he talks about the school's reputation, how important the upcoming exams are. It makes her feel uncomfortable, as he repeats again what a huge privilege it is to teach here, how grateful he is to get a chance to *mould these young minds*. How lucky the girls are. Sam could swear he stares straight at her when he says this. She stares back.

Right then Sam decides today is going to be all types of wrong, so she might as well ramp it up.

In class, after Travers opens all the windows and repeats his podium speech verbatim, he presents the students with new work. All smiles. Sam flicks through the handout. Colonialism and Neo-colonialism. Resources. Education. Tables comparing countries. One question grabs her attention: *Describe and explain the relationship between the educational attainment of mother and child mortality*. It's like a gift. Sam asks Mr Travers if the fact that she doesn't have a mother means: a) she doesn't have to answer it, based on emotional distress; b) it doesn't apply to Sam, therefore she doesn't have to answer it; or c) in Sam's case the *idea* of her mother is spread out over Dundrum Bay, part of the greater ecosystem of the coastal dunes, the beach environment, the essence of a million living organisms, looked over by the Mourne mountains themselves, but even though Fionnuala Malin has contributed to and created life – Sam is proof of that – essentially her mother is tatty bread. Completely and utterly dead, dead, dead, dead, so that also means she doesn't have to answer it.

Do you think that's funny, Miss Malin? Travers barks.

Not really. Do you?

No. Do you like school?

Do you like teaching? Do you think you're good at it?

A few people snigger, they can't help it. Becca is trying not to giggle. Sam flicks her hair off her shoulders.

I'm the Teacher here, you're the studen—

Are you sure? Sam is warming up now. Sits up straight. Waits for it.

That's enough.

Enough what?

Enough challenging behaviour for one day.

Um huh. Who isn't, challenged? Are *you* on an even keel, Mr Travers? Everything perfect in your so-called life?

My life is none of your business. If you don't want to learn you can go to the office.

I don't think so, Sam says.

Everyone laughs nervously.

I won't be spoken to like that.

Sorry. I. *Won't*. Think. So. *Sir*.

Right, that's it. Out. Now.

Sam doesn't move.

Or would you rather the whole class got held back?

There is a sharp intake of breath as he hauls Sam out of her seat and manhandles her through the door. Becca is throwing her daggers. Jesus, Sam, Becca whispers under her breath as Sam goes past her, trying not to laugh.

Sam knows he can't possibly win this, that sending her to the office is futile.

After class Sam sees him, Mr T, teacher tail between his legs, blister past and demand to know why his authority is being flouted. Notes his body language change through the fuzzy glass window that divides Nearer-My-God-To-Thee-Sister-Principal-Eudoria from the rest of the school domain. Sister PE puts her calm, cold hand on Mr T's shoulder and helps him find his seat. Sam watches the nun take a deep breath to explain the way things are for Sam. She lets Travers respond. Waits. Then rises from her desk and stands behind him. Sam has noticed Sister PE does this a lot when she's trying to get her point across; a kind of where-would-Jesus-stand approach, she guesses. Sam thinks, Jesus, even Jesus would think Sister Eudoria was a right cow.

Sam wonders if he was any craic, Jesus; he must have been: twelve fellas plus followed him around, hung on his every word, then wrote it all down after he popped his clogs for the second time. But where were all the women? They might have given JC a more balanced review. Surprised JC didn't come back to give

56

a revisionist history, like a religious R.F. Foster. If Sam had that power she would. She *so* would. Before Sam can tune into the Lord to get an answer, Sister Eudoria has appeared at the door to her office, apparition-ready, standing there like the Gary Oldman of nuns. In fact, if Francis Ford Coppola had released Gary Oldman from set one day for a wee walkabout and Gary Oldman randomly ended up here, no one would have copped him for a vampire, Dracul or anything, just some oul one locked up in the convent for too long. But of course *Hollywood* is a long way from here. Holy wood is more like it. The Holy One beckons Sam inside and naturally, like any good virgin, her blood runs cold.

Nits and Pies

Sam, 1994

With her mother gone, Patsy took the razor to her. It was a long time ago, but still. Some days it's like she can feel the nicks fresh on her scalp.

Merciful Lord, Patsy! Merciful Lord! Margaret Caher said. She's a child, not a sheep!

Her father had taken the shears and shaved her head. PJ had lost all his hair already. Together they looked like refugees, refugees from the world. Which she supposes they were.

Now, in the school corridor, Sam sees the girl's skinny face and shaved head and feels instantly sorry for her. She knows there's something wrong somewhere, there's something very wrong, because normally they take a metal comb and they put conditioner in your hair and they smooth it down and someone sits with you, probably your mother, sits with you and picks those things, those nits, out of your hair. But no one did that for Sam and no one has done that for this girl and so she's shaven, like a monk.

Everyone at school's tormenting her, tormenting this little first-year and pushing her, and Sam wants to take her under her wing and say, I was you, I was you once. But then Sam thinks about how, about how that girl might look at her, and think, Will I grow up like you? I don't want to be you, Sam Malin. I don't want to be any of you. So Sam stops, stares, says nothing. Says nothing to the bald-headed girl, and the shame grows on her, like a cancer.

It reminds her of the day, well, the story Margaret tells her of the day, that she and her mother went to Belfast shopping and the husbands, John-Jo and Patsy, nearly burnt the house down. Margaret always points to the spot above the cooker when she retells this story. Sam almost feels it is her memory now. She could tell it like she remembers it. But she doesn't. She remembers so little of before.

The men were late to put on the dinner, of course – animals came first, always. The weans giving out about being hungry and sure they couldn't listen to it, so off they went, forgetting about everything, the two of them heading into the town with the kids in tow, all in John-Jo's wee blue car, for fish 'n' chips and then thinking, sure, was a nice evening, they'd take a dander out to the shore, let the kids run about for a while, tire themselves out.

How when they got back Patsy had nearly burnt the hand off himself taking the incinerated, black-as-your-boot shepherd's pie out of the oven, the good casserole dish cracked, the kitchen filling up with billowing smoke.

Little Miss Madam here bawling her head off. Margaret laughs.

And where were you? Patsy would say to Margaret, joining in – off galivanting in the big smoke yourself!

When I got back Patsy was off in the surgery getting the hand looked at. John-Jo had the four of ye in our bed. Himself passed out in the chair, sandy boots on and everything. God bless him, that man, she'd say, and she and Patsy would anoint themselves without thinking, a blink of Catholicism, before returning to their story. The black soot on the wall. Airing the house out for days. Patsy's tiny scar. From cooking, of all things. Finding out the children had nits the day after. The adults too. Sure, it was all sorted in the end. Was a good laugh all the same. Except they always managed to tell it without mentioning Nuala.

Malapropos Magnetar

Sam, 1994

She slips under the ultra-blue current of light, small talk easing her quick entrance to the throbbing body of the pub, the gig underway already, ripples of music calling out comfort to her body. She can't be alone tonight, needs the safety of other people. It's difficult, like every year, wanting to remember, trying to shut it out – the last days she saw her mother. Her body won't let her forget even when her mind shields the date. The loss remains fixed inside, and grief irritates; like an insistent child, it won't be ignored for long.

Naoise wasn't in when she called. Often Naoise doesn't even turn up before she has to leave for her evening shift at the newsagent. She'll hang on, waiting to the very last minute, race out of the flat. She feels dumb, stupid, at wasting her time waiting on Naoise. But even waiting is better than not waiting; that what she felt before she met him was irrelevant. This thing between them is taking her over. She tries not to think about it. What it means. What he means to her. That she needs to see him today of all days.

She throws herself towards the pace of the music, welcomes the thud into her heart. A throb in her chest extinguishes the thoughts rushing through her head, undercuts the agony inside her, dampens the blackness of her frame. She's an empty silhouette set against the smoke and heat and sweat rising and falling around her, soaring out of the indescribable logic of the crowd, which comes together and breaks apart like the undercurrents of the sea; she jumps in, not stopping the moment for anybody, because if she does, she would have to admit she doesn't like to be alone, would remember the first time she touched herself in a dark room, when she knew she shouldn't. And that would be too sad to admit to, to anyone at all really. All their faces, all their tongues, all that pleasure, just enough denial to let it be real enough for her to come, a cast of characters appearing between her legs on demand, conjured up by her desires. She can do that, worship her own body, a temple, entered and willed into submission as required. But what happens when she's with him is different. A reaction she wasn't prepared for. Something she can't control. It's consuming her.

Sam looks for those possible faces, someone to sabotage this feeling she can't handle, searches the crowd for other people to be part of her but they might not be what she has imagined. Might not say the right things. Might not look the right way. The resolution of their hands, the way their fingers lace together, covered in litmus-paper skin changing colour with desire, the sure small spread of lust blotting out from their palms into fingertips, seeping into everything they do. She thinks about his hands around her neck, inside her, the way he holds on to her, always pulling her towards him. She has become a spinning top of a girl. His toy. His beautiful hands. Her pain.

Perhaps no one can tell these things about her. Perhaps no one notices. Or perhaps everyone does. Perhaps everyone cares about these things. Perhaps it isn't the cattle-market rub against nightclub walls in a darkened auction of affection. Maybe there is more to all of this. She leans against the vibrating walls, watching the audience thrash themselves around. Most of the way she has to crash up against herself, or someone else, anyone else, to find out. Most of the time she is left in a frenzied state of deep disappointment.

She needs to see him.

She feels the inside of her mouth go sour.

She sinks to the ground. A girl she knows vaguely from the Prod school sits down beside her. Sam thinks the girl says she knows Becca. It's too loud to hear but Becca knows everyone. Sam smiles anyway. Her head hurts. Her chest. A tightness. The girl produces a joint from her bra and lights up, takes a long deep inhale. Smiles, takes another, taps her lips, then she cups Sam's face, and blows smoke into her mouth. Sam lets the kiss of smoke take her over. Anything to numb the pain welcome. The du du du duh guitar string starts. Soars. She closes her eyes and conjures the singer. Kurt appears. All the space in the room is filled by his voice. His face.

Hey! he sings.

Wait! The crowd performs like a choir.

His bleached blond halo swinging, his perfect weak discoloured smile, graded Pisces-blue video eyes.

Hey! Wait!

She just wants to reach out and touch him.

Hey! Wait! he responds, voice carrying above the swell of the audience.

He's like a priceless painting in a gallery. A wired alarm will go off if she loses control, reaches out.

Hey! Wait!

He pushes a hair caught against her cheek away, his guitar-string-calloused fingertips fizzing against her skin.

Hey! Wait!

For those few seconds, touching something real, they forget themselves. Their faces move together like pages in a closing book.

Hey!   Wait!

She opens her eyes and he is gone.

Hey! Wait!

She closes her eyes again. Only pulsating red-hued darkness remains. She can't get back there. To him. She blinks back into the room. Condensation soaks from the sweaty wall, solid against her back, his song ending, another starting. She tries not to think about her. Photograph in her head as if she is above herself watching everything below. Wishing she could change something that might matter. A Polaroid developed over time exposing all the sadness in the world. This world wasn't enough for her mother. Or maybe it was just too much.

Everything is rotten, everything is ending. She stays there, watching the dance, wanting to betray herself for this feeling but knowing, deep down, that she can't.

She heads back to the flat, bangs the door, stands there, shivering in the cold. Drunk. She wants to sleep with him, she does, but she wants it on her terms. She wants to be sure. Sometimes everything feels so overwhelming, so huge, rare, special between them, like they have expanded out and into every part of her life. She is obsessed. Intoxicated. She lives or dies on every little gesture, on the smallest look, dissects his words, their meaning. He is all she wants. He knows her body better than she does; they talk for hours but she holds back. Sabotages herself.

No one comes to the door. She hammers it again. A sinking feeling blooms inside her. There is a chime – not an alarm exactly, but a pause. Nobody wants you. Nobody loves you. Just like the North. No one willing to claim her. So she stops giving herself away. She wants to let go. She wants him. She wants him to feel the same way she does.

She slumps down on the step, closes her eyes, falls asleep.

Sam.

Sam.

She opens her eyes and Naoise is there kneeling in front of her.

What are you doing? He pulls her up. She kisses him before he can ask more questions. He opens the door and they go inside. The flat is quiet. He traces his fingers against the contours of her face. I don't think you should be here tonight.

Can't I stay? Please? Don't make me go home. She starts to unbuckle his belt, her fingers shaky.

He catches her hands. Stop. Stop. I'm tired.

I lo—needed to see you. The words tumble out as he places a finger against her lips. He studies her, his face neutral.

It's late, you should go home. I'll get you a taxi.

Naoise.

She feels awkward, out of place in this room that has become so familiar to her. She starts to take off her clothes; her cardigan, her shirt, fiddles with the skirt buttons, the shaky sensation inside her let down by her feeble fingertips.

He smirks and stops her, pulls her towards him.

What are you doing? You don't have to do this.

He says this holding her delicate mouth close to his, his steady palms encircling her entire face. She doesn't have an answer.

Go home.

Naoise, she pleads. Today's when my mum—I mean. I dunno when she died. Where. Exactly. I remember when she went. When she left us.

He says nothing for the longest time. Eventually, when Sam starts to cry, tears impossible to curtail, he kisses them away. Kisses her lips, the salty sweet taste of the possible.

You need to be with your family.

They don't care. He never talks about her.

You can't stay here.

I need you, she says.

Naoise sighs.

This isn't going to work, he says as he kisses her mouth. She kisses those words away, trying to capture something she can feel leaving, kisses him so hard, almost biting his lip.

You should go.

He traces his mouth against her dipped lashes, one blaze from his eyes into hers. Then, nothing. He leans away from her. She reaches for him, even though she knows she shouldn't; it is weak, her muscles move in jerky panic, straining for him. She wants him to stop. Is desperate for it.

She needs to touch him. Comfort herself. She tries to kiss him again but he pushes her off.

Tomorrow.

Let me stay.

Sam. We need to talk—

I think I love you, she says. A sigh, desperate and needy, escapes, her response moulded; she has waited for those words for what feels like the longest time, starved herself for those words. Words she finds herself saying. Words she wants to hear from him.

Words that make him stop.

He stares at her, deciding something in that moment; she thinks he has absolved her mess, accepted her flaws.

Show me, he says.

In that instant, he makes everything they have sound cheap, disposable.

He kicks her right leg open and lies down on the floor, his head between her legs. Waiting. She looks down at him and laughs. Then blushes as she begins to understand.

Show me, he says, his expression serious, resolute.

She lifts her skirt slowly, heavy gabardine fabric twisted up in her left hand, and slides her fingers inside her white knickers, inside herself. She is a little self-conscious, even in the gloom, as she gives into this feeling but his eyes light with pleasure as she touches herself while he watches. Her body bows as she comes.

Just as she wants to collapse against him, he pulls her down. Kisses her in the dark. Something has changed in him. She can feel it.

She tells him she loves him. He just says, Sam. Sam. Sam.

They almost have sex. Everything but. She tenses up every time he tries. Shuts down. Her hands spread wide, hard in his chest.

You sure about this? he says.

She nods. Yes. I want to.

Eventually, he stops trying. He can't stay hard.

I'm sorry. I don't know why—

You're not ready.

I am.

Seriously? he sighs and she is left shivering on the cold hard floor as he moves off her, dresses. She feels stupid and young and ugly. Did I do something wrong?

No. It's never happened before.

She reaches for him but he brushes her off, hands her her clothes.

It's *me*. You think I'm disgusting.

It's not you.

It is.

Christ. Sort yourself out. You said you didn't want to have sex with me. Remember?

She has nothing to say but before she can deflect, Sam hears the door bang open downstairs, smells grass and hears Chiz's slippy, curling laugh. She grabs her clothes and races to the bathroom. Naoise couldn't have sex with her, even when she wanted him to. There is something so wrong with her. She is a fucking joke. Disgusting. She bites the meaty part of her palm, to stop tears, then wipes her watery eyes because Chiz enjoys weakness, the cracked parts. He picks at you like split ends, wants to snip you.

When she comes out Naoise is smoking too. He offers her a beer; she sits on the edge of the sofa, sips it. Eventually he pulls her down on his lap. Acting as if nothing has happened. So she does the same. Resets herself for him.

When she leaves later that night, she fixes her face in the wing mirror of a saloon car on the street. She feels bruised. Beaten up. Hollowed out. But she can't understand why. She wants all of this. She tries, she tries, tries to be everything he wants, but somehow it is not enough.

Sediment

Nuala, 1982

The children are like gold and I'm the stream. Sometimes I flow away alone but in the morning I wake up and there they are, deposited around me, one curved into my back, the other under my chin, my arms like low branches around each, entwining them to my heart. I fear for the day they don't settle with me but slip upstream and out to the wide wild world. I fear and I yearn for it, remembering that I want them to leave me as much as I desired them into this world. I deposit stones of discomfort and stir up the sediment of their hearts, muddy all ahead of them, but for now they slow at my bend in the river and settle into my sides, little slips of love and want and need until they outgrow me, are mine no longer, and we slough back into sleep.

Mother's Day

Sam, 1994

She doesn't do Mother's Day. Mother's Day is to be avoided at all costs. Sam hates Mother's Day.

It's as though every part-time job Sam has ever had has forced her to engage with the full horror of this man-made celebration. Of course, the Church created it; like most horrors in this world, it originated with them. Victorians took it over, then some American woman who wanted it to be a day for mothers *and* peace. Well, that is an impossibility here.

She knows this morning at the nursing home that sad-sack sons will rock up to see their near-dead mas, some looking hopeful that *this* year might be the *last* year. It never works like that. It's really true, the good die (relatively) young. The newsagent gig in the afternoon is no better: reams and reams of cards. Awkwardly wrapping last-minute overpriced chocolates which little boys and old men, who should know better, pay for with warm coins, metered out one by one, bacteria-laden currency, giving you all of their DNA, shit and sweat in every little bit of their hard-earned cashola.

Sam always hopes the tainted money will make her ill. A vomiting bug. Infernal stomach cramps and bloody diarrhoea, enough to make her unconscious, to send her careening out of this day. So she'll wake lighter and cleansed and the tomorrow that she's been praying for will have arrived, it will already be another day. No longer Mothering Sunday. The day when the fact that you don't have a mother is no longer possible to ignore. Unavoidable. So the ones who know, remember, after all this time, hesitate just enough, to let you know their immense pity, that they haven't forgotten, and oh, how they love a good tragedy around here. As if there isn't enough in the province to go round.

The local papers print the same old slogans. Vapid beliefs repeated like prayers. *Mother's Day is a time for tradition. Flowers make the day complete. A time for the family to get together.* No one mentions the unwanted gifts. The crap spur-of-the-moment purchases. No one mentions fathers across the province destroying the kitchen and using every pan in the house to make a dinner that takes six hours and tastes slightly off. Then too tired after to do all the dishes – some pot always left steeping and unwashed for the next day. Which they wholeheartedly promise to wash but never do. Every day is Mother's Day.

Each year Patsy makes them go, en famille, with a large bunch of white carnations, and place them ceremoniously at their mother's grave. Except Nuala isn't in that grave. Her name isn't even on it. It's the only place her father can think to bring them: to their grandparents' grave to think about their mother. Sam wonders what is the point pretending after all this time. Eleven years of this charade. They'd thrown ashes into the sea, ages ago, when her aunt, Sara, had arrived back with an urn. Ashes from a fire. Her mother wasn't in the urn, it was symbolic, Sara said. Ceremonial. Last Sara had heard from her sister was in Gambia, the spring of 1983, six months after Nuala had left them. Sara said Nuala told her she was coming home to get her kids. The line was bad. Nuala mentioned it was hard to stay in touch. Then the line went dead. That was the last time the sisters spoke. Sara thought Nuala likely died on a dirt road in the Gambia. But she didn't know for sure.

Sam notices other weary families coming to pay their respects to their dead mothers who actually have graves. They exchange small glances of recognition. Clutching their white carnations. Sam has always detested carnations. Cheap, petrol-station flowers used for hurried apologies also happen to be the same flowers you give to your dead mother, if your mother is dead, on Mother's Day. Makes sense somehow.

Naoise's parents are here too. She stood at the barren grave and read their names out loud. He doesn't visit, though. He never talks about them. He doesn't have to worry about Mother's Day presents, either.

This year, though, Patsy has got them a present for Mother's Day. He tells PJ, after years of asking, that he's going to put Nuala's name on the stone. This year.

Finally put Nuala to rest.

RIP, Mummy dearest.

Happy Mother's Day, Mrs Malin, you're officially dead.

Sam says it is stupid. Years earlier, before Sara died, she gave Sam a postcard that was sent on a road somewhere in Africa. It had arrived months after her mother had left. Sara had kept them to send on. Addressed to Sam and PJ. Sara had presented the postcards, photos, mementos, like a gift she didn't want, when Sam was eleven. The battered card stamped with faint pink kisses that used to smell of something: love, maybe. Faded photographs of her stunning mother leaning against a battered jeep in bright sun, her eyes light and her mouth a smiling orange coral. She looked so happy, so free.

Her aunt had gone there, visited the place in the picture. Talked to locals. Her mother had been working on a wildlife reserve. The owners of the complex told Sara she'd gone travelling and never came back. They thought she'd moved on. People did that apparently – they promised to come back, volunteer again, but they hardly ever did. They said Nuala had been great with the animals; the ones that had no chance – the outliers – she nursed back from the brink. The unbelievable irony of that. Acting like she was on a gap year.

No one knows what really happened to her.

Aunt Sara swore right up until she died that her mother was going to send for them. Swears it would only have been a matter of time. All Sam knows is that her mother left and she never came back. So she point blank refuses to visit the grave on Mother's Day. She knows her mother isn't in there.

Patsy wanted to destroy her mother's memory in those early years. Erase her from their lives. Her da was sentimental but he wasn't stupid, yet Sara wouldn't give up.

The rancour in Patsy's words made him sound drunk sometimes, even though he never touched a drop. The hatred slurred over the sounds, ice-cold – *she* only cared about herself – abandoned the job lot of us – only loved *herself*. You hear me? You hear me? Your sister. Your precious fucking sister. Where is she? Huh? Huh? Eventually Sara stopped fighting his version of events. Gave up. Gave in. He beat her down. Dismantled her defence.

Cancer took Sara in the end. Sam remembers Margaret minding them, waving Patsy off out the door, her da awkward with a new haircut and his good suit hanging loose on his shoulders. Margaret had fussed but Patsy had no patience for her to put a few tacking stitches in to make it neat against his back, as if not fitting in was part and parcel of the penance for losing Nuala. Contrition he carried with him as he hurried off to catch the boat from Dublin to make the funeral across the water, already regretting the journey, constantly wanting to turn back.

There's no reason for it that Sam can see but Patsy still uses Sara's name like it's a bad word in their house, curses her with every breath.

She wonders is it because she gave up, like their mother.

The Other Side of the Mountain

Patsy, 1982

He put down the letter and left PJ in the kitchen, ran through the house calling their names, his voice sounding almost foreign to him, panic soaring through it. He found his daughter, Sam, almost instantly, quietly rocking back and forth on her mother's chair in the good room, bubbles of blood and dirt on the side of her face, the dog's bloodied body a few feet away. He tried not to look at what was written on the wall, it made his insides run cold. Nuala had spent money on this room. Making it all white and pure. She'd made him take his work boots off to use it. It had always annoyed him. Her habit of making him feel dirty. He reached out to touch the bloody letters but then his hand recoiled and he forced himself to turn his back to it.

He picked Sam up, checked her over as if she were a small, injured animal. Once he was satisfied it was the dog's blood and not her own, he brought her to the kitchen and put her down beside her brother. Sam was thankfully silent for once. The boy noticed her and stopped crying, stared and stared at his sister and then started to scream and scream and scream. Screaming for all of them. Patsy left them there and ran around the house yelling his wife's name. Echoes of his own desperation greeted him but she did not appear. When he came back downstairs the children had wandered back into the dog, in the good room. He lifted her up and carried her past his crying children and lowered the animal onto the ground outside. They followed him out. PJ sat squealing on the step. The girl gone quiet again. He picked up the boy, then got down on his hunkers to his daughter's level. Trying to talk to her. Samantha kept going back to the dog, lifting its head up, the blood staining her little face as she hugged her, painting her crimson.

72

Where have you been, pet? he asked her. With Mummy?

Daddy, help Whiskey, Sam said.

Sam, Patsy said. Whiskey is dead.

Please, Daddy! Daddy! She kept trying to lift up the dog's head, blood leaking out onto her clothes. She started screaming. No, Daddy! No. No. I want Mummy! I want Mummy! Mummy! Mummy! Mummy's gone!

He wanted to do something, comfort them, but all he could think was, Where is Fionnuala? Where is she? He left the kids there outside and went back in. Ran through the rooms in a frenzy, calling her name, again and again. In the good room he stared again at the word on the wall. *CUNT* daubed large and red and frightening against the heavily embossed wallpaper. Trickles of blood had run down the wall and pooled in the thick white shag carpet where he had found Whiskey. It made him think of senseless animal attacks, packs of dogs maiming sheep and their lambs in a frenzied bloodlust, just for the sport of it, because it was their nature. To kill. He tried not to think about the calf in the field, the cow.

He ran outside and looked around the yard. There was no sign of her car, and he finally accepted that she was gone. He threw up, almost immediately, vomited once and then retched, kept retching. His empty stomach pulling him over he buckled, knees hitting the ground.

Back inside, he drank water straight from the kitchen tap, rinsing his mouth. When he came out he had his car keys in his hand but he didn't know how they got there. He put the children in his car, on the floor, behind him. Wedged in tight, his daughter blotting blood on her brother's clothes.

Fionnuala wasn't dead. No. She was gone. *No.* She'd come back. She had to.

He kept thinking of the cow in the field. She couldn't have been saved, she was too far gone. Images slashed in his mind's eye like in those horror movies. The field, the cow in the field, the calf, the calf in the field. Fionnuala. Nuala. His Nuala. The calf, destroyed, deformed, like, like, the cow, the dog, his wife. No, his wife was fine. She was not here, so she was fine. She must be fine. Fionnuala had left him. He would have to come back for Fionnuala. Find Fionnuala. Nuala was gone. She might never come back.

Whatever had happened next had somehow made him guilty. The police took her note to the station. Photographed all the rooms. The vet said the calf was born deformed. Would have died anyway, the cow probably too. Then removed the animals. *His* animals taken from *his* land. Evidence. Then all of it disappeared, just like his wife.

So you have no idea. Who did that to my property? Patsy said to the detective, Peter Savage. Any news on my wife?

Patsy, we've told you, we've no leads. She could be anywhere at this stage, Peter said. It's been two weeks already.

Maybe she'll come back, the younger officer said.

I hate to ask this, but was there any trouble at home, Patsy? Peter said.

No. There was no row, if that's what you mean.

No one strange hanging around at the house?

No. What do you mean by that? Patsy said.

Could she have been having an affair? the younger officer asked.

An affair? With who? Catch yourself on, Patsy said.

No offence, Patsy, but she was a good-looking woman, the younger officer said. We have to ask. There's talk.

Officer Clements, that's enough, Peter said.

Talk. What talk? Talk is all you are good for. No. She wasn't having an affair. Is that it? The height of your police work. Jokers, the lot a ye. Patsy tutted but even as he broke into a mistimed laugh, he could see what they were really saying, what everyone was thinking. That she'd never really been his in the first place.

Officer Clements pressed him. What kind of woman leaves her children behind, Patsy? What kind of mother does that?

That's enough, Peter said.

What are you trying to say? Patsy said, getting agitated.

74

It's just, you know, mothers don't leave their children behind, normally. It's unusual.

I said that was enough, Officer Clements, Peter said again.

I didn't kill her, if that's what you're thinking, Patsy said. I didn't do anything wrong.

No one wanted to hear that Patsy was giving her an opportunity, a window for Nuala to see sense, to come home before anyone noticed she'd gone. Patsy could never find the words to explain he loved her enough, he was trying to make room for her mistake. That he felt she'd simply gone astray. Believed she'd come back until she didn't.

A month later, they had even less to go on. Officer Clements had a big mouth. Liked to gossip. Wondered what Patsy had done to make her leave like that? Then other people wondered. There was talk about what was written on the wall. Dirty words. Grown men fell into sniggering like young ones behind Patsy's back when he would arrive in somewhere, till after a while he couldn't stand to go out the door atall. People said, thinking of it now, Nuala had looked under pressure before she left. *Under pressure*. What was going on, up at that farmhouse? It became not why she left, but what had Patsy done to make her go?

Patsy asked himself the same question. He felt guilty without a real reason. In the wee dark hours he chastised himself; for what, he couldn't figure out. He wasn't enough for her, somehow. He was easy to leave. Sometimes he thought of the children; maybe they had been all that kept her here until they didn't anymore.

No body. No body was ever found. Nothing to hold against him. They tried, though. They marked him out. Even though it was clear after a few months he was innocent, when the first postcard arrived. He'd considered briefly going after her, leaving the weans with Margaret, heading to where the post mark was. Africa. Eritrea of all places. He'd never even heard of it. Pride stopped him. Patsy had done nothing wrong. He would go into the police station every once in a while with a postcard from her. They'd log evidence. They told him she was gone and there was nothing they could do. The postcards stopped after six months. The last one came from Gambia. Finally, the police put her down as a missing persons case. They kept a close eye on him for the rest of that year and the one after. Near-silent raps at the door late at night. His car always getting pulled over at checkpoints. That strange click on the line when he picked up the phone to make a call. He felt like a terrorist. He went silent, into himself, after. Hated the feeling of being on show. The sense of being watched. It was the not finding her, Fionnuala, that soured everything after. Like the whole place was waiting for him to make a mistake when he hadn't done anything at all. He hadn't done *any*thing wrong, but once they start, those quiet whispers never stop.

Two years after her mother left, when Sam was seven, he had told her she had to do her bit, make dinners, washing, all the things her mother did. He had said it was just the way it was, he needed help and she was old enough now. She had said nothing as usual, just stared at him in that unknowable way of hers that echoed her mother so intensely it brought him to anger every time. Margaret helped teach the girl. The Caher woman had been good to them but was getting on. Eventually she sat him down and suggested perhaps they might get a housekeeper.

A stranger? In my house? He'd laughed. Sure, the young one can earn her keep. About time. Margaret had said no more about it then but had appeared weekly with jam and tarts and whatever else would do them. He had a mind to say no, but in the end he needed the kindness more than his pride.

They lived on fish 'n' chips and anything with eggs he could make. The boy started playing Gaelic a few years later – good, but not a county player. Lost all his hair after, the boy did, bald since he was three. He could not even remember his mother. Patsy blamed his sister, her quiet blood-soaked face and body, smoothed out like the best Sunday china, set out once and then broken apart.

Still, no one could say Patsy didn't try, didn't do the best for his girl. Didn't he let her go to the fanciest school round here in the end? PJ didn't get into grammar school straight away. This had never sat right with Patsy. His boy slow. A half-wit. No point telling him that the exam system was a joke, testing children at ten and eleven, marking them out for life as good, or not good enough, bright, not quite bright enough. Not enough to tick the Protestant or Catholic box – let's add a smart or thick label, early enough to really damage you.

Sam had found her uniform for the other girls' secondary school – the not-the-grammar-school school – stuffed in his wardrobe in a white plastic bag from Clobber. Margaret had asked him would he not wait and see, not listen to that jumped-up headmistress, blowing that her own daughter would be the only one who would pass. Samantha was easily distracted and had trouble concentrating, she said, and, well, you know yourself, Patsy, a lovely girl, no question, but not quite grammar school material.

When she had passed the big exam, Patsy had acted as if she had done it to spite him. Margaret was thrilled, but no one from her primary was going; the few friends she had all heading to the secondary in the town. Going to the convent grammar school in Newcastle meant lots of buses. It meant leaving the other uniform back. It meant money. Patsy was incensed. Margaret had kicked up a big fuss and Clobber's manager had given in and changed the uniform in the end.

Patsy got a size up before Margaret could get around to fixing that, though. Margaret had given out stink to him – She's swamped in that uniform, our Lady in Heaven, she said in a highfalutin' tone, up to high doh over a pinafore. For God's sake, Patsy, Margaret had gone on. You might as well have painted 'Bully me' on her forehead on the first day.

Give over, he'd told her. She'll grow into it. Sure, it'll toughen her up.

It didn't quite work out the way he thought it would, though. In the end, with Sam, it was always that way. She did her own thing. Never listened. He couldn't be responsible for that, for the way she was.

In Down, Three Saints One Grave Do Fill, Patrick, Brigid and Colmcille

Sam, 1994

Normally, when she finally arrives at the cathedral and then St Patrick's Stone, she pauses, respectfully, like it's an open coffin, with a dead relative laid out, waiting for her to mutter prayers and kiss the cold plastic skin of the recently deceased.

Sam blesses herself, then splays out on the slab, cadaver lite. She lies back, luxuriating in the sun-warmed exterior of the stone as she proceeds to smoke as if she were on a beach somewhere in France. Cannes. Mont-Saint-Michel. Île de Ré. Places from travel mags that she pores over in the newsagent. Locations they'd use for *Vogue* covers. Except she's never been to France.

Cigarette artfully poised at her thin-lipped mouth. Modelling and pouting as if her lips belonged to Sharon Stone. A show without an audience. Normally, this place would be hers. Today there is a full complement of tourists, Christians and idiots.

There are still two hours before the parade finishes and the place is packed. Her cigarette smoke catches in the sunlight, mingling above her. She wonders what Patrick would have made of all this. He lies, apparently, below their feet. *Saint* Patrick, so they say, a slave that made us all believe in God, is what gives this town its name, hard-won against the odds of terrorism tourism. Other places argue that this is not true. Like Armagh. *Other places* want to claim *our* Paddy for themselves.

A brand-new sign explains Patrick's final journey. Apparently Patrick wished to die in Armagh but the angel Victor ... *Victor?* Whoever heard of an angel called Victor? Anyway, the angel Victor came to Patrick in a dream, persuading him to let two untamed oxen carry him to his final resting place.

The chances of 'two untamed' *anything* pulling him *anywhere* past the townland of Saul was a bloody miracle in the first place. What a fool. Guided by the will of God ... to *Downpatrick*.

Sam smiles to herself as she reads the blurb. She blocks out the earache boom of American accents faltering over the parish place-name pronunciations. Imagines some local boyo back on approximately 16 March 461 AD dying to get back for his tea. Sees him calling time on the whole thing. Now, town councils argue back and forth the decision of some Yee-haw with two big 'untamed' cattle. What the hell did they expect? Tourism boards have yearly meetings around who 'owns' St Patrick and all that comes with that ownership. Sam finds it funny that anyone would want to admit they had a slave in the first place, and that he was basically a rent-a-kill bloke from Wales who vanquished Ireland's snakes and gave us Jesus as a replacement. He was about sixteen, bit younger than Sam, when they took him into captivity. The poor sod. Imagine that. At least Paddy's not down there on his own – there's Colmcille, massively into the rowing, and Bridget making her bloody crosses – loads of craic.

Every year some poor unfortunate Yanks end up in Downpatrick instead of Dublin, freeze-watching overloaded Massey Fergusons, crowned with hay bales and children of the corn, done up with their ma's best lipstick on their cheeks and a few old bedsheets, led by a local eejit with a few pints too many on board, staggering along with a big stick pretending to be the aforementioned saint. Followed, in no particular order – at least none that was clearly visible – by pipe-bands/ baton-twirlers/insert-random-musical-slash-gymnastic-act-as-appropriate and a few other unlucky foreign sods brought over by the council. This year's special tourist is an American patriot named Giuliano. It's embarrassing. In the middle of Lent Paddy's Day is an oasis of hedonism in a desert of giving up stuff you love for forty days and nights. The kids get chocolate. The adults, alcohol. Teenagers just get the hypocrisy. Because even Jesus Christ himself would have walked out of that sand pit and taken them twelve disciples and got shitfaced in whatever pub he found first. Christ, he could have turned that water into wine into green beer.

Paddy's Day is just an excuse to get steaming drunk like the rest of Ireland. An annual chance to fit in with our southern cousins, shake off the yoke of our Northern brethren, disguise our little bits of true-blue Protestantism that we secretly love, wee signs that we aren't the same type of Catholics as southern *Cath-ol-ics*. Our own breed, our own special mixture just across the border, washed and rinsed and polished by the BBC and British high street shops and sterling claiming us, no matter how much green we possess. Identity is a bitch.

Oi! Dickhead! Becca shouts at Sam across the throng. They squeeze through. Meet in the middle.

I have to show my face and then I'll meet you here later, Becca says. You wanna come?

Naw, I'll just get super chips, Sam says. Did you see Naoise?

No. You try the flat?

Yeah. Sam smiles, goes quiet.

You sure you don't wanna come for food? Becca is expert at changing the subject, pirouetting away from uncomfortable silences. My da doesn't mind. Actually, he'll be half-cut, he won't even notice.

Sam knows Becca's da will pass judgement. They always do. She doesn't need that today.

I'm good, Becs. See you later.

If I see Naoise, I'll send him this way.

Cheers, Sam says, and pushes her way through the throng, away from the centre of the town.

'St Patrick's Festival of Culture' really gets going in the evening. It's dark when every shade of teenager seeks refuge in Paddy's graveyard, awaiting the mild west stand-off with the cops, who inevitably come and find them, but only after the peelers have their tea of whatever-'n'-chips cop special. The minor armed forces announce their arrival like the Second Coming, giving almost everyone the chance to escape along the railway lines or out to Inch Abbey or the Quoile river. The newbies always head to the water, which is a massive mistake. The railway lines are much, much easier to navigate and there's always someone down there with a bag of something speedy and a fire going.

Sam makes her way there, necking whatever she has left of her bottle of multicoloured dolly mixture, the alcohol a tie-dyed kaleidoscope of her friends' parents' good cupboards' exotic summer holiday booze. She wants to make sure she is just a little bit flying as she bounces over railway sleepers and away from the fight. She hasn't seen Naoise or any of his mates, even though he was meant to meet her. Technically, he's stood her up. It stings less the more she drinks.

She walks for about half a mile before she hears them: disembodied male voices, egging each other on, sparks shooting up from damp branches dumped on the fire, that smell of cold cut with smoke from old trees, cigarettes and hash.

He is not there. She misses his silhouette. Instead, she hears Chiz and she finds herself shivering at the thought of joining him.

Hi, Sam calls out. You seen Becca?

Naoise with you? Chiz calls back.

No.

Chiz walks towards her then, smiling and smoking.

Haven't seen Becca. More's the pity.

Hi, Murph, Sam says, relieved to see his soft face appear behind Chiz.

Come on and sit down. He hands Sam a cigarette. He offers to light it for her but she declines, fishes her own lighter out of her pocket.

Chiz, Murph and the others sit around the fire on three long seats made from old lumber, the tops of the logs worn smooth with use, the flaky wood removed, like bald heads with bushy sideburns of bark. The girls with them are not from her school; their mouths hard and shining orangey-red alarm, even in the dark. They talk about Sam, brash enough to say something but not loud enough for her to hear, their mouths turned up like Crayola'd children's smiles, not without charm, simply unsophisticated. Sam doesn't know where to put herself so stands awkwardly on the edge of the group. Her shoulders rise ever so slightly as Chiz calls her name, makes the lads budge up for her to join them. She stretches out her hands and warms them on the fire.

How come you're on your tod? he asks. Where's your mates?

Sam holds her hands out to the flame for as long as she can bear it.

Everybody scattered when they tried to lift us. This one cop went mental and beat the head off that Wheeler fella, and Tony Odongo's little brother, David. Total pig. I just legged it, she says. Did Naoise go to Belfast?

Did he, Murph? Chiz says. Sam thinks he is making fun of her, but she doesn't know why. She just doesn't like it.

Chiz sits smiling as he watches her. Dressed in faded denim, the washed-out colour of silver birches. He bends forward to get a better look at her. He is looking at her in a way that she doesn't want. That Naoise wouldn't welcome.

Chiz offers Sam a joint, waggles it at her. She stubs out her ciggie, inches over. He's the only one with any gear.

Chiz waits.

Say please.

What? Sam says.

Say, pretty please, Chiz. I'll give you a little hit – and he leans into her, pulls her towards him, so no one else can hear and says – if you let me come in your mouth.

I should go, Sam says, as much to herself as the others. Chiz sniggers as she abruptly stands up. He curls his head towards his chest in laughter. Sam watches him and decides Chiz is a stretchy sort of human being, like chewing gum, tall and stringy, able to fold himself in on himself. You'd take in too much air around him and make yourself feel sick. She moves away.

I was only joking! Chiz calls out. Gets up. He's laughing as he follows her. She instinctively tries to hurry but she's too drunk to move as fast as she needs to. He catches her forearm and then grabs the other. Holds her arms cuff tight. Her chest is caught, her breathing fast, and he is still laughing but not as much now. He pulls her close to him.

Just let me stick one finger up your fanny. You'll love it, I promise, he whispers. Naoise doesn't have to know. We share everything. Family style.

His hands are on her arse, fingers digging into her flesh, pulling her against him.

Fuck off, Chiz, Sam says, struggling to free herself. The moment seems to go on forever but suddenly Naoise arrives with a very drunk girl hanging off him.

Chiz drops his hands. Mate, he says, where the fuck have you been? Sam's been worried bout ye.

Sam recognises the girl. It's her friend, Lena, from school. The most beautiful girl in their world. She is so drunk she can barely stand and Naoise hands her over to Chiz, who half carries her back to the fire. Sam needs, wants to say something but no words come out.

Naoise stands apart from them all, across from the fire, watching silently. He lights a cigarette.

We were supposed to meet in town? Sam says eventually.

Something came up, Naoise says, giving nothing away.

You mean something came up with Lena.

We're just friends, Sam.

He doesn't move towards her – she has to go to him. But she waits. Angry.

She watches Lena wobble herself up, almost coming down again she's so unsteady on her feet, Chiz beside her, handing her the end of his joint.

Can we get out of here? Sam asks.

I just got here, Naoise says. What's the rush?

I've been waiting on you all day, Sam says.

I'm not your keeper, Naoise says back.

He is angry when it is her who should be annoyed. She feels unbalanced but goes to him. Stretches up on her tiptoes, places her head against his chest, her arms slung low across his waist. She wants to kiss him but she is unsure, hopes her proximity will settle him. She can feel his heart steady.

Have I done something? she whispers to him. I'm sorry. What's wrong?

He listens while looking at Lena, the fire burning between them with little sparks breaking off into the night. Sam starts to sober up. He kisses Sam hard on the mouth and she tries to ignore her feeling of despair. Like she is not the newest, shiniest thing in his world.

I want to fuck you, he whispers back. I don't want to mess around anymore. He is slipping his hand between her legs as he says this.

Stop, she says. Everyone can see. Naoise. Stop, not like this.

Like what? he says.

He picks her up, throws her over his shoulder, her legs swinging in protest, helpless like a little kid's. Naoise puts his hand on her arse, roughly sliding it over between her legs.

She is livid. Struggles on but he carries her across the stubbly ground easily. Deposits her under a huge oak. In the distance she can hear Lena and the others laughing.

What are you on? Sam asks.

What does it matter? Naoise says. He is all over her, his body weight pushing her against the tree, and she wants him, the familiar buzz all over, this ache he makes in her, but she's angry. She doesn't want to fuck him, here, like this. Not now. Not after what happened before. She wants it to be special.

She shoves him off. Her knee catches him in the stomach. Just a little, but enough to make him step back.

Why are you being like this?

Lena wouldn't do this.

What? Sam says.

84

Make me wait.

What is that supposed to mean?

Oh, you're a smart girl, you'll figure it out. But then again, so is she. Beautiful too. Isn't she? He glances over in Lena's direction, takes his time looking away.

Are you trying to piss me off?

No. Are *you* trying to piss me off?

Stop it, Naoise.

I'm not doing anything.

She's my friend.

She is, is she? He releases a little gasped laugh, mirthful. Good friend?

I have to go.

What?

You're off your head. See you Saturday.

She turns and runs down the tracks towards the lights of the town.

Sam! he calls after her. Sam! Fucks sakes!

She can still hear them all laughing, the sound at her back, following her even when she disappears from their view. She desperately needs to pee but wants to make sure she is far enough away from their little gathering. She speeds up, feeling less and less drunk now. She shouldn't have left but she can't go back now. Her pride won't let her.

She drops off the tracks to the gravel stones and then into a ditch. In the half-moonlit night she picks her way through the reeds and thicket, careful not to go too far; last thing she needs is falling into the bog. She pees – Christ, the relief – and as she pulls up her knickers she hears what sounds like footsteps approaching from downwind.

She crouches back down. Maybe that skanky shit Chiz has come after her. It won't be Naoise. She was too drunk before, she's more careful now. He's getting fed up.

She wants to talk to Becca about what happened before, or more like what didn't, with Naoise, but she doesn't. Too embarrassing. He's not embarrassed. It's alright for fellas, there's no consequences for them. They can just walk away, because if you'd shag one, you'd shag all of them, so you are the slut and you're left holding the baby. Becca is on the pill. Her mum took her up to Belfast, practically insisted according to Becca. Better safe than sorry. No GP around here will give her the pill without parental consent because they've all been indoctrinated by the Catholic Church. Like she could talk to Patsy about contraception anyway.

Sam waits, listening to the sound of her own breathing. Must be squatting there ten minutes before she comes out. It is easier since her eyes have adjusted to the dark. She moves spiky fronds of blackberry plants away from her, new growth ready to reclaim this bank, clambers her way up the slope to the track, brushes sticky-backs from her clothes and continues to walk back into town.

Sam.

It is Lena. Drunk. Stoned.

Didn't want to stay there on my own. Lena hiccups and smiles. She possesses a smile like Naoise's – all is forgiven when she turns it on you.

Sure, Sam says, let's walk back together.

Oh, shi—

Lena pukes everywhere. Sam holds her hair back as she empties her stomach on the railway lines. She wipes her mouth with the hem of her dress and Sam sees that she's not wearing any knickers. She wants to say something. She wants to accuse her. But she doesn't want to be like everyone else, making up stories about girls, thinking the worst of them always, judging, labelling, pointing the finger. So she says nothing.

Episiotomy

Nuala, 1982

He is in town today. My daughter points at him in the street, her still chubby but not quite baby fingers unfurling from their fern-like curl on the stick she is holding. I push on past the throngs of schoolboys hanging, smoking, making comment, mitching from school on that Wednesday morning. Their presence jars, jars me from my safe, cosy world.

He is leaning, louche against the red brick of the oldest building in town, smoking steadily while he watches me approach, unblinking as his comrades chat on, egging each other on to piss-take some passer-by. Shame them for not being young.

I trudge on, feeling my years against their lack, an embarrassed flush rising, spreading from my cheeks, down against the skin of my throat, coating my chest till I feel the colour red like a tight hand inside, gagging my heart, the pushchair dragging on a broken clip of stone that has escaped its lines and lies waiting to trap unsuspecting pedestrians.

I haven't noticed the stick fall until the wailing starts. I bend down to see what is wrong, feel his presence first before I can bring myself to look at him, conducting that energy between us, cable fast, kneeling and talking to my four-almost-five-year-old daughter like he has always known her. Been at her conception. Held my hand as I pushed her out, my insides screaming as they cut, midwives and doctors and all manner of hospital staff flushing me with the urgency of panic, dripping slow release as the surgical blade, torment-sharp, sliced me open to let the baby's head out – You don't want her to die, do you? – a cut that slashed my previous existence as not-mother, opening me up as a mother.

That was the mark.

Not the first double pink lines like ballerina laces. Not the swollen tender breasts and stomach racing ahead of my shadow, not the fluttering kicks, or 4 a.m. rendezvous with the toilet bowl, or the endless check-ups and unasked-for touching. Good, bad and any manner of advice. Not any of that. It was the destroying of me that made me mother, the severing of one world unto another. A line that could not be traversed, a badly sewn-up scar under the shaky hands of an intern, who might as well have been sewing his name on a sack. That was the line between me and motherhood.

The line they'd promised was a subtle nick, a fine line, had become horizontal pain that pulsated every day for months afterwards. A tattoo of her arrival bestowed on my body forever. A slicing of my desire from the day she arrived till the day I would die.

His lips rested there on the raised edge that underscored my life.

In the ecstasy I had forgotten that I couldn't hide motherhood from him. He'd felt the tremor as it hummed from me, caught it all on his sweet mouth. His breath had escaped hot and slow on those lines, knit together like the promises I made my daughter the moment she arrived. Promising I would not cause her pain. Promising I would love her forever. Promises I never made to my son, because by then I knew the truth: there are promises you cannot keep, words that should not be spoken aloud.

Our hands meet as I take the stick and give it to my daughter. We stand apart but I can feel his lips on my scar, like he is dissolving the stitches, warm tip of his tongue wet, lick by lick, absorbing the fear and tasting the pain under my trembling frame, giving me back something I had lost, given up on. Under him I am transforming, soaring again, becoming solid and seen. His friends are calling him now, jesting. She tugs on my dress. I have forgotten he is not quite a man. He strolls away and I see the confidence, that sway, the swagger. I see that and I'm afraid for myself.

Nuala. Nuala? I hear my name but can't locate the voice. We've never used each other's names. Never spoken them aloud, because that would make it all too real. I think it, though. I think his name. Think it all day long. Think it more than the names of my children.

I can't be alone with my head these days. Can't trust myself. My friend Margaret approaches with hugs, hugs me and hugs Samantha who has run to her, Margaret lifting her high in the air.

You need a coffee, Margaret says.

I smile weakly.

She's getting so *big* every time I see her. Will we get a wee bun, missy? Have you been a good girl for your mummy? Margaret says, a judgey tone breaking through her goodness.

Sam hits Margaret's legs with the stick, a light tap. Laughs.

You wee rascal! No buns for you! Margaret says.

Sam cries then. A sudden gust of tears and Margaret's face drops.

Sam. Stop it now, I say, gathering her up. Sam. Jesus Christ, stop crying.

She's just over-tired, Margaret says. She's the best girl. My girl. My wee sweetheart.

Where are your two? I ask.

Bonding with John-Jo. Child psychologist fella said I had to let them at it. Good for him and the weans. I dunno though, John-Jo is very soft—

I let Margaret talk. I know she wants to talk, so I let her. She pushes the buggy full of groceries without being asked, while Sam fusses. She's that kind of friend. I smile but I'm not listening, I'm barely able to breathe. I think of all the things we do, he could do to me. I think of the danger of it all and I don't think I can stay standing up: I want to lie in the road and stop everything. Stop being a mother. A wife. Stop being a friend, a sister; stop being myself. Stop thinking stop feeling stop stop stop.

Then I catch him, a brief head turn to smile at me, and it is desire as glorious as the sun, as simple and as full of wonder as the sheer amazement that it rises every day and shines on all of us and all I want is to fuck him until I can't think or feel or stop anything, anymore.

Growing Accustomed to Falling

Sam, 1994

Sam feels utterly stupid as she hoists her friend onto the roof. Becca sways dangerously. They have taken way too many drugs. Murph had invited them to his twenty-third birthday party and Sam felt she couldn't say no. Now she wishes she had.

She hasn't spoken to Naoise yet. Although she doesn't know if they are even still a *thing*.

Herself and Becca clamber along the slippery roof tiles, finding the slate edges with their freezing, pink-tinged fingers scrabbling in the dark. She was going to make him search for her. Play her game for once. When they reach the chimney stack, Sam stops, looks up. The sky's not as clear in town as it is at home, where there are few houses and lights to detract from the stars. The sky here is dirty, a grime-covered stocking, baggy and loose, like the ones a woman over forty might wear; like Becca's mum, her legs losing their muscles, making saggy gaps where tight flesh should be. Sam lies back and closes her eyes. Everything swirls around her system. She remembers they haven't shut the roof light so technically someone could come up and find them. Becca sucks in closer to Sam, as usual wearing too little of everything. Sam is wearing a black catsuit, revealing and concealing everything all at once; up here she disappears into the night. She is wearing it to wind *him* up.

Drunken voices gurgle up from below and Sam feels guilty for bringing Becca here. It was a bad idea. Becca has a broken heart because the twat, Gavin, who she's been seeing for what, almost three years, the boy-child Becca has given everything to, ditched her for some wee girl two years below. At the cinema. In front of everyone. Destroyed Becca out in the open. Becca has become a

90

smaller, quieter version of herself since, and Sam detests that boy for it. Rages at him while desperately trying to find some way of dislocating him from her friend's heart and head. Nothing has been working, so she'd suggested they go to the party. Get pissed, smoke something, flirt with older boys. Forget.

This is not a place to bring a broken thing, and she has spent her night delaying, moving, prodding, pushing away those young men from her friend.

But she wants Naoise to forgive her. Or notice her. Take her back.

Naoise is fed up with her. Fed up with their little dance. They've fooled around enough, come so close to having sex, yet since that night something, some part of her has kept him, it, at bay. Something that says: no, don't do this. She wants him but Sam is really saying no to herself. She handles him. Transforms his desire into faith, hones this idea of herself as his almost-girl. He can't help coming back for more because no one says no to him. Not the pals, not women, not girls. She can't think about Lena. Everyone seems to do what he wants, but not Sam. Sam is always out of reach.

She lies up on the roof listening to him call her name. Smiling to herself that he hasn't thought to look up there. She is just that little bit cleverer than he is, but he is prettier than her. She seems to have grown up next to a town with the most beautiful boys in the world. Unsure young men who can take their pick and be cruel. She isn't smart enough yet to see a way out of that.

When the row starts beneath them it wakes Becca up; she had drifted to sleep on Sam's chest and she starts to cry immediately, sobering up. Sam hugs her, cradles her friend's puppy-fat face with her cold fingers. They are going home, one way or another. They crawl over the tiles, towards the sound, without knowing why really, the comedown getting the better of them.

The yellow unmasked light of uncovered bulbs roars out through the rectangular space of the roof light and blinds them momentarily. Below, Naoise is swinging a baseball bat and knocking through beige walls like a toddler biting dry crackers. Northern Ireland buys more baseball bats than anywhere outside America. No baseballs, though. They don't play ball here. Someone has got in the bat's way and the bloodstain spreads up the wall, in spurts. The guy lies, head propped up against the skirting boards, wailing. Sam and Becca see friends and strangers gathering at the top of the stairs, not wanting to stay but afraid to turn away. Sam rubs Becca's back as she suddenly vomits, puke rolling down the roof tiles like unsavoury rain. She starts to drag Becca away, her body moving of its own accord. Sam doesn't notice the silence until the yellow light distorts behind her as he pushes his lean body out against the dark sky.

Sam! You fuckin little bitch, Naoise roars.

Go. Move, move! Sam says as she frantically pulls, pushes Becca along the tiles. Becca's crying uncontrollably now, snot and half-digested pieces of Chinese food from their silver carton takeaway dinner forced out her nose, smeared across her face as they try to move quickly to the end of the roof.

Sam looks back.

Someone has caught his leg from below; he would have already been on top of them by now. He is struggling, kicking, lashing out. Murph. It must be Murph. Sweet, stupid, bloody foolish Murph. She hears the clash of boot and bone and a cry and Naoise pushes himself up over the skylight like a swimmer emerging from a pool. He appears, naked from the waist up, the baseball bat dangling from his left hand, playful. Sam knows he doesn't need to run after them. She knows he knows she'll tell Becca to go, knows she isn't the type of girl to let him hurt her friend. Becca can't stay, doesn't have it in her to fight him. He'd win. Easy.

Becca is well ahead of her now, has gotten to the other side of the chimney when Sam decides to turn and face him. Rain starts coming down, soft drops at first, then growing larger, like the fear spreading through her body. He moves deliberately, slowly towards her. The chaos below doesn't stop him. The sirens, the sounds rising to meet her become unbearable as other vehicles join, red and blue and green security services, a rainbow of concern lighting up the dark.

She can just make out his eyes, coffee black, illuminated by buzzing white-hot edges. She takes a deep breath, pushes her arms and fists tight, out from her body, turns and runs. She knows she will fall but in that moment falling is better. Better than getting caught. Falling is the only thing she can do. Falling away from him. Because then he won't have done anything at all. She will have very little to forgive him for. She hears Becca scream her name and his swears descending, smashing roof slates against the agony of his voice, tiles dislocating, removing themselves haphazardly like last orders in a pub. She catches something, a part of the building, dangles momentarily trying to hang on but her freezing fingers weaken, slide, and she is tumbling, her body slipping past her head, beyond her control, hitting her ribs, knocking her breath out of her lungs, all so fast, so quick. She covers her face, all she can remember to do is try to cover her face, because everything is black and descending with her, nothing solid, everything moving, moving away and then nothing, nothing anymore.

It's Good to Talk

Patsy, 1994

Bob Hoskins could go and jump. Patsy still hated talking on the phone, no matter what those ads on the telly tried to tell you. The phone in the hall, on its own mahogany perch beside a seat only big enough for a child to balance on, was hardly ever used by the men of the house. Sam, when she was at home, seemed to live on the phone. She'd pull the cord into the kitchen, or splay herself against the wall, bum on the Yellow Pages, and talk for hours on end.

He could see the school had rung again this week. Margaret had left a note in the wee address book she'd got them. That no one used but Margaret. It was like she'd bought it for herself really. He watched the phone ring and ring. Probably someone telling him something he did not want to know. Selling something. Or a bloody survey again. Sunday after Mass was the best time to catch people out.

It might be the GAA manager, though. Last season Patsy had heard someone slagging PJ from the sidelines and he'd knocked out McGarry's da over it. The fuckin head-the-ball, they had called him. Then the young lad refused to play anymore, said Patsy had made a fucking show of him. No matter what anyone said, his son was marked out by that day. What happened at the farm. His mother's leaving. Set apart from his peers. His daughter had sat with calm cat-cold eyes, watching them grow to hate the sight of each other, and he'd wanted to knock her block off. She could have helped. Put them back together. But she just surveyed all the damage.

The phone kept ringing. He sighed, resigned himself to conversation, picked up.

Downpatrick 5427, he said.

Hello, is that Mr Malin? I'm calling about your daughter, Samantha, said a practised young voice on the other end of the phone.

What's she done now? he said.

I'm afraid she's been in an accident.

As he put his cap on and headed out the door to the hospital later that day, he accepted that he couldn't tell where she was half the time. Treated home like a hotel. This was a new low though, even for her. Early morning phone call to say she was in the hospital. She can fucking stay there, he said. Detective Peter Savage had called around on his way back from work – off-duty visit but still – told Patsy if he didn't go in the newspapers would get wind of it and all that shit would start up again.

Couldn't have that now. Wouldn't be good for you, Patsy, for anyone, for the town, Peter Savage said.

The town, is it? I'm not from the town, Patsy replied, thick with rage.

For the girl then, Peter said. For your daughter. I'll come with you, Patsy, if you like?

He drove them in, put the flasher on his car even though he was off duty. He even knew the ward Sam was in so Patsy didn't have to go asking.

Patsy stood at the door and regarded his daughter. Samantha looked so like her mother now, lying in the hospital bed, comatose.

Is she going to be a vegetable? he asked a passing nurse, who blanched at his question.

I'm sorry, you are—?

Her father.

Oh, right, no … I don't think so. She's very very lucky, this one. Just concussed. Miracle nothing was broken. We'll have to keep her in a few days, but you can talk to the consultant about that. Were you away? Terrible to have to come back for something like this, the nurse said. Smiled in that reassuring way they had all been trained to do as she moved off.

Something like that, yes, Patsy said quietly.

He didn't bother to watch her return to her colleagues. Just waited. She came back moments later, her puss rotten with a bad smell, that brusque manner so familiar to him now, and he knew someone had taken it on themselves to say something. Rumours bloom like stinkweed. Peter Savage arrived up to the ward then, detective cap in hand, escorted Patsy into the room proper. He handed him a heavy brown paper bag, then left Patsy on his own. Patsy could hear Savage charming the nurses with his fabric-of-the-community chit-chat. Bloody peelers. Knew everyone's business. Patsy looked into the crumpled brown paper bag Peter had given him – pop magazines and a large bottle of Lucozade, wilting grapes. He thought it was a waste of money but Savage had insisted. He watched his only daughter breathe in and out, her pretty face painted ugly with bruises. The buzzing whirr of the machines ate away at him.

Suddenly he stood up, couldn't stay there, put the bag down, felt like his heart was going to stop, the rushing of blood to his head, lurched and made it to the door, then barely got out from the room when he fell, stopped as the floor appeared out of nowhere to meet his face. Savage was there all of a sudden, beside him, catching his shoulder, stopping the impact, talking at him, about him. The words didn't register.

Take a minute now, Patsy, Savage said, but Patsy was already brushing him away like unwelcome dandruff from his shoulders.

It's your nerves, go easy.

Nerves? I'm not a bloody woman. He found his stride, unsteady but taking him along. Call me when she comes round. I'll come get her.

I'll drive you, Patsy, Peter said.

I'll walk. I've two legs, haven't I? Patsy shouted back.

Every step out of the hospital got easier as he went away from his child and her pain. He was no kind of father and he didn't ask for this, this difficult daughter.

He didn't ask for this.

For any of this.

Postcards from Sam

PJ, 1994

PJ is drinking in a field with his mates when someone arrives in their older brother's car to tell him that she's fallen off the roof of the drug den in town. He doesn't even ask if she is dead, he just presumes she is. It's like she has lived life constantly only to find a way to extinguish it and she'd been like that forever. He feels the friction off her; she couldn't just settle in the world. He has been hoping she would leave soon, not die, just go, leave them all in peace, and he loves her, he does, but she isn't meant for a place like this and it can't hold her, contain her, it is slowly sucking all the life outta her. He didn't want to be the buffer between her and their da anymore. It is too hard.

He wants his sister to be postcards from exotic places they would never visit, crackling broken-up, short-lived stunted telephone calls; not coming home for summer, two, three days for Christmas at the most – till the rows simmering away underneath it all would blow up like always, and she'd leave in a storm of tears and recriminations, vowing never to return.

He wants peace.

He wants it to be just the two of them, easy, like it was before.

He used to want them all to get along but he is growing up now and knows that in life, like Christmas, you don't always get what you want. A few things from your list if you're lucky, Margaret likes to say every year. Not a thing if you are bad, his dad would shout back, but Margaret would smile and say every boy and girl is a good child in Santa's eyes, there's no such thing as a bad child. And he believed her, he did, but he knew Sam didn't, knew from when they were little kids that Sam felt there was something

97

wrong with her, something bad, something awful, and he knew too that he could never fix that.

He tried, though. Kept trying.

When he sees her lying in the hospital, he finally gives up on her, stops trying, just like everyone else. That's when he lets her go. Says it out loud for himself, to her, You're not *bad* but you're bad here. *Here* is bad for you. And that's when he wants her gone and he doesn't feel bad one way or the other about it. It's just what is best for everyone. Best for her. He wants her to live somewhere else, rather than die here.

Milk for Tea

Patsy, 1994

He got a call a few days later to say the consultant was releasing her. She had a few bumps and bruises but she'd be fine.

Dr Stephens is recommending your daughter attend counselling services, the secretary said. Do you have a pen to take down the details?

Hold on a minute, Patsy said. He sorted through his coat pocket, dug out a chewed orange Bic biro. He rubbed the nib across the newspaper rapidly, till ink appeared like blood from a wound, blooming black on the page. He scrawled down the number of a woman in Belfast on the top of that day's paper, above a headline about another random punishment beating. It never seemed to end, Patsy thought, all this hatred.

She'll be expecting your call, the secretary told him in her haughty telephone voice. Please make sure you call her this week, Mr Malin.

Right, Patsy said, and hung up before she could tell him a third time what he should do with his own daughter.

It was almost six-thirty when he picked her up.

Patsy sat waiting impatiently, car engine running outside the doors of the hospital emergency department, parked arrogantly in the yellow-lined criss-cross meant for proper crises. He didn't give a shite. He just wanted to get out of there as quick as he could. Unlocked the doors as she approached. She eyed the mess on the passenger seat and huffed in the back. He knew he was late but he had to get things sorted on the farm first. She could just wait. Lifted and laid that girl was.

Right? he said.

Yeah, she said.

They barely talked on the way home. He occasionally glanced in the rear-view mirror, watched her hug her ribs. He could scarcely look at her, swollen up, battered. She'd destroyed her beautiful face. Saw her rub her dark-ringed eyes. She was trying not to cry. Trying her very hardest not to sob. Not to suck in air through her mouth like a child lost. Every breath bit into him.

He swerved off the road to the garage. Any excuse to get out of that car. Give her time to shape up.

Getting milk. You need anything? he asked, without turning round. He waited, her silence his answer.

Patsy took his time. She could just sit there and wait on him. Halfway in the door he decided he'd better top up the diesel and not wait till the morrow. When he reached the car she had her hair pulled around her face, head shoved up against the window, half asleep maybe, or pretending to be, he couldn't tell. Could not tell you a damn thing about that there girl who was supposed to be his daughter. Flesh and blood. He wondered sometimes what that meant. You could love a thing that didn't have to be yours – he'd seen animals do it, take on a wee orphan and bind it to themselves and then other times push away their kin, as if it had no spit of life from them.

He thought of his daughter as a baby, hooked up to beeping machines, come early from her mother, wan and sallow. She would not go to him after the incident on the farm. There was no way to explain they'd never taken to one another, always her mother's child, rooted in Fionnuala. It just looked bad. Looked as bad now as the battered teenage girl slumped in the back of his car. People would talk. People were talking. He would be blamed. Again.

The queue in front of Patsy melted away. He put down the milk. If Patsy didn't know better he'd think the young one who worked in the garage didn't want to serve him. Joe appeared behind the counter. Joe was the kinda fella who was born old before his time. He was almost seventeen years younger than Patsy but it was hard to tell most days. He was an odd sort of being. Patsy saw Joe hold something in his face, watched Joe suck and turn his lips in as if it would stop the conversation that was waiting just ahead. Joe blew out, a slight colour rising in his face as he clicked his jaw and put through the milk. Patsy realised Joe must have seen the girl in the car already, and Patsy only just in the shop.

Patsy, Joe said.

Joe.

Heard about the young lass.

Joe waited for Patsy to fill in the blanks. Patsy stood quiet, money in hand, refusing to budge. A man stuck in the mire of conversations that pulled him deeper into the heart of the community, yet no one knew him at all.

The last time Patsy had seen Joe was Sunday two weeks past. Patsy had stopped the car after Mass and helped Sean Davey and the boys pull a pregnant cow from the shuck. Unlaced his polished brown brogues, placed his good fine wool socks in each corresponding shoe, rolled up the legs of the trousers, no panic, slow and steady and measured, to reveal white cold feet, skin translucent, the sheen of it like raw chicken, sheathing blue veins that pulsed with every step, feet unused to light and air and being on display.

Patsy swapped his church cap for a trusty green tweed thing that looked older than him, but fitted on made him a sergeant among men. He strode into the squelching mud, his face giving no concern for the freezing cold, magnifying the yelps that Joe himself had made moments earlier as he went in to help. Patsy waded in, big, firm strides, to the swollen flank of the by-now fierce distressed animal, and talked to her first, hand on her nose, soft, soft words, like whispers to a child. Then slowly, tenderly, he checked her belly, running his hand gently under and through the mud, checked the hind legs and front, considered a moment and then passed a message to get the rope from the boot of his car, the bigger one mind, and a few more of the bigger lads to the back to push. Everyone did as told, and it seemed to Patsy that at times like this, at times when they needed a firm hand and a quiet mind, everyone forgot about Fionnuala and everyone forgot about the constant questions swirling around him.

They hauled gently under his watch, his constant lowing at the cow's ear, a wearing away of the glar and dirt and stuckness that had trapped this poor foolish animal. Finally she came out with such a pop that everyone shook with laughter and relief, half hauled herself, half pushed out by the men, then walked off quite unsteady but still upright to a patch of green, immediately started chewing.

The men followed and as chat turned to the pub, a pint and sandwiches maybe, Patsy just came out with it, told Massey loudly to mend the bloody fence so it didn't happen again, rubbed his two feet on the stubby hard grass, and marched back off to his car, words of thanks lost in his telling off, his proselytising, his lack of pleasant comradeship. He acted as if he hadn't been involved at all, and all the good feeling that had held them together, men saving a living breathing thing, through sheer will and whispers of care, disappeared into the sharp shallow air that caught your chest as the day closed, caught any semblance of goodwill towards Patsy and snuffed it out. He was a breath you couldn't take. He couldn't be liked by anyone. Couldn't give them the slightest reason to warm to him. And that was the way it stayed.

Desperate business. Is she alright? Joe said now.

She is.

Joe rang up the diesel and handed Patsy the change.

Did Massey's cow come right yet?

Gave birth last night, Patsy. Fine, fine wee calf.

Good. Did he fix the fence like I told him?

Well, he hasn't had—

There's always time, Joe. Time before another cow gets themselves dead in that bog.

Patsy took the change tight in his hand. Stood slightly to the side and counted it before he tipped his head at Joe in goodbye, felt the queue stiff at his back. Earrywigging. As he exited the shop he realised he had forgotten the milk. Fuck it, he thought. Black tea. Fuck it all.

Joe crumpled Patsy's receipt in his fist as he watched him walk to the car. The man never took the dockets but Joe figured today was not the day to start bothering Patsy Malin with paperwork. He wondered would the oul man not just say something, speak up for once, put paid to all the rumours. The state of his daughter in the back of that car and him enquiring about Massey's cow. Jesus. People needed to see that he cared for the girl. They had no faith, all these bloody Christ-lovers, they needed proof. Patsy should have been a Protestant, Joe thought. That would have given him a bit of space at least, protection, one way or the other. He noticed the milk then, lifted it and made his way out to the forecourt, knowing fine rightly that he wouldn't say anything to Patsy, one way or the other, about his difficult daughter.

Sauce

Sam, 1994

Sam wishes her brother had come to collect her with her da, create a buffer between them. PJ gives a fuck about her at least. Patsy makes some excuse about her brother checking on the new lambs in the top field. Indicates that it's a hassle coming to get her in the first place. She wants to crawl into her bed and shut the day off. She can't believe it when her da swings into the garage. People peer in on their way past to the shop. She lets her breath sink deep and low, trying to fog up the windowpane. Her breath keeps hitting the small glass triangle, obscuring it for a bit but fading again just as quickly. It should work but it doesn't.

Sam closes her eyes instead. She does not expect a rap on the window. She panics as she sees Mr Malone, her religion teacher from school. He puts his hands in his pockets, waiting for her to roll down the window at least. He takes a hand out, repeats the motion again. Slower this time. His well-fed finger twirling over and over, and she really does wonder has she done herself some actual damage with the fall, the sustained concussion taking its toll. The window sticks and shudders, catching on built-up dirt on the way down, his big, happy, concerned-teacher head on him grinning back at her, until he sees her cheek, tinged with large traces of her tussle with the side of the building, a watercolour of bruises soaked up by her sponge of a face.

It's much worse than it looks, Sam says, half laughing. *Your* face, Mr Malone.

Sorry, Samantha, it, it just looks … it looks pretty bad, to be honest. How are you? I mean, I'm surprised to see you out and about. Rebecca Donnell said—

Christ, sir, you really can't listen to anything Becca says, she blows everything out of proportion. You really have to learn to trust those old, new, whatever, teacher instincts you have going on, or at least some of what they taught you at college.

Mr Malone laughs loudly and even Sam can see that he has a soft spot for Becca. In fact, in a few years, when Becca has got all those teenage boys out of her system, Mr Malone – *Gary* – will be just the type of guy Becca will go for. They'll probably bump into each other some night in Belfast, she'll be at Queen's studying law or something pretty sensible and will have started going to the gym and they'll both be far enough removed from school that no one will bat an eyelid. He is, after all, only a few, maybe six, years older than them. He is younger than Naoise.

Naoise is going to be twenty-nine soon.

Gary will be funnier. Becca will be slimmer; hotter, enough grown up. He'll meet her when she is six months out of the latest disaster and not really looking for someone. It will be hilarious at first and all her college girlfriends will giggle that her old religion teacher is *such a ride* and Becca will say, Stop it, Mr Malone – *Gary* – is so, *so* nice, but still, they'll glance over at each other all night and Becca, a few more drinks in, will think, Maybe, maybe. He'll be encouraged by his mates, a few married, a few still looking, to chat to her at the end of the night, casually outside the pub. Those mates will gradually fade away, subtle as taxis on a wet street. Everyone will. Becca and Mr Malone will go get chips, both a little drunk and before they've even opened them, they'll snog in one of the back streets, salt 'n' vinegar and fat becoming the most erotic smell in the world, Becca's back taut against one of the little redbrick houses full of students from Tyrone, a funeral of forgotten chips in white plastic bags dropped at their feet. They'll grab a taxi back to his flat, and fuck like rabbits. She'll wake the next day, after doing all the things she swore she never would on a first date – if you could even call it that – survey his house, wearing one of his shirts, a shirt he'd probably wear for teaching, baby blue, stiff collar, single-cuffed, super cas. And Becca will sigh and pause at every little item. Hum with contentment over lovely soft furnishings and matching plates, rugs and throws all in the colour of adulthood bought from a chic (for Belfast) high street store. Stalk his place good and proper and then make them both coffee. But she won't let him drink his; instead, she'll wake him up by straddling him, and he won't – can't – believe the tectonic growth in their previously flat, non-existent relationship, as he, she, they, shift back and forth.

All the while Mr Malone talks incessantly about Sam coming back to school, about getting her some help and maybe counselling, have a chat with him even, if that's what she wants, and she isn't really listening, not paying attention, until he says, What are you going to do when school finishes next summer? And nothing pops into her head at all. A blank space.

For the first time in a long time she is grateful to see the scowling face of her father appear from the shop. She watches Mr Malone flounder, drown really, trying to make pleasantries with a man on whom pleasantries are as wasted as fancy tray bakes.

Give me a wee iced bun, her da would say, none of that fancy sauce covering things up, hiding something, making it look like something it's not. Plain. I want plain.

It was the bizarre idea that there was something hiding there, covered up in plain sight by curry or Bolognese or parsley and white wine sauce. That someone was trying to *conceal* something; a bad piece of fish, say – a not-straight-out-of-the-fucking-sea crustacean; a bottom feeder that lay in wait for you, *just* for you to eat it, and that the person – the chef, the cook – was hiding something from you too, some *terrible* secret under the pretence of an insipid, or well-made, or shop-bought, sauce. That *all* is not well under this *illusion* of sauce. That flour and butter and milk cooked together with some herbs sprinkled into it signify a greater malaise, a bigger problem, an unspeakable wrongdoing behind it. White sauce as the Axis of Evil.

Sam sometimes thinks of this when she looks at the photo of her mother. Plain she was not; she was not a plain wee bun. The day Nuala Malin got married she looked like Elizabeth Taylor. Sam often feels like saying to her da, this plain man with his plain tastes, Why the hell did you marry such a shiny show-off of a thing? Why did you taste the sauce? He probably put the plate to his face and licked it clean, savoured it, couldn't believe that he could have sauce every day, couldn't believe his luck, until it ran out. Patsy's problem was that he should never have tried that sauce in the first place.

Now her teacher is Patsy's problem. Mr Malone stands tall to face her father, like it might help. The ingratitude of her da makes him quite a treat to deal with. She slinks back down to watch the mismatched fray but Joe arrives from the garage with a pint of milk and Mr Malone realises that the conversation he wants to happen isn't going to and he makes his goodbyes, apologies really, and leaves. She waves at her teacher's disappearing back, unsure if he has even seen her, then Joe winks at her as he goes back in the shop. Fucking chancer, she thinks, but still, he's brought out the milk and neither she nor her da can stand black tea.

Boeing 747

Sam, 1994

She recovers at home on the sofa watching Jeremy Irons in reruns of *Brideshead Revisited*, wishing he was that *actual* character and not a real person, who apparently, according to her English teacher, Miss Denvir, has been married for years and has two sons. Jeremy Irons's character in *Brideshead* is about as far away from here, her current life, as it is possible to be. She closes her eyes and listens; that voice is everything. It isn't just the razor-sharp cheekbones or his impossibly symmetrically beautiful face. Everything seems gravelly sharp about him, like he is a favourite knife being sharpened against your skin. You'd let him cut you just to hear those words. She adds him to the list of people – like Michael Hutchence – whom she might one day meet and who would, somehow, find something amazing, mysterious, unforgettable about her – inexplicable, given their star quality, incredible lives, fame – and that an inferno-like desire would entice them to leave their once considered thrilling lives, draw them here – the arse-end of nowhere – to rescue Sam.

She does not fully realise that the chances of meeting Michael Hutchence on an economy flight are slim. Having an intense but meaningful chat with him en route to Australia, or somewhere else suitably exotic, during which the plane suddenly crashes yet they, miraculously, are the only two survivors. And, both being amazing swimmers and somehow unscathed by the destruction, swim many, many, nautical miles to a nearby tropical island where they fall in love and live together in paradise. Maybe a trusty canine companion joins them. Sunsets and coconuts and happily ever fucking after.

When she daydreams, she deigns to leave out the incomprehensible amount of damage that would occur should a massive Boeing 747 crash-land into the sea. The slim, nigh-impossible chances of anyone, especially those two alone, surviving. She refuses to think about the smell, a smell that comes with bombs, a certain exploding type of death, that too many people round here, in this wee place, in this land twisted with decay, know. That smell of burning rotting flesh, and the trauma that those smells, sounds, sights would have on a relatively normal person like her. Thousands of people have died here. Many in explosions, many in other ways. Sam doesn't know the exact figure, it changes all the time, daily, but she knows people who know people who have died, because more people here have died than is normal. It is only *here* at the relatively normal part of the fantasy that she pauses and wonders how she would explain to any of these fantasy lovers – possibly Kurt might be the most understanding – about her missing mother. Her mother wasn't a statistic of the Troubles but the trouble within herself, consumed by her own war. What if the truth was that she left them all behind so she could save herself? All that left was shame, shame that your own mother didn't love you enough to take you with her when she left. Unclaimed.

How could she expect anyone else to love her?

D'you want tea, love? Margaret Caher calls from the front door as she lets herself in. I've brought soup as well, and some wheaten, Margaret continues through breathy exertions as she removes her coat. The shutting of the door snaps Sam back to her stuffy room, and Jeremy Irons's lovely airy face recedes into memory. Sam hears Patsy rise from his seat in the kitchen and Margaret chase him out to the yard as she sets up. Margaret has brought the same soup she makes for wakes and funerals. Clear, thin, hot broth with barley, sliced fine carrots, leeks and slips of chicken that disintegrate as soon as they touch the inside of your mouth. The smell filters through the house, warming Sam before it reaches her.

Am I dying? Sam asks when the bowl arrives, white batch spread thickly with butter tucked on the side of the too-small plate Margaret has fished from the cupboard, the Dutch blue pattern of willow escaping at its edge. The chipped good china, used and reused because nothing is ever really put aside in this house.

Ah, away a' that, child, Margaret says. Just something to get your stretch up. Sure, you know, I might take a bowl with you. I suppose I should, it's lunchtime somewhere in the world, isn't it? She moves across the room, pops open a window without asking and heads back into the kitchen.

Margaret never seems to have time to sit down and eat anything, so Sam figures it must be serious when she reappears back in, doorstep of wheaten bread sweating under all the butter it can carry, her own big bowl of soup ready to perch on her knee. She positions her large frame at the foot of the sofa, careful not to move Sam's feet too much. A wave of tiredness comes over Sam just then, but it is probably the sense that she knows what is coming, knows something has to be said, and Margaret is the one to say it.

They eat in silence for a while. Sam finds it funny that, for all Margaret's attempts at good housekeeping genteelness, it is the pure deliciousness of her own soup that undoes all her properness as she slurps with undistinguished pleasure.

Your da's fierce upset, child, Margaret finally says.

Sam keeps her eyes fixed on her own soup, studying the floating bits of barley brushing up against parsley, the blue edge of her bowl reminding her of the coast nearby, stones and seaweed.

Sam, love, I know, I know he's not the best at … but, you know, he really does. He's never been good at …

Margaret does not know how to go on. So she just takes hold of Sam's ankles and sits there rubbing her feet, absentminded, figuring out what words might land best. Before she has another chance to get started, PJ bolts in the front door, bag flung on the hall floor, the smell of muck and grass and sweat filling the space where all Margaret's concern has been waiting.

Sam. Sam! PJ shouts through the house, his voice booming. He bursts into the living room and is about to launch into something but seeing Mags catches him short so instead he just beams and says, I'm starving, Margaret, is there any left or did old bendy legs there eat it all?

Margaret taps Sam's toes lovingly and rises to meet him. Christ, child, would you ever stop growing. C'mon now and leave that sister of yours alone, and I'll get you a wee bowl. Or a trough more like, Margaret adds, shooing him out to the kitchen. PJ is trying to mouth something over Margaret's shoulder as she moves him out. Sam can't understand what her brother is saying, half thinks of calling after him but her father appears then, pauses, casts a cold glance over her and shuts the door, the whole world out, as far as Sam is concerned and she can finally relax. She pulls the blankets around herself and drifts off to sleep.

Like Mother, Like Daughter

PJ, 1994

PJ wants to tell Sam, needs to tell her – he's seen that shithead Naoise Devlin fawning over Elena Owens. When he should have been here visiting Sam. Wanker. Word has spread by now that it was an accident, her fall. Sam as much at fault as anyone else. Everyone knows her boyfriend is the local drug dealer. She has never been short on any substance since Naoise took a shine to her.

Tainted. That's always been her problem. No one ever takes her side. *She must have done something wrong. Why was she on the roof in the first place?* Soon it's been turned around, twisted, so it became *all* her fault. Soon Naoise turns out to be the fucking hero. The town has decided she's her mother's daughter alright.

He really can't understand the attraction. Naoise Devlin is a dick. Margaret has been wittering on about his sister's nerves and not to go upsetting her. So he's left it alone. He wants to say something but knowing Sam she'd tell him to fuck himself. That it is none of his business. And it isn't really, but her fucking swollen-up face and that sly prick sitting smoking and laughing and not giving a bollocks ... Girls PJ's age wouldn't give him or his mates the time of fucking day but they'd probably give Naoise Devlin a blowjob round the back of the bus station if he asked nicely a few times. They are magnets and he is metal.

Later, Sam ever-so-casually asks him, Any craic after school today?

No, nothing. Everyone's still going on about you.

You see anyone? Becca?

Yeah, I forgot. She's gonna call over the morraw.

PJ, fuck sake.

You talk to her every day on the phone anyway, wha's the big deal?

PJ watches as Sam rolls her eyes. Anyone else about?

Nope, he says.

Okay. I'm wrecked, Sam says, as she turns over, pulling the covers around her, but PJ can tell she is disappointed. Like a wee kicked dog looking for a scrap. Would take any wee bite. Naoise is the absolute last thing his sister needs and, knowing her, probably the only thing she wants.

Home Visits

Sam, 1994

Margaret nearly falls over herself saying a young gentleman is here to see her, with flowers no less. Margaret winks across the door frame, and Sam thinks, Fuck, don't let Naoise see me like this. And then, No, no, he should see what he's done. But when Chiz appears, cocky and breezy, at the bedroom door she hopes she's rearranged her features quickly enough to mask the hurt.

Chiz, with a mix tape and some roses, sent by Naoise, no doubt. Roses that look like he's picked them from someone's garden and wrapped in the local newspaper, which carries a picture of screaming ambulances and chaos on the cover. Sam knows it's not a coincidence, but a pointed thing, a little stab of a thorn in her finger to remember that prick by. She is upset and angry that he hasn't come.

Hey, Sam.

Chiz sucks the next words in as she purposefully pushes her hair behind her ears and turns her damaged face towards him. He shifts a little, his lanky frame twitching uneasily, and then gently places the roses and tape at the foot of the bed. He always looks like he's about to flee, never settled anywhere.

Sore?

What do you think?

It looks cat.

Yep. It is.

Her words are plucked, staccato. Chiz. Of all people. Chiz, who is just a little bit stupid and a little bit sly. Sending Chiz is a slap in the face. Chiz will have to explain why *he* hasn't come. She isn't going to ask. She is going to make him say the words. She imagines the conversation in the flat, Chiz refusing – Ah, for fuck sake, Naoise, come on. But then she realises that can only mean one thing.

Where's Murph, Chiz, doesn't he like me anymore?

He's in the hospital, Sam.

She sits up straight, stumbling around in her own head.

What?

Ah, he and Naoise got into a, a, a, altercation ... Broke his arm, real bad, he's up in the Downe, plaster right up to his fucking neck. High on painkillers. Operation last week, got pins and shit in it, be out in a week or so. Going on the disability, lucky shite. Probably six months if he plays it right.

Sam waits. Digesting. She can't help herself. Spits out the truth. You mean *Naoise* broke his arm, right? *Naoise* broke Murph's arm. Chiz?

Chiz shoegazes, his loyalty deafening, looks unseasonably glad when Margaret arrives with a tray of scones and china-cupped tea.

Thanks, but I'm not staying, Chiz says.

Margaret ignores this and hands him the tray and busies herself clearing the dresser, then takes the teapot and pours, blushing when she starts to ask if he is Sam's young man. Chiz nearly chokes on the jam-laden scone in his mouth. Sam laughs, first proper laugh in ages, and Margaret berates her, pulling a long face at Sam's rudeness.

Samantha, that is no way ...

He's not my 'young man', Margaret. Sam rolls her eyes.

Well, it is very *nice* of this young man to visit you at all, Margaret chips in, handing Chiz a cup of tea, and then she flits in and out between them and exits the room like she's interrupting the romance of the century, a little chuckle to herself on the way out.

Well, at least you've given Margaret something to talk about, Sam says, grinning at his embarrassment.

Sure. Listen, I'd better head, Chiz stammers, mouth still half-full of scone. Sam really can't stand people who talk with their mouths full.

Chiz glugs his tea. The china cup looks ridiculous in his hands but she can see some part of him at ease here, Chiz older, a grandad in a nice house with small kids and some old woman who has saved him, someone who has finally made him realise that there is more to life than drugs and dole money. There's something funny about the delicate way he balances the delph against his bony fingers that links him inextricably to this future self, and Sam is beginning to think she's misjudged Chiz somehow, that he's put away all his manners and potential and stepped into this other life, tried it on like dress-up and he can just as easily shake it off and continue without it ever showing on his skin. He's cleverer than she's given him credit for. This, this is what makes Chiz so skittish. Chiz's just playing, future's waiting on him to catch up, walk out, move on. She's heard that Chiz has started studying again, night classes at the tech, on the sly. He'll be twenty-seven soon but he doesn't look it. He can still get a grant. Go to college. Leave all this madness behind. Suddenly she feels a jealousy fall over her, a rage that he will be able to remove himself from all of this so easily and then out of nowhere she is crying.

He's shaggin Lena, right? She struggles through the tears. Admitting it to herself only when she says it aloud.

Chiz pauses, and that familiar smirk arrives. Then he says, I didn't tell you. Okay?

Okay, Sam says. She has been picking petals off the roses, crimson red flower heads gathered in her palm.

Look, you're better off. Chiz puts the cup down, stands up as Sam wipes her snotty face with the sleeve of her dressing gown.

Take these back, will ye? She pushes them off her lap with a flick of her knee, the loose petals scattering on the floor, red tears.

No, Chiz says. I don't want to get in the middle of this. He gathers up the debris. Bin? he asks.

Just leave them on the dresser.

He puts the petals on the china saucer he hasn't used.

She is looking at the back of the mix tape, at Naoise's beautiful handwriting. His penmanship is gorgeous, all full-marked lettering on such a tiny card. And then she notices the songs he's picked, a curated list of break-up songs, a musical diary of their short time together, and something sharp dismantles in her chest and escapes, sits there, a heavy feeling pressing on her emotions and in that moment reveals its presence.

Did he tell you to come here and break up with me? Is that what you're doing? What the fuck, Chiz?

Like, you were never really going out, Sam, Chiz says. Lena's worried you'll make a scene. Like, at school. You know. You know how you are. Chiz stops. I was trying to be *nice*. I owed him a favour.

A favour? I'm a fuckin *favour*? Sam says. And Lena? *Lena's* worried? Elena. Is. Worried. That two-faced bitch is supposed to be my friend.

Don't shoot the fuckin messenger, alright? Chiz says and Sam can't tell whether this was planned or not. Chiz shifts, a bounce not a pop, one foot then the other. He looks like a sketchy rabbitty fuck.

Get out! Sam finally says, and then everything in her body screams. Get the fuck out! Before she knows what she's doing, she's throwing all the china, roses, anything she can get her hands on, at his head.

You're a fucking mentaller. I said it from the start. He always goes for the mad ones. Crazy bitches, the lot of ye. He ducks as she throws a book at his head. Waste of fucking space. Fuck this. Wise up, will you, Shambles!

Don't fuckin call me that! Sam shouts.

Everyone fucking calls you that. Look at the fuckin state a ya.

The delicate bloom-covered china smashes with a beautiful crashing sound against the littering of Chiz's expletives.

Fuck you, Shambles! Chiz shouts as he bundles past Margaret.

Cunt! Sam screams at his back.

Sorry, missus! Chiz calls back at Margaret, who is so surprised she doesn't know what to say.

Sam, language! What on earth …? Margaret looks at the state of the room. She is about to give out stink about both of them until she sees Sam is in convulsions of tears on the bed, sobbing sobbing sobbing, and Margaret's heart shatters for the child, like the china.

Acid Bulge

Sam, 1994

She needs to stop thinking about Naoise.

Initially, she felt triumphant whenever she sailed past him outside the bus station. Ignoring him. Chatting to whatever pretty boy she could. But that bit, that part of her that wanted him to notice, to make sure he was taking in every bit of her performance, began to bruise as soon as he failed to react to her antics. Then he stopped turning up altogether. On the rare occasion he was there, he spent his time smoking and laughing with Lena, teasing her mercilessly, so that the sound of Lena's laugh could be heard all around the station. It made Sam sick.

One afternoon Sam gawped as he'd pushed his two fingers, a cigarette in their grasp, against Lena's pouty mouth. It seemed to Sam that her exhale took forever, and in that moment she wanted to hurt him, destroy him. She realised she was jealous. She missed being looked at that way.

Sam stupidly thought he would grovel, beg her forgiveness, plead for her to take him back. But it hadn't been like that and he'd cast her adrift on a sea of teenage girls, who all raised their hands, a beautiful wave, hoping that he'd float towards them.

Becca swears she got the drugs from a fella in Belfast who her sister Lucy knows. We are not giving that prick our business, no fuckin way! Becca said and all the girls agreed. Solidarity. Plus Becca was paying.

On the tip of Sam's finger is a little square of coloured paper that will change the whole universe. She stops one more time to consider what her life is now and what it will be after. She does not know the elasticity of her brain or the way everything can snap and disconnect and reform. Sam considers that she might never be the same again, if all the synapses refuse to knit back together, considers being permanently left in a plane of misunderstanding, but when she hesitates she feels the ache, the ache that nothing will stop.

Her friends sit in a circle, Sam joins them and they stick out their tongues in unison, mimicking Mass on Sunday. Fervently she places the square box of paper and promise onto the tip of her tongue.

Acid. Unknown. Unknowing. Her birth day trip. Besides, it's Easter Sunday. Resurrection. Rebirth. The end of the world and the fucking start.

A way to reset, re-become herself. A short cut through her pain and out the other side. No more wallowing, just a short, sharp slap to her nervous system and rational brain and boom! she'll be herself again. Deforestation of the mind.

The others know she's sad. The marks on her face and body have almost gone, faded a lot. Only traces of the physical remain. It still hurts a little to breathe. The kind lady doctor checked her out a few days ago, and asked again would she talk to someone now, mentioned good people, tried to hold her hand and was so like the type of mother that doesn't fucking exist in real life that Sam just knows she can't be one.

Somehow Sam is now standing in the dense centre of Tollymore forest, spruce pine leaves running through her fingers. Their smell becomes hers, fresh and clean and heady. Her stocking-like body contains one hand curled inside her, the other in the tree. She is wedded to him, unable to move.

The tree that had introduced himself, politely. Shaken her hand, said hello, so nice to meet you.

His tree face is tender. He doesn't really have eyes, but she feels like she should be kind, so lucky to meet this tree, absorb his vibrancy. The tree man strokes her face, her hair, his piney veins throbbing with life. High in his branches perch little blue-feathered birds calling out to her and him, shrieking their birdsong until it becomes unbearable, but she can't cover her ears. She leans in, tired, and the tree draws his large arms around her. They silently love each other, her and this tree. She might stay here, sleep a little, settle in. Get swallowed whole.

Snap.

She feels tendrils in her hair, sinking into her ears, moving towards her eyes. This tree is trying to possess her, branches grabbing and clawing at her, trying to make her his. His long green fingers, thin tributaries, have taken up residence in her mouth. She can't cry out for help, can't move. She is becoming branch and bark, realises she is going to let the tree have her, feels herself giving in, becoming heartwood and sapwood, bones and skin crumble and transform, her teeth falling away. She is okay with this – she is not going to fight, she is going to be the tree's parasitic wife. A hand finds hers, soft fingers she trusts peel away her own from the tree man's sinewy grasp. Release her.

Not today. Words float up. Today is yours. Birth day.

S n a p.

Hands. Lots. Multiples of laughter. Her friends' disembodied heads run like antelope through the forest, lashing their legs out like they are fleeing something swift, feetless in their running, soaring, heads flying above them. She feels for her own neck but it has gone. She accepts this disfigurement, it is okay, it helps with the flying past, running through the tree lovers, who call out as one to her now that they love her, and no other, and won't she stay with them, but she is a neckless girl heading towards . . .

Snap. Snap. Snap.

They stand in the car park looking at the shore. The forest still calling to them but fainter now.

Her friends with no necks are smoking, the grey plumes create fake skeletons. X-ray girls. Hers is a fine and long stack, but Becca's turns burnt orange in the fading magic sun, a thatched-cottage throat. Sam is laughing, guffawing – which is not real but they do it on the telly in English dramas – she thinks the colour will not work with school uniforms – blue and orange – it is wrong somehow. Becca will turn into a Jaffa cake girl. She wonders if Jeremy Irons will save her, with his plummy voice and laugh, come with a teddy and linen suit and take her away from all this. Jeremy Irons never held the teddy. It was Sebastian Flyte.

Sebastian Flyte isn't real, she says to Becca.

I don't know him, Becca says laughing.

Snap.

She is sailing through. Jumps. Is watching herself go. Flying up up up like Mary Poppins, they are soaring together, safe like birds they land in the water. The parked cars survey them, headlamp eyes squeezed almost shut, sneering, devoid of illumination, but in the seas, holding hands, they are safe. Girls giggling on the waves like debris. They are floating away to the free state, *main land*, foreign land; to oppressors, saviours, conquerors, subjects. The chastity of water protecting them from everything, every person, every ideology that wants to hurt them.

Snap.

Everyone is gone and the sea has spat her out. Bladderwrack seaweed has become part of her hair. Little barnacles and cockles are lodged inside her, just under the surface, skin like a cheap gift in a tourist shop, manufactured and made somewhere else, only an estimation of this place but not this place. She scores at her skin, digs her nails in, but the pattern just moves away, along, up, scuttles from her fingertips. Fear releases itself from all her cells at once. SNAP.

Snap. Snap. Snap.

She is a trapped *Her* forever. The orange-brown-green carpet swirls and makes her sick, rolls and rolls and rolls and she cannot even tiptoe because it is moving up and down, swelling like waves. She clings to the walls and edges her way out of the monster carpet room but just as she leaves it is moving higher and higher with bigger and bigger waves, a squall of hate and love and she falls into the carpeted sea and decides to die.

Snap.

She is walking the roads of her home place, eating ice cream from a tub with a fork. Walking walking walking. They are happy to see her, the roads, and they tell her. She doesn't think they should be, they are changing, moulting leaves turning from thick green to the beautiful decay of umber, then black and she is broken-hearted that their leaf babies are dying. When she looks again they are full bodied, bright shining green. They are alive but they won't speak to her anymore. She cries as she walks, or maybe she walks as she cries, she can't tell. There is a canned light shining on her and she can hear her brother's faraway voice and she walks and walks and eats endless ice cream, the tub refilling like she's always wanted.

Snap snap snap snap.

She is in school.

She has washed hair and shiny shoes and the royal blue of the day and everyone is getting on the bus home and she is smoking again but it tastes like shit and she can't remember anything but vague details of why they are in this system.

She hears Becca tell her it's Tuesday. She sits beside her and holds her hand, which feels bigger than her whole body. Huge. Big enough to crush Becca and the whole bus. She sees herself reflected in the bus windows. A grotesque, massive hand attached to her tiny body – looming and awful. Pawing her. She throws up. Throws it all up, head out the emergency door of the bus while it's still moving. She feels unsteady. Raw. She sits beside herself on the bus like an identical twin and follows her twin around for the day, repeating and refracting her twin self.

She still hasn't had enough and realises she's stuck in this trip.

Never coming down.

Never going anywhere.

Always being eighteen.

Always turning eighteen at a terrible party that she made. And she throws up again and again, throws up parts of her head and eyes and her limbs until there is nothing there; she is not there. What remains lies in her bed and thinks it will never

ever sleep again and she will always be this day, this moving, unflinching time, and she decides to go back and live in the forest.

She wakes up and she is all whole again, all herself. She is so fucking sad.

You still in there? says Becca, laughing as she knocks on the side of Sam's skull like an open door, misplacing air for sound. Sam shrugs and Becca shifts, starting to entwine their arms together like Medusa's hair on the hard navy seats at the back of the bus into school the next morning.

Sam stares at Becca, vacant, a sponge waiting for the feeling of water.

I'm so glad you're okay, you totally freaked the shit out of me, Becca whispers in her ear, finishing with that loopy comic big grin of hers, the one that is used when everything is too serious to be taken completely seriously. Becca's words reverberate like a friction burn in Sam's head. She forces a smile, feels the muscles in her face pull apart her mouth, every sinew working, a biology textbook movement, pushes her lips into the familiar security of an emotion they give away so easily. She's not living, just existing. Muscles and bones and nerves forming nothingness.

After school, Naoise is there. Waiting. Watching. But not for her. And it still hurts.

Sam pulls at Becca, says, Don't go anywhere, okay? She feels translucent, thinks everyone she meets can see all of her insides, squirming and moving underneath her cheap gift-shop skin. Knows he can see through her.

Becca hugs Sam with something approaching life or death. Don't worry. Just ignore him.

Naoise.

They walk on. She can feel him watching her back. They go into the library, sit in the big windows, flicking through fashion magazines until it's time for them to head back to the station and get the bus home. He's gone when they come out. They walk back holding hands, make promises Sam knows she won't keep.

Naoise.

Sam remains diaphanous, fingering the small pale shells bunched under her wrists, waiting to collect all the little squares of coloured paper her heart has to offer, peel off her skin and start again. A portrait of a new, shiny thing without past or hope, with nothing to fade into or out of, framed entirely by her own loneliness.

Solstice

Nuala, 1976

I should never have met him. If I hadn't gone out that solstice night. A stupid English twat philosophy student had left me behind to make my own way home after we'd rowed about Baudelaire. I didn't even know the land belonged to Patsy, owned by his family for generations. I was sitting half-naked on the wishing seat when he arrived. I didn't attempt to cover up. He took his coat off and approached me, and as he tried to cover me up, I kissed him. He smelt of work. I wanted him. Wanted sex. Rough and open fields of barley sat behind us and the smell of meadow grass, loose and sweet, rose up again and again as we spent ourselves against the stones. In the excitement I think he might have asked me to marry him right there and then, and I roared out laughing, giggles rising with the morning sun, our sweat mixing with dew and coming cold and then he frowned, serious, and asked could he see me again.

We walked up the lane together and he was so quiet. The narrow loney was covered over with powdery flowering hawthorns, prettified by basic little offerings left for the local spirits: braids of children's hair, straw dolls and rusted horseshoes twirled on fine ribbons and bits of blue fibrous string in the breeze. The branches of the trees met each other and their canopy shaded out the view of the mountains that rose to the south-east of his land, and the only thing he said was that he looked on them and they looked on him every day of his life. At the time I thought it was a silly, wistful thing to say, him trying to be romantic, but he was letting me know he was this place and would never leave it. Had no desire, no adventure in his belly.

He drove me all the way home to Belfast, in his beaten-up old car, the burgundy Rover that lies on blocks in the yard now, since replaced by bigger, bolder vehicles. I stupidly told him where I lived, fell asleep under a multicoloured crocheted blanket he fished from the boot.

That should have been it. It should never have continued, me and Patsy, Patsy and I. I should have given him back his blanket, followed by a thankful, graceful peck on the cheek, a sly smile for the great sex, got out of his car, slammed the door and never seen him again. Floated back to my uni life and middle-class mates, to smoking pot and talking politics and trying to pick out which lads were soldiers in the clubs at the weekend and which were not.

But I was weak.

I was in some sort of transitional phase, a yawn between my current life and my future ahead, and i fell into that solidness he offered in the face of so much uncertainty. Plus, Tony the prick tumbled out of my flat at the exact moment I was about to say no to his succinct offer of so-I'll-call-here-next-Saturday-and-take-you-out-for-dinner question. Instead of the frivolous laugh, the peck and the brush-off, I found myself grabbing Patsy and violently kissing him, yes, and then leaving, huge smile on my face as a gob-smacked Tony ranted and raved about my duplicitous nature until I slammed the bedsit door in his face.

That was my first mistake.

Thinking I could tame myself.

That I was the circus master when I was actually the lion.

Tollymore Forest is Full of Midges, All Looking for Giant Michelle

Sam, 1994

The geography trip is going ahead with the local Protestant boys' school at the end of the week, Mr Travers announces at the end of first period, and as they pack their bags a quiver of anticipation moves across the class. He starts to talk about cross-community policing, peace funding, and the proposed syllabus and all the other malarkey around the excursion but a hive mind of virgin-blue-soaked uniforms can only focus on one thing. Peace is great and all, but lots of hot boys is a much more realistic prospect.

It's actually a mixed school, smart-arse Michelle pipes up as they file out of the door, ruining the concurrent onset of bodily secretions and sending all the blood back to their heads instead of to their collective hymen. Michelle douses the burn of potential fun with her casual throwaway gloom, as usual.

Michelle has a peculiar ability to see the negative in everything, every little fucking thing. It's a gift, really, to be that focused on the bad, shite, poor, bringing you right back down to the depths of despair with that laser-gun loaded with bleakness she carries around with her. Sam often wonders how it would be to go around like that. Michelle looks totally normal on the outside and she seems happy enough. Maybe she likes bringing everyone down to her level. Maybe that's why Sam irritates her so much. Can't let her words settle – Sam is Tippex on her notebook of misery.

Most of the class walk in herd-like formation towards the outdoor classrooms at the back of the school grounds, girl buffalo waiting to cross the river. Every single person knows their place and they move as one, listening intently to the slagging that happens in the centre of the pack, all the while pushing forward up the slope towards the main building. The younger form girls break their early attempts at copying this older dominant formation and move around the senior girls, ultra-careful not to interrupt them as befits their elevated status, as the social pecking order works its invisible magic and the rest of the school body splits open for them, a holy hill of hierarchy. A crucible of teenage girls. A hive of Mary Warrens swarming together, but then every day at a convent grammar school could be the Salem witch trials. No one wants to get on the wrong side of that. Even teachers wait until they are clear. It's safer that way. When they finally reach the brow of the hill, Michelle says, So, they'll be bringing their girlfriends with them because it's a co-ed.

Might be a problem for *you,* Michelle, but personally I've always been interested in a threesome with some tasty Prods, Sam says back.

Michelle rolls her eyes.

You're a dirty minge, Samantha Malin.

Careful, Shell, you already look like your ma. You wanna sound like her as well?

Both girls have stopped now, squaring up like TV gangsters. Sam would never fight with anybody, she's just touch-paper skin, bones and tits, but Giant Michelle is a proper monster, an incredible six foot four girl/woman hybrid who scares all of them (and most lads), a porcelain doll-faced grown-up version of Annie gone to the dark side, and she is in a real fouler today. Sam should back down but she won't. It's a Wednesday that feels like a Monday and she's sick to her guts of school already this week. They are almost at the back of the huts and the non-smokers drop away, to study hall or another class. Exams are in five and a bit weeks. Everyone feels it. No one says it.

Christ, look at you two, there will be plenty of boys. Becca takes a little theatrical pause, curtsies and says, And they will *all* be fighting over me. Me! Me! Me! She shrieks with laughter.

Everyone splits at Becca's diplomatic narcissism and the tension drains away. The remaining girls take a seat on the wall or a stump and dig out battered packets of cigarettes. The tall pines that cut into the walls at the back of the prefabs shelter them from the wind. Mary Rose Stewart pulls a lighter from her bra. She has room in between all the toilet paper she's stuffed it with, but Sam does sometimes wonder if she will accidentally set herself and her boyfriend on fire as they dry-ride each other against the bus station wall, so she always gives them a wide berth.

Give us a fag, then, Becca says. Sam gives her one, and Mary Rose lights it.

Are you two on your period or what? Big grumpy knickers, Becca says, as she knocks Sam on the shoulders. It's then Sam realises that both Michelle and herself are the only girls in school who don't yet have a boy to bring to the formal. No one has asked them. There's not even three weeks to go. Franken Shell and Shambles. It is easier to feel sorrier for Giant Michelle than for herself. She could still take Petra's brother Pauric. She'd have to ask him. It's so embarrassing. Giant Michelle has no one. Knowing her luck she's been asked by the town midget. And then Sam thinks of Murph. Murph could take her, he's almost tall enough, and not that bad-looking, and before she knows what she's doing she starts a conversation that she shouldn't have and promises Michelle an introduction.

The guy with the broken arm? I thought he was riding you, Michelle says to Becca. Sam silently signals Becca to go gentle in there, it's like defusing a bomb. Becca takes a long drag on her cigarette to give herself time to answer.

Becca's back with Gav, Michelle, true love never runs smooth and all that bollocks, isn't that right, Becca?

Do you have to say his name like that? Becca says.

Like what?

Like shit on your shoe?

Look, I think he's a dick, alright, you know that. Sorry, but he totally fucked you around.

And yer man didn't do that to you?

That's different, Becca.

Different how?

Sam starts to wriggle off the wall when Michelle puts her hand on her shoulder. There is no option but to stop moving.

So, who's taking you? Michelle says.

Michelle, are you trying to be funny? The nuns are in the convent praying every day to Saint Anthony or the patron saints of lost causes or whatever, that some poor fucker takes me just in case I change my mind and decide to give the religious orders a go.

If you joined, Giant Michelle retorts, they'd send you to Africa and make us do two sponsored walks instead of one to pay for your airfare. Those poor wee black children, things are bad enough without you turning up.

Becca joins in. One-way ticket.

Ha, ha. Besides, Africa is massive, it's not *all* like that. It's a gross misrepresentation, what we see on the telly. It's like saying all of the North is like Derry.

Alright, David Dimbleby. Enough of the *Question Time*. Can we get off your high horse and back to rea—

I'm just saying—

And *I'm* just saying, if he's so *great*, why aren't *you* going with this Murphy fella? Michelle asks.

He's my friend. It'd be weird. It'd be like going with David Dimbleby.

How would it be like going with David Dimbleby?

Sorry ... what the fuck are you two talking about? Becca says.

Men and women can't be friends, Michelle says solemnly.

Er, what? That's not ... we weren't talking about ... look, we're teenagers, we can't actually be friends with anyone who isn't also a teenager.

Michelle stares sadly at Sam.

Are you, like, *sad* all the time, Michelle?

No, she says, puzzled. Piss off, Shambles.

Just thought I'd check. *Anyhow*, I can totally introduce you. Or will I just get him to ask you? Roses and all that shite.

So, who are you going with? Michelle repeats.

Don't know.

I heard Petra's wee brother was going to bring you, Michelle says.

Yes. A pity date. Thank you for the reminder. Fucksakes, Becca, who'd you tell?

No one. Must have been Petra, Becca says.

Sam sighs. Great. Fucking laughing stock. I just don't see why I can't go on my own.

Because you can't. Look, her brother's really sweet, Becca says. They have almost forgotten Michelle is still standing there.

Well, are you going to talk to Murph or not? Michelle says.

They both look up.

Yeah. I can go to the flat today, Sam says.

The first bell rings, signalling the start of next class. They can hear doors open and girls spill out, bringing their own particular brand of teenage symphony with them.

Fine, Michelle says and walks away into the din.

Er, *thank you* would be nice, like, Sam half shouts after her.

You haven't done anything yet, Michelle roars back, her voice carrying all the way without turning her massive head. They watch her go, her curly red head bobbing above everyone else's like a danger sign.

How is her voice so loud? Do you think everything about her is supersonic? Sam says. Like supersonic hearing? Do you think she has a supersonic vagina? Hellloooo in there? I'm lost in your supersonic vagina, Micheeeeelle.

They splinter into fits of laughter.

Witch, Becca peels out the words.

Supersonic ginger pubes, woooohooo, a forest of exploration, deep into the depths of Michelle's undercarriage ... I swear, sometimes when we go to athletics meets I think she's going to swallow up all the other competitors. Or just terrify them with her colossal ginger pube forest.

Stop it, I'm gonna wet myself, Becca says, crossing her legs and giggling.

Another quick fag and just tell Carson you had your period and it was really bad and there's blood on the walls? Sam says.

Euuughh, gross. What are you in now?

Study period with Malone, Sam says.

Once they have lit up again Sam scoots across and Becca leans on her shoulder, like the sister she'll never have. It is quiet again. Settled. They smoke. Sam blows big perfect circles of smoke, a cheap trick but people love it.

Please don't go there. To the flat.

Becca, what the actual fuck, Sam says, shifting Becca off her shoulder, turning to face her. I'm not a total loser. I'm not going to talk to *him*. What do you take me for?

Sorry. I didn't mean it like that, but how are you gonna avoid him?

They're not joined at the hip. Sam hops off the wall, bag in hand, stubs out her fag. You comin?

I'll talk to Murph, Becca says. You don't have to go back there at all then.

Great, you do that.

Sam. Let's not fall out about a fella, especially him.

We're not. C'mon, hurry up.

The bell rings again. Becca jumps off the wall and catches up to Sam. I'll go round the side just in case PE is on the prowl, Sam says. See you after.

See ya.

Below them a blue and white porcelain life-size statue of the Virgin Mary calmly watches all the proceedings. Mary V looks like she is standing in a big clam shell, like she's been caught, hauled there for penance, or has just taken a break from all the admin in heaven.

Becca catches sight of Sam turning at the bottom and waits a sec. When she reaches the statue she looks up at it and says, Some fucking help you are. She pulls her bag tightly around her shoulder, feels the strap cut in but leaves it there and walks slowly back up to chemistry trying, but failing, to figure out how her smart beautiful friend can be so stupid.

Daze

Nuala, 1982

It's Monday. At least I think it's Monday because every day is Monday in its ordinariness. The baby is not really a baby anymore and since we, he, really I, decided we aren't having a third, I sit in coffee shops wondering about things I didn't have time to think about before. Or didn't want to. There's not *that* much time. I read an article about how the man you have children with, the father of your children, is not necessarily the best life partner. Hunter-gatherer types don't make for the most interesting bed fellows. Monogamy is not normal. A hundred different ways to feel good about yourself. I slide the brightly coloured magazine away from me and order another coffee. A daze descends. Stuck. Sam slurps juice and plays a game with her funny Lego men, she chatters to them as they fly into the air. PJ stirs, still drowsy in the buggy. People see my children like it's the first thing about me, the only thing, like the hue of my eyes, or that I'm afraid of crocodilians but once stood among hundreds of them just to get over that fear. Meat in their busy trap. It's not their fault, my children. I cannot blame them. I cannot blame anyone but myself.

I talk about them sometimes. *He* never speaks their names out loud. I know he wants to separate me from them, from this business of motherhood. I think I want him to name them, shape us together, but I know it's far too much to ask.

He treats my body like a map, a list of the places he'd never been to. He took his time, learning, ever so painstakingly slowly, to orient his way across the landscape of my belly, fine silver lines telling the stories of my body's loyalty and betrayal, that battle to remain one thing while becoming another simultaneously. The viciousness of all that. The glory in it.

He told me it made him angry sometimes, and afraid, that he couldn't do that – transform and mutate into something completely new, would tell me he was glad that he would never be invaded, taken over, consumed by another the way I was. Then he hurts me just enough to make me like it. Demand it. Covet the pain. Stolen time we get together.

He flips me on my belly, grabs my hips roughly, pulls me up, pushes inside me, his breath ragged, determined, heavy against my back. He pulls my hair taut.

I can't get enough.

He pulls my head back all the way, trying to control the force of what happens between us.

There's never ... enough ...

I want him to smother me, keep me dizzy, dislocated. Raw from too much possibility.

Don't stop, I beg.

Fuck ... ah fuck ... fuck. He shudders and is done.

I'm petty with him, sore with yearning for things that are out of my grasp. I try to keep it to myself. I'm asking too much and I know it. I pull my dress on. He drags me back.

I have to go.

Go where? He is starting to get hard again, smiling. His body a weapon. I touch him because I don't want to help myself. I want to give in. Sometimes I think I want to get found out.

What do you expect me to do? *What?*

Leave. Let's just leave.

I stay silent. Not for the first time. Hand him his clothes.

I don't belong here, with you. We can't do this anymore.

Then go.

He dresses quickly. I follow him out. Watch him leave from the safety of the barn.

Wait! My voice hisses, whispers out my desperation.

His slight body stalls in the dark. His shape just an outline, yet darker than the night that surrounds us both. His figure seems to become more solid as I beg him not to go. I get on my knees, bare skin embraced by a deep carpet of debris, the dirty leaf-strewn ground cold. The shoulders of trees sway above us, naked, the hard bones of winter set upon them, their soft bodies of summer gone, shadows of that season. I cling to him, wanting him to stay even though I know it is impossible. Behind us the lights come on in the upstairs of my house and it seems that we will burn right through each other there and then.

He unpeels my fingers from his slender torso. Tries to hold my hands. Don't go back to him. To them.

I let go of his hands. He turns from me as I run back to the house.

I lie to Patsy as easily as breathing, telling him the dog wouldn't come when she was called, that I had to go looking for her. He is half asleep as he gives out, hands me PJ and closes the back door sharp at the dog's heels, disappears back up to bed. I can't go back outside with PJ already in my arms. I settle. Feed him. I knew *he* was watching me rock back and forth in the chair at the window, breast held in the child's mouth. He had told me before he ached to be that mouth, to be held there by my soft hands.

He tells me he would cut himself open for this feeling. He says he doesn't really have me, not really, not in the way my children do. He knows I'm lost to Patsy. Knows *he*'s the thing I'd cut myself open for. Satisfies himself with that.

Our disease. A stain that won't come out. A precious, cultivated thing that we cannot stop wanting, in thrall to each other, caught permanently between glory and agony.

When the cigarette smoke fades I know he has gone.

We are already failing each other with the words we say and the ones we don't. Making unspoken agreements into memory, marrying the past with empty promises.

I've had more endings than him. I should let go. I know how.

*

135

Without him every day is Monday.

I take another sip of coffee but it's cold. Before I can order another Sam drops her Lego on PJ's head. He starts to scream. So does she. An older woman turns and tuts loudly for my benefit. As I pick my son up onto my lap, I spill the coffee. The cup rolls away from me and smashes on the floor. The milky liquid runs across the newspaper, soaking in, drips flow, catching and collecting in the words, finally fall onto the floor. Under the day's date the spill stops, swelling the print beneath blurry and illegible, leaving the masthead solid black and bold in relief. I struggle with the two kids, ignore the minor chaos around me, let the mess unfold.

Today is Monday. Monday the third.

There is a feeling in me, hibernating, that staggers awake, registers blind panic. Bile rises in my stomach as I try to soothe my children.

I'm late.

Mourne Mountains

Sam, 1994

Sam and Becca roar when they see Mr Travers arrive at school with his maps and compasses and fanny-looking backpack for the field trip on Friday morning. Sam takes one last pull on her cigarette as he comes into view, stubbing it out on the oversized pillar that she and Becca are lounging against. She can hear the cacophony of the other smokers as they cough and finish, a choir of nicotine filling the air. Too many illicit smokers to single Sam out, yet he still glares at her. Sam enjoys this back and forth with her teacher and she straightens up, plants her feet in front of him, scattering tiny pebbles with the surprise of her runners. Mr Travers places his rucksack, bright with newness, on the ground.

Do you think you're going up Everest, sir? Sam says. Or maybe staying the week, get a wee break from Mrs Travers, is it, sirrrr?

Everyone laughs as his face flushes. Sam can see it takes some nerve on his part not to tell her where to go. Or hit her in the mouth. He really wants to hit her. Instead, he tightens a strap that doesn't need fixing.

Hilarious, Samantha, but you won't be laughing if anything goes awry up there. Best to be prepared, Travers says back, words snapping off like dead branches. Their sound is meant to be enough to shut her up. She absorbs their noise because that's all it is to her, the noise of a man used to people listening to him, revering him. She's been around men like that her whole life.

Mr Travers orders them onto the bus. Starts his safety talk. Sam and Becca make their way down the back and Sam sits cross-legged, watching the twisted twig of Mr Travers' mouth crack out words, bending and breaking their meaning to suit his own.

She gazes out of the window, studies her reflection. Her eyes fill with the colour of granite, then shale grey, changeable, moving constantly, as they reach the foot of the mountain. Margaret swears the mountain gave her those eyes. Sometimes Sam's are blue like the break of sky at the summit, set with the cast of lilac heather in mid-winter, blooming and altering as the sky runs across it. Even on the brightest day the range can gather storm clouds when just moments before it was bathed in sun. The Mournes a law unto themselves, looking down on everyone, fiercely beautiful yet savage, barren and overflowing, a juxtaposition of a thing.

They get off the bus and eye the boys from the other school. All of them know they are really there to use up the cross-community fund. Some of them know each other, at least to see, but for now they just pretend to have never met one of the other side before. Brace themselves for the talk about difference and togetherness.

Travers introduces himself to everyone, launches into his plan for the ascent to the summit.

Ladies, does anyone want to add any local knowledge? he asks.

Sam doesn't hesitate.

Ach, sir, round here they leave you out on the mountain overnight when you're a baby to see if you'll survive. It's all Romulus and Remus, here, sir. Mourne people are the mountain. If it doesn't kill you it claims you as one of its own. Loves you even, you could say, sir, and you'll be besotted back. My one true love, sir. So, you know, just do like the Romans do, sir, and you'll be fine.

Everyone laughs. Even Travers pretends.

Samantha, he says again.

Yes, sir.

Do you know the *composition* of the mountain range you love so well? Exams are in just over five weeks. Travers gets louder, so everyone can hear him. Sam sees that some of the boys she knows are paying attention now. All of you should know these subjects inside out. Anyone? Caroline? Can you explain the—

Sam interrupts, starts to reel off all she knows, long loud clear sentences. She spits out facts and figures like she collected them herself rather than copied them from a book. Everyone is stunned. Becca has to stifle a laugh as Mr Travers adjusts the strap of his backpack again, to its original position, the plastic material in a hideous surge of orange stark against his pale soft fingers. Something about Mr Travers buckling and unbuckling the strap, the light and dark of his hands, makes Sam's stomach churn yet she can't look away as she finishes her sentence about the Silurian roof, of which only a tongue of Silurian rock remains, penetrating deep into the heart of the high Mournes themselves, at the entrance to Deer's Meadow. That the only thing left of the roof of the mouth is the Spelga Reservoir, the dam closing it off forever. That the mountains lay like little granite teeth, intrusions, held fast in that mouth, until eventually the weather revealed all twelve peaks together, a gummy granite smile.

Well, Travers says, surprised but stopping her there. Thank you, Samantha, that's a very comprehensive knowledge of the topography. A *very* creative way of remembering that. Right, ladies, gents, we should make a start.

Girls, keep an eye out for changes in habitat, local fauna and flora, wildlife. Think about the logistics of transporting the stones to the Mourne Wall, the process now.

It's basically the same as it's always been, Sam says under her breath.

Get out your notebooks, girls. Note down questions for later.

Becca digs Sam in the ribs as they walk. Fuck, you showed him, didn't you?

Suppose, but I'll probably still fail the bloody test. Sam sighs.

No, you won't. Don't *say* that. You're smarter than me, nearly as smart as old sugar-tits Dornan over there. They both laugh at that.

Stop it, says Sam, through her giggles. All she's got is that. She never gets out, never goes anywhere. She's probably under massive pressure to be a doctor or whatever.

What? Where did you come from? She *totally* hates your guts, Becca says.

Yeah, but I can take it and she can't, Sam says.

They drag behind, barely keeping time with the line ahead. Caroline Dornan is up the front, hanging on Mr Travers' every word.

God, look at her. She totally has a crush on Travers, which is pure wrong, Sam says. If that's the kind of fella she wants for the rest of her life, well, you have to feel sorry for her.

Rank. Imagine Travers on top of you. Big mad geography head on him. Oh, Christ, I think I'm gonna be sick, Becca says.

They dissolve into fits of taut laughter. They start to howl. Travers asks them are they okay and they are worse than before. Caroline shoots them a filthy look and Sam is creased over, bent in convulsions, neither she nor Becca able to walk.

Sam knows things about Mr Travers, things that would temper Caroline's schoolgirl fantasies. She had mooched along to a house party in Belfast two weeks after Travers started with Becca's sister Lucy's girlfriends, who are so beautiful they transverse any religious fault lines – the pretty people pass. They all stuck together from a love of getting totally fucked-up. And music. People get over all the other stuff for a dance and a wee bit of speed. Lucy took pity on them that night but had to leave early to take Becca home when she got too fucked up too quickly. Sam stayed. She had sat smoking weed in a corner, and that was when she'd first spotted Travers.

That Monday, at school, Travers told the girls he thought he was getting the flu, after Caroline, naturally, told him he looked ill.

Rough more like, sir. You have a mad one at the weekend? Sam said, half under her breath, half loud enough so he and everyone else could hear it.

Travers' eyes had flickered with some whirring cog of recognition while he lied that he was definitely coming down with something – the flu or a head cold.

Sam thought to herself, Oh yeah, coming down alright, you were really flying at that party, free as a fucking bird, *sir*, she wanted to say, practically had *sex* in front of me, *sir*.

It had been like an X-ray, seeing him reveal himself right down to his bones, the spiral, that badness in him, the bile, the endless cascade of drugs. He was sloppy. She was fascinated, dissecting the deranged behaviour of her buttoned-up teacher, enthralled by the otherness of him, as if someone had put on a live re-run of her favourite TV show. She'd remained politely slid up against a wall watching Travers, entranced, her own little channel come good.

She's seen him every so often since then, in Belfast at late-night parties, eyes rolling in his head, his body grimy with drug-induced sweat and a ramping need to get further and further away from his reality. She has seen him in a chipper on the Ormeau. Then at one in East Belfast called 'For COD and ULSTER'. They have a thing for puns there. Like an art. We might be killing ourselves, out of our heads on drugs, but look at the use of language.

In school these last few weeks she felt Travers cautious and uneasy and unsettled around her and she wound him up, good and proper, any chance she got, and she shouldn't have, but it was like a game she was good at, a thing that she needed to do, to have power over at least one person in her life. Just one. Even if they didn't know or understand. Just knowledge.

That is all she needs.

Travers huffs and puffs his way to the top, the majority of the students breezing past him with ease.

Keep up, sir! Sam says, smiling at him as she passes him out.

She still has time to change, they all do. Still forming, porous like limestone, able to absorb what they need, let go of what they don't. Nothing is set in stone. Yet.

CAO / UCAS

Mr Malone has told her she is smart, smarter than she knows, special, if she wants. He suggested a while back that she should talk to his friend; there was time to apply, make a late UCAS application, she could still go to college. Mr Malone – *Gary* – has arranged it so Sam can talk to his friend Matt and decide for herself, no careers guidance, no pressure. See if she likes the sound of it. College.

Mr Malone and his belief in her.

Special. What does that even mean? Something another person says about you, a collection of letters in a certain benign order. Like Belief. *I believe in you, Sam, you're so special*. They aren't real things and yet these words, two drops of language, matter, like whether you take sugar in your tea or bless yourself when an ambulance drives past.

All the things you need to be a person that no one can see, no one can feel. She has learnt that you are always alone. Alone in this life. No one can help you with that, you can't *feel* specialness, she can't share *that* feeling or pain or love. You can appreciate it, like a painting, but you cannot know what it is like to put the brush in your hand, the hours it takes, the surety or un-surety of each stroke, what the artist feels. You just get to look. Observe. Everyone else's life an exhibition, all on display but unmoored, unknowing. Empathy is a bad joke but still some try. Like Mr Malone. He spends his life trying for kids like her and she really can't fathom why.

She meets his friend, Matthew – *Call me Matt* – who is in his final year at Edinburgh Uni, doing law, on the Saturday, when all she wants to do is be morose and get shit-faced and cry about

Naoise. She thought her feelings would go away but they've grown. She thinks of not turning up but then she thinks of Malone and his hopeful teacher face and decides to go. It will be free drinks anyway.

Matt is wry, lopsided-smile funny with doctor parents, posh, the kind who sing in choirs and do house visits where they mostly drink tea and sympathise. The decent kind, who have some money but not through any fault of their own, and Matt is *so fucking hot*, honestly, she probably should just sleep with him there and then and get it over with.

Matt seems genuinely interested in answering all her pathetic questions. Something in the way he looks at her when she talks makes her feel that she is the only other human on the planet in that millisecond, that they are both trashy, bruised things who have found each other, beaten up in different ways by life, but beaten up all the same. Despite his carefully kept exterior, he has something missing too and now that they have met everything will be better for it.

Margaret would call Matt a 'tonic'. A prescription to numb all the hurt Sam feels over Naoise. Becca had practically prescribed it. Under over. Like a pill. A person as a pill. The drugs don't always work, though.

They spend the night chatting shit in a random old man's pub in Saul, a parish a few miles over. Saul was also known as the centre of Christianity in Ireland back in 482 AD. Sam remarks that they should probably revise that if the shoddy measures from the barman are anything to go by. Good chance everything is watered down in there.

Matt stops at one drink. She downs three. She might be trying to impress him but free drink is still free drink. The bar starts to empty and Matt says he'll drop her home. The song 'Something In The Way' comes on, and she turns up the car radio so loud it seems to swell and fill the space with Kurt's languid voice and slow dull strum of a guitar and she can feel herself breathing in time with the music, heart thudding because she wants to kiss him so badly. She asks Matt to stop the car ten minutes from her house, directs him down a lane, her hand on his leg, like she is moving a horse, gently, a slight squeeze to go left or right or to turn the engine off and let her manoeuvre herself into position.

He has to let her do all the work at first – that glance that says it is alright, she can always see it clearly, there is an artfulness to it, her tenderness consumed by all his feelings, feelings that she is sure aren't about her, trapped feelings that she can feel sing through his body. He kisses her neck her stomach her thighs. He kisses her over and over. She knows they won't see each other again. She would probably let him do anything to her in that moment but he holds back, holds on to whatever girl he is thinking about, keeps himself far enough to be a gentleman, a blond-haired Cary Grant who drops her to her door and tells her to look him up when she gets to Edinburgh.

Apply, go start the rest of your life, he says.

Cary Grants aren't that common round here.

What If Kathleen Turner Was
My Mother and She Ate All the Bombs?

Sam, 1994

Sam wonders: how did Kathleen Turner go from *Body Heat* to *Serial Mom*? Is it like growing up? Does everything end up ridiculous? Is that just reserved for Kathleen Turner? Or will that be Sam? It won't be Kurt. Kurt will stay forever perfect imperfect twenty-seven.

Without fail, every Sunday evening, Mags arrives up like clockwork on some pretence or other, a forgotten scarf, a cup of sugar, an urgent message, but really she is just in desperate need of female company. Sam makes Margaret tea and she lets Sam lie, head in her lap on the sofa, cat curled, and they watch telly. It's a funny routine, one Sam considers questioning, but truth is she likes their unspoken once-weekly appointment just as much as Margaret. The ritual every Sunday is that she sits there and Sam gets up to change the channel, flicking through the stations.

Sam doesn't really feel like it tonight. It's one of those evenings when Sam thinks she could end up on the roof for hours, trying to get the static yin and yang that passes for reception around there to turn into Raidió Teilifís Éireann, when the set flickers into clear bright images and a woman in a white dress with the deepest voice she's ever heard comes on the screen.

Margaret gasps, *Body Heat*. Oh, this is a great film.

Really? It looks ancient.

It's a classic, Margaret retorts, slightly put out.

Okay, alright, cool your jets, Mags, Sam says and smiles to herself as she flicks the lights off and sits back down, cross-legged in front of the telly.

That's Kathleen Turner, Margaret says excitedly. There's William Hurt. Like she knows him personally, when the impossibly handsome blond guy appears beside the actress in white. The actors shine out from the screen, the glow reflects in Margaret's eyes, a flicker of her hopes and dreams, hazy reflection of someone else she once wanted to be that Sam will never get to see. Someone who Margaret can never become now. Desires that had been sewn up with every passing week. The ingratitude of this place bleaching out her possibilities. Washing out her dreams.

She lies there watching Margaret watching Kathleen Turner, and sort of falls in love with her.

Do you think Kathleen Turner is Kathleen Turner in real life? I mean, there's no Kathleen Turners in Northern Ireland, Sam says a while later, at the ad break.

Oh, there are, love, but they are always getting blown up, women like that. They can't be in the house too long, they can't be contained, and they love everything that might kill them, Margaret says.

D'you know Kurt Cobain died?

That singer fella you liked, with the wee wean? It's all over the news.

Yeah, Nirvana. I was supposed to go and see him in Dublin. This weekend.

Terrible shame, though. So young. Awful sad altogether.

Why? Like why would he do that? Leave them.

It feels like Margaret waits a full minute before she replies, shifting her weight like the silence between them.

I don't know, love.

Sam lifts her head up and swings her feet around so she can get up but before she can escape to the kitchen Margaret takes Sam's hand. The gentle warmth is unbearable for Sam, the brief feeling of comfort, so she jumps up, before they let any smidge of grief settle.

I'll make tea, Sam says.

Alright, love.

Do you want a biscuit? she shouts in from the kitchen.

It's coming back on, Margaret calls back, as the ads end and Kathleen Turner appears again.

PJ's eaten all the biscuits again. Sorry! Sam shouts again, realising tea without biscuits feels quite close to sinning.

So, Margaret says, way too breezily at the next ad break. You got a fella to take you to the dance yet?

Sam has no more tea left to sip. She puts the cup down.

Formal. They call it a formal. It's not the 1950s.

Right. Formal, dance, same difference really, love. Are you going with someone? I bet they are all dying to go with y—

No, they are not. I'm not exactly flavour of the month, Margaret.

At this point Sam wonders should she explain to Margaret that she'd rather punch someone in the mouth than let them slip the hand when she can get herself off quicker than any stupid boy she knows. Because that's what asking one of them to the formal means. They *will* try it on.

Lena's bringing that really tall fella, what's his name ...? Becca told her down the phone earlier. Oh, right – Davy Bell.

Davy Bell, Sam said. She felt huge relief it wasn't Naoise.

Yep, Bell-end, Becca laughed, then continued. She'd already asked him before. Her parents would have gone mental if Naoise had turned up. Imagine their golden girl with the town druggie.

Sam was quiet on the line.

Oh shit – sorry – I didn't mean it like th—

I know. Look, he's not going with me anyway, Sam said. But he might gate-crash.

Why would he do that? Look, who cares – you're bringing Pauric, though, right?

Who knows? It's not like there's a queue.

They didn't speak for a moment, then Sam said, Here, I better go. Later, Becs.

Bye. See you in the beano, Becca said.

Margaret had arrived as she put the phone down. Now she was staring at Sam, expecting an answer before the ad break ended.

Penny for your thoughts, love? Mags says.

Nothing, Sam says, settling in beside Mags.

Sam Malin. Not a good bet at all. A lot of work. Every bloody boy in this town knows it. Pauric knows it but he wants to go anyway. Pauric fancies another girl in their year, but this girl hasn't even noticed him and is going with someone else. All kinds of fucked up. Pauric absolutely understands that this is just a thing – go in together and eat our dinner and don't even acknowledge each other for the rest of the evening, and then Sam'll just go and get totally fucked up on her own. After, he's on his own. She hopes he gets to kiss that girl he likes, or feel her up or whatever. She can't even remember who it is he likes. He deserves that much for going with Sam.

What she'd really like to do is bring Matt. Open him like a present with huge, overwhelming excitement in front of all the teachers, Malone, PE. Watch their faces gape as Cary Grant escorts her in, his perfect manners, his blond hair and blue-eyed smile dazzling them all.

But Sam's certainly not going to bother Mags with all that.

Sam knows it will be mortifying getting the pictures taken. Knows everyone in school has taken pity and are scrabbling to get her a date like she's leftovers, which she is. Left over before you even get to nineteen, how the fuck is that possible? How can she already have a sell-by date in this small fucking town?

It will never change, this place. Someone should line up all the bombs along the border and blow the six counties off towards Greenland, let them become little green and orange felt-hatted insignificant tribes again, murdering away at one another until it's just the beauty and quiet of this place left, our bones all whitewashed down into the beaches, an island of mementos, free from hate or love, a habitat of forgetting, left to the animals and the sea.

Petra's brother might take me, Sam finally tells Margaret, but I think I should just be able to go on my own. The nuns are encouraging us all to bring someone.

Well, you wouldn't want to disappoint the good Sisters of Perpetual Succour, now would you? Margaret says, playfully nudging Sam's elbow.

They stop talking and watch Kathleen Turner's character get away with murder. Ned Racine and Matty Walker. Well tended. She wonders if Sister PE has ever been well tended. She thinks not.

Sam knows Sister PE would just like to get rid of the event wholesale, ban formals altogether, but she can't. The parent-heavy board think it's a good idea. A final celebration for the girls before exams. Even after what went down last year. Which no one talks about. So they have all agreed to move it to late April, strict age checks at the bar, chaperones. Like that will make any difference. There will be so many ways to smuggle drink into that hotel that the level of organisation involved should qualify for a small business grant.

Sam's only really going so she can see Sister PE's face curdle with dismay and disgust on the night. PE has already given them the talk about *relations* outside of marriage. Which basically adds up to abstinence. The pregnancy cycle of elephants. When you kiss a boy place two Yellow Pages telephone directories on his knee so you don't get up the duff through the power of osmosis. Knowing full well every house has only got one copy. Nothing useful or practical. No mention of AIDS or HIV or STDs. Just the virgin birth, tiny gold or silver baby feet pinned onto lapels with a pro-life pledge. You've only got this bit of yourself to mind. Like anyone pays attention. Well, the girls on the pill don't. So at least fifty per cent don't listen, the rest just pray or don't give it up. It's a sin. Did Jesus really think it was a sin? Or just those four fellas that wrote the story of his short life? She can't imagine life was much more fun in Judea back then, and sex is free and Jesus made it off-limits. Really? Why did he stick a load of shame around it? There's so little in this shit-soaked fucking place to feel good about, couldn't Jesus have outlawed something else instead?

*

As soon as Mags goes home, Sam wants to get a little high. PJ and her da are out. She cries her eyes out each time she listens to Nirvana so she puts on the Smiths and inhales industrial quantities of poppers, starts swinging jumping shoe-gazing dancing around her room. She's dizzy from screaming and singing. Catholic guilt is a dose. No one enjoys it, it's like boiled cabbage.

She needs to either wear this guilt or burn it to the ground. Protestant guilt must be different. Maybe Prods don't get given it. Of course they do, though. Everyone suffers here. There are whole generations washed with trauma from the moment they're born, by a fault of geography, a misstep, an accident of birth, that colours their entire lives. Catholic guilt has nothing on that, and it's hard to let go of the psychological brainwashing of your entire life in one evening, but drugs, drugs always help.

She's not scared of the pain, the physical opening up anymore, of actual penetrative sex. That's not what worries her – she's kind of looking forward to finishing that part now she's figured it out. It's the aftermath, it's the fucking with your head. Sex isn't love. Knows it. Those fairy tales they've fed her since birth, stories laced with good girls and bad girls, girls who wait and girls who are waited on. Women never get to be in charge in those stories.

Sam's terrified because she's already in charge and doesn't know what she's doing in this life. Fucking it up before it's even started. Men get fixed first. Or they are allowed not to be fixed. To make mistakes. Women mend. Support. Accept. Men tell us all the stories about ourselves. Even the good ones. Especially the bad ones. Create tight circles of need.

What is it like to step outside all of that? To escape?

Family Planning

Nuala, 1982

We'd stood in silence in the lie. In the line.

Margaret had listened with her head held down, face turned slightly away from me. Focusing on her small feet shuffling forward in the queue towards the policewoman. Finally, when we got through the turnstile and out the other side, she turned to face me and said, How will you get back? I'm only doing this the once, Fionnuala. This one time. You're making a liar outta me. He's a good man. He has his faults. They all do.

Margaret.

I faltered. I knew she'd react – it chipped at the heart of her.

I can't have any more kids.

So that's why you wanted to come up to Belfast again. More fool me, eh?

I could see the hurt. The lack in her, the gap she was always trying to fill.

It's just the coil, Margaret. She is already marching off, I run after her. Margaret! I get pregnant at the drop of a hat. Patsy wouldn't understand. I'm sorry. You know I don't mean it like that.

More's the pity we don't all get to choose. Those beautiful children.

Can you just tell him I bumped into an old university friend? Can you?

You must think I'm blind. You think I haven't noticed how you've been, the care you're after taking. Then the way you shy away from Patsy. That unbroken mare in the top field has more sense. You're asking for trouble.

I'm protecting myself.

From what?

If I say his name.

Margaret. Please.

You need to go back to work. The university, researching or whatever it is that you do.

I've been at home for five years. I can't just walk into a job. There's no jobs to go to. Lucky we're making ends meet as it is. I didn't even complete my course. There aren't that many places—

I'll mind them, you can go part-time. Finish it.

It's not as simple as that.

Sure, it's only a few more years and PJ will be in school. Then you can do whatever you want. Go back to school yourself.

I purse my lips, to stop myself from saying I can't last that long. That I can't cope. Stop myself from saying his name.

I. Can't. Say. His. Name.

Tears come without warning. My body betrays me at every turn. I know it might be too late already. Margaret is my priest but confessing won't save me.

Margaret immediately searches for a tissue, shoves it into my hand. The hardness in her face remains when she asks me will I be alright getting home, after? Will I be too sore?

Nothing a painkiller won't fix, I say. Or a drop of whiskey.

I could do with one now, she says, and we both smile a little, feeling our way back to each other.

Gimme those bags?

Ah, no, it's—

Bad enough. Worse with you hauling that in with you, she says, taking them from me.

I glance at my watch again.

Go on, she says.

Thank you.

Don't thank me, she says and walks away.

I watch her trudge off, stooped, laden with bags of clothes and new sheets, heavy white cotton, stretched, pin-tucked tight over flimsy cardboard. You have to be careful taking out the sheets, the sharp pin concealed so artfully, you could forget yourself, wince as you lanced your fingertip, sully their pristine newness with your blood. Ruining the sheets you haven't used yet; soon they will be soiled with your sweat, skin, no remnants of the factory smell will remain, the gift of freshness and tender sleep lost to the washing basket. I imagine Margaret hurting herself, the tiny sting of pain. It's nothing to what she carries around already. She holds all the pain she's never had in her shoulders. Pain she longs for. The ripple of labour, embracing agony with joy for your child. The hurt others want to forget, she calls it in. Tries to get as close as she can to that pain, punishes herself for every little thing. Pricks her finger for your lie.

It's busy at the rank. The rain. The rough way the streets feel today with closing time looming.

Where to, love? the taxi man asks before we get in, bunching us altogether depending on destination. I share a black taxi to the Newtownards Road. Less chance of being recognised up there. When I give the name, the real one, not a street away – stupid, so stupid – I see the taxi driver recognise the address. If he has feelings one way or the other his face doesn't betray him. His accent leans south, across the border. Maybe he knows what it's like to fit in and stand out.

Nice day for ducks, he says to everyone and no one as he pulls out onto the road.

Another woman is going near the same place. She's older than me. Nearer to Margaret's age. Careworn. She's been unlucky. She rubs her lined hands together, small gold band glinting on her finger. I try to catch her eye but she refuses to engage. The gable-end murals fly by like a mix of cultural celebration and sectarian ticker tape blurred into one. William of Orange is the man around here. Big Bill. With his white horse and wig. The taxi stops a little short but as we get out I see why.

I'm not prepared for the protesting women gathered outside. A new kind of hatred. I'd read about it – the abuse the staff and clients suffered, but it was so far away. Easy to ignore when you could close the paper. Like so many things here.

They are gathered in groups of three and four, creating a morbid modern frieze, like animated Stations of the Cross, devoted to the neglect of anyone's redemption. In thrall to an invisible father figure. They carry their crosses, heavy wooden posts with messages of women's failures.

I stall, but I know I have to move past them, walk this Way of Sorrows, and it takes all my effort to force myself on. Closer up I can't help but study the sad faces of the women on the road who hoist baby dolls in the air, perfect manicures clutching plastic foetuses, strange, stretched mouths open, giving voice to bile and Bible. Words and pages twist in the wind; they are reading, chanting, praying, shouting abuse. They are normal. Women of all ages, who you might see in the supermarket, at school, on the beach. Most mothers, some young girls barely old enough to know what they're vilifying. Minds too fresh to recognise that in a few years they might end up here. The oldest women sit politely on canvas fold-up seats. Dressed for a church service. Holding court, hair set, warpaint applied like they'll be judged on their appearance first before they open their mouths to condemn others. No one will be saved today.

Slut!

Jesus will absolve you! Repent and be saved!

Murderer!

Satan's whore! Slut! Slut! Slut!

I step off the footpath and walk on the road. Spittle lands on my face as I pass. The vitriol in their words makes me stumble, a fallen woman. As if I'm not guilty enough.

I nearly close the door on the woman behind me in my rush to shut them out, their harried, barking voices. The woman from the taxi. She acknowledges me, just, but there's no smile, no solidarity now that we're inside the place of our resurrection.

*

The staff are warm. Professional. Everything is done in a measured, helpful way despite the demand on their time. I shudder relief when the test comes back negative. The place is busy. Desperation never takes a day off in here. They let me break down a little. They don't need to know the why of things. They offer options calmly. I sign forms. Consent. A female doctor and nurse explain the procedure. Getting the coil will hurt a bit. Not as much as giving birth, I joke. No, says the GP, her delivery steady. Just some cramping. Light bleeding over the next few days. Anything heavier you need to go to your own doctor. She hesitates. Or hospital, if you're more comfortable with that. Gives me a tight, reassuring smile. Good luck, Mrs Malin.

I take painkillers afterwards with a cup of tea, sit waiting for them to take effect. I see others who have not been so lucky, their tear-stained faces drawn into acceptance or realisation that other steps, new plans have to be made. Resolution forming. In their future, secret tickets being purchased for procedures under fake names in anonymous cities a boat ride away.

When I leave the family planning clinic I feel lighter. Lucky. The hateful women and girls are still outside in the grey cold. Shouting. Spitting. I walk on past.

The surge comes over me so quickly that when I swing around and walk back and spit right in their faces it's like it's not me doing any of it at all.

Fuck you! I scream. Traitors!

Their faces are frigid with shock. They stand open-mouthed, stripped of their indignation for a moment. Traitors. Traitors to our sex, to those women who came before them and raised them and the girls and daughters ahead of us. In a place where sides get picked before you are even born, hatreds laid down like heirlooms, with so little choice, they choose to destroy, to blame, refuse kindness.

A woman, she must be my age, her lipstick the same colour as mine – she could be me – hesitates. Something about facing me cracks open a squalid fissure of silent interrogation that lets the buried doubt creep in. All her certainty questioned. I know this place. I see her waver. The others gather her up in their name-calling. Draw her back in. She is full-throated now, as if thunderous noise will apostate me. Elicit an idea, form a woman who doesn't exist, as if I, her perturbing reflection, will disappear. My disappearance will shore up the lack inside. Allow this version of womanhood to hide in a man's world, where they don't have to look at themselves up close, to ask What do you want? To listen to the secret answer. She bellows her beliefs. She thinks she won't be forced to make changes, in herself, in her home, in this world. She thinks she will be safe. Spotless. Venerated. Righteous.

She has picked a side. Her choice.

The door of the clinic opens and they turn, a mongrel wave, and direct their bile at another and I walk away. Quietly.

Courage is hard to find in such an ugly place. Courage is a choice.

Better to Burn Out than to Fade Away

Sam, 1994

She guesses the way Mr Malone looks at her Monday morning that Matt has probably not spilled the beans. He still looks at her like she is special. Matt is not a blabber, it seems. Good for him.

Mr Malone is called away from study period and asks them to keep working, which no one does. She is sitting on Becca's desk busy telling her various details about Matt when Malone arrives back in and ushers the girls outside. They expect a fire drill but no bell comes.

When they arrive at the special lunchtime assembly Mr Carson is fussing at the edge of the stage, a polished mahogany platform that definitely contributed to the destruction of the Amazon rainforest, which they had *not* held a sponsored walk for last week. It was just the usual money for African missions so the nuns could torture little black girls. God's work knew no bounds. Education for everyone, served with a huge dollop of religious indoctrination on the side. Huge blue velvet curtains hang glamorously across the stage. Twin peaks of fabric are pulled slowly back to reveal the cast of the divine and Satan's representative on earth, Sister Eudoria Regina Boyle. All the lay teachers are seated on one side of her, nuns on the other. Carson takes a free seat on the end. Sister Eudoria strides to the podium.

Sam thinks, Oh fuck this, if they ruin this, if they take Kurt's death and *jesusify* it, I'll kill my fucking self. She knows the nuns are about to steal her now deceased potential boyfriend and it breaks her fucking heart.

Instead, they don't mention Kurt, they talk about the *peace process* and the IRA ceasefire and a whole lot of other cross-community bollocks. Kurt's memory remains sacred, like the standardised painting of the Sweet Heart of Jesus.

They ask them to pray for peace.

Kurt is dead but peace is here.

Sam prays but not because the nuns ask her. Or because of God or the Church. Religion is what causes all this bollocks. My god, your god, their god. Whose god is it? Whose peace?

People from Ulster love to say no.

No. No. No.

No will be back, carried by a gun or a bomb. Sometimes Sam thinks *No* is engraved on our hearts – branded with the preface *Ulster Says*. Regardless of religion, contrary fucks all, that's our true communal nature. First word she said as a baby. Not Ma. Not Da. But no. No is the nation's dummy. Our safety blanket of negativity.

Peace can't last.

We can't have nice things.

Good. Things.

Here.

The powers that be picked a Wednesday after Easter. Last week. One of the other powers that be killed someone on the Thursday because they could. It wasn't their peace. So one of them beat someone to death. Stuffed her body in a wheelie bin like rubbish because he thought she was one of the other sort in the wrong part of town. Thought the Protestant lady was a Catholic in a Loyalist place. Mistaken identity. Battered her to death. One of their own. Innocent.

For three days a temporary cessation of hostilities. Catholics won't kill Protestants. Protestants won't kill Catholics. Then *they* start up again and *they* kill each other all over again. The man, the member of their organisation that murdered one of their own, is shot dead in the Shankill by the organisation. Murder as reparation. Tit for tat. Killing themselves. Killing the other. Violence resurrected so easily. Killing killing killing.

She wonders why *they* waited till after Easter.

Why? Because it's a bloody miracle? The mere idea of no one dying here for a few days? Or because of the theatre of it all, the pomp, the ceremony, the puns? Because the powers that be think that the only way to get through to *us*, six counties of pain, is the nearer-to-thee-god circle of it all? Because *our* Lord Jesus saves? Because Jesus our Lord and Father and Son and the Holy fucking Ghost have to be involved in every little thing here? Not Gerry, John, Ian or Martin. Our Beatles. Not Albert. Not the Brits or the States or the God-Awful/God-Save-Us (depending on your point of view, where you're standing, who's listening) Southerners lodged in our throats who agreed to abandon us in the first place. Who don't want to know.

The powers that be have all been whispering behind backs, talking about the good people of Northern Ireland.

We the People. Like anyone gives a shit, what we, the people, want.

It's a trial run. Then *they* wait and watch for all the shit that would happen after.

Because there can't be good without evil. Hope without despair. They let we the people *believe* we did it.

This is the diatribe Sam inhabits every day. Was raised on. Her daily bread. Sodden with milky promises of what's never been possible. The putrid taste of lies makes her gag. Every line she's been fed. She has to swallow the medicine because people died for this temporary peace. On both sides. While those other people over there sat in their high towers and watched. Unmoved.

Yes to peace. Yes, sir. Yes, missus. Yes to being locked in a system. That's all she's ever known.

Yes. Yes. Yes.

Yes feels good.

The nuns say the peace process is fragile. They say it is a long road, this path to peace. They preach to a sea of blue. Girls fidget in their uniforms. Everyone has heard this narrative before but they sing a hymn of hope anyway. The ceasefire is over. People already shot. Already kilt. Yet the bus station after school is jubilant. Happy. It's a perfect April day. No one cares anymore that Kurt is dead, an ocean away, that someone's peace is lost.

This temporary peace doesn't really change anything. There is a spate of sectarian killings after, booby traps that fail to go off, rocket bombs, petrol bombs, punishment beatings. Attacks. There is reparation and condemnation and assurances and grandstanding and talk of ongoing talks. The dialogue doesn't stop. The news reports don't stop. Doesn't stop baby-faced soldiers at a checkpoint waving down school buses on the way home, boarding, guns strapped to their chests, marching up the aisles, trying not to make eye contact with school children. Doesn't stop you smiling at some of them and some of them smiling at you. Asking pretty girls like Sam and Becca where they went drinking. Because they're lonely at that camp. Because they just want to feel normal. Doesn't stop soldiers second-guessing themselves and being afraid when they go out at night to mingle with civilians. Promises of peace don't stop people being afraid. Worried they'll end up a news story on the BBC or UTV.

Her family sat quietly last Wednesday night, watched the news of the three-day ceasefire. Patsy said little. Probably all across the province families sat together and said little. Numb to the possibility of it. Some probably laughed and some cursed it and some turned off the telly. Mostly, they didn't believe any of it. Waited for the awful, crushing deadening that followed. Waited for someone to say the peace process has died.

Sam knew it was coming. Knows that peace spoils. A divided nation got their treat. Good little boys and girls, seen and not heard, who can't understand each other. The smack after catches people out, surprises, knocks kind words from tight mouths, breaks tiny hearts. And they can't look at each other anymore.

The fallout is epic. Not enough condemnation. Vitriol. Sadness. It is so easy to say yes, but no is etched into the very heart of the conflict here.

No. No. No.

Anything you know can help.

0800 666 999 Secrets.

You can stop it – now.

Don't suffer it, change it.

No.

No more.

The quiet whispers have to stop.

Kitchen Clocks

Sam, 1994

Margaret is gone. Her exit from this world was not trumpeted; she just died in her sleep. Death had the good sense to copy Margaret; for her it was gracious and quiet. There was no production in Margaret's dying. She was here, and then she was gone.

The days after her mother left have not lasted in Sam's memory. They are patches of time and grief. Margaret Caher was her only constant then. When Sam thinks of that time now, when she forces herself, when she has to go back there, she thinks of being on the floor with Margaret, their heads touching, their bodies like the arms of a kitchen clock, held at different points of time.

She was five, almost six. The little hand to Margaret's big hand.

Sometimes they would be joined by PJ, like a little second-hand marker, who settled into Margaret's side, and the music would come on. Margaret was always humming something under her breath, and then one day she said, Have you ever listened to this guy? and took out an old 64 cassette tape and made them lie down in the living room. Sam remembers hearing David Bowie on that floor. Dylan, Elvis, John Lennon, Roy Orbison. Sometimes Margaret would sing. Margaret only sang for them. In between all the domestic, the everyday blindness of the mundane tasks that bound her to their world, there was something rising and falling inside Margaret, a mystery perhaps even to herself.

Margaret helped Sam get ready for a life that Sam didn't want, but all the same she put it all out there for her. A dependable, stable sort of love; no troughs of hidden feeling, everything set out in its proper order.

Now Sam lies on the same floor, headphones in, listening to The Cure, tears coursing down her face, a broken clock, unable to tell the time without Margaret to count the hours.

The funeral was a sombre thing. Mags' boys, heavy with community expectations to act like men, reduced to quivering lost children at her graveside, after getting plastered as quickly as possible. Drink to tamp down the hurt. Sam could barely look at them. The soup was not Margaret's, it was a bad replica made by a woman who only has a bad word to say about everybody. Sam slumped the contents of the bowl into a dying plant in the kitchen of the community hall.

On the back of the splintering door hung a flowery, faded apron that Margaret used to wear when she came into the hall to make tea for bingo or soup for funerals and wakes. Sam reached into the pocket, hoping to find something, anything, but it was empty, just a crumpled tissue. She pushed her face into the material, but she couldn't smell anything.

It was like all the sound had gone out of her world: noise bubbled in her ears, as if under a veil of water held in from jumping in the swimming pool. During Margaret's wake she had filled up with a blast of oxygenated sound, a dim hum of noise-bathed anxiety.

She hadn't cried at all for Margaret, and now as she lies on the floor in her best black clothes after the funeral, she weeps until she feels her ears pop and the sound of a new world without Margaret enters her head, a miserable hollow sound with no love left in it. She cries until she falls asleep and wakes puffy-eyed and bereft and even though she knows she shouldn't, she goes to find *him*. Something to help numb the suffering and dull the sharp pain every time she takes a breath in this new world, a space without Margaret.

She stands outside the flat but can't go in. Hangs around till she realises nothing on earth will make this better. It just is.

Missing Margaret

Sam, 1994

Sam wakes in Naoise's bed the morning after the funeral. She lies there for a moment, looking at him sleeping.

She needed someone to be kind to her last night. She'd waited for what seemed like an age and then walked away from his flat, cursing herself for being so stupid, when she felt his hand on the small of her back. She turned and collapsed into him, sobbing without care for how she looked or sounded. He'd heard about Margaret, of course he had. It was a tight community and Margaret was well liked. He joked that Mags had been a good-looking old broad in her day.

She'd be rolling in her grave if she heard you say that.

You wanna go for a walk? he said. Let's go to Inch Abbey.

He stopped and bought cans and ciggies in the shop and they walked there, slowly, chatting along the cow-parsley edged road.

I know this must be difficult for you, he said to her, when they got to the ruins. I know what she meant to you.

Thanks, Sam said.

He stood in a broken church window, framed by the view behind him, the Quoile river, ancient and high, hugging the banks of the fields, flowing past.

My ancestors arrived here, on long boats from Normandy, Sam said.

Huh. Raped and pillaged, did they? Naoise said, pulling her up beside him.

Something like that, yeah. Sam ran her fingers down the walls of the building like it was his spine, her fingertips skimming the grey flecked stones, white lichen growing upon the surface, mimicking a pretty cathedral wedding veil, hiding all the flaws concealed within. These were the same walls that monks had prayed to God to keep safe all those years ago. It had worked; the abbey remained almost intact, with a sky for a roof.

She'd thrown herself at him then, her body her offering, kissing him and losing all sense of reason till he pulled away gently.

Sam, he said. Stop.

Her face flushed.

I didn't mean … it's not that … Sam … you're upset.

She got down from the sill. She wanted to leave, but he stopped her, caught her hand.

Just have a drink with me, he said jumping down.

Mates? He opened his arms for a hug and she sank into him, breathed him in, his solidness.

I'm sorry, she said, looking up at him, though she was not even sure what she was sorry for.

They sat in the ruins and talked for hours. She got a little, then a lot drunk. Her head rested on his shoulder.

I've missed this, she said. Missed you.

Look, about that, I had stuff going on. Too many drugs. That night. At the party. Things shouldn't have ended like that.

It's fine.

It's not. About Lena—

I don't want to talk about Lena.

He stroked her hair and they sat in silence in the dark. She could feel the tension between them and when he finally slid his mouth over hers she thought she would scream out. The terrible need she had for him rushed over her, their bodies colliding in the dark. Stopping all his words. Shoring up all her doubt.

I can't control myself around you, he said to her, and laughed. We should go.

They walked back to his flat. Giddy, holding hands and laughing like they had no history together. Like it was all new and shiny and pure. Stopping to kiss, their bodies tightening against each other, fitting together so easily. No one else was in when they arrived back and she was relieved. Time was severed when she was with Naoise. Like no time had passed at all.

He made her forget everything.

It's about 5 a.m. when she sneaks out of his flat. Above her the early sky is being washed out into daybreak. She borrows his bike and cycles home. Leaves it in a side building, were her da might not look. Lets herself in using the key hidden just inside the post box, her slim fingers still just about fitting in the slot to retrieve it. She jumps in the shower, washes quickly and shoves on her baby-pink carer's uniform, her body half-dry. She can't find her shoes and it's then she remembers that Margaret had washed her white plimsolls. Sam hasn't worn them since her shift last weekend. Margaret has left them stuffed with last week's sports pages in the hot press. She feels tears coming to the surface again as she empties the balled-up bits of words from their innards, and laces them up tight enough to pinch her feet. Margaret would have pored over this paper before she reused it. This weekend's pages will carry Margaret's obituary. Sam throws the paper into the bucket beside the fire and grabs a banana from the bowl in the kitchen. She gets her own bike from a pile of rubbish in the shed, moving the lawnmower and spades and shovels that seem to grow around it from one weekend to the next.

She pushes off the feeling that this first day without Margaret properly above ground has no right to be so beautiful. All around her things blossom and shine out, Technicolor happiness that today should not exude. She speeds up, using the lanes to quicken her cross-country cycle, hitches up her dress, practically tucks it into her white cotton knickers in case it gets dirty, dry mud flying up against her strong legs that race, using every little hill to fight against the lateness that's coming.

She cycles onto the main road. The village of Ardglass has not woken up yet, apart from the clatter of boats in the harbour, busy like a toddler's bath, gently batting one another against the lapping waves. Her hair has come undone and whips her face as she skids around the corner and pumps momentum to get up the final steep hill to the nursing home.

If she is only five minutes late her boss might not notice; she can time it so that it looks like she has been in the loo or making a coffee or chatting to one of the residents. She could always blame Margaret. Start to cry. Alive Margaret wouldn't mind, so she can't imagine the dead version would have an issue with it. Margaret can save her again, one final time. Her boss will have nothing to say to that. She parks up her bike, pulls her hair tight enough to make her eyes water. It isn't hard. She tries not to think about Naoise at all.

The Study of Encopresis, or
The Shit that Resembles My Life

Sam, 1994

Sam knows there is a name for it. She sits there seeping in the smell of shit, trying to remember the terminology, but she never listened in biology GCSE because Mrs Muldoon believes in the natural rhythm method and the only rhythm to her biology teacher's life is that every other year she has a baby.

I don't think that method works, miss, Sam piped up in class one day, years ago, as Mrs Muldoon sat looking forlornly out of the science block window, her bleached lab coat stretched button-popping tight over her bump, explaining some function or other of reproduction to the class. The girls could hardly repress their sniggers at Sam's quip, but when Mrs Muldoon started to cry large fat tears, eventually no one laughed anymore and Sam went to get Sister Agnes. Then the hard-faced nun took their teacher away.

Everyone sat in shocked silence for a few minutes afterwards, but by the time Sister Agnes returned to the lab they had stopped whispering quietly, reverently amongst themselves, and reverted to teenage girl loudness, as if nothing untoward had occurred. Sam had dawdled back to the classroom. Arrived in after Sister Agnes tried to pass off what had happened as the *joy of pregnancy*. A hormonal blip. Asked the girls to join together in prayer for their teacher but Sam couldn't help herself.

Yes, Sister, course I'll pray for her.

That's lovely, Sam, Sister Agnes said, as Sam took her seat beside Becca.

I'll pray to God she wises up and has no more babies.

Everyone laughed suddenly, too sharply.

Samantha Malin!

I was just at the toilet, Sister? Time of the month.

Sister Agnes practically dragged Sam out of there, her normal nun-white visage ruined red with rage.

No more babies was the right *and* wrong answer.

Sam's papers scattered where Sister Agnes had manhandled her, yanking her off the high stool. Sam knew the sister thought she could drag her, because Sam bore that scent, a fragrant lack of care that enabled people like Sister Agnes to commit these slights. Cruelties doled out to counteract the slips of unsanctioned thoughts that escaped from the quick mouths of those that question. Sam was that kind of girl: trouble waiting to happen.

Now, as the foul smell of shit hits the back of her throat and she gags repeatedly, she wishes she had just shut her mouth and stayed in the classroom back then. Finally learnt something useful. She should have been studying this Sunday, she needed to study, but Sundays paid double time.

Sam could have gone home that day after school and looked up the only encyclopaedia they owned, but what if the word she needed wasn't under the letter *F*? The salesman who had sold these treasure troves of knowledge was *so* clever, and *so* insistent, and *so* 'Is your mother in?' and so in praise of the benefits of education for girls and 'look-at-the-state-of-the-place' without saying *look-at-the-state-of-the-place*, that her dad had bought one book to get rid of the fecker. And all Patsy had bought was the letter *F* and Sam felt it was her mother smiling down on her – F for Fionnuala – but of course her mother was not a benevolent spirit but an unclaimed, missing-presumed-dead person, and what if the salesman only had *N* – Nuala was her mum's pet name, short and sweet – would she have seen her mum in that too?

Becca had, of course, got every flippin one of those encyclopaedias. Cost her parents a fortune. Enough to ensure she went along to college just to pay that back. Sam used to wonder how Becca managed with all that stuff sometimes, the expectations it brought. *Bought*. Be good, besmartbekindbebeautifulbecareful. But not anymore because one day, not so long ago, Sam realised she's expected to be all those things too but there is no one on her side keeping score in a positive way. Maybe they are keeping score in a negative way. There should not be anyone keeping score at all, but they are teenage girls and all anyone does is keep a silent scorecard on their lives, the comings and goings and subtle shifts that a hair style, colour, hormonal development could make.

Boys played rugby and football and ran races, but girls are set to compete forever, no team support, no trophy in sight. A never-ending race and she knows already that it isn't fit for her, she doesn't want to play by any rules that she hasn't vetted herself, because she's been questioning everything since she could speak, the language she was given, the way she was spoken to, the colour of blood in her knickers. Why do girls have to bleed and boys don't? Why? It doesn't matter what it is, she has to know the why, the essence of a thing and then wonder can it, she, he, they, be another thing, another way, another person altogether, because someone, somewhere, sometime, has made her believe that anything is possible. Her mother just up and left, so why couldn't she? She could escape.

Steam floats above them and Mrs O'Keefe's face looks sort of serene and beautiful for a brief moment before she starts smearing Sam's baby-pink carer's uniform with shit again. Sam hates that uniform with its insipid feminine shade. Shit-brown is worse, though, much worse. The thing about being raised on a farmstead, the practical side of Sam, is that she didn't throw up straight away, but it is rising up, the disgust, the fear, and she keeps pushing it down, away, trying to remain still and just listen, *listen* to what Francesca O'Keefe is trying to tell her.

Listen to Francesca.

Francesca has something to say.

Something important that Sam needs to hear now.

It could have been anyone trapped in that bathroom, on that day, could have been Becca, but it isn't. It's almost inevitable it is going to be Sam she tells. Sam is a person to whom things like this will always happen. She just has that sort of life. Interesting to everyone but her.

Best behaviour, Francesca says.

Turned inside out, upside down.

My best *best* behaviour, Francesca says.

Francesca is not on her *best behaviour*.

All those words kept tight inside, now tumbling, pouring out. Francesca had smeared herself with shit, smoothing it into the creases of her skirt, which she lifts like a little girl to reveal she'd rubbed all the crevices of her body, rubbed raw with shit and blood, hidden her belly button with faeces, laced shit into her pubic hair, dyeing sparse white wispy hairs mucky brown. There is no way to wash tenderly. It has quickly descended into scrubbing, scrubbing, scrubbing, the filth away. Mrs O'Keefe is the oldest person Sam has ever seen naked, a body of dripping flesh, like candles melting downwards, almost to the point of flickering out. Francesca has practically melted away, skin and bones washed with time. This shit is paying for college, Sam thinks, literally. A temporary *shit* job.

Sam got this job because Becca couldn't handle it. Sam had tagged along and Becca barfed the first day and never made it past the first weekend. Two jobs and no fixed schedule was always going to work best with a da who didn't really give a shit where you were, so Sam had stuck.

Sam soaps the sponge and runs it against Francesca's back, knobs of bone popping out to greet her, unearthed from the brown scum. Some of the shit has dried. She has to clean this old woman's cunt and she really can't face it. Every time she dips the sponge into the water it muddies and swirls with chunks and clumps of foulness floating and disappearing under her delicate hands. Sam gags again.

She doesn't get up, instead she shuffles her bare knees across the sweating lino. She rinses her gloved hands under the double tap at the bath's end and wonders if even the tiniest bit of Francesca's shit would get into her somehow. She hands Francesca the sponge.

You need to clean there. Sam points between Francesca's legs. I'm not doing it. You have to do it. Do you understand?

Francesca just stares ahead at the white standard-issue hospital tiles. Rectangled, ordered, pristine. Unlike Francesca's mind. When the muddied water darkens Sam heaves and staggers backwards from the tub, but it is only when she feels the first little stab, the pinch of pain as the blade of a pair of scissors strikes her, that she realises it is blood not shit that is colouring the water. When Francesca stands up, Sam sees she has been plucking at her inner thighs, thin little lines, old scars, opened up with ease and practice. New scars appear on Sam's forearms, tiny little nicks, that let the blood stream out.

The red emergency cord isn't working. Sam yanks it so hard it comes away in her hand. Sweat trickles along Sam's neck.

She feels the little edge of the blade dig a little deeper into her and she misses Margaret. Sam doesn't even say stop. One cut for Francesca, one for Sam. Sam watches, held as if in some temporary slow motion, as the two women settle into a conversation of pain. Elder educating the younger. Leading her astray.

She doesn't think she has screamed or made a sound but she has. She has. In all the chaos Sam finds herself holding the shivering naked damp bleeding woman on the floor, holding Francesca's hand tight, holding it until they drag Francesca out, holding on as needles puncture her skin, sedation putting all Francesca's secrets back to sleep.

Sam tries to tease out answers after. No one really knew. Margaret might have known what to say but her grave doesn't give many answers.

In the aftermath Francesca sits motionless in her room, drugs trapping her in an easy world, all her scars unable to surface. Even though Sam doesn't have to care for her again, she pauses, studies the old woman's now tranquil face. This new routine chops up her days at the nursing home, so despite herself, she always pays the room a visit, perhaps thinking if she looks long enough some wound will reveal itself to her, some chance to help, the possibility of resolution, but nothing ever does. Nothing ever really heals in this place. She feels guilty about Lena. About last weekend. She has thought about him every day since and knows it has to stop.

Maybe that was wisdom. Knowing when to give up.

Formal Adoration of the Sacrament

Sam, 1994

The formal is in a posh hotel in Belfast. Her face has just about healed, swelling gone, and she covers up the fading yellow stain of bruises with make-up. Margaret never got to see the end result. The frock turned out well. Made her fit in with the string quartets and Italian marble draped columns. Giant Michelle is also doing her best impression of a human column; if there is a worse dress for Giant Michelle to wear to the formal it would be hard to find it. Sam gawks at the burnt bronze monstrosity, which clashes so vividly with Giant Michelle's entire colouring that it's difficult to look at her for more than a few moments without experiencing some sort of face blindness, triggered by all the umberness. Her horrendously bad fake-tan job seems to bloom and grow, sunshimmer reflecting in the disco lights, as Giant Michelle moves her limbs around in the hysteria of the dancefloor.

Basic Instinct was shown on the telly months earlier, inspiring at least fifty per cent of the girls to wear no knickers to the formal, and to cross and uncross their legs at Mr Travers at a moment's notice. Sam really hopes Giant Michelle is wearing knickers. Even those awful 'natural tan' ones. In the weeks after the movie was shown on the telly there was a surge in broken VCRs being brought in for repairs, the rewind and pause buttons worn out, while doctors' surgeries overflowed with repetitive strain injury emergency appointments. As far as mothers, video repair men and GPs are concerned, Sharon Stone has a lot to answer for.

Bronagh Kerr got a wax done up in Belfast and can barely walk properly – burnt the fanny off herself, Becca says. Told everyone she had to put on her ma's girdle and one of those massive pads they give you after childbirth, and use a load of Vaseline and painkillers, just to get out the door.

If you have to pick one, the most Northern-Irish version of Sharon Stone, Becca would totally win. She has slicked back her hair, tight and low, and wears a pure white frock with a big slit up the leg. It has a high neck and goes straight to the floor because even her da had seen the film and informed the sales assistant in *no uncertain terms* that his daughter would be wearing the longer version. No discussion. No surrender. Daddy says no. Still, she looks great.

While the body of white-clad girls surrounding her make the colours drowning Giant Michelle all the more ghastly, the thing that really makes Michelle a true laughing stock is the state of her date. In all the excitement Sam had forgotten one thing; Murph still has a broken arm. Not in a big fuck-off metal triangle anymore, thankfully, but the unruly cast is resplendently tattooed with expletives and badly drawn penises. Sam had told him to paint over it with white paint, advised him to clean off the cast's original inappropriate artwork with white spirits first. Becca had helped. They met in her house and attempted to remove the worst of it while the fumes made them giddy. It was as they watched telly afterwards, smoking copious amounts of grass, that they had hit upon their *amazing* idea to butcher a tux to fit the arm in. Murph was like, 'I'll be Charlie Sheen in *Major League*, Ricky "Wild Thing" Vaughn rocking a sleeveless tux.' Even Becca thought it seemed such a good idea at the time. Murph would look amazing – guns out. But this is south County Down and not California and Murph is a pasty lad with so-so muscles and a big dopey head on him. They'd rough-cut the sleeves off a charity shop tux and vowed to get it sewn up properly, but it never happened.

Now he stands shivering in the line for photographs, frayed cut-offs hovering around his shoulders, a full head shorter than Giant Michelle, who is both pissed and pissed off. Both he and Giant Michelle had bare arms in the photograph. Ebony and Ivory. Or maybe more like Tango and Cash. Sam hasn't even bothered to queue up for photos. Pauric is long gone, trying to talk to the girl he is mildly in love with but still gawping at all the other beautiful creatures whose existence he's just become aware of. He hasn't even lasted until dessert. The whole evening is like being on a diet.

Sam smiles as she watches Jennie McVerry, the school's token lesbian – or at least the only one who has admitted it for now: some people can't take their eyes off other girls' tits in the changing room but divulge nothing. But when Jennie snogs her girlfriend from Derry, who goes to art college and is such a fucking ride, the energy in the room changes. Every boy and some girls and at least a quarter of the adults in the room will be dreaming of those two kissing the faces off each other for months after, shiny satin sucked around their curves, completely lost in one another in a way that a lot of the local teenage population have not yet achieved, that perfect space of fresh young lust.

It sets Sister PE on edge and provokes her to ask the videographer to leave early, hilariously accosting him and escorting him out the double doors, wires trailing behind his red and grey chequered shirt back as Naoise appears.

Sam tries not to watch him make his way slowly towards her, stopping to speak to people he knows, taking his time, turning heads. An exhibition of confidence. Being so close to him again leaves her breathless. She watches Lena dissolve into drunken tears after he kisses her on the cheek, avoiding her pretty flushed mouth in a hit 'n' run movement of betrayal, a practised collision on his way to his real target: Sam. Sam knows he isn't invited but he doesn't even flinch at the stares from the nuns. Just before he reaches Sam, she can see Sister PE shake her head. Not a movement of disappointment, but expectant. The nun knows Sam is the destination. Attracting chaos, courting danger. Sister PE is gunning for Sam to get burnt. Teach her a lesson. Put her in her place. Sam sees it all over her face. Sister PE wants Sam to learn the hard way.

Naoise lets out a loud wolf whistle as he reaches Sam, tries to spin her around, draw her into his shiny orbit of showiness. She wrenches back her hand, turns back to the bar and continues to order her drink. She's already pretty drunk. She can see Naoise is high.

Ned, Naoise says, addressing the barman. How's tricks?

Ah, Naoise, how's it going? You know yerself, same oul shite. Usual?

Aye, get hers as well, and yourself one.

Thanks, mate.

No bother, Naoise says. He pushes a tenner topped with a little white baggy across the counter. It isn't enough but the barman smiles and pockets both.

Naoise swivels around and leans up against the bar, his arms props. So, who you planning to fuck tonight? It could still be me. His irises swell with coke as he looks around the room. This is a fucking bust. We could get out of here. I've got a key to a mate's house in the Holy Lands.

You're off your head, Sam says.

Guilty! He laughs, pushing his hair out of his eyes. He's buzzing.

Sam watches the barman lay out the drinks, an expert in appearing not to listen to their conversation, but he purposely catches her eye as he hands her a drink. It's swift but it's there. Concern. She smiles that she is okay and he moves on to his next customer.

Well, that was rude, Naoise says softly, and traces a finger on her bare shoulders, moving his fingertips down her back, joining the dark brown beauty spots together, making her quiver a little as he trails his fingers back up the blots, connecting each one with a tiny pulse of desire.

Some people might say these are ugly but I don't think that. I think they mark you out as beautiful. Dangerous, though, because they can change, develop into something that might kill you, if you're unlucky, or careless. Did you know that the Chinese believe moles on your back indicate struggles in life? No? Look at you. All the struggles ahead written all over you like pointless graffiti. Lena doesn't have any moles. Not one.

What about Lena? she says. Doesn't she mind her boyfriend ditching her?

She's got Davy to keep her company. Always about Lena with you, isn't it? Neither of us really gives a fuck about Lena, do we? You made that pretty clear last weekend.

I was grieving, Sam says. Fuck off.

He leans into her, pushing his head against hers. Hey, Sam, he says. His words run hot and he grazes her ear imperceptibly with his tongue. Just admit it. You can't get enough of me.

She flinches away from him. Straightens out her back, pulls her hair around her ears so he can't do it again. She can feel the buzz of want needle her body, and she takes a swig of her drink as he reaches around her waist, hand grazing below her belly button, pulling her towards him. She reaches up with her free hand and pushes her fingers into his, meaning to pull his hand away, but she finds herself holding, locking tight.

Not here, she says, and they leave the ballroom.

She freezes in the hallway, not knowing what to do next. She looks down at the ornate swirling royal-blue carpet, the same colour as her school uniform, her feet planted at the head of a bird, a peacock, with shimmering tail feathers and one widely cocked eye. She focuses on his hand held tightly in hers. Her breath is sparse and unsteady, like she might flee this decision at any moment. Naoise doesn't let her pause last, and she feels his grip change as he pulls her through a fire door, the exit light above broken, only the I illuminated.

On the fire escape stairs, coldness hits her as he starts to kiss her. He feels like a stranger inside her mouth, not familiar. Frenzied, rushed, almost sloppy. She tries again, kissing him harder, trying not to think as he pulls her dress up, pushes his hand inside her knickers. His fingers take moments that feel too long already to find her wet, screaming out for him, her biology reacting despite herself. He smiles his warm, wicked smile and she feels everything spinning as he gets down on his knees, his face buried in her, the crêpe de chine falling over his body. She desperately tries not to let go of all her need too easily but she can't get enough of him in that moment, his tongue bringing her, making her come, and she clutches his shoulder, afraid she might collapse on top of him.

He takes her hand, unbuckling his belt with the other, pushing her hand inside, his trousers coming down. She feels the rub of concrete against her spine, panic rising a little. Cold. So much feeling. Something is tearing. Fabric dragged against the ground. The feeling that this is not right, too fast, this is all wrong ... She starts to say, No, no, not like this. He is rough, kissing her mouth, stopping her talking, he's high and forces his weight against her. She snaps back to herself, a drunken shake, starts pushing him off her. She realises this – he – is a mistake. Wrong. Everything wrong. Wants to pause. She needs him to stop.

No, Sam says again.

Get off me.

She tries to push him away but he isn't listening, or doesn't hear her, his body insistent. She pulls herself higher up the concrete steps away from him and he catches her by the shoulder, his face leering, manic. She buries her head against his chest, lips purse in a kiss, bites him with every ounce of strength in her body. The shock of his blood hitting her teeth, metallic, the flesh giving way underneath her incisors, his scream, the feeling of her head banging against the steel railing, his shouting, the blood spilling down and blotting out through the heavy cotton of his shirt. She is scrabbling away from him, laughing, drunk, stupid, frightened, backwards up the steps, using every fibre to will herself: move, move away, go.

Sam flees up the staircase. She races towards an emergency exit door on the next floor that's propped open with a plastic wedge, crashes through it into a faceless corridor with the same blue carpet, plain, no birds. She hesitates, doesn't want to take the lift just in case he has decided to look for her. Then she notices Mr Malone walking towards her, swaying, probably a little bit tipsy. He stops short when he sees her and then moves very quickly towards her. Like fast-forward.

Samantha, are you alright?

She touches her fingertips to the part of her head he is looking at, feels the dribble of blood pumping loose against her skin. She comes to a halt.

It's only a little nick, sir. Be fine.

She sucks the blood from her fingers and dabs her head again and again, moving the blood away.

Mr Malone reaches her and fishes out a clean handkerchief from his pocket, hands it to her.

You're kind of old-fashioned, aren't you, sir? Sam says, as she holds the cloth to her forehead.

Well. What happened this time? he says, an annoyed tone sheltering in his voice.

Larking about on the fire escape, knocked my head against the railings. Her voice is high-pitched with the lie as they walk back along the corridor.

Uh huh, Mr Malone says. He leaves it at that. The sound of a heavy door opening makes them both turn and she sees the expression change in Mr Malone's face, like cloudscape moving above the Mournes. She shifts alongside her teacher, a pivot to put herself closer to him and Mr Malone takes a step forward so that now she is slightly behind him, not in Naoise's direct line of sight.

You lost, son? I think you're at the wrong party.

Ah, no. I'm exactly where I'm meant to be, mate. *You* have just what I'm looking for.

You know him? Mr Malone says.

Aye, sort of, Sam whispers, then: I'm not with him. Tonight. He's not my date.

As Naoise walks towards them, his jacket opens and they both see the splodge of red, too bright for wine.

Were you on the stairwell, son? Mr Malone insists. Sam wonders why Mr Malone keeps calling Naoise 'son'. She knows Naoise is older than her teacher. Pretty confident Mr Malone knows it too.

Naoise's laughter carries down the hall towards them. His hand outstretched. Naoise, he says to Mr Malone. And you are?

180

Naoise, don't you think you're a bit old to be gatecrashing a school formal?

I'm old enough to tell you to fuck off, mate, Naoise says.

The two men stop abruptly and Sam reaches out for something to steady herself with, finds herself tugging on the back of her teacher's dinner jacket, dragging the weight low like a child who wants something so badly it can't let go.

I think you should leave, Malone says again, louder this time.

I'm leaving – with her.

Samantha's not going anywhere with you.

Naoise, just leave it. I'm not feeling so good and he's getting me a lift home.

Naoise reaches out to her but Mr Malone steps in and says, very steadily, I think you should leave it alone. I think you've had a bit too much, son. Samantha is not going anywhere with you. I think you should leave before I have you thrown out.

Oh. Okay. You playing peelers now? Naoise takes his cigarettes out from inside his jacket pocket, fumbles opening them, takes one himself first, then offers one to Mr Malone, who declines. Naoise sways as he lights up, takes a long drag and smiles, deeply content with himself.

Come on, Samantha. Mr Malone turns Sam around and starts to walk away.

Naoise starts shouting, following them down the long corridor: Hey! I'm talking to you. You love it, don't you? The thirst on you, for some really young, keen, fresh virgin pussy. A few at a time, begging you for it. All in those box-fresh blue uniforms. Tie them up. Beat them. What you wouldn't do, if you only had the balls.

Sam can't help it, she looks over her shoulder at him. Naoise's lips curl around the word *balls*. Curl against the viciousness of his insults, forming into his disarming smile so easily again that Sam shrinks looking at him.

So, you're going to fuck her, is it? You missed that boat, she's damaged goods, this one. Rotten.

Sam swallows, runs back and launches herself at him, screaming. I wouldn't sleep with you if you paid me! Fuck off, Naoise! Just fuck off, alright? Leave me alone. It's over, it's fucking over.

Naoise raises himself to her but Mr Malone puts him to the ground with one hand, pushes him down and grabs Sam with the other. Sam is so surprised Mr Malone can do that. Naoise stays down. Her teacher puts his arm around Sam's shoulder, turns her around and starts to walk quickly away from Naoise.

Did he hit you?

Just pushed me. He's drunk.

Are you sure you're okay? Malone asks.

Sam looks up, mouth held tight in an unspoken promise.

Did he do anything else?

Sam hesitates, then shakes her head in a blurry no.

You sure?

You belong to me! Naoise roars down the corridor, still lying on the ground. You're fucking mine, do you hear me?

Sam freezes but Mr Malone holds her steady.

You have very poor choice in boyfriends, Samantha. Sam starts to shake. She wants to look back, but her teacher's hands grip her shoulders tight.

Don't turn around, that's what he wants. Don't.

I'm going to fuck you. You're mine, you are fucking mine, you'll always be mine. You belong to me. Do you hear me? Do you fucking hear me!

Mr Malone's chunky frame starts to move at pace, taking Sam with him, her feet bouncing pebble-like against the carpet. He pushes their bodies around the corner and through double doors that open onto the cavernous ballroom. Sam is overwhelmed by the sound of music and dancing, loud bursts of laughter, familiar faces that contort as she speeds past with their teacher; all of these things blur together, a tableau of surprise that momentarily absorbs Sam's shock. She's still shaking as Mr Malone calmly walks her down the stairs into the lounge bar and tells her he is going to get Naoise removed.

Naoise's words take hold inside as her face flushes with embarrassment. His words. Her body. She feels exposed. Mr Malone shakes her, just a little.

Samantha. Don't go anywhere. Okay?

Okay.

He lets go and looks at her for a shade too long, concern etched on his face. She watches him approach the security guard at the door near reception, who in this high-end hotel probably rarely gets bothered, and certainly not at an all-girls' grammar school formal. There are a few out-of-town businessmen chatting at the bar and looking over, casting casual glances laced with sex, and she feels sickened then, all the events unfolding upon her. She sees a door at the far side, pushed open, letting cool night air into the stuffy lobby. Her teacher is still engaged. She can hear him describing Naoise, the receptionist looking over as Mr Malone tilts his head in Sam's direction, the tone becoming hushed as he impresses upon them the urgency. She sees Naoise appear, then Murph behind him. Mr Malone looks back over at her and then points towards them, and the security guard and her teacher look away from her and start to move towards Naoise and Murph. Sam knows the rest of their confrontation will last just long enough to give her time to flee.

Flight of the Earls

Nuala, 1982

His family had a caravan in Donegal. Near Rathmullan, Lough Swilly. A place tainted by exile, still grieving the end of Gaelic Ulster aristocracy, a place marked by leaving, used to goodbyes. I'd been placing the suggestion for weeks, with both of them, trying to figure out how not to spend too much money, because leaving required money, squirrelling it away, going without, making things stretch so I could escape. I thought Patsy would baulk at the idea of me taking the children to Donegal to catch up with an old friend, but the harvest was late that year and he accepted that the kids and I were better off out of it. His words.

Pamela who? Patsy said in bed a few weeks before, absentmindedly pawing my damp hip, his rough fingertips tracing the silver stretch marks he'd given me along with our children. We'd had quick rough sex, the grateful unexpected kind that makes married people suspect each other of a betrayal. Hoping it's only some petty infatuation. Nothing serious.

English Pamela. She came to the wedding and wore that ridiculous wide-brimmed hat and slept with your cousin, Mark.

I started to touch him again, a cheap exchange for my time away.

The handsome one. I whispered in his ear as I moved on top of him.

Yeah, yeah, he moaned. Sure. Not listening, not hearing anything anymore, lost in my body. I let PJ cry while he finished. Patsy didn't feel the pull of those cries like I did. He barely registered the distance between us.

I didn't think about my husband when I was with *him*. With him I was thinking of ways to say goodbye, how to break his heart in increments. And he was thinking of ... what? Sex-fuelled days, staying in bed, sweat-saturated want dispelled and growing again in us, not enough ways to find each other in that mobile home. A weekend would feel like we had all the time in the world when actually I was saying my long goodbye. Taking us both to a place we couldn't return from unchanged. I was more worried about leaving him, about what it might do to him, to me, than my own husband. I don't know what he said to get away, I didn't ask. I tried to insulate my life from his reality.

He hadn't been around my *real* life. It hadn't flung itself into our pretend paradise. He'd never had to deal with transporting small children, nappies, toys. A journey from hell. Sam full of questions he couldn't be bothered to answer.

He's our babysitter because Daddy can't come, I told her. He's going to help me. This lie. The domesticity in it, made me blush, when nothing else, none of the depravity between us, had. The idea that it could be true. Real.

Is Daddy milking cows, Mama? she asked.

Yes, darling.

I miss Daddy, she said. I wish Daddy was here.

He pouted. It was *too* real. The drive was never-ending. Six hours of squealing kids in crappy pubs shovelling chips in their faces and breastfeeding PJ on demand. Dusk came and when the crying protests finally ended we stopped in a layby and fucked outside, up against the car, as they slept. Maybe that was the best way – no decadent fucking but silent holed-up sex in small spaces beside my children. Maybe that was the way to wake us all up. To shake him out of this belief that *I* was love, *I* was real, *we* were real. The smell of dirty nappies, the locals thinking my teenage son had come to help. A single mother on her own, with three kids. A saint not a sinner.

I was grateful to him, I was open, but he wasn't enough. He was a conduit and I was stepping through. He was a seventeen-year-old boy in my car. Who I was fucking.

Naoise? my daughter had said. Trying out his name, the vowels forming on her tiny tongue. Nee shaaa, she says again, enjoying the way it sounded.

Naoise is Mummy's friend, I said. My friend. Mummy's friend.

He was a friend to me. He was more than a friend and I would always love him but he wasn't enough. He wasn't what I really needed. I needed myself first. I needed what no one could give me. I needed love that wasn't his to give or mine to take. I needed to be alone. I would break him so I could fix myself. I knew I would and I loved him and I didn't care.

I am a terrible person. *I* am the only way I can be.

I was inventing myself all over again. Saving myself. Just for me, for no one but me. When I kissed him, tasted him, I cried because I knew this was the first and last time he would be like this with anyone. I was destroying a part of him that was beautiful and good. I was taking it with me forever because it was fuel I needed to survive on, to get me through the next part.

I was very clear and I could see how the fire would die between us, burn out if we had to make this real. I could see a teenage girl, his own age, coming into view. I could see her, siren-like, calling out to him, and I could see him slowly killing, murdering, turning me to carnage as the years passed. I could see him drunk and angry with a shit job, hating my kids, struggling to leave, cheating. I could see me forgiving him and him abandoning me and the mess of returning and coming and going again. Until we were finally done. Destroyed by each other.

I could see. Finally I could see and I was sorry. Sorry for who? For me. For me mostly. I couldn't have the things I wanted. Staying would only torment him and me. This wouldn't stay hidden. I thought I wanted everything revealed but I didn't. I didn't want to hurt Patsy like that anymore. He didn't deserve that.

I thought all these things, and more, as he moved inside me, the kids asleep again as we fucked in the car, one last time on the way home, the small of my back shoved against the dashboard, my knees buried against hard plastic on either side of the passenger seat, my shoe dangling from my foot, our bodies caught in an awkward embrace, surrendering to an old rhythm now, the newness and excitement of the thing fading, but still we moved against each other, willing it to spark, to stay alive.

Mama! Sam cried out and we paused. I froze. He still moved. He didn't want to stop. I looked at her over his shoulder and he didn't stop. I smiled, and stretched my hand out to hers and he didn't stop. I let him. I let him silently fuck me.

Mama, she said.

I let him. I let him.

Mama, she said again, when his breathing quickened and I knew this was working for him, something about me being trapped, me being a vessel, for him to pour himself into, me on top of him, rigid and tight, holding my daughter's hand. I pushed my free hand over his mouth. I tried to silence his noise. I dug my fingertips into his soft face. I could feel their worn roughness mark his jaw. I could feel a thousand times I'd washed the dishes and touched his cock and put my fingers in his mouth. I was trying to drown his desire out and I forced my fingers between his lips. I was trying to choke him, trying to stop him, trying to save myself, but he pulled me down and shuddered and I felt him come inside me.

I moved off him carefully, the slick wetness slipping out of me. I went to my daughter. Crouched between the seats, batted his hands away as they reached for my nakedness under my skirt.

Shush, go back to sleep, Sam. I rubbed her little face and then sat back down. I wanted to wipe him away but I didn't have anything. The cold air hit as he left the car.

He was leaning against the car, smoking. Pleased with himself.

I wanted to drive off and leave him. Leave him stranded there in the blackening cold of the night, the Blue Stack mountains at his back. He was more dangerous to me than freedom because I would let him do anything to me. Anything at all. That was the shame of it. That even when it was terrible I still wanted him. Even when it was wrong. The person I was leaving most of all was the one who couldn't be trusted around him, the one who would do anything for him, destroy herself for him.

He got into the car, kissed me long and hard on the mouth. He wanted other things but I drove home. I'd let him touch me again, here, in this car, I knew I would. So I drove home. Drove home to the remnants of my marriage, while he slept, peaceful, undisturbed, content.

Silent Valley

Naoise, 1982

He was not expecting to find her daughter in the house. Her little face mooned up at him now every time he closed his eyes. She had been crying, like she'd woken alone from a bad dream, then walked in on him painting the word *CUNT* onto the wall of the good room.

Where's my mama? she said. Her voice pinched at him. He got down on his knees and said *Sssshhh!* The dog prostrate between them. She petted the dog, hugged it and started to screech as the blood came away on her little hands. She ran over to him, hugged his legs and rubbed her hands clean on his jeans. He let her. Stood stock still, hands, arms, raised out above her, afraid to touch her. Then watched her go to her mother's rocking chair, climb up, struggle her way onto it, in that precarious way young children do, when it looks like they will fall, the moment before they catch themselves. Reaching the summit she started to cry again, buried her sob-heaved little body into the blanket as the chair rocked back and forth, a gentle ache for her.

He walked past her, she looked up, eyes bright with crying. Your mum's gone, he said.

Habit-ual Offender

Sam, 1994

Even she knows that turning up at school in her formal dress, barefoot, heels in hand, at eleven o'clock on Monday morning is a *bad* idea.

School is still a better option than home. Just because a search party hasn't been called for her doesn't mean that she won't be in deep shit when she gets back to her da. She'd stayed out the whole weekend. He'd have expected one night; two was pushing it. Still, it was no big surprise that Patsy hadn't even bothered to look for her. No surprise either that the whispers started early and spread to include the rumour (untrue) that she arrived on the back of a motorbike, or that she had been smoking dope, blunt in one hand, bottle of vodka in the other. The legend would swell and develop over the years until it wouldn't even be about her anymore but would create a creature so incredible, so outrageous and powerful that it wouldn't matter, a myth for all the little girls to aspire to.

For now Sam is a tiny bit hungover, tired, and cold. She heads for Mr Malone's room but it turns out he is off sick that day. Just her fucking luck. She has almost reached the furthest prefab classroom when the second-form teacher spots her, turns her around and escorts her to the principal's office. Becca bangs the window as Sam is marched past and then blasts two high sharp whistles, resulting in a slow clap from the other girls and more whistling, so Sam duly does a twirl and takes a bow and frankly this just makes things much, much worse. PE for once isn't in her office but her secretary, Christine, looks at Sam with a *You've done it now* gaze. Sam slinks down on the hard chairs inside Sister Eudoria's office and hopes she can have a little nap to settle her hangover before the inevitable onslaught of the god-botherer starts.

The nun must have come in when she was asleep because when she shakes Sam roughly on the shoulder there is a pile of clothes on the coffee table beside her and Sam is told to get dressed. Sam sits up, still half asleep, noticing something odd about the clothes. Then the sister has Sam on her feet, elbow hooked, out the door.

Nice of you to join us, Miss Malin. Want to tell me what happened to you? PE says.

Not really. I missed my bus home. Stayed with a friend. Before you ask they don't go to this school. They are – Sam exaggeratedly blesses herself – a *Protestant*.

Very funny. Get changed please.

Sister PE shakes her head and points at her own personal toilet. She stands outside while Sam pees. After, Sam holds up the clothes. Oh fuck, she thinks. Well played.

When she appears ten minutes later, fully clad in a nun's outfit, Sister Eudoria barely hides her smirk. Christian as fuck, PE, thinks Sam.

Lovely. Now, PE says, as she holds the dress with the very tips of her fingers, like she'll catch some sort of venereal disease from it, we'll get this washed for you.

It's fine, Sam says. I'll do it at home.

Oh, you'll need shoes.

The brown tights possess a level of scratchiness around the crotch that Sam did not think possible. They pool around her ankles in folds like those small fancy dogs with big wrinkly faces but Sam is too hungover to recall the breed's name. Sister marches Sam back into her office and sorts through a lost-and-found shoe box.

Ah, these might fit.

A too-small pair of rank trainers are given forth and Sam smiles gloriously, just to spite the old fucker.

We'll have a spare gym uniform washed for you later, to go home in, but for now this will have to do.

Sister Eudoria waits for Sam to speak. The expected. Two little words. *Thank you.* Sam sits silent. The two in a wordless game, neither giving in. Sister Eudoria fixes her glasses. Sam smiles at her, unblinking. Eudoria's phone finally rings, piercing the sharp stares between them. It must be important as she eventually shoos Sam out with a wave of her hand. Christine, the secretary, can't manage the poker-face response and bursts out laughing as soon as they turn the corner from the office.

I'm sorry, Sam, but what did you expect, turning up to school like that? And you know Sister Christy-knickers in there has it in for you.

Tears come to the surface.

Oh, love. Don't give her the satisfaction.

Christine takes Sam to the staffroom, checks quickly that no one is inside, and shuffles her in. Tea or coffee? Tea. You'll want some sugar, it'll help with the hangover. I think there's bread in here somewhere.

She makes Sam toast with honey and they both sip on mugs of tea in silence.

So at least tell me it was a good night, Christine asks.

Sam sighs, shrugs. It was, I think. What I can remember.

Christine smiles wanly and ten minutes later they are standing outside Mr Travers' geography class and Samantha feels like she wants to die.

Good luck, Christine says, as she pushes open the door and Sam's performance begins.

Tune into the Lord, motherfuckers, Sam proclaims in her best clipped Jesus voice, not that she knows what Jesus sounded like, plus he probably didn't speak English, being a Jew and everything.

A volcano of laughter erupts as every girl in the class swings around to face her. She is ready to square up to Mr Travers but it's not him. The sub turns from the blackboard and his smile shifts from open to closed as he recognises her as the girl from the weekend. Shit, they both think, and Sam, dressed as a nun, finds a desk at the front and sits down.

Student Teacher Training

Sam, 1994

Sam lets the laughter wash over her as she tries to figure how this might play out. She has not yet spoken to Becca about what she'd gotten up to and feels caught out. Blushes hit every part of her body where he'd touched her; watching him, she could see it was mutual. He pulls his collar from his raspberry-hued neck and sweeps his brown hair behind his ears. How old is he? How old did I say I am? Older than this, obviously. Older than sitting in your class on a Monday in a nun's outfit because you've turned up in the dress he had taken off you. She exhales all those thoughts out of her body as the laughter turns to stifled noises somewhere between fits, coughs and giggles.

That's not a radio station I'm familiar with ... Miss . . .?

Samantha Malin.

Okay, *Samantha*. Ladies, simmer down. Shall we start again? As I was saying, Samantha, I'm Laughlin Trainor. Mr Trainor to you lot, and I'm a student teacher. I'll be subbing for Mr Travers this week while he takes some personal time.

He is about to continue when Michelle starts up. Maybe you could *train her*, Mr Train-or – Michelle points to Sam – to come in in normal uniform.

It was a terrible pun but given the ridiculous circumstances – the fact that Mr Travers is out sick, the impossibly handsome replacement, the absurdity of Sam's get-up and the heating that makes it feel like Nicaragua not Northern Ireland – the room explodes again.

Through it all Sam tries and fails not to look at Laughlin Trainor. After the initial shock, he now seems completely unfazed by her presence. Everyone eventually settles down and everything carries on as normal. At the end of class, just as Sam gathers up the pad and pen Christine had given her – the tights are really at her, Sister Eudoria really *was* a godawful scratchy cunt – ready to traipse out the door, he calls her back.

Samantha, can I have a word with you, please? Won't take too long. Where are you due next?

English, sir, pipes up Becca, all teeth.

Rebecca, isn't it?

She fixes her posture and smiles at the same time, shiny ponytail swinging like the tail of a dog that knows it's been good.

Would you mind letting your teacher know that I asked Samantha to stay back for a few minutes? I don't think Samantha wants to get in any more trouble today.

Of course. Becca smiles all over, mouths the words *Lucky cow* silently at Sam when Laughlin turns his back, and bounces out of the classroom.

He closes the door behind her and turns to Sam. Smiles. Waits. He speaks first. You told me you were at university.

Did I? Well, I am, I hope to, I'm probably going, it's almost the same thing, right? You didn't tell me you were a teacher.

It's not the same thing, and I'm a *student* teacher. This – he motions back and forth between them – is the kind of thing that stops you becoming an actual teacher and ends with you getting arrested.

Look, Sam says, I don't want *this* – she mirrors his body language, finger pointing and all – getting out, either. I'm in enough trouble as it is. I mean, look at the fucking state of me.

He smiles broadly, reaches out and touches the waist of her skirt. Two fingers slide over the thick bunched band, stay there, resting against her waist, as if he is going to pull her towards him.

You like nuns? she drawls, raising the hem of her long brown skirt so he can see the tights gathered at her ankles. The brown rolls wrinkled together like the faces of Shar-Pei puppies – *that*'s the breed.

I'm only here for a week. I don't want to get too used to the charms of the religious orders, he says.

You sure?

His smile grows. He releases her, tucks his hands under his armpits, holding himself in a straitjacket of cashmere. Sam wonders do all teachers get their jumpers from the same shop, bought in unspoken agreement, a uniform just like the students.

Habits never really did it for me, Laughlin says again. His hands go to his pockets and he moves behind his desk. He takes a moment to study her. I do quite like red-lipped girls in stockings, though. Or did the nuns get rid of those too?

An image flashes up of her prancing around his apartment with only that on. She must have been very drunk to do that. Drunk and a bit full of herself. He is flirting with her, though. No mistaking that.

Huh, Sam says. This is not really what I expected for a second date.

Well, I didn't expect to see you here either.

He picks up her hand and writes his number on it. Clear black roller pen. It hurts a little but she doesn't mind. She gets the feeling that he wants to kiss her as badly as she wants him to.

And we talked about?

Oh, you're having trouble with understanding tectonic plate formation.

Hah.

You might need to stay back this week for extra tuition. Apologise to Miss—?

Miss Denvir.

Miss Denvir.

He moves towards the door. Sam looks at the number.

So I'm going to have to ring you?

Only if you want to. When I don't teach here anymore. Like, next week.

What if someone notices this on my hand? She waves her hand in the air, teasing.

Everyone's too busy looking at your habit, Sister Samantha, he says, deadpan. Oh, and Sam?

Yeah.

Not a word to Rebecca, she's—

Becca has the hots for every teacher in this school, you're not that bloody special. You're just shiny and new.

He really smiles at that. Sam reckons he thinks she's a cheeky little fucker but he likes her anyway. Today is bringing her one small good thing. She remembers more now. They definitely didn't have sex, but they did everything else. Spent the day in bed. Watched old movies. He ordered Chinese food, then they started drinking again. She got dressed and meant to go home but fell asleep. She hadn't meant to stay another night. She had called him Naoise by mistake and he'd flinched but said nothing. Maybe just repeated Laughlin. Embarrassed when she woke up, realising she was still there, she'd snuck out super early that morning before he got up. Got up for school, she now realised. Christ Almighty.

She had tried to get a bus home from Belfast but ended up falling asleep in a café. Somebody woke her and told her she couldn't sleep there and a truck driver regular intervened, took pity on her and offered her a lift, which she took. A lift from a truck driver she didn't know. That was a terrible idea, she realised now, but he seemed lovely, seemed like he wouldn't do her any harm. Trusted her gut. Like that ever means anything. What a complete child she is. All those people who trust their guts and end up in the worst situation. You could only say you'd listened if you survived. What about all those poor fuckers who listened and their guts told them the wrong thing? No one ever heard from them. Still, he seemed nice. But she'd sobered up enough then to feel like she should get out. School was closest. He dropped her off on the outskirts of Newcastle, she said the school was just around the corner, lied just to be on the safe, her sense having arrived back by then, realising her hangover was in control and not her gut. She'd hobbled the half a mile back along the road to her actual school, and back to the stranger she had just spent a day and night with.

Driving Lessons

Sam, 1994

Malone was covering for Travers now. There is something seriously wrong with that man but because it is the North there is something seriously wrong with everyone here. The whole of Northern Ireland needs therapy, so no one discusses it. Malone asks Sam's class to start on this week's topic: Mount St Helens. Becca's favourite. He asks her to read to the class. He sits back in his chair, distracted, Sam can tell. He's always so eager to learn but it seems like he's not actively listening. About halfway through the text his face crumbles and he makes a cough that on another day, with another teacher, might sound like muffled crying. The girls shuffle in their seats.

Becca pauses. He tells her to keep reading. A crack in his voice too sharp to hide.

David A. Johnson died at—

Malone stands up. Excuse me, ladies. Caroline, you're in charge. Answer the questions on page nine everyone, he says, referring to the passage Becca has just read. I'll be back shortly.

Becca looks at Sam. She shrugs, has no idea what's up.

Anyone? Becca says.

Malin? Michelle asks.

Again, how would I know?

Becca, just finish reading, Caroline says. Some people grumble but for once Becca just does what Caroline asks. No questions.

When Malone gets back Sam can see he's washed his face. Tiny wet patches around his ears, curling ferns of unruly hair, pushed back. Later she lets the classroom empty, takes her time to pack her bag. Malone is in and out of the storage cupboard. Busies himself.

Ignoring me, sir? Sam asks on her way out.

Not at all, Sam, he calls from behind the door. Just a lot on, trying to cover the extra classes.

I applied to Bristol as well in the end. Just wanted to let ya know.

Bristol? Malone says, popping his head out the door. That's great.

If I'm lucky. Or Trinity. Wouldn't have applied if it hadn't been for Matt. You tell him I said thanks next time you're speaking to him.

Sam ... Malone sighs. Sit down, he says, in that concerned voice of his. She feels like if he had drink he'd give it to her. She braces herself for news. The way people here are used to. She flinches when he says Matthew, youth already disappearing from her teacher's voice as he matures right in front of her.

Matt is dead. Car crash.

She tries not to cry but when it feels like he might hug her and instead hugs himself, the tears come. Malone's face is ashen.

I'm fine, Sam says, he was your friend. Sorry. It's so stupid ... honestly. I'm—

Life's not fair, is it? Malone says.

Thanks for telling me, she says brightly, like nothing has happened. No one special lost.

She moves away to the door as the bell for next class rings. She is still reeling when she leaves the classroom. Defends herself from further offers of kindness that will only hurt her more. Feels sorry for herself. What a sap. She isn't sick. Or dying. She has a place to live. She has people, some people anyway. She knows, some small part of her, she's done a good job, getting this far. Surviving till now. When so often all she has wanted to do is stop. Stop it all. Stop the utter nothingness that claims her. Quiet all her thoughts.

Matthew's death was not quiet, she thinks, but she doesn't know. Doesn't know enough about car crashes, about Matthew in that car crash, some Highland road, hoar frost, late at night, or

Kurt's shotgun suicide in the sunny U S of A. Sam doesn't know about these things.

She swears she won't go back to Naoise.

Laughlin agrees to meet her after school on Friday in Downpatrick. Someone might see them in Newcastle, tell the school. She gets off the bus outside the *Down Recorder* offices and dawdles. When she finds herself outside Naoise's flat she goes to the door but leaves again straightaway. Hesitates. Hopes he hasn't seen her. Then hopes he has. Laughlin picks her up at the bottom of the street. She could have picked anywhere.

His car is messy.

Unlike Matt's.

Littered with notes and Snickers wrappers and drinks cans. Laughlin shoves aside papers, throws them into the back seat so she can sit down.

Your car is worse than my room.

Music is what Laughlin spends most of his money on. In his apartment she saw vinyl from every band she's never heard of. In his car, CDs of the same. They both went to Féile last July.

Stiff Little Fingers, best performance of the weekend, Laughlin says as they drive to the airstrip.

I dunno, That Petrol Emotion killed it. And INXS.

Laughlin starts to laugh.

Fuck off, they were amazing! Sam says.

Okay, and the Manics!

Look, I don't remember most of it. Alright? she sighs.

Yeah, he says. I get that.

Someone slashed my tent and then I just got fucked up.

Sam sees him catch his reflection in the rear-view mirror. There is doubt behind his smile. A question. Why he is here, with her. She switches tack.

Okay, this is getting awkward. I missed the bit when INXS became deeply uncool. Let me drive, she says.

No, he says, but relents when she sits on his lap. He pushes the seat back to make space but she is so slight that she fits right in the space between his legs. She pushes herself back against him as her feet find the pedals. She loves the feeling of him tense up underneath her lightness, the solidity of his thighs against her, the rise of him against her knickers as she settles into his lap.

Teach me how to drive, she says, leaning her neck and head back into his shoulder. She is in her uniform. This is dangerous, if anyone sees them. She made him drive out to the deserted scrap of an airport that no one uses, but still.

People come here to learn to drive all the time, she told him on the way. But not after school.

What time do you have to be back? Laughlin says.

No one's keeping tabs on me, if that's what you're worried about.

She runs her slender fingers over his hand on the gearstick and he releases his grip like a moth that's been batted away from a light, returning as soon as it's safe, her hand now under his. Her right hand rests on the steering wheel. She can steer perfectly but stutters through the gears, the car stalling and stopping. She doesn't get angry or annoyed, just bemused that it's so much harder than it looks. Every time her arse slides into his crotch she feels him tighten against her. He's very patient with her. Teacher in him, she supposes.

His hand has been draped, resting on their thighs, and as she starts to get the hang of the low gears, giggling as she feels the rush of actually driving, of making the car move, like magic, she feels his fingers brush and move beneath her skirt. She makes a little gasp as she feels him push her knickers aside and his fingers enter her, his body crushing hers against the steering wheel a little.

Careful, he whispers in her ear. Careful.

He's good at this, she thinks, and she wants to turn and kiss him full on the mouth but she has to concentrate, has to try to drive. She stalls the car, the engine cuts out and they shoot forward, bodies smacking against each other and the car, but she doesn't turn around as he makes her come, quicker than she had thought possible, and she breathes ragged into the steering wheel at the intensity of it.

They stay kissing in the middle of the airfield afterwards. He had come all on his own just at the thought of her, and she doesn't know what to say.

Come back to mine, he says.

I can't, Sam says. What she means is, I can't trust myself around you. She knows she can't. He drops her half a mile from her house and she walks home in the dark.

Naoise, 1994

He woke up Friday afternoon, happened to look out the window and there she was. Her hair tight in a low bun, slim shoulders, demure in her uniform. She looked almost innocent in the colour of the virgin, moving like a gentle tide to and from his door, waiting to come in.

Murph, he called.

Murph came in to his bedroom, hungover, half-cut still. His arm pasty from where the plaster cast had been.

Told you she'd come crawling back.

He waited for the knock. He was cocky as he pulled Murph over to the window.

Ah, she's gone, mate, Murph said and Naoise shoved him out of the way to look. She was headed down the street, stopping at a shiny red VW that had pulled up on the kerb. He knew by the way she opened the car door, the way she tilted her head, the way she fucking got into that car, that it was some other fucker, the prick.

Naoise's weekend ahead soured like milk. Everything cloudy, thick, raw-tasting. He didn't leave his room, barely slept.

Just after four on Monday afternoon, he picked up the phone and dialled the school's number, racing thrill rising as it rang, the familiar click. He could hardly contain himself as he cleared his throat. A pure sharp English accent appeared like a stranger in his mouth. Puritan vowels.

I'm calling about a troubling incident I was privy to.

Quite sensitive, actually . . .

A student, yes . . .

Maybe sixth year.

Yes.
A pause taken up like confession on the line.
She was with a teacher, I think. A male teacher.

Entente Cordiale

Sam/Patsy, 1994

The school hasn't seen Patsy in a few years. He doesn't darken their door. In some ways it made it easier that Patsy never bothered turning up for anything. As Sam's behaviour gave way there was no cosy-toed parent who knew all the teachers by name to keep an eye on her, there was only Patsy, a sure-fire nightmare of a parent who no teacher wanted, needed, or had the skills to talk to. He missed all the good early years and now is being dragged in for the bad stuff at the end. Naturally, Sister PE has taken Patsy on as a personal project. Fix the father and the daughter, ease your entry into heaven, assemble some Jenga-like structure of seemingly good deeds to hide the fact you were a total cunt. Or at least that's how Sam sees it.

Sam chats to Christine while she waits on her da. He is late. His speciality. There is probably some problem with an animal, which would of course take preference over his own flesh and blood. Mr Malone turns up early, barely making eye contact with her as he passes her on his way into the inner sanctum.

Christine?

No.

You don't even know what I'm going to ask you yet!

It's no, whatever it is.

How much shit am I in?

A lot. Christine swivels around in her chair as she finishes the letter she's typing. Then files it.

Is there a file in there about me?

No.

No! Really?

It's in there. Christine tilts her hair-sprayed head towards the office.

Sam blows air, puffing her cheeks out like a toddler.

And it's a big one, Christine finishes.

I'd be *very* disappointed if it wasn't massive.

Well, you'll be happy to know it is.

Sam grins at her. Christine starts another letter, trying to ignore her. Sam hears raised voices and looks over her shoulder through the plexiglass. Sister PE and Mr Malone are both on their feet. When Sam turns back Christine has also been watching, but she immediately drops her head and starts to type.

C'mon, Christine, we're friends, aren't we?

No, we're not.

My da hasn't even turned up.

Sam.

Please. Margaret's only been dead a couple of weeks.

Margaret's not family, Sam.

Technically, she's not, but she's the closest thing I had to a ma and everyone knows that. Do you think Margaret would make a good ghost? Haunting people on my behalf, like?

Look, how many days have you missed this week?

This week … er … I did Tuesday and Thursday.

Last week?

Monday, Wednesday, Friday.

Exactly.

Exactly what?

You've missed a lot of school.

So?

Sam. Honest to God. When are you gonna wise up?

A knock, sharp and thrice, interrupts. Sam quickly sits back in her seat and the door swings open and after a long pause Patsy half appears, suited and booted, like he is on his way to Mass or a funeral.

Has someone died? Sam says.

No, Patsy says, disgusted, leaving a seat between him and his daughter as he sits down. He takes his cap off and places it on the seat between them. Not that she has any plans to move beside him. He runs his rough hand over his scalp, fixing down his unruly hair.

I'm sorry for the delay, Miss Hunter. Trouble with the dog.

Patsy settles his hands on his lap. He can still see dirt in his fingernails; he curls his fingers in, shy. He is raging: one black grubby nail, like a slug on his hand, that fuckin nun will see it, no matter how he hides it. Maybe he should just show her his dirty hand and get the judging over with straight away. She's never done a day's hard work in her life. Labour. She'll never know what any of it means. He hates them. Nuns. Bloody good-for-nothing nuns. Nosy as the day they were born. It was nuns had picked on him as a small boy with big ears. Big ears that would hear things. Big mouth. One of them had locked him in a cupboard once. All day. Left him there and then forgot all about him. His mother, a woman no one crossed, had threatened to break that nun's legs. She'd called her – Sister Candice, that was it – names he would never use. Cursed her to hell.

Christine knocks into the office then. Patsy watches her tell the principal, Sister Eudoria, he is here. Heard the bint's reply: Finally made an appearance? Like father, like daughter.

Christ, Patsy shook off a little shiver that passed across his shoulders. When he'd hung up the phone yesterday he asked her what the hell was going on but she'd slammed the door in his face. He told her he wouldn't put up with that messing, off on out of it. His house. His rules. Now here she is sulking under this microscope of manners, even the fucking pictures on the walls follow him about the room, everything watching, judging, measuring.

Sam watches Sister PE through the glass. Somehow she is always backlit, like a saint. It isn't just a case of good lighting, it is a stubborn element of timing and ambience. Sam wonders how the hell she manages it. PE is a formidable opponent and battle is about to commence. It would help an immense amount if Sam knew what she is fighting. It's clear that she *might* get suspended for mitching and really that's fair enough, but it's Mr Malone's shouting – there is no other word for it – that brings a little tremor to her demeanour. She finds it hard to sit still, gets antsy. Worried. Would he shout over a suspension? He seems *way* too even-keel for that stuff.

Ah, Mr Malin, you're here. Please come in.

Samantha rises with her father.

No, dear, you can stay there. We'll call you in a little bit.

Isn't this a meeting about me?

Sam sees her father shoot her a look that makes her hesitate momentarily, but she forces herself to remain standing. Shouldn't I be involved in any decisions that are going to be made about me?

Sister PE smiles. Sit tight please, Miss Malin. We'll call you in presently.

It isn't a request and Samantha plonks her ass back down on the hard wooden seat. Round one to you, Sister. Round one.

The meeting about her lasts twenty minutes. Sam can see Patsy says little. He stands up once and then sits down almost immediately, like he's errant punctuation. It all seems a bit tense. Christine refuses to answer any more of her questions. She actually puts the answer machine on hold and goes for a sneaky fag out the fire escape that the sixth formers get blamed for smoking on. Everyone, even PE, knows the staff use it, yet she seems happy to blame the students but never does anything about it. One of the blessed little mysteries. Sam guesses that even PE understands the pitfalls of dealing with seven hundred adolescent girls might require some nicotine-induced respite.

Mr Malone finally appears and guides Sam inside. Fuck. He's being super nice. She knows this is going to go badly. Her father won't even look at her, his face set at an angle, his own personal ninety degrees of rage.

So, what's up? Sam asks.

Manners, girl, Patsy barks.

Sister PE raises her hand and he obeys, like a little trophy dog.

Miss Malin ... why do you think we've called you in today?

I haven't done anything wrong, Sam says, and regrets it immediately. I've missed some days. Okay? I can make the work up.

I'm sure you can, Miss Malin, and isn't that just the problem, an incredibly intelligent girl acting so stupidly, damaging her reputation and that of the school's.

I'm not damaging the school's reputation.

There was a phone call. Someone saw you with a man. Older. A teacher, they thought.

Sam sits open-mouthed. She has fucked up Laughlin's entire life. She doesn't know what to say.

We know that's not the case. Mr Malone explained about the incident with your boyfriend at the formal – which I would have appreciated knowing about earlier – but, regardless, you were engaged in activity unbecoming to the school's ethos and values, Miss Malin. Whomever this older man is, you should know it's frowned upon.

That's one way of putting it, Patsy says gruffly.

You are putting yourself at risk, PE says sweetly. We are concerned for your moral welfare.

By snogging someone? Sam says.

Samantha, I swear to God. Patsy is on his feet.

Sister PE remains smiling, calm, hands folded in her lap. Her gaze gently focuses on Patsy's shoulder; he twitches like she touched him and obediently sits down.

Mr Malone inches forward, coughs before he speaks. We're just concerned for you, Sam, especially after the formal. Your boyfriend—

He's not my boyfriend, Sam says.

Yes, but he's considerably older than you, Sam. It's not appropriate, Malone continues.

I don't have a boyfriend, Sam says again.

Be that as it may, we've all discussed it, Sister PE says. At length. Your father and I have decided it's best, given your many and prolonged leaves of absence, that you repeat upper sixth.

What? Sam says.

As I said, there are multiple reasons, Samantha. Multiple concerns, Sister PE says.

Did *you* agree with this? Sam accuses Mr Malone. He tries not to look at Sister PE, rubs his finger along the side of his nose, fixing an unseen itch. What? Are you fucking joking me? Exams are in a few weeks.

Samantha, language! Patsy shouts.

Jesus Christ, Da! She grabs her bag. I'll pass my exams. Sam turns and spits the words at her da. He does not look at her now, keeps his gaze low.

Sam, sit down and listen. Please, Mr Malone says. I'm sure we can work something out.

Why should I? You've already made up your minds about me. I'll leave first. I'll quit and damage your perfect results table and mess it all up. I'll go to the bloody tech.

Miss Malin, sit down, Sister PE says.

You sit down! I'm not *listening* to this crap. I'll pass. This year. Or not at all. I'm eighteen. I'm an adult. You can't make me repeat. Do you hear? I'm not doing it.

Samantha. Patsy speaks slowly. Sit. Down. Now.

No. NO! I'm not fucking up my life so you don't lose face in front of a fucking nun. Sam turns, she's almost crying, opens the door, hard, flings it so that she has to catch it as it swings back to her, closing in on her, like its hinges swing only towards her complete and utter humiliation.

She's just like her mother, hot tempered, Sam hears Patsy say as she thrusts her slight frame against it, creating enough space to make her exit and storm out.

L'Année Dernière

Nuala, 1981

Some days, a lot of days, it's too much. Too much, all their need for me. Overwhelming. Some weeks, most weeks, these two hours are all I have. I stop things here. My little stopgap. I stop nursing PJ, come here with Savoy cabbage leaves tucked in my bra, their curled fingers cupping heavy, aching breasts. I can't manage cold turkey. I can't take the severing completely, the swelling loss, the pain, so I cut down. Do it sensibly. Measure out my love. No more feeding on demand. I train him. Make space for myself. Loosen my body away from his.

I could never sing but somehow Margaret persuaded me to join the choir. Or forces everyone else to let me in. She's their star. All tones, all pitches, every note, low to high. Margaret conquers them all. She's giving me access to a thing that is just for her. They need her and she knows it. It's so unlike her to take advantage but she does. Does it for me.

Singing together with these women becomes a beautiful disconnect. It becomes a sonic first love I'm tumbling in, infatuated by my ability to connect my adolescent offering, which they bend and transform into a regular harmony.

I close the distance between myself and these strangers. I don't believe in God but I like his house. I like the way our voices fill the space, wrap around us. I like watching the coloured light of glass saints spill on our faces. I fall in love with these women, who give me so much, for so little effort on my part. We move our mouths and the words that appear clear my head. I cannot think of my loneliness, my children, my need to touch someone, anyone other than my husband. I cannot think of anything at all, and it is bliss.

I'm going out with the girls from choir, I tell Patsy. He believes me. I don't know why I lie to my husband.

I go to Belfast. I get the bus. Tell Patsy I'll be late. He goes to one of his friends. I don't care what he does. I just need time. I go to the Queen's Film Theatre. It's a Sunday. I buy a ticket for *Last Year At Marienbad*.

Good choice, the clerk says. He has olive irises, the same colour as the hard seats in the cinema, but his soft eyes widen as I make safe small talk.

Have you seen it then?

It's a sixties classic, he says back.

You don't look that old, I say. Laugh. And it is cheap, cheap flirting, but he exchanges it for something better.

Save me a seat, maybe I'll drag my old ass in beside you. His smile is dangerously open.

I blush everywhere, aware of the queue forming behind me, and move away. I'm so grateful for the moment. The acknowledgement. The flimsy interaction. I'm so enamoured with the possible, fantastical. With patterns of behaviour I'd forgotten about. What may be, what will never be, what has been. Between us. When really it's nothing at all. When everything that is happening is happening inside me.

I sit on the hard seat, my ankles draped lazily over the row in front, and watch the unnamed woman on the screen struggle with her fragmented memories of the unnamed man. It is all black and white, precise imagery against the grey area. Did she have an affair? Is she his lover? Or is this their first meeting?

I let out a small gasp when he sits down beside me. My smile is too wide, too happy, too hopeful. Instant like bad coffee.

Tout bon? he whispers in my ear. I realise I have taken a seat at the back, everyone else – not many people, it's an arthouse French film after all, showing on a sunny Sunday – sitting in front of me.

Bien sûr, I whisper back. I can feel it then, that pull, between us, like static. We are not looking at the screen anymore. He moves towards my face, making sure it is okay, slowly, like he's asking me but he doesn't say anything, closes the dark between us, kisses me.

Kissing a stranger in the dark. Absurd. A stranger I met an hour before. A stranger who sought me out. A stranger with his tongue in my mouth. Whom I want more from as each moment passes, pulling our bodies towards collision, a daring impact. He kisses my neck. I wonder can he feel my pulse ascend as he moves his mouth across my skin.

I can hardly wait. I am trying to be patient. I am trying to slow down. Feel everything. Hold myself together but I need things from him. I pull his delicate hands down. He rubs his fingers between my legs. I can feel myself getting wet and I want to reach for him. I hesitate. Like I have forgotten what to do. I want him all over me. We are breathing so loudly I'm afraid someone will turn around. He swells under my hand, I struggle with buttons, fingers tread fabric and find his zip. Then he stops. A sharp intake of breath. His hand falls away, takes mine and I feel the wedding ring, shallow metal under my fingertips. A pause. He is already somewhere else. Looks shaken, pushes his hair off his face and moves away. Creates a divide between us. He looks frightened for himself as he stands up, fixes himself and walks off and doesn't look back. Like he has just done something he never thought he would. He has broken all the rules and I have helped him. I close my eyes and know I am broken. Bereft. Because I didn't want it to stop.

The ticket booth has a closed sign hanging on it when I leave.

I hang around. I shouldn't but I do. I am so desperate. I don't want to go home.

I stop going to choir. I miss a few meetings. Margaret adopts her boys. Ruddy-cheeked twin four-year-olds, who cry at everything, anything, like babies. She asks me to mind them as she tries to keep singing. I do. I want to tell her about the cinema. I want to share it with someone. She asks me advice and I give it to her. The boys come around. She tells me that they were neglected. She can't imagine anyone being bad to a child. Sometimes she sheds quiet tears that no one ever sees. She treats me like I know something. Like I have something special to give her. She looks at me and I know I can't share anything that might change how she sees me. I need her to think I'm *that* version of me. It's so precious.

I go into stasis.

I order in expensive fat green olives and suck the salty flesh from their pits. I make the jar last as long as I can. I eat them at night, alone in the dark. I wish myself away and I didn't even know his name.

So I wait.

The next time he has a name.

Bilateral Agreement

Sam, 1994

What the fuck did you say to my teacher? Sam bursts into the living room behind a sheepish Chiz. Becca follows. Naoise is lying, feet propped up on a cushion, white sport socks on, his ankles crossed. He closes his eyes and finishes his smoke.

Chiz slinks past the girls. He goes to apologise but Naoise waves him away, so he perches at the end of the battered leather sofa. Murph smiles at Becca. Becca ignores him. Naoise blows smoke circles in the air. He taught Sam how to do that. A cheap party trick.

Well?

Well, what? I was high. I don't know what the fuck I was saying. Come and say hello properly.

He turns and lies on his belly. Smile brewing on his lips. Broke up with Lena.

Lucky her.

For you. I. Broke. Up. With. Elena. For. You. Naoise props himself up on his elbows. That's what you wanted, isn't it? Stop all this fucking about and c'mere.

No. You reported me?

Shit, they took it seriously? Naoise laughs.

It's not funny. You know how much shit I'm in. Why did you say that about me?

It's funny. Winding you up.

It's not funny. They can't prove anything about the teacher but when they add up days off school and my much older 'boyfriend', it equals making me have to repeat a year.

Who's this boyfriend? Anyone I know? Naoise smiles to himself. Drive a red car?

What's so bad about repeating the year? Murph asks innocently.

Sam rolls her eyes at him.

They were *really* pissed off. Like, they would have called my ma in, if she wasn't, like, dead.

You look just like her, you know that? Chiz says.

Sorry, what?

You're the spit of her, Chiz says. Isn't she, Naoise?

Sorry, did you know her? Sam asks Naoise, but before he can respond Chiz answers.

I didn't *actually* know her. I remember her face from the paper, though. Everybody knew her to see.

What do you *mean* everybody knew her? I didn't fucking know her. She left when I was five. I don't know a thing about her.

Naoise sighs, stares at Chiz.

You used to deliver papers up to the house back then, didn't you? Chiz says, stirring, and Naoise shoots him a look, makes his lips thin like a muzzled dog, a little show of teeth, distorts his pretty face to shut Chiz up.

Right, everybody out, except you, Naoise says, looking squarely at Sam. He gets to his feet, bouncing like a kid on a trampoline, high from too much sugar, the crash waiting just around the corner.

Sam shrugs her shoulders, hardens her jaw a little against his orders.

I'm staying too, says Becca.

No, you're not. Naoise is directing them all out the door, his hands on Becca's shoulders, turning her around and pushing her out after the others.

Out. Go to the pub. He shoves twenty quid into Becca's hand. Don't spend it all at once. Just make sure you put a pint on for me.

You sure? Becca says softly to Sam.

Yeah, it's fine. I'll just ... I'll be fine.

Naoise paces around the room as the others shuffle out, then closes the door behind them. Leans against it, listening to them leave the apartment. Murph grunting down the stairs. The heavy door slam.

So what are we going to do, you and I? Naoise says. His body is still, serene, but his words start moving towards her, impatient, casting out to catch her. Can't we sort this out? I was just having a bit of fun. I swear. Those nuns are mental.

You're not my boyfriend, Sam says, moving away from him. So, you knew my mum?

Naoise leans back into the door, his palms pressing against the wood, fingers splayed out like supports, scaffolding himself in place, safe from her question. It unbalances him.

Not really. She was popular, though. Like you.

I'm not popular.

Sam once thought this skanky flat was the coolest place in the world. It's funny now to see it anew, almost for the first time: the shabby threadbare carpets and worn furniture. Walls that haven't been cleaned or painted in years. Circular teacup stains in overlapping crescents covering the coffee table, its edges chipped away, looking like someone has nibbled on it like a chocolate digestive biscuit. The debris of a joint in an overstuffed nicotine-stained ashtray. The clashing flowery curtains discoloured by sunlight. It is a kip. She sits on the sofa. He joins her. They listen to each other's breathing. Waiting for something to happen.

She kisses him full on the mouth then, savouring it, sickening herself, reminding herself that this is the last time she will ever kiss him, the last time she will ever be in this place. She feels him get hard, relax into her and, as soon as he does, she tenderly breaks free, another brush against their velvet softness. She pulls back. Smiles.

She is letting him go, he's already in her past. He moves to pull her closer but she says, We're done.

Naoise laughs. Jesus, Sam. What do you want me to do? Did I really get you into that much trouble at school? Is it my fault that religion teacher totally has the hots for you? He's jealous.

Grow up. Sam pushes him away.

He mock-falls off the sofa. Okay. Okay. Alright. His hands shoot up, peace-loving. He lies down on the floor in front of her, prostrate at her feet, mock-begging. Sam, Sam, Sam, he says, over and over again, kissing her bare legs from the ankle up, taking his time, apologising slowly past her knees, tiny tiny kisses that disarm her. It was just a little joke that got out of hand, he says.

His kisses and words meld together, dismantling her conviction, kiss by kiss, as he runs his fingers along the edge of her thighs, kisses so soft and subtle it is like she can't be sure that he is kissing her at all, and she feels herself come undone and she has to jerk herself back from the reverie, from the desire for him.

Stop.

She pushes her skirt smooth and straight across her knees, slams them together. He lays his head on her lap, gazes up at her. She can't resist the urge to touch his hair, finger the delicate curls. He is so much older than her, he is so good at this, because he's had so much practice. So many bodies, so many times he's said these words. Made these promises. Broken these promises. He closes his eyes. She knows he thinks this has worked. He's waiting for her to kiss him. She leans down towards him; she wants to kiss him, to taste him again, despite everything, one more time, but as she leans in she sees the trace, the slight upturned corner of his mouth, betraying him, thinking he has won, and she retracts, recoils, gets up roughly, shoving him off her lap.

Sam moves through the flat, picking things up, putting things down, giving herself time. Naoise props himself up on the sofa. Lights another cigarette, watches her. She had planned to give him a little speech, had practised over and over again what she was going to say. Me and you, it's never going to happen. I am fucked up, but *you*, you are completely fucked up. I thought I was just like you. I thought we were the same, but we're not. You're stuck. Stuck here. In her imagination she has played this scene out again and again. In her little production Naoise catches her wrists – Sam can feel the marks already, the way he grabs at her. Naoise would shake his head and laugh at her performance. This little bit of theatre. Goodbye, Sam was supposed to say. Good riddance.

But that's not how it plays out.

217

Was she really beautiful, my mother? Sam asks, catching her own reflection in the out-of-place, oversized faux gilt mirror set above the mantelpiece. The glass has mottled specks, bubbles of copper coming through to the surface, distorting her face.

She was, Naoise says quickly. Not as beautiful as you, though.

Did you all fancy her?

Huh, not really.

What was she like? Really? Do you remember?

He hesitates. Shifts his body around. He seems to tense up, his loose limbs straining against the effect her question is having on him. She doesn't ever think she's seen him feel this uneasy. It's disconcerting for her as she watches him pull images from his memory, tries to see from his face if what he's saying is true.

She seemed nice. Smart.

Nice. Smart?

Yeah, like you. Too smart for her own good, maybe.

Thought you never talked to her? Sam watches him in the mirror; he looks distorted too now, dirty, ragged.

I used to chat to her when I dropped the papers up sometimes. He pulls hard on his smoke, exhales. She was lonely, I think. Bored, maybe. Lots of people talked to me on the round. You know how it is.

Sam can see this line of questioning is making him uncomfortable. She turns and faces him. So you must have met me when I was a kid. Sick, isn't it?

He stubs out his cigarette with one hand, pushes his hair back from his face with the other. Gets up. Goes to her. Sam. Look. About the formal. He coughs, clears his throat. We both went too far.

Oh, fuck this. She moves to leave but he makes himself big, filling the space.

Okay. I went too far, but you bit me.

You deserved it.

Fair. I was bang out of order. Off my head, but one minute you're all over me and the next … your man tried to get me arrested, you

218

know that? He is standing right in front of her now. Her arms clamp across her chest, a criss-cross of limbs marking her heart. Fine. I was jealous. Okay? He deftly moves his fingertips along the outline of her shoulders, arms. He is not touching her yet, he just wants to, and she can feel the pull. The thought of you being with someone else, anyone else. Everyone looking at you. That teacher. Made me a little crazy.

Mr Malone? Christ, what do you take me for? You were with Lena. You're *sleeping* with Lena. She's *your* girlfriend and you … like, what the fuck was that?

Sam. I broke up with Elena. I told you. He reaches out to touch her arm. I can't stop thinking about you.

She feels her conviction wobble.

I'm seeing someone. She waits, knows this is dangerous.

I don't care. It doesn't matter. He puts her hand on his chest. His heart is pumping so fast. She's never seen this side of him, his whole body pleading with her, begging. She seems to crumple under the force of his want and finds herself folded into him, his arms origami-tight around her tiny frame. She lets him kiss her.

She keeps thinking, One last kiss and then I'll go. But something is coming away inside her, separating her conviction out like loose, unwanted change. He whispers, I'll never leave you again, and something breaks in her in an instant, and she kisses him back. Surrenders to this feeling for him. All her focus on his mouth, his lips, her body going there before her mind can agree.

The buzzer throbs and throbs, rings in her ears like a wake-up call and she tells him she has to go but doesn't move. She listens as he lets Becca in. Becca, all accusations and concern. She doesn't come up the stairs. She hears him calm, ask does Becca want tea, tells her that Sam will be down in a minute.

I'm going back to the pub, Becca shouts up to Sam. Going home after one more drink, Sam. See you in school tomorrow.

Sam can hear the condemnation in Becca's tone.

I'll be there in a sec, she shouts back, but hears the door already slamming shut. She hears Naoise piss, bare feet pad into the kitchen, fill the kettle. She realises that everyone must hear her moaning in that tiny space. She is starting to sober up from all the need for him, feeling stupid at her lack of self-control.

She quietly leaves without letting him know, opens the door onto the street, into the relief of fresh air replacing the stale smell that inhabits the flat. She inhales and exhales deeply. This is not what she had planned. She doesn't trust herself or whatever this new feeling is. They are not back together in her mind but they are not apart. She doesn't understand what has just happened. Who was at fault? Was she to blame? Her lack of willpower. No wonder she is a terrible Catholic.

Chiz and Murphy are sitting at the bar nursing pints. Only them and an oul fella huddled in the corner. It's getting close to six. Chiz raises his eyebrow at her entry. He is such a pain in her arse.

Where's Becca? she says.

Ladies, says Murph.

Lovers' tiff, again? Chiz chuckles to himself.

It's over.

Yeah, right. They all say that. Tell him where to stick it, then beg him to take them back. Christ, girl, what makes you think you're so special?

Fuck up, Chiz.

You can get the ride off me if you'd like. Chiz gulps his pint, sniggering into it.

I'm not that desperate.

Don't be a dick, Chiz, Becca says, as she arrives back from the toilet.

Can we go? Sam says.

Can I finish this?

Nope.

Okay, then. You wanna tell me what happened?

The girls start to talk like no one can hear them.

I'll tell you later. Let's go. She picks up Becca's bag.

Okayyy. Are you okay?

Ecstatic, Sam replies, deadpan. Can we just go?

Sure.

Bye, Murph, the girls chorus as they leave the bar.

Chiz moans, What about me?

They raise their hands in one-finger salutes.

Oh, fuck you too, very much. Another slug of his pint. Bitches. Blue-blooded stupid wee virgin cunts.

The doors smack up against each other as the girls exit. It's just past six and Becca decides to treat Sam to super chips, so they hop on a bus to Newcastle.

Sam tries to compress what happened but it still seems like she is talking for ages. The whole story. Sam's version of it. Only a few clipped sentences in and she finds herself saying it aloud for the first time: I think he knew my mum more than he's letting on.

What do you mean, knew her? Like how? Becca says.

I don't know. Just ... something ... in his voice ... the way he talked about her. I don't know. It's nothing, probably.

Becca is speechless for a moment.

Becca, I know, it's hard to get your head around.

Try impossible. He prank-called the school and told them you were shagging a teacher. Have I got that right? Sam? Come on. Seriously.

He didn't mean to get me into so much trouble ... it was just a joke. And Chiz was just fucking about, Chiz didn't even know my mum. He's just repeating rumours. Naoise said it's—

Naoise said? Oh, so we're trusting him again. That was quick.

He thought I was with Malone. As if.

Eeeew. Hold on.

Obviously not. Come off it, I'm not that bad.

You were supposed to be having a go at Naoise for nearly getting you suspended and instead you snog the face off him. Fucking hell, Sam.

Sam doesn't meet Becca's gaze.

It's not what you think, Becca.

Fuck sakes. You are a first-class idiot, Becca says, exasperated. I just want to say that I think this is a bad idea. Okay. So when it all goes tits-up I don't have to pretend like I didn't warn you. Agreed?

Sam doesn't respond.

Okay. I'm going to help you right now. He is going to hurt you. Again. Worse this time. You know that, right?

Becca is very serious now. Sam knows she is warning her.

You made me promise to stop you from going back with him. You made me swear, Becca says. At least wait till after exams. Can you at least do that?

I know, Bec. I *know*. I'm sorry. I can't help it. I lo—

Don't fucking say that. Do. Not. Say. That. To. Me. I thought I *loved* Gavin and look where that got me. Years on the pill and more spots than the chicken pox. None of them are worth it.

Why did you take him to the formal, then?

There was no way I was going with some randomer. Gav couldn't say no. He thought I was a sure thing too, cheeky git.

Becca smiles to herself and suddenly Sam sees something about her friend she's missed. Oh my god, I know that look. Who'd you get off with?

Becca draws an imaginary zipper across her lips.

Ah, c'mon on, tell me? I know who it is anyway.

Yeah, right. Early days. We'll see how it goes. She pauses. Don't sleep with Naoise, Becca says, suddenly serious. I mean it, Sam. Gav was a dick but Naoise's, like, another level.

Would you like to check my hymen's still intact, mother superior? Becca. Gimme some credit.

Fuck off, you know I don't mean it like that. Shag all round you, for all I care. It's just … he … I don't want you to get hurt.

Sam sighs. Becca joins her. Sam pulls her hair around her face, like she always does when she is hiding from something.

I know, Sam says, I know that.

Exams first. Becca repeats. Exams. Promise.

Promise. Malone says I have to apologise to PE. I'm gonna have to, aren't I?

Do you really want to spend another year in this dump?

No . . . Will you write my apology?

I'm not a miracle worker. Naoise or the Nun. Pick one.

You sound like my ma.

Sam.

Okay. No more Naoise, Sam says, and realises in that moment she might actually mean it.

Carrot and Stick

Sam throws up a little in her mouth when PE insists she has to read her written apology aloud, in front of her, Malone, her da and even Christine. Luckily her father does not turn up. Make it meaningful, Malone mouths, so Sam milks it like it's her Oscar turn for the Academy but she's also sincere, is desperate to sit the exams. There's no need to fake that. The sad truth is she would say anything they want to hear and PE knows it.

The sanguine sister enjoys pressing Sam's buttons in the days that follow, mandatory check-in's each morning, monitoring her uniform, scraping a finger against her skin for make-up, making unannounced visits to her classes. Sam has been on her best behaviour since the agreement that if she misses a day she will defer exams and stay back a year. PE tells her to lower her expectations. So she does. She is very good, very careful, very polite for the next two weeks. Takes nothing for granted. In school she is the model student. Outside she still stays the night in Belfast. Tells Patsy she is going to study at Becca's.

Laughlin is a safety valve, a catch-and-release mechanism that prevents her making a fool of herself. Keeps her away from Naoise. His flatmates don't even raise an eyebrow anymore when she arrives in her uniform. They lie on his bed and she recites things off. Facts, figures, passages of text. He will only give in after she's learnt something. Best carrot and stick ever. He cooks sometimes. They both know what this is. That's okay. They might meet again, years from now. Or never. That's okay too.

Laughlin helps drown out all the noise. Chatter. Naoise is always there, in the background of her mind. Remains a deep thrum that she carries around with her.

She can't focus on anything when the want starts. Can't study. She's trying to figure out what she's done wrong. Analyse the problem. There's no one she can confide in. She lies to Becca. To herself. Lies to him. Margaret's dead so it's not like Sam can tell her. Not that she could have told her. She wants to tell someone. About this need.

Becca's words echo in her head.

Exams. Promise.

So she distracts herself from the noise. She focuses, despite, because, to show herself she can. Takes extra classes. Help where it's offered. Mr Malone at school. Laughlin in private. Of course, her English teacher, Miss Denvir, does not comply. She is on her own with that one. It surprises her that she's not the only one who needs support. Faces that she does not expect to see arrive into the study hall. Giant Michelle for one. Giant Michelle, who threatens them all casually, when Malone leaves the room, with an I'm-not-fucking-stupid stare. Don't-fuckin-say-nothing face. No one does. They all just agree to feel silently stupid together.

Patience. Will I Pay For Who I've Done?

Naoise, 1994

Naoise waited for Sam. Every single day. The idea of getting Sam back on side was the best part of his day. The tiny bit he looked forward to. The first time, in fact the only time he saw her in those weeks, she ignored him, jumped straight on the bus to Belfast before he could catch her. He banged the doors but the driver wouldn't stop and she had turned her face from the glass. He wanted to follow her but he wasn't sure where she'd went, so he left it. Let her cool off for a while, Murph said. Leave her alone was what he meant, had actually told him as much. Murph had warned him off. Fucking Murph.

Then exams started and everyone disappeared. Study. Maybe he'd gone too far, maybe, but he couldn't tell because Sam didn't arrive on the after-school bus with the other girls.

Sam staying behind again, is she?

Why do you care anyway? Becca said. You're part of the reason she's so fucked up. Just leave her alone, will you.

How's she getting home?

Bus, Becca said.

She's never on the late bus.

Stalker.

I'm just concerned about her, Naoise said.

Yeah, right, Becca said.

I care about her.

My hole, Becca said.

That's way harsh, Becca. Way harsh. I'm worried about her, you know that?

Does Lena know that?

We're just mates.

Yeah, right, Becca said again. You shouldn't even be asking about her.

Free country. An' look, I know things ended badly. He holds his hands up. But I thought we sorted everything out.

You think? What does Lena think of that?

What? I told you—

Don't be a dick.

Becca had ranted and raved and he'd let her. He'd said a few well-placed things about missing Sam, that he couldn't stop thinking about her. Made a show of remorse. Every. Single. Day.

You see her today? he'd ask.

Obviously, Becca would snap back. I know what you're doing. I'm not a child.

It's just, with Margaret gone … must be hard for her, you know.

They'd smoke and then Lena might arrive and he'd slope off. He still had sex with Lena all the time. Like every other girl he knew she wanted to give this a name. A title. Like he was a fucking book. But he was just on loan to her.

Naoise knew Becca well enough to know she wouldn't tell Lena what he'd said, just filter back the information Sam needed to know. Teenage girls and their bessie mates. He waited. Another week went by. More drip-feeding of his longing. Becca started to soften, tell him things back. How broken-hearted Sam had been.

He orchestrated a very public fight with Lena. Everyone saw. Everyone talked.

Yet, still no sign.

So he waited.

The afternoon her exams ended he watched from a distance as Sam and her mates arrived off the bus from Newcastle, the girls elated as they lit up cigarettes, then plastered each other with flour and eggs in the bus station; some got off with a light dusting, others drenched, their uniforms ruined forever, discarded blazers left to bake in the sun, fetid with the smell of dried egg. Later he sat above The Grove, listening to gangs of them giggle hysterically as they lay in the grass and drank cider under the huge leafy trees that had stood there for hundreds of years, snogging their boyfriends and ignoring the tuts of passersby. A rite of passage. They weren't in school anymore. They were free and they wanted everyone to know it.

As he watched Chiz and Murph amble over to the girls, he considered joining them.

But he had waited this long.

He could hold on.

He jumped from the high wall and made his way past the museum and the old county gaol. The tall grey buildings still held the majesty of long ago in this part of the town. He finished off his afternoon nursing a pint in Denver's. He knew that in the evening the now ex-schoolgirls would arrive in, dolled up, still giddy, with all their possible futures ahead of them. He didn't stick around to see if she was with them. She would be. She might even expect to see him there. He trusted in his absence. Let the nothingness of this place do the work.

Answer All Questions in This Section

Sam, 1994

The exams are a blur.

Cramming.

Cheap caffeine tablets.

Desperation against the smug faces of those who studied, those who pretended but still studied, and the ones, like Sam, who are winging it.

In some ways she doesn't want them to end. There's a rhythm to her days, all lined up with desks and shuffling papers and quiet concentration. Ticking clocks and the heels of the examiners buffing the hall floor with their boredom. There's a weird comfort to the intense regime. Even Patsy cuts her slack. Leaves off. It gives her time and distance and space.

She hopes her and Laughlin might actually date in the summer but he's going travelling because apparently that's what teachers do with all that time off. He only tells her after exams have finished. Thailand, Cambodia, Laos. Places so far away as not to be real. Laughlin is gone as soon as school ends and she is unmoored again.

And Naoise is waiting.

Post-exam High

Naoise, 1994

He knew she'd be surprised when she answered the door of the farmhouse that evening and found him standing there. But so was he, his heart stammering in his chest as he rapped the door.

He half expected Nuala to answer.

Hi, she said.

Hi, he said. If the mountain won't come to Mohammed and all that.

What? she said.

Nothing. I wanted to get my bike, he said.

Oh, shit, yeah. It's in the shed. Hold on, I'll just be a minute.

She left Naoise standing, peering in the door. He shivered with recognition at the unchanged hall: same sideboard, same bowl for keys, just Nuala's familiar boots missing, her slouchy yellow cardigan, which she'd made herself, knitted naked in bed with him once.

Naoise longed to go inside, just for a moment, to feel the solidity of the place, run his hands along the lime-covered walls, feel the wear and tear of the years, the abrasion of now and then, but Sam came clattering back along the hall, breaking up his remembering. She had an oversize Aran cardigan on, dotted with wooden peg buttons, like a little kid might wear, bare lean legs, her feet inside Dunlop men's wellingtons, their insides turned out aways, like a half-peeled under-ripe banana. They would have looked ridiculous on anyone else but Sam, or her mother.

He hardly ever let himself use that word. Mother. Nuala. It was always Nuala. She was no one's mother to him.

Naoise tipped back and forth on his heels as he waited for Sam to pull the door behind her and step outside. Without even meaning to, he set off apace in the direction of the shed. He had to stop himself. Slow down. The smell of the place was heady, intoxicating after the rain. Honeysuckle in bloom everywhere, the sweet golden scent dragging him backwards into the past. His memories and her presence melded together. He had thought it would be simple coming back here, back to her, but his head ached.

How's Lena? Sam said.

Sam, he said, there is no Lena. I just wanna get my bike. How'd your exams go?

He offered her a cigarette. She declined. He went to light up but she batted the fag away from his mouth. You can't smoke up here. My da'll go mad.

Where is he?

Out. Helping bring in … something. Hay. I think. I don't actually care.

He shrugged, put it back in his pack and into his pocket. It'll keep, he said. How'd exams go? Really?

Don't know. Guess I'll find out in August. At least I had nothing to distract me. Where do you think you're going? Sam said. She'd stopped dead.

Naoise had been walking in the direction of the side entrance to the shed, the one he was familiar with. He swivelled around to face her, smiled. He could feel himself sweating. He wiped the sheen from his forehead, the rush of pungent memories pulsing out of his skin like odour.

We haven't used that entrance in years. It's been boarded up. How'd you even know you could get in there? Sam said.

Just looks like you could … farms all look the same to me, Naoise said, the toe of his boot worrying a stone out of the ground, back-tracking as she observed him. He felt her studying him, trying to uncover some secret about him, something she'd missed before. Her gaze was unrelenting.

Didn't know you spent that much time on farms? Sam said, puzzled. Getting your hands dirty isn't really your thing.

231

You don't know me that well, he said, flashing his smile.

No. I don't, Sam said. Bike's in here. She opened the shed door, slid it back on its rail.

You must have come up here a lot, back then? she said.

Yeah, I split the deliveries with Joe, Naoise said quickly.

Joe Walsh. You're the same age as him? Sam looked appalled.

He looks like shit, doesn't he? Naoise said. He was grateful she laughed, took the opportunity to duck past her.

She stood in the doorway, watching as he walked into the shed, breathed it in. He could feel her observing his movements and then turn away. His eyes adjusted to the half-light. It wasn't the same: the machinery that had hung in the eaves was gone, the smell of hay and oil replaced by must and dusty forgetting. He could tell the space wasn't used as much anymore. It reeked of being closed up, shut off. Things had changed.

He shook off the feeling that he was in a memory and grabbed his bike. Pulled it outside. The wind had picked up and Sam's cardigan was blowing open, back and forth, her body bending in and out with the breeze, like she was a washing line. He tugged her cardi down from her shoulders, playful, and let the bike bang on the ground. The wind whipped her hair across his face as he pulled her towards him.

Stop it, she said. What's got into you?

Nothing, he said, letting go of her. I might cycle down to the beach. Come with me?

I've got a puncture.

I can put you on the bar, you weigh nothing. He tapped on the metal as he picked the bike up.

She hesitated. It was almost nine.

I've got work in the morning. In the home.

I've got some really really good grass. Post-exam treat?

I can't miss it. Money for college, sorry.

No hangover with this stuff, but I'm easy, whatever.

She twisted her hair, and he knew it meant she was considering.

Okay, but only if I get to cycle, you sit on the bar.

Do you know how painful that is, for a man?

You'll survive. She laughed and took the handlebars from his grasp, swung her leg over. Even though she barely balanced on the ground, the tips of her wellies moving from side to side as she tried to maintain her position, he could see she was determined to carry him. Once he was on, she jumped back onto the seat, her arms barely managing to circle his body. They flew down the lane, dust scattering behind the bike. Naoise was yelping as she steered over every bump in the road. The sound of her laughing at his play-acting filled his head as she skidded the bike sharply into the corner and rode quickly onto the road towards the beach.

He had a Polaroid camera with him, told her he was trying to get his act together, apply for art college. Get off the dole.

The camera is an extension of me, he said, laughing. I can capture the real you.

Oh, piss off, Sam said, as she took it off him.

You make me want to be respectable again, he told her.

I doubt you've ever been that. She laughed as she snapped the mountains meeting the shore.

He'd wrestled the camera back from her and taken pictures until the film was used up: in the magic hour between day and night, he had held the blocky camera high up above them, strong hands stretching past the horizon towards the sky, and taken shot after shot, trying to get her to smile. He gave her the last picture.

Tyrella

Sam, 1994

He insists on cycling her home that night. Eventually she hops off and he wheels the bike alongside her as they talk. She has agreed to watch the big match with him, as friends. Ireland v Italy in the World Cup. Everyone would be watching it somewhere. Better in the pub than at home with her da. It's no big deal, she tells herself while he hugs her for too long before he disappears into the dark, whistling 'Goodnight, Sweetheart' as he cycles off.

Sam stands in the cold listening until the sound of him fades and the orchestra of night takes over, a chorus of creatures waking up the sky, navy blue and starless above her. Every call seems to be pitching for rain as clouds appear like billowing sheet music above the farm buildings. Eventually it begins to pelt down and she finds a use for the wellies she's worn all evening. As she runs across the yard, the photo falls from her pocket, the flicker of losing something so flimsy that she almost doesn't stop, but then she swivels to the ground, not knowing where it has landed, her hands searching in shadows for an instant memory. Her fingertips pick at the white edges, muddy water dripping from it.

She lays it on the kitchen table, sees his smile, arms around her, up to the camera. She tries to clean the image, wipes it with more water. Her face in the photo is receding below his as she tries to clean the dirt away, her features becoming a faded blur, eventually invisible, his smile taut and huge above a blank space, his arms encircling nothing.

They Think It's All Over, It Is Now

Patsy, 1994

PJ ran in and got Patsy out of bed. They stood there dumb. On the streets of the town a while earlier, lads had come roaring out of the pubs, football crazy. Now cars blocked the road outside – Catholic cars. To make sure they couldn't strike here. It was only a few miles away. That pub. So close to home. It could have been. It doesn't bear thinking about, Patsy said out loud, to no one at all. A mixed pub. But so was the other, up in Greysteele. So was the other. Men with guns shot up the bar. People just having a pint and watching the match. Innocent people. Catholic people. Protestant people. People.

There was blind panic in the town when Patsy arrived. Couldn't find her. Couldn't find her at all. Wouldn't let him in the pub. Hammering the door. A crowd, but the doors would be shut till it was safe. That appeared to be the plan. He had left PJ at home with a loaded shotgun. He'd kept it ever since the incident on the farm. For shooting rabbits. But everyone round here had a gun, all with the same excuse for having it. Rabbit numbers never dropped. He was taking no chances.

Joe spoke through the locked door. Calm down, Patsy. There's more than you looking out for their weans. Go home. The fella she's with al' bring her back.

What fella?

There was too long a pause before Joe finally said, Naoise Devlin.

Ah, give over, Joe, Patsy said. Naoise fucking Devlin. She's more sense than that.

Look it, Patsy, you don't know who's on the roads. Go home, I'll drop her back, Joe said again.

Naoise Devlin. Are you sure, Joe? Patsy said. He saw the old nun's face, her know-it-all grin. He'd defended his girl. Stuck up for her.

Ah, look it, Patsy, maybe I'm wrong about it, Joe said. Patsy could tell he was delaying him.

I'll hold you to that, Joe, Patsy said.

It'll be late but I'll make sure she gets home safe, Patsy, Joe said, after a pause.

Right so, Patsy said, and he moved from the door.

Now would have been a good time to have a cigarette if he'd smoked. They were dirty things. Cancer sticks. Naoise *fucking* Devlin of all people. The type of fella who was always around when bad things happened. The girl had not an ounce of sense. And a liar to boot.

On the way home he doubled back around the town and drove past the pub his daughter was in. Police had gathered outside. Not many. Most had been sent over to Loughinisland. There should have been antics on the streets, drunk lads singing 'Olé Olé Olé'. There should have been celebrations. For a beautiful game. Instead it was shocked people sobering up, talking in quiet hushed groups. Patsy saw Margaret's two boys, splutoored. He slowed the car down.

Boys, he called out. Jump in and I'll drop you on the way.

The younger one, as Patsy thought of him – a full two minutes younger than his twin brother, he constantly boasted – full of drink, bellowed, Ah, Patsy, you legend, as he opened the door.

Both in, Patsy sped through the streets of the town. He listened to them talk.

Peace talks, what fuckin peace, they said to each other in the back of his car. I'll agree to murder any fucking one of them.

Scum.

Cunts.

Two boyos, still drunk, blathering bravado.

They haven't a fucking clue, Patsy thought, but said nothing. Let them get it out of their system.

Just loud-mouthed children.

This place makes children of us all.

Patsy waited up for her. It was late when she got in. Drunk. The face on her when she saw him sitting there at the table.

They barred the doors, she said. We all had another drink. Becca's dad drove us home.

He ignored the lie. This once. Just this once, he let it go. She'd been out most of the night. He could see she was in no fit state to have that conversation. It would have to wait. She didn't move to sit down, just peered in at his cup and decided to make tea.

The early news came on the radio, in-depth reporting.

Loughinisland. The Heights Bar. Massacre. UVF kill six Catholics in a gun attack, wound five others, one seriously. The men were watching the Republic of Ireland playing Italy in the World Cup in the USA at the time of the shooting. Reports from the scene. Commentators. Rushed heated panicked words and then silence.

She finally sat down.

Some people cried, she said. Some people punched the wall. Mostly it was quiet.

Father's Day

Sam, 1994

It has never been a good day. Father's Day. There were socks. Maybe a cap. A rotten overpriced dinner in a local hotel. Last year PJ had ordered egg harlequin and spent the rest of the night throwing up at home. Good money down the drain, Patsy always said. Father's Day became just another day, mirroring Mother's Day with its badness. They ignored it as much as possible every year. This year they cannot. When Patsy gets back from Mass Sam has cooked breakfast: veda bread, eggs sunny-side-up, and thick bacon. There is a card and a hastily wrapped book. The world has made her feel guilty when she is busy trying not to feel anything at all. There is no ignoring fathers today. Not with those fathers waiting to be put in the ground. Not with the images of blood-soaked benches and bullet casings spilt like birdseed across the carpet tiles of that lonely little pub.

That scene replays again and again, remnants of life turning into death, so everyone can watch it blur into another tragic Troubles television report. All the bulletins are full of it, each news reporter's accent heavy with intonation that it is not Father's Day for these men, for their families, forever. Will never be Father's Day again.

This atrocity will become a memory you hold in your body. Returning each year like an unexpected blow to the head. A thing you feel even if you don't understand and then all the after-effects will roll around to surprise you all over again, those bug-eyed reflections, the off-white coloured porch, policemen in rifle green uniforms, the tape instructing you not to cross police lines, white and blue, and not that it matters because you'd gone to a place that you can't come back from. Changed. Changed and that is it.

Screaming angry women, collapsed in on their own heartbreak, a minister, a priest, sad politicians stumbling over their words, all conveying an infinite sadness that will never really close.

That should have repaired things between Sam and Patsy. That shock. The shake of that echoing around the community. It only let cracks between them split further apart, the turning away from each other shattering them both. There is nothing left to repair. Nothing to fix up. They had lost each other years ago.

Her da sits holding her hand afterwards and she wants to sit, to stay, to stop the distance growing, but she does not know how to accept this, this opening, his paternity, and so she slips loose of his grip. Breaks his heart to save hers, moves away just when he needs her to love him the most, repays him with the nothingness he has given her, takes all the barren years and deposits it with him, that dissident despair. An unwanted gift.

Joe told me, Patsy says, after she stands up. Who you were with.

She pauses at the door but doesn't look back.

Patsy Tries So Desperately

Sam, 1994

In the days after Loughinisland, Sam sees something shift in Patsy. Something serious settles on his chest and there are no words at first and then the anger comes in waves. She waits for him to ask about Naoise again, but he's distracted, adrift.

They have found no one for it. Six Catholic men dead. A red car abandoned in a lonely field is all they have. Murderers, Patsy says. Living here.

They show the victims on the telly. The youngest thirty-four, the oldest eighty-seven. Murdered by the UVF. She sees the face of a man she looks after in the nursing home flash up, but it is not him, how could it be? She realises then it is his brother, his brother, who jokes and gives her a quarter bag of sweets every now and again. Drops them at the nurses' station and says help yourselves. She thinks of his brother and what she will say to him. How they will explain. How they will have to explain every day that his brother is dead because he cannot remember.

Like so many other Northerners he will be given a made-up version of the truth but not the actual truth, just a diversion from it, a cul-de-sac of swirling answers that never really let anyone get anywhere. Stuck in a hellish circle of deceit, all for their own good. Decided truths doled out by those in charge. The British Government. The RUC. The Army. The Provos. The Red Hands of Ulster. Lies. Lies. Lies. Only their official version of the truth exists, simple straightforward answers unpalatable.

They would have made an announcement at Mass. It's a small place. They know. The words are hard to get out because no matter what anyone says it won't change anything. The boys' school is worse; her brother's friend's grandfather. The grieving families ask for no reprisals but they also ask for information. Someone must know something. Traversing those dark knotted lanes needed local knowledge. Someone knows more than they are letting on. Someone is always someone's family, they are never just a nobody. There are no strangers here. Everything and everyone is connected.

She knows this place is rotten, rotten to its core. No matter how hard they try they'll never be good enough, never ever get over this place, no matter how much they want it, no matter how much they need it, no matter a thing about that, and she knows she's going to leave, has to leave, and knows she's never coming back.

The weekend after, Naoise is waiting for her when she finishes her shift at the nursing home. She protests, tells him she doesn't need a chaperon but there's a sourness in the air these days, everyone can taste it. Everyone is on guard a little bit more than usual, double-checking doors, looking under their cars more often for devices. Extra security measures. Worried there will be more attacks. Suspicions linger like a bad taste. Pubs let patrons in then lock the doors till closing time. Till the police arrive to escort everyone out safely. Some fucking use the cops are, Naoise says, and Sam agrees but says little, is secretly glad that he is there, every night, even though she teases him – Don't you have anything else better to do? You afraid of my da? – when he leaves her off at the bottom of the lane.

It didn't seem possible to her that she had missed him at all. Maybe she hadn't let herself miss him. Maybe she had been holding him at arm's length for so long, she had forgotten how quickly things can catch together again, how the space around someone can reel you in; and you forget yourself when you should be on guard, bend those rules just for a moment and then there are no rules anymore.

Malocclusions After Massacres

Sam, 1994

She puts the damaged photo of them at the beach, which is really just a photo of him – she is just a smudged and watermarked blur beside him – in a box with pictures of her mother. She resolves not to encourage him. Insists to herself every walk home is a once-off. Promises herself she won't look forward to seeing him, but finds herself racing through the last few minutes of her shift, checking her reflection, changing out of her uniform if it gets too manky. She expects him to let her down but he doesn't. He is there, every night, leaning up against the wall, bright against the grey cinder blocks outlined with green moss, a poster boy for the visual benefits of smoking.

Her mother smoked. Sam only has one photo of her smoking – she didn't like people to know, apparently. It's in one of the photos Aunt Sara sent her; images of her mum before she was married. It was something. Something at least. Her mother was smiling in them. Smiling, always smiling. It annoys her. Margaret made Patsy keep some family photos around the house: christenings, stiff formal rituals of their lives with blown-out blue swirls behind her parents' heads, standing in the centre of the badly framed universe that only existed in the time-warp of the early seventies and eighties. The pictures on the wall charted their arrival, first her, then PJ, both drowned in a lace-laden christening dress, frilly bonnet to match. Her infant fists were raised in baby protest, while his appearance remained placid, the perfect baby; later her toddler frown sang cute against the high bunches of her hair. She never quite had the right expression but her mother was always smiling, relentlessly, through it all.

*

Naoise tells her he has to go away for a week.

Short notice, he says. You won't even miss me.

Other way around I think, she says, but when she finishes her shift the next evening and he isn't there she lingers, wishing he'd arrive, late, dishevelled, out of breath, smiling apologies coming from his mouth.

That week she takes his photograph out but when she does, underneath she sees the pictures of her mother. She lays them out on her bed and studies her mother, her flawless Hollywood smile, her pouty cigarette mouth, visible in the black-and-white images. When some people get old, their jaws get smaller; she's seen it in the nursing home. Sam thinks of the old man's sad mouth, how his teeth would be yellow and chattering if they had told him his brother had died, if they had said the word *gun*, how at night he might grind his discoloured canines through the projectile of unspoken grief, into bullets. She imagines some future morning when he will expel teeth like empty cartridges after he has processed the ache, his bones dissolving with sadness, wearing away the pain and rage and despair as he sleeps every night. That never happens because the powers that be in the nursing home decide not to expose him to the devastating truth that some coward shot his brother dead in a pub for no good reason except hate.

Naoise visits again, less than a week later. Surprises her, calls to the house. She thinks he has balls. Her da would lose his mind if he knew. He rings the bell, his frame visible through the wavy amber glass. They cycle to a cairn on a small hill a mile from her house, sit with their backs against huge warm stones and get happy. They take their time going home, she cycles in huge figures of eight around him on the deserted roads back to her house.

Wait here, she says, before he can leave.

Alright, he says.

She races up to check if Patsy or PJ are home yet. Then she remembers they are staying out to watch evening point-to-point races at the beach. She can picture her da and brother in the crowd, other punters' salt-licked faces, the strut of excited horses, coloured silks rippling against the breeze, skinny jockeys sat atop their mounts like dolls, kids and dogs being roared at to get outta the way in case they got a clatter; later, hooves kicking up putty-coloured sand as the crowd's cheers jostled against the wind to be heard.

When she was little she thought they were magic, believed for a long time that the elegant horses she watched were flying along the stretched spit of sand, sea and sky, floating above the horizon, feet clear of the ground.

She makes him stash the bike in the hedge, just in case, links her arm in his as they walk up to the house.

They won't be back for ages but you can't stay long, she whispers.

Why are you whispering? he whispers back, and they dissolve into fits of laughter, both still high.

She's never brought anyone home before Naoise. She brings him to her room. Puts music on. She fools herself that this is safe, a minor interaction. Mates. That is all she wants, what he wants. That is enough. The closeness. Yet she hasn't told Becca, hasn't broken any promises, has kept their meetings for herself alone. A sweet-tasting secret. She gets up to make them tea and he arrives in his bare feet to the kitchen. He comes up behind her, presses himself into her, pulls her hair back and kisses her neck. She can see their reflection in the rain-flecked windows, his smile growing as she says, No, no, stop, we can't. But she doesn't really mean it, really doesn't want him to stop. He moves away then, his hand gone from her waist, his mouth from her ear, and she reaches her left hand backwards, groping for him in the failing light. She feels his lips kiss her palm, tongue taste her skin, before he appears out of the shadows. He goes down on her in the kitchen, his hands on her hips, fingers grabbing her insistently.

She watches him stroll away from the house afterwards, pushing his bike, one hand gripping the centre of the handlebars, one in his pocket. She has an urgency to see him leave before her da and

PJ arrive, but he doesn't rush. Her reflection seems to cover his shape, his body dances in and out of the shadows filling the yard, until he slips out of sight, becomes a spectre.

It takes a while before she feels he is gone, isn't out there watching her in the dark. She likes the idea of him being unable to look away from her.

She studies her face in the windowpane. Worries about the spread of freckles on her nose, bares her sharp teeth, forces a small imperfect smile. She has read somewhere about Hollywood starlets forced to have their teeth fixed, replaced by dentures, implants or worse. Noses smashed and elastic hair bands pulled brace-tight, plied with horse tranquillisers, cocktails for their calm complexion, all to look pretty. The cost of living in the spotlight could just be the cost of living for everyone. Sam runs her tongue along her teeth and smiles in the lurid mirror of the window. She will never have a perfect smile and there is something brilliant about being broken almost straight away.

No one can fix you.

No one will even try.

See Something. Say Something.

Patsy, 1994

Even Patsy knew where to find that fella. Patsy sat in the car after early vigil Mass on Saturday evening. Waiting. If he waited long enough, he would come out eventually, to get cigarettes or booze. He lived in a bloody dive and the thought of his daughter, anyone's daughter, going in there, left Patsy cold.

He'd read the paper twice over and was almost about to leave when he saw him, coming up the hill. You couldn't miss that bloody swagger. If Patsy was quick he could get to him before Naoise knew what hit him. Patsy locked the car and walked briskly down towards him. He reached the Devlin fella on the brow of the slope, launched into his speech before his feet came to a standstill.

I want you to stay the hell away from my daughter, you hear me? Patsy said. He was right up beside him now.

Naoise had kept walking, seemed bigger than Patsy had expected, more solid.

What? What did you say?

You heard me. Stay away from her or I'll knock your block off. Patsy squared up to him and Naoise stalled, started laughing, opened a packet of cigarettes.

Listen, man, you'd need to be telling me her name, before you get carried away, Naoise drawled back.

Patsy could see that he wasn't even bothered. Suspected this wasn't the first time someone's father had had a word. Wouldn't be the last, either. Just stay away from her, you hear me? Patsy repeated again. A part of him hoped Joe was wrong, had made a mistake, but it would be just typical of Sam to be with this article. She's eighteen years old, Patsy said.

Again, Naoise said, as he lit his cigarette, could be anybody—?

Jesus Christ, Patsy muttered, and turned back up the hill, towards his car.

Fuck! Naoise said, as Patsy walked away. You're Sam's da. He started to laugh. Fucking hell! You've got old, man.

Patsy stopped and said, Old? Sorry, do you think you know me? Do you think this is a sick joke? Stay away from my daughter.

It's a free country, *mate*. Maybe you should tell her to stay away from *me*? Naoise smirked, took a final drag and then stubbed out the cigarette butt under the sole of his trainers. Patsy was transfixed by his casual littering. He marched back down the hill as Naoise took the keys from his pocket to open the door to his flat.

Pick that fucking up, Patsy said, too loudly.

What? Naoise said, in disbelief. Pick it up yourself, prick.

Pick it up. Or I'll make you pick it up, Patsy said. I'll rub your fucking nose in it.

Oh, will ye now? You're fuckin mad, d'you know that? Naoise turned the key in the lock and Patsy lurched after him, grabbing the door with both hands, pulling it back, blocking his entry. Naoise struggled to keep it open, the two men jostling for position.

Fuck off, will ye! Naoise was shouting now. Chiz! Chiz!

You yellah coward. I'll break your bloody neck! Patsy roared back.

Patsy felt a hand on his shoulder, looked around. It was Joe, trying to pull him back, and for the briefest moment Patsy loosened his grip on the frame. Naoise elbowed him in the ribs, shoved him out of the way and slipped quickly past him, as Patsy and Joe stumbled backwards on the uneven street. Naoise was in through the door and started to push it closed, as Patsy fought to keep it open, Joe still trying to restrain him.

I'm fucking your daughter, d'you know that? Naoise roared, his words escaping through the gap before the door slammed shut, their force overpowering Patsy, like a punch in the chest.

Patsy lost his footing, staggered. Joe too, and the two men swayed, hunched over breathless on the street, as the sound of feet on cheap wooden stairs and receding laughter filtered through the closed door.

Patsy banged on it, repeatedly, louder and louder. Come out, you coward. Big fella, eh? Come out and face me! Out, you bastard, and I'll show you who's old!

What's got into you, Patsy? Joe said. He's not worth it, he's a big mouth, Patsy, winding you up. That's all.

He's a bad fucking apple, Patsy said.

Come away on outta that, Joe said, pulling on Patsy's arm. It's not gonna do any good, Patsy.

Bugger off, Joe. I know my own business.

I know, but there's no point in making it worse. That fella's not budging. Better off talking to her, Joe said.

And say what? Huh? Say what exactly, Joe? Would you like it if it was your daughter? Well, would you? Patsy said, still flushed with rage.

Patsy walked off up the hill then, his whole body shaking with anger.

Joe came after him. Take it easy on them roads, Patsy, Joe said, as Patsy got in the car.

I'm a better driver than you. Been driving forty-odd years and you're giving me advice.

Ah, Patsy, that's not what I'm saying, it's just you're a bit—

But Patsy didn't stick around to hear Joe's safety lesson. He clicked his seatbelt in, turned on the engine. Joe stepped out of the way as Patsy indicated past him and drove home.

Patsy knew best. Joe hadn't a clue.

Talking never got you anywhere.

Loowit Leaving

Nuala, 1982

I love my children but I love me more.

I am standing at the line, hanging out washing. I am standing there taking in the absolute beauty of this place and I am thinking about leaving. The clothes move like quick clouds against a blue sky reckless in its rapture of the colour. It will be the bluest sky I'll ever see. The sky seen from this place, on this day, before I make up my mind. All that is possible will be there. My children play on the grass, unable to see the terrible future I am planning without them. I am thinking of taking my daughter. I am thinking I could manage and that Patsy dotes on the boy, adores him and then I am thinking that if I take anything that belongs here I will have to return, I will not be able to escape. I catch a reflection of me in a window as I enter the house, apron slung over an odd patterned dress, an empty woven basket, older than me, handed down, wooden pegs in my hand. My hair is dragged back from my face and I know I could be looking at my grandmother. Time stops here, stands still and catches you in it and you become buried in it, heartsore like this landscape. I don't belong here. All the wordless matryoshkas are coming out of me, pointing to my release; all my secret hidden worlds revealing themselves to me, and no one is more surprised than me when they keep coming, an infinite hidden world. I am dying here, the countryside is killing me, my whole body longs for a city, not a town or village, not bigger roads and better transport, but the chaos, strangers rushing past, the throng and desolation, rush hour and dirty streets, rubbish. The infrastructure of coloured faces, accents mixed like leftover soup, but even that's a lie.

The truth is, I need anywhere but here.

I'm not honest with myself. I have been saving strength for a long time, hoarding my resolve like money, keeping things just for me.

The kind of mother that makes me is the kind of mother I don't want to be. I put these feelings away like boiled eggs in the fridge, gone cold and smothered in mayonnaise, cayenne powder dusted on them too early, so it cakes and cracks like lava, the pretty colour gone soft, the sharpness of the moment lost forever, everything made in advance for an easy life, not set out fresh.

We are lying on the grass in bright sunlight as I think these things; I kiss their precious heads and the smell of them is like every good thing I've ever had. And yet I still want to leave. I have no heart, I think, no heart at all.

Last year in the papers every day they wrote about the men starving themselves, starving themselves for freedom, for justice, for love. We are all starving in some way, all empty and gnawing and raw inside. They had been hungry for such a long time, hungry for that cause that some say will die soon, a cause that has lived and died for hundreds of years, has taken hopes and fears and lives for hundreds of years. This year is no different. People keep dying, and belief breeds from that decay, a faith that in this sacrifice, in this offering up of bodies, corporal destruction, resides the will, the ravenous hope that others say will change everything.

I doubt that. I doubt that a man, alone, can change anything, can change the minds of other men. I wonder if you go down a path so far that you cannot come back, cannot step back from your intent, even if you are afraid, even if you get lost, even if you know you will win, win against yourself, supplant your own desires. It is a curious thing, I think, the certainty of death, the will to hold out against every cell in your body screaming for nourishment, to overpower your biology. All for a belief, a cause, a future you'll never see.

I have not taken much now that I have decided to go. The few things that I cherish, the things that matter most, I have to leave behind or I can't leave at all. When the report comes on the radio over the space of a few hours I am shattered. I cradle a cup of tea as the children sleep and weep silently in the kitchen as the posh Northern tones of BBC Radio Ulster propel me to London, and even though it's just talk, condemnation and interrogation and disbelief, the only sounds in my head I can hear are the cries of the young men and terrified whinnying of injured horses, hooves clattering on sharp tarmacked streets in distress, their riders thrown in the air or dissolved by the brutality of the bomb, nails wedged into their beautiful, shiny black shoulders and forelocks, blood trickling along their flanks, their insides visible to innocent bystanders. I see polished brass ceremonial bridles destroyed, while smoke and bodies and bits of car debris shatter and divide all around them. I think of those horses wedded to the ground, dying with their riders, man and beast locked together in agony. A few hours later the bandstand bomb goes off in Regent's Park, while the smell of death is still present in the air, young men played the defiant music of the monarch, and someone with killing on their minds, in their heart, with destruction bubbling up inside them, must have stood in the bushes and pressed a button and watched them light up, like pushing play on a VCR recording, except there is no rewind facility. There is no going back.

Selfishly I think of my trip today. I wonder will they stop the flights, prevent people coming in or out from here. I am going from Dublin anyway, going from there because this place is so small, someone will notice me, find me, someone will see me in Belfast airport or the ferry terminal, someone will ask about the children or Patsy, and then I'll be snapped out of my stupor and I won't be able to go through with it.

No one knows what I'm doing. I barely know myself. I can't tell Sara. My sister wouldn't understand. I promised to bring the children with me, to visit London. She thinks we are all coming at some stage. She does not understand, yet, what a life can be like and I have let her think whatever she wants. Perhaps in London she can't see the smallness of my world. Smallness can be like death. Small world, small people, small lives. Smallness can suffocate you. You can be dying from the smallness of your life. I need to go somewhere I can be free. No one looking at me and wanting things from me. Placing motherhood on me like a funeral wreath. I need to be me, not anyone's wife, or lover. I need to remember who I am.

I will put the children to bed tonight and live the lie of my life one last time. Patsy will watch telly and then fall asleep on the sofa as usual. I will sleep in the spare room like I always do. He will only wake when the first of our children cries out for me, and then, and only then, will he panic, think me dead, not gone, but later when he calms down he will find the letter in the kitchen. He will read it and he will understand. Or not. Unable to comprehend. To see who I am and always was. I can't wait another day. I can't have another tomorrow, another day, another dinner, another row. He comes home the same time every day, like clockwork, his life an hourglass: no matter what way you turn it, the monotony never runs out. I will spend one more night here. It won't matter now, one more night, because when I leave he will dye my name blue forever with his curses, as blue as the sky today, on my last day in this place, but it won't really matter because I'll be gone and this part of life, the stranglehold this place has on me, will be over.

But before any of that there is Naoise, and Naoise will not be as easy to let go.

Cemetery Sunday

Sam, 1994

What no one likes to talk about is that it wasn't simply an accident. Nuala Malin was running away, running away from them. Patsy, PJ, Sam. This place. No wonder it doesn't suit Sam. You're just like her, people say. The spit of your mother, Chiz said, but what does that actually mean? That Sam looks like her, that Sam can't stick it out, that this place is killing Sam?

Sam's never understood why one Sunday a year they all come here and parade around their dead. They're not flippin Mexicans. Sweating in the middle of the summer, the one guaranteed 'hot' day of the year, trussed up like it's a catwalk not a cemetery. The smell of incense wafting over everyone, raining down holy water from the trainee celebrant, who is always some saddo local boy done good and come home to show off. And Father Give Over. He has an actual name, a destined-to-be-a-priest name like Smith or Fitzgerald or Murray, but everyone calls him Give Over. The reason being obvious even to his most fervent parishioners. Father Give Over likes to whine on in that special priest voice that no one can understand, intonation that sits somewhere between a toff and a regular person eating toffee really loudly, continuing to chew, as the sweet gets stuck on their teeth, while they drone on and on and on.

There's also the six-week prep beforehand or, if you're like their 'burial-pit' neighbours, the Morrisseys, who basically run a gardening centre out of their grave, it's honestly like a religious version of the Chelsea fucking flower show. Sam's da, never wanting to be accused of giving too much of a fuck, detests their showiness. There's no need for that. There is, though, a need for every fake emerald-green stone to look brand new. So they wash them by hand. Religious levels of cleanliness. As perfect as the day her father laid them on the bizarre concrete patio that constitutes Sam's grandparents' grave. Not Sam's mother's grave. Granny Malin wouldn't have stood for that. Her power over her only son seems to have grown even though she's been dead for years.

They go to a grave that holds the past. Buried nothing. Buried a ghost. Buried themselves. It's an empty ritual. The gravestone is black Mourne granite, old, holds a slight grey fleck, classic and carefully chosen, by her da and his brother, Sam guesses. They live closest so they do all the work. Patsy's brother is older and lives abroad and Sam and PJ never really see him. He can never make the summer religious reunion. He's fond of the drink is all Patsy says about that.

There is a black flower-holder to be cleaned and polished, covered with an upside-down steel colander-type thing from which the carnations stick out. Only white. Never any other colour. Especially not red.

Margaret always used to provide tea and sandwiches on Cemetery Sunday. Normally, before these uncomfortable family gatherings to praise, raise, rile the living and the dead, everyone headed to the local shop, joined the queue for ice creams. Idle in the lines filled with screaming children, ready to terrorise their Sunday best with the smoothest whippy 99s that money could buy, while old men queued opposite for their piled up papers, smoking and chatting, dispensing the odd wink, the odd tut. Most wouldn't attend Cemetery Sunday Mass till they were in the ground. A summer pageant that has always played out the same. Except this summer there's a lot here who don't really give a shit and Sam thinks they are starting to see. Rituals are shifting.

It's not like when she was fifteen and practically giddy with who she might lay eyes on – one of the Finney boys back from Queen's, total dicks but still so handsome, who spent the afternoon getting the preppy backs slapped off them, egos swelling with all the golden chat about the GAA, the cries of, We'll do it this year, lads. These last few years the young people of the town and local surrounds seemed to slip under a spell, most teenagers dressed in black or tartan all year round, slouching fellas with hair long, pale gothic girls like statues, and Margaret had blamed the jumped up family of the local curate for cutting the hawthorn tree down on purpose. Whether you believed in it or not, she had said, there was a change in this place, a lack of respect, a change in the young ones, that she lamented. No one had the heart to tell Margaret it was a musical wave called grunge and it came from Seattle via Dublin and Belfast.

Patsy still made Sam go. As long as she lived under his roof she would go and make herself presentable. It wasn't a discussion. She had to make a sort of middling fucked-up effort, funeral black but a dress.

You'll die in this heat, Margaret would have said. Really, Samantha, don't you have anything else?

Sam sat on the side of Margaret's grave. Freshly dug, flowers still alive, barely. It was right beside her mother's. Organised years ago. Margaret bought it so the gossips wouldn't. Now she joined John-Jo in it. Margaret's useless sons coddled together, uncomfortable in their unironed shirts and crumpled suits, Margaret's domestic influence already sorely missed, the two lads like batch in a toaster, big thick musty sweaty heads on them, getting grilled alive on top.

For Christ's sake, stand up girl, Patsy seethes at Sam through a hollow in his poor teeth, they're coming to bless the grave. She wears cheap blown-out black sunglasses that Becca had brought back for her from holiday, pouts at him as she stands up, stroppy and hot and fucking bored. This ritual is a waste of time and it is never going to last. Does he think when he dies Sam will stand here with her children, not that she's even considered having any, and mourn him every year? Do any of them? It seems so impossibly stupid. As Sam smirks at the thought of a half-empty graveyard and some shambling priest with no one knowing the refrain to his badly pronounced prayers, Patsy sees. Maybe sees everything she is thinking. Patsy raises his hand. It hovers above, hummingbird patient, before his arm descends in a slash of black against the blue sky. Sam doesn't have time to move aside. No defences against such a precise motion, a motion men have used for centuries to hit women. He knocks the glasses off her face and they clatter and break on the earth below, the ground hardened, dusty from weeks of unusual sun.

The force of his gesture in such a crowded space can't be seen by anyone except those closest to them and Sam can tell he doesn't care what the neighbours on either side of the grave think. Some women flinch, draw their children tighter against their skirts, but the older men simply sniff and rub their faces, plenty of practice at ignoring, oblivion a familiar friend. Patsy folds his hands back into prayer, as if he's done God's bidding. Sam touches her face, feels the redness rise on her cheek. She doesn't think she has ever hated him so much before or after, but in that moment it is everything.

Fuck you, Sam says, and pushes the shattered glasses further into the ground as she steps on them and moves past her brother onto the tiny track that leads past speechless neighbours. Margaret. Margaret would have scolded him and stopped her, but Margaret is dead. Gone. Just below them, rotting in the earth. Sam thinks she sees Becca's face, her mouth gape open and closed, and hundreds of other parishioners who know Sam to see, who knew her, not well but local, the way you read a face you've seen every day since you were born.

Father Give Over and his entourage have nearly reached the path to the Malin family plot. It is an airless day, no wind and the priest stops abruptly like he is going to curse Sam. She glares at him as the other parishioners continue saying a decade.

Fuck you too! she roars. Fuck the lot of ye!

Father Give Over drops the microphone in shock as Sam's curses reverberate, stun the place to silence. For once he has no words for her or anyone else.

Everyone turns to watch her leave and the congregation mutters a thousand words of whatever good or bad thing they have to say about Sam Malin and her family and her dead mother, but she's done something that afternoon. She's shown her da up for the heartless fucker he is. He can take lots of things, her da. Lots and lots of talking behind his back. Can deal with all the whispers, the pointed silences and squirrelled-away conversations, but what he cannot take is being shown up in public, shown up by his only daughter.

Love Knots Inside Us All Like Bindweed

Patsy, 1994

Patsy and PJ came into a quiet house after Cemetery Sunday. Half relieved Sam was not there and half concerned she was not there. They didn't know what to do with themselves this year, since Margaret usually did a spread at her house. So they ate chilled gammon slices and cold boiled egg halves smothered in beige salad cream, scallions chopped roughly and a tomato split in quarters with a shake of salt, some sliced batch. Patsy put down two mugs of steaming tea in front of them, waiting till his turned the colour of freshly cut peat before adding his dash of milk. Patsy missed Margaret's feed, the smell and warmth of a kitchen that loved to be used. He would have been batting away another slice of pavlova at this stage, heavy with cream and Irish strawberries sweet with summer in every bite, but the trade-off was small talk and pleasantries and that was something he had no stomach for.

D'you think she's dead, Dad? PJ said, when he had almost finished his tea. Mum? He'd never asked this question outright before and Patsy knew he must have been getting the courage up after what happened at the graveyard. Patsy blinked a few times before he answered, needed a moment to point and lay his words out in his head, ready a solid response.

Aye. I know she is.

How? How'd ya know?

Patsy sniffed.

She would'a come back. He speaks as if he is addressing the table, then looks up at his boy. Come back for you, his voice falters, for you and your sister. She loved you.

He gestured to his son's plate then, to see if he was finished. Lifted them both and put them in the sink. Patsy stood there for a moment longer than normal, his hands gripping the white ceramic. There was no tell-tale sign he had ever been married. He hadn't worn his ring. It wasn't the fashion back then. Too good for every day, so it just sat up above in a green leather box. At that moment he desperately wanted to see its tawny gold band appear below the red lines that criss-crossed the joints of his hand, marks of time, of a life that nothing could bleach away, no pressure could erase. There might have been a comfort in that. If nothing else. He crossed the room and reached for his coat and cap from the back door and went out to see to the yard. PJ followed him moments later. The two worked silently in their usual routine, side by side, settling the animals, in the quiet way they had always done.

Misnomer, Misnamed, Named

Sam, 1994

She's a snivelling mess when she turns up at his door. He tells her to wait there and vaults back up the stairs two by two in his rush. She has been trying to be good around him. Slow everything down, be in control. They haven't given this a name, this thing they are doing. No expectations, except that she has made him come to her this past while. She'd made weak, silly excuses not to go to his flat but he didn't complain. Yet now she finds herself in the doorway, waiting on him. She thinks about leaving, but then he comes bounding down.

Let's go, he says, shaking Chiz's car keys in her face. The tiny bell attached has a tinny ring, impossibly loud for such a small trinket.

Naoise drives the long way, veering off on hilly, winding back roads. Like he is mapping out something on the way there.

He hands her a cassette that he's fished from the pocket in the car door. She turns it over in her hands. Depeche Mode, *Violator*. They wait for the album to start and he speeds up, cornering the twisty tree-lined roads like it's a rally. He turns up 'Personal Jesus', blasts it from the speakers. He reaches across and moves his hand up her naked thigh, pushes his fingers against the cotton fabric.

Take them off, he says. They speed past Spelga Dam where you can leave the car on a slope and take the handbrake off and it rolls up hill. Magnetic force pulling them all along. She shimmies her underwear down, lifting her frame up off the seat and unhooking them from her ankles. He takes them from her, makes like he's going to eat them, then throws them out the window, laughing uncontrollably at her shocked face.

You shouldn't litter, is all she can think to say, mock disapprovingly.

We'll get them on the way back, he says, and almost makes her come while he drives the car one-handed. In those moments she would do anything for him. Everything potent, spinning, unstoppable, but by the time they arrive she finds some semblance of control again.

They climb over thick stone walls towards the Silent Valley reservoir, inhale the lush smell of gorse and heady summer clover as it catches on their clothes and spreads from the edges to the centre of the hay fields where he lays her down and buries his tongue in her cunt again and again until she can't breathe.

She can see he's trying so hard to get her to give in and the more he tries the more she wants him to try. This is the version of him she needs. She tells him she touches herself when she doesn't see him. Whispers it and trails it around with her like promises. Everything between them is moving so fast again, she's giddy with it. She tries to be in charge but she's slipping, intoxicated, into his world. He uses her body in a way that is reckless and corrupting and brings her to the edge of what she thought she could feel. All she wants is more of him. She is running out of reasons to say no.

She is on her knees when he says it. Has him in her mouth. She used to think she did this because she liked it. She is certainly good at it. She does it so she doesn't have to do other things. It's a compromise. Fucks her mouth. They are outside. Evening never seems to arrive. In the summer it's almost turning into night for hours. It feels like she is on display but the place is deserted, everyone with their families.

Her knees are in the long grass, the dusty lilac seed heads of the blades are bunched under her dress, their featherlight touch tickling her thighs as she moves herself up and down and it makes her want to laugh. She can't. His cock is in her mouth, his hands on her head, rubbing and pulling her hair, the bobble lost somewhere in the grass, another elastic gone.

An image from earlier, of everyone she knows, standing at graves, mouths full of prayers, flashes in her head.

Nuala, he says.

She shudders, tries to unhear it, stop it from entering her head; he is moaning above her, lost, and she thinks she is going to get sick, he comes in her mouth then and she does. Spits him out. He sinks to the ground beside her, tries to kiss her, his hands reach under her dress, fingers searching for her but she pushes him away. He's on top of her now, smiling, getting hard again, his desire for her never seems to dim. He is touching her and she is letting him and he moves her dress up, his body moving down, mouth above.

Stop.

She pulls him back up to her face. He mistakenly tries to kiss her.

Why did you call me Nuala?

He smiles. What?

She pauses. Breaks. Breathing words out slowly.

You called me Nuala. You said Nuala.

No. I didn't.

You said you didn't know her.

I didn't.

He pulls his jeans up. Levi's. Takes time to button up, the silver coins pop out and his thumbs push them into the corded holes. He doesn't wear underwear. Ever. Before she thought it was cool. She's starting to think it's repulsive. Expectant. She stands up beside him. Looks at the lake. She crosses the field and swishes the tall grasses apart.

Sam, he calls after her.

She ignores him.

Sam, come back. Fuck sakes, he says under his breath. He follows her at a distance, like he can't be bothered.

She strips off her clothes and walks in. It's sparkling cold but she doesn't squeal. Gets far enough out and dips her head under the water.

She wills violence. She wants the water to fill her open mouth, strangle her darkness, drown her rage. She rises to the surface, faces away from him and opens her mouth, silently screaming into the night. Her dark hair slicked to her shoulders and back. Waits for him. She knows he'll join her. He has to. It's too much to resist.

When their bodies meet in the water and he kisses her she knows if he doesn't fuck her soon he'll go mad. Lose all reason. She feels his hands on her breasts and wonders did he want to touch her mother like that. She pulls away, back towards the shadow of the mountains as he treads water and watches her.

I need you to be honest. Just be honest and you can fuck me right here, right now. You knew her, didn't you?

He swims to her. She feels his hands on her waist pull her towards him. She takes his look, long and deliberate as he searches her face. Then she asks the question.

Did you sleep with my mother?

What? he says, breathing heavy, No. Kisses her hard on the mouth. He can't feel the cold anymore, just her, slicked against his skin, like vernix, like she's being born.

Sam clamps her thighs around his waist and he sinks beneath. She releases him, watches him surface and lets him catch his breath. He holds her tight as they tread water. Then he gently, softly kisses her neck, pushes himself against her, his body adjusting to the cold.

Yes, Sam, yes. God. He tries to push himself inside her. Yes, he says, tries again, is kissing her neck, but she shoves away, pushes off him.

You fucked her, didn't you? Her words echo around them when he doesn't answer. She slips under the water. Stays under as she swims away from him, and when she surfaces she's already far, swimming back to shore.

Chiz wants to fuck you, you know that, right? Naoise shouts after her. His voice echoes in the massive space. Murph too. Don't you get it? They aren't your mates. They just want you to suck their cocks and take you from behind. They … He stops shouting across the expanse, realises there is no point, watches her nakedness break the water, rise, slip straight into clothes. No looking back.

Finally she walks down to the water's edge, carries her shoes in her hand. She still wears her black hard-capped school shoes. Can't afford a new pair for summer. Buy them yourself, her da says. Her shoes look like clown shoes, huge rounded toes and clunky heels, brutal, as if they are mourning something. Flecks of mud and grass cling to the edges of the soles.

There are huge white pavers of Mourne granite underneath her bare feet that make it look like a Roman bath, not a reservoir. She thinks about the men who broke their backs to bring them here. Imagines them swimming in the man-made lake. Rinsing off the sweat and grime from their tired bodies, fine white dust pooling around them in the water, icy coldness cutting their lungs, same lungs that had breathed in this place, breathed in alabaster powder that would continue to mill away at their insides, turn their coughs opaque with bright red blood eventually, years later, make the invisible visible. Sam wonders, when they died, did they ever think of this place, its grand silence, intoxicating magnetic pull, and curse it? Everything truly beautiful is deadly. Pretty things kill you the most.

Tell me the truth. You called me by her fucking name. She crouches down on her hunkers. Finds his eyeline. Waits. He floats towards her slowly. Why'd you say that?

Naoise says nothing. Sam watches the outline of his face, small breaths escaping, his body submerged in the silver dark water.

I fancied her, okay? Naoise says. We all did.

I'm not an idiot, Sam says.

No, you're not. You're obsessed. Trying to find meaning in any little thing. Trying to find any excuse to push me away.

Fine. Fuck off, then.

Aw, Sam, don't be like that—

Like what? You called me by her name. What am I supposed to think?

Sam. Stop.

Stop what? My questions? Breathing? Putting up with your stupid shit? What was she really like? Was she chatty? Funny? Good in bed? Am I like her? Was she like me?

Sam stares at him. Puts down her shoes like she's going to step into them.

Well? Sam says.

Can I come out first?

No one's stopping you. You can do what you like.

No doubt. Naoise shakes his head. Disappears under the surface of the water. Sam stares out over the empty space in front of her. Waits. He plunges back out, gasping. Throws water on his face again and again. She can see he's freezing.

I'll get your stuff, Sam says.

Sam saunters back with his clothes. Naoise is shivering; he looks sheepish, vulnerable set against the violet mountains; they leer over him, solid and fearless. He's stayed in too long, the landscape has conspired to weaken him, he cannot overpower this place. His hands can't manage to button his jeans, she watches him fumble. Wrings out her wet hair again as the temperature drops. She has to help him walk back to the car, he is shivering, he leans into her, his arms around her. Silent.

They get back to the car, tumble inside, and Naoise turns the engine on, blasts the heat. The car headlights catch insects confused by their counterfeit brightness. He moves to touch her face but she flinches.

I barely knew her, okay? She had a nice laugh.

Bullshit.

He breathes in slowly, like he is calming horses.

Fine. Fuck it. She kissed me once. Just once.

What the actual fuck?

She was a wee bit tipsy, at Christmas, giving me a tip, it was an accident, Naoise says. His voice shakes. She can't tell if it's the cold or confession coming out.

Kissed you? Sam asks, lets out a little nervous laugh. You accidentally *kissed* my mother. You lied to me. Drive me home. I want to go home now.

Okay. Listen. Let me exp—

Now!

He turns the engine off.

Why did you call me Nuala? Sam screams.

His hands grip the steering wheel but he doesn't look at her as he slams his forehead off it. The bang makes Sam jump but she doesn't try to prevent him, curtail his violence. She lets him do it again.

Nuala!

It stops him, her name, and he rests the side of his face against the wheel, looks up at her.

Why? Her voice falters as she pushes him, slams her bunched-up fingers into a fist, lashes out. He lets her strike him once, twice, then catches hold of her hand.

I messed up ... been trying to tell you. Figure out a way to say it, that didn't sound wrong. That didn't hurt you, Sam.

Oh, *right*. You sure she didn't give you blowjobs on a regular basis? Because, you know, if I was a rational person, it might make more fucking sense than your sudden concern for me.

Sam. Listen. It didn't mean anything. It didn't matter. I didn't know—

It didn't matter? Didn't mean anything? To you maybe—

I wanted to tell you. I didn't want it to ruin stuff between us—

Fuck away off. You're a fuckin liar!

I should have told you sooner.

Told me what? You haven't told me anything. Tell me what she tasted like? What she smelt like? I don't believe you. You fucking liar! She half hits him again, thumps him with her other hand, tears at his fingers. He releases her fist.

They sit in a hard silence. Naoise doesn't move. She stares at him. He has a small red lump on the top of his forehead. He looks older, strung out in this light. He starts the engine again. She gets out of the car. Walks around it, her body flickering in and out of the headlights, a shadow of who she was before. She gets back in the car.

Drive me home, she says.

Sam.

Her hands cover her mouth. Then her face. I want to go home.

Sam.

He sounds small and far away.

Stay.

He uncurls her fingers, presses his forehead to hers.

She can feel the first salt of his tears. She knows that this moment will become knotted in her bones. Dark slow growth like you see when you cut open a tree, the mark of a hard year, heavy line of a difficult time, lighter circles spitting out from it with promise. You survived the bad thing. You grew anyway. You lived.

I love you, he says.

He sobs and sobs, heaves himself inside out, anchoring himself to her tiny frame. Cries like a child putting itself to sleep. Sam holds on to him, not knowing what to do. What to say. She has waited for those words. She listens to him cry as if she is outside herself, she is not here, she is watching from a distance. She waits for a feeling to come. Any feeling. Wills it to overtake her, this crushing want she had held for him. She takes his hand. Spreads her warmth across his skin. Kisses the inside of his wrist, leads him towards her, refusing to let herself shy away from this need they have for each other, thinks she can confuse herself, her emotions. It is like a sickness coming out of her. Wonders if this is real or just the effects of cold-water shock. Wonders did he ever cry for her mother like that. Wonders if he is crying for her still. Wants with every bone in her body to believe him before he breaks her completely.

My Bonnie Lies Over the Ocean

Nuala, 1982

I put them down for bed, kiss their pretty, perfect little foreheads, motion to leave but my body betrays me and stays rooted to the spot. I light a match prematurely to smoke a final cigarette outside their window but I think of them too long and it burns down to the quick, searing the delicate skin at the base of my nailbed. A blister forms there and throbs; I try to suck it away but then leave it throbbing, an echo to my children's gentle shallow sleep. PJ's lashes are straight, fan out from his lids like sweepers. Make him look cartoonish, too perfect, like someone wished him into this world. Like your dreams made real. I hold my breath as I kiss his eyes, one for sorrow, one for joy. My magpie boy. Sam's curl upwards at the edges, double lashes, ink black, made to trap tears and frame her fierce little stare. And I can't kiss her goodbye. I can't. Her hair's still damp and she smells of No More Tears and talc. Wake up. Wake up and I'll stay. I'll stay if you need me.

Before I go I tenderly place my ruddy red-tinged thumb on their chests and feel them rise and fall and finally I take a breath. Let go of all I have been holding in, remove my hand and simply leave.

I don't look in on Patsy. He's in the past now. I hear him turn in the bed.

I go to the kitchen, letter in my hand. I let myself out. My bag in the car already. Everything sounds huge as I turn the engine on, like all the night crawlers have come to see me off, serenade me one last time with their dark music. The house remains asleep as the tyres crunch the gravel of the driveway. I edge out into the wide wide world, roll the windows down, infinite possibilities rush over me, giving me goosebumps in the midnight air. I turn the car out of the drive and start to cry. I take a different route than normal, old back roads, but before I reach the town I have to stop. I feel queasy, lost, but then I recognise the swell; it's hope. I had forgotten it could scare you.

In the morning, Patsy will rise like clockwork, to feed the livestock. He'll find my note first. Or he won't. Find it when he gets back. They will be fine till he gets back. They will all be fine. They will all be better off without me. They will. I will.

And I am not losing anymore. Hope is taking me further. I am going far away and starting all over again. I am breaking up my heart into tiny pieces and no one can stop me.

I find myself outside Naoise's house. I know he is waiting for me. At the usual place. In the dark, on the edges of my home. When I think of him, lean, waiting, wanting me, I almost can't bear it. I suck my thumb hard, teeth biting the burn, bursting the blister, breaking the skin, leaving a scar. And I drive away.

Cowed

Naoise, 1982

Circles of light as she drives away   abandons us
                    fill the blood-soaked dark
                              hot damp fear like a coating

                    sweating her out of him

her words, lies, promises, broken

          words   forming   and   reforming in his mind

                              like birds
                    his skin slick with need.

a sing song of the boy
patsy's gruff squeezed-out laugh
heavy steps on hard ground, kicking stones,
the boy sweet, old macdonald, old macdonald had a cow, *ei ei o,*
he hears them   lost   their own little world, laughing,
and it hits him,
what he's done   violence like a stitch he had
                    breathing rapid still,

ei ei o,
the cow, the calf, the dog, the girl   heart-shaped silence
sun across a pinking sky
face the same as her mother.
ei, ei, o
and he runs
away   away   from that house.

False Negative

I love you.

His words rattle around in her head for days.

She tells Becca. First about the love, later about the kiss. They spend hours on long winding conversations, time wrapped up in hard plasticky telephone coils that Sam twists and tightens and loosens around her fingers, their stricture depending on the version of the truth she is selling to Becca.

He snogged your ma? Becca says.

She snogged him. Once, Sam says. At Christmas.

So he says. What was it, part of his present?

Very funny.

It's totally mental, Sam.

It's fine. It's just a *bit* weird, like, Sam replies, but the strained lies glare pig-pink on Sam's fingers for hours afterwards. Indents of truths she can't say out loud.

She doesn't tell Becca that she had pushed him for details, ransacking his memories for any speck of information about Nuala that he could reveal. Things that her father, her aunt wouldn't have known. Things that only a stranger would know. That a person might observe about another. Small points of interest that made them come alive in the world. She doesn't say she thinks he might be lying. That he tells her things she already knows. Like her mother always smelled of almonds and had beautiful handwriting. That she is waiting for him to slip up. Give himself away. That he knows more than he's letting on. Ignores the small insistent voice inside her head that tells her she should just walk away because she is fascinated by him. Drawn to him more than ever. The danger in it. A dark thrill.

She doesn't tell Becca how he is cold afterwards, brooding, quiet. When he tells her things, it's like a shock. The shift is almost imperceptible to her, his fingers stroking her spine as he kisses her after, flares of feeling running through her, edging her closer to staying, to giving in, and he is always pulling her towards him and then, with subtle force, an imagined shove, away from him.

She doesn't say that it seems to cost him something to remember these trivial things. How it makes her uneasy when he touches her sometimes now, how he acts like nothing has happened, nothing has changed, but something has shifted, some truth revealed between them, something shared. She purges herself and him, pushes them closer and closer to a place they can't return from. He's euphoric, manic, chaotic. She is punishing herself. She craved the certainty of his love before but there's a thrill being this close to him, to the maw of him, that she cannot get enough of. She asks too many pointed questions he doesn't want to answer. She needs to talk about her mother all the time, every time. It leaves her unbalanced.

Minute humiliations have been piling up. She lets them take root. His bad behaviour penance. She so badly wants to fix him, *them*, she absorbs all the sorrow that lives in him. Resurrects all the need she has for him, buries all her doubts again and again, persuades herself, flints faith against her malleable desire like cheap coal. Tests herself.

It's no real surprise to her when in the weeks afterwards there's a bitterness that grows on him; silence takes him over. A twisted kind of hurt she encourages, which he fuels with drugs. He hides away from her. Tells her he's ill. When she sees him again, he looks spent, broken.

He isn't waiting for her after work one day, so she goes to his place. The sounds of a raucous party meet her, busy feet, bodies squeezing past each other, people laughing, banter, music so loud it makes the walls throb. In the living room she sees Murph and Becca slumped over each other like dirty dishes left overnight in a sink, a chore she hadn't got round to sorting out yet. Naoise is not here. Naoise is not anywhere in the house, Sam realises, after walking in on Chiz and some random bird, whose name Sam should really get to know because she's becoming a regular fixture.

Bit a fuckin privacy, mate, Chiz shouts, throwing a boot to shut the door in her face. She cracks it open, just enough to let her words sneak through.

Where is he?

Lover boy? Chiz pants. Sam knows Chiz is revelling in this, having sex while talking to her. How. The. Fuck. Would. I. Know.

C'mon, Chiz, don't be a dick.

He's your boyfriend, not miiiiine.

A photograph would last longer? The girl sniggers underneath him.

You wanna ... join ... us? Only he laughs now between his grunts.

Sam shuts the door, nauseous.

She goes downstairs. Sits on the step outside. Smoking. Waiting.

It is half an hour later when a car she doesn't recognise drops him off with two girls. College girls. Girls who are not from here. From Belfast, maybe. The blonde one has beautiful clothes, her boots fall just below the knee in expensive leather, tan, middle-class brown, the colour of money. He has seen her and so he takes his time getting out of the car, goes back, leans in the window to talk again to the driver, dragging it out, smirks as he saunters towards her, girl on either arm. Walks by as if he doesn't know her at all.

Where were you? she says, and the girls look past her like they can't hear her voice, like she doesn't exist. Naoise, I'm talking to you?

She follows them up the stairs, pushes her way past acquaintances saying hello and strangers staring, ignores Becca's confused expression meeting hers, then rips the lead out of the speaker. The collective *ah fuck* drops to a hush when she screams *Where were you?*

Naoise finally looks up. Stares at her.

I had to see a man about a dog, he says, and they all start to laugh, especially the girls, hysterical uncontained drugged-up giggles. He joins in but he is only interested in Sam's reaction, she can see that now, he wants to see her explode, he wants to make her angry, he wants her to lash out, hit him. She does. She saunters across the room, seemingly calm, unconcerned, and slaps his face, in front of everyone. And when he laughs at her, her pathetic little smack, she lunges at him, pulling fistfuls of hair, startling herself as the stark black curls come away in her hands.

Imagine if I'd a bought the fucking dog? he says, his mates roaring laughing, as he picks Sam up easily and hauls her off to his bedroom, everyone suddenly quiet as he slams the door.

Rompers

Sam, 1994

You wore rompers as a kid too, he mouths in her ear, his voice sluggish with early morning.

She had meant to go home but he had fed her. Divulged little pieces of her mother. Titbits of knowledge so sweet and sad that she'd been unable to leave. Soothed her with his memories of a past she couldn't get close to. She'd woken up to his voice, his hands on her body. His fingers are almost inside her, slipping past the puckered buttons that clasp each other tightly underneath her pelvic bone, everything above taut against her febrile, urgent little body. She is half dressed and he hasn't even bothered to unclick the buttons on the bottom of her bodysuit.

His words come out like a whisper. A glimpse that curls her frame away from him when it was right there, resting impatiently on top of his hand, rising, falling, disturbing itself in order to achieve that sensation, almost fucking, but not quite fucking, she is wet and he tries to pull her back to him, tries to put his words down, move them out of sight, like his fingers pushing their way in again and again, but he knows he's lost her. They move apart. His eyes like cats', feline shadows move in the dark of his irises, deciding whether to return home or stay away.

What do you mean I wore rompers when I was little? Sam says.

He is pushing Sam onto the bed, again, his decision made, but she finds herself stall, something folding up inside her. He starts kissing her then, kissing her, and it is as if he is preventing her saying more words, asking the next question, and it *almost* works, that sensation *almost* overtakes everything else, even the feeling of uneasiness that has started up in her, she is losing herself too quickly, and then she pushes him off her, sits up.

What do you mean, rompers?

I saw you at the door once. Wee blue suit. Naoise tries to kiss her. Look, it was just a joke. Babies wear those. Little kids. Now women. It's sick.

He laughs.

It's not even funny, Sam says.

Jesus, Sam, it was a joke. Maybe you shouldn't wear anything anymore, save me some time. He smirks but she doesn't laugh, arms folded across her chest. Put out. He goes to light a cigarette. He is half-dressed, his jeans unbuttoned, his dick still semi-hard. She hasn't fixed herself properly yet, bodysuit pulled clumsily to one side of her pubic bone.

Was it with my mum? The time she kissed you—

You wanna talk about your mother? Again? Sam, what the fuck? We stayed up half the night talking about your mother. I thought we'd got over this—?

He lights a cigarette, waiting for her answer. She can't look at him.

I barely kissed her. She liked books. She left. *Enough?* He sits up, tries to pull her towards him. She leans away. Get back into bed, he says, the command stark in his voice.

She feels naked, talking to him like this, and pulls on her skirt. Fixes herself. Shy, almost trying to make it look like nothing.

He regards her, sucking hard on the cigarette, hunched over, his muscly forearms resting on his legs.

We can't just get over this, I can't, she says quietly, trying to manage her anger. I should go. I'm tired. She turns to kiss him goodbye but he doesn't even look at her.

Your dad paid me a little visit, Naoise says. He isn't happy.

What? He had a go at you?

Told me to stay away from you. He chuckles a little, leans back into the bed.

When?

While back, so why don't you be a good little girl and go the fuck home.

I didn't know he was hassling you. What'd he say? She sits back down on the bed beside him, barely touching his side, her body pleading all the same. Naoise, come on.

Come on, what? Come on, let's have fucking sex. He turns his head, blows smoke in her face. You're a fucking cock tease. Why are you here?

Don't talk to me like that.

Cock tease, he says again. He sucks the cigarette out, flicks it into a pint glass by the bed, full of dirty mangled butts, stands up. You think I need this? I need you, with your tiny fucking tits and stupid friends? He straddles her on the bed, takes her by the jaw and kisses her roughly, forces his tongue inside her mouth. She tries to push him off, but he shoves her back, his body heavy on top of her.

Naoise, stop, what the fuck do you th—

I'm fed up of this – he grabs her crotch – and this – he grabs her breast. He squeezes hard, and she squirms underneath him but he's too heavy, a deadweight on top of her.

Naoise, this isn't funny, she says. You're hurting me.

He doesn't let go, brings his velvet mouth to her ear. He's so strong it doesn't feel real, not possible that he could do this.

What about what you've done to me? What you're doing to me? He laughs, a language of disintegration descending from his mouth as he sneers at her, licks her neck. You want to know what your mother liked? Is that what you want?

Her hands pinned under his weight, he opens her bodysuit, one slow pop at a time.

Naoise, stop, stop, she says again. Get off me. She struggles, her hands fluttering, useless, as he pulls her underwear away, rolls himself on top, pushes himself onto her.

His fist lands against the side of her head and she stops, rigid, as his mouth, a mouth that she worshipped, is transformed into a colourless abyss of every bad thing she has ever believed about herself, ringing, rasping into her skull. She feels his weight dig into her bones, every bit of shrieking pressure, pull of that bile, takes it all into her skin, down screaming into her bones through all her cells, a bleached-out projection exposing how this is all going to end.

He is telling her she wants this.

Is telling her he's going to make her beg for it.

Telling her he's going to live inside her head and she'll always belong to him, pillowcase mouth on hers moving to hot breath at her ear. She's saturated with the demise of anything good between them, incapable of stopping everything shattering and breaking apart, preventing this forward momentum as he moves on top of her. Draws quick little breaths each time he presses and releases his torso against hers, willing all time to stop, rewind, to unmake this.

Then he calls her Nuala. Nuala ... Nuala ... Nuala again.

He crushes her, suppresses her last vain attempts to escape this, rubs himself against her, frenzied. She stops moving, frozen as he takes layer after layer of her clothes off until she is completely naked, shivering in the cold beige bedroom.

She is perfectly still. In her mind she is quiet. Willing him to stop. To survive this.

She notices how it is *so very bland*, this space. Layers of beige, magnolia, pale custard. The walls, the sheets, the wardrobe, his skin. Jaundiced layers of bland, everything blending together, suffocating her in the mediocrity of the colour. He is still half-dressed, trousers lowering with each attempt, his cock out, overcome now, overwrought with a need to humiliate her.

Each time she thinks he is going to put himself inside her, force her, he never does. He simulates sex until he comes all over her and finally, when he's done, rolls off her.

She waits, his body slowly falling into sleep. She wants to smash his chest in. In that moment she hates him, wants to hammer every bit of breath out from his chest, break apart his ribcage. She feels herself cleave apart lying beside him, waiting to feel solid enough to get dressed. Steady enough to leave, to be whole again.

She realises that she has been holding on to herself. Marks have been left. Indents in her skin where she held on so tightly, her sheer will cementing her to life, to this moment.

She stumbles from the bedroom, stark naked, bruised, clutching her clothes against her chest. Chiz stands slack-jawed, smug, watching her as she races past him toward the bathroom to clean herself off, her eyes filmy and wasted, every murmur of his gaze upon her. Her veins pump and push shock and fear around her body, rising startlingly close to the surface. Closing the bathroom door feels so good. Safe. She wipes herself down with toilet paper, what is left. Every towel she picks up stinks of men and their bodies and their rancour, their bile, their desire for what they have to possess, and she can't let anything of them touch her.

The water feels like a baptism. When she is done, she regards her pale face, swallows up part of her that he has claimed and she wonders if she will ever get that back. Realises then that he has devoured a part of her that she has no name for; it is gone and never coming back and she sobs then, for everything that is lost and the person she was and her shocking, stark, unspeakable, unexplainable lust for him and knowing that she doesn't know what to do with all of it.

She wishes her mother were alive.

Take My Name in Vain

Patsy, 1994

Patsy was waiting on her in the kitchen. His tea had gone cold thinking about what he would say to her. It was at times like this he wished her mother were here. Or some sort of mother. Margaret would have known how best to deal with this.

He'd sent PJ to Belfast with his friends. Knew the boy needed new boots. There was a fancy over-priced sports emporium. Told him they could go to the pictures after. Gave him too much money, when he thought of it now, and the boy was bound to be suspicious. Anyhow, he needed a bit of time to confront her when she got back from staying out all night. He'd rung Becca's first thing, looking to speak to her, and it was all Becca could do not to lie. Awkward silence that only meant one thing. Her mum had finally said she was very sorry but Sam wasn't there. They were both at a party but Becca had left early. It was easy enough for Patsy to figure out that Sam was somewhere she shouldn't have been last night. With someone.

When she arrived in the door, hours later, his anger had stewed, till the inside of his head was stained and the state of her tipped him easily towards a grievance. She rushed past him, her face flushed. She smelled of men. Of sex. It sickened him.

Where have you been till this time?

Not now, Da, she said, a whisper as she fled down the corridor.

Out all night, Samantha. Out. All. Night. Sit down now, I'm talking to you!

Just leave me alone, will ya?

Get back here, he bellowed after her. She didn't stop, headed straight for her room. He barged his way in. He could see she'd been crying, her slim face swollen, eyes slitted. That didn't matter. Now was the time, he told himself, to get through to her.

279

Tell me where you were!

Da. Please. Stop.

It's drugs. Is it? Is that what it is?

No. She laughed, and the sound of her mirth set off a stabbing, burning fury inside him. A sharp pain winced inside his stomach, an undigested fear coming to the surface.

The realisation he could not control her.

There's nothing funny about it. You're a child and he's a grown man. Patsy could feel himself getting wound up further, all the hurt parts of him fitting into place, justifying his rage. He could not control his own daughter.

I'm eighteen. I'm hardly a child.

What would Margaret say?

Ah, she'd probably say if you can't be good, be careful.

God forgive you.

I don't believe in God. Remember?

You're not to go back near that kip.

I'm not *doing* anything wrong. I just want to go to sleep, okay? Leamme alone. She lay down on her bed and closed her eyes. Took a deep breath.

Think you're the only wee girl he takes back to that dump? You're special, is it? He's using you.

He watched small silent tears run down the side of her face. A performance as good as any. Once started, he knew she couldn't stop. It was all too much for him, this way she had of weaselling out of his concern. Don't try the waterworks on me, girl. You're gonna get yourself in trouble. When you do, when you do—

When I do what? I'm not going to get myself in *trouble*. Wise up, Da.

Don't speak to me like that.

Like what? She sat up.

I'm your father—

Seriously, *Patsy*, wise up. You wanna have the birds and the bees talk? Now? How does it go … errr … get married … have

280

children … die alone. That's the only way. Or, what if I'm gay, or maybe PJ is? He sucks dick. Would that be worse?

Don't you talk about my son like that—

Fuck off, Da.

You're just like your mother—

Wondered when you were going to bring her into it. Well, how the fuck would I know? She left because of you.

You don't know a thing about it.

Well, tell me. Tell me!

Making a fucking show of yourself, whoring about the town—

She swung her legs off the bed, grabbed a bag from the floor, started stuffing clothes into it. Then stood up. She was close, standing poker straight, looked like she wanted to attack him as she spoke.

Yeah. I'm a slut! I fucked Naoise Devlin all over town. Fucked *him* and Joe and the twins and *all* your fucking mates, and their wives too while I'm at it. I'd let them do anything they fucking want for a few drinks. Bitta coke. As many times as they fucking like. Is that what you want to hear? What the *fuck* do you take me for?

It was like someone blew a whistle. A red flag dropped and he lunged, grabbed her, words spilling out of him. You're a disgrace. A dirty whore! Get the fuck out of my house!

He flung her flickering shape against the wall of her bedroom as hard as he could.

His daughter had felt so light as he picked her up, as he cast her aside. His violence was casual to the point of insufferable. Her tiny body hitting the wall sounded like victory one moment and despair the next when he realised what he'd done. He moved to help her up, but by then it was too late.

Get your fucking hands off me! she screamed, her voice hoarse with fear. She scrabbled for her dropped bag, raised it almost in front of her face. His only daughter looked terrified of him, all her bravado slipping away yet resurfacing momentarily as she said, Is that why Mum left? Because you knocked her about? Because you're a fucking bully? Because you're fucking boring? Because she didn't love you anymore?

Patsy stilled, caught himself on, as if he had got sight of some part of himself he kept hidden away. His legs went from under him, like a lame horse, and he found himself sunk into her bed. A choked sob came from her throat as she got up from the floor. He watched her try to put it away, cover her small mouth with her hand, as if to sever the sound. A hardness passed across her face that reminded him of her mother – resolve – as she inched past him. He took a breath, closed his eyes, tried to let the feeling pass. No, he finally said, to an empty room. No. I never touched her.

He came to in a stupor. Hours later. His denial spoken aloud, Sam gone. There was no one there to hear the truth of it but him. He went out and looked after the animals. Gave her time to cool off. Expected her to slink back in after spending the day with Becca bitching about him.

He started to worry that he had done something so bad, so very wrong, that she was not coming back. That he should have set out straightaway, that his pride was a foolish bitter thing that he was not the better for. He called Becca's house again, but no one answered. He let it ring out, tried again. He realised there was only one other place she might be. Even though it sickened him he went there, but no one came to the door.

He drove round the roads looking for her then. He wasn't used to driving at night. He wore odd-shaped glasses that he hated. The glare of the headlights reflected in them, the white light of the hi-beams making him dizzy, and he rubbed his eyes. It was the lights, the muggy air that summer held in this part of the world. It was tiredness.

He went back to that dive in town where the Devlin fella lived, parked at the top of the hill, but after watching drunk teenagers and old men he knew vaguely coming out of the pubs half-cut, he thought better of hammering the door again. The men pissed in doorways, then sidled up to the young ones outside the chipper with offers of cigarettes, sleekit banter while trying to steal chips. Acting as if they were only lads themselves.

He saw other fathers there. Men he knew he'd see at Mass tomorrow. Their own daughters not long after making holy communion, daddy's girls, their small hands reaching in prayer, small mouths presenting themselves for the body of Christ. Their fathers sitting proudly watching them from the pews, because it was still new, they were still feted. When did those girls become old enough for these same men to prowl around? When did they replace one type of brightness for another? Or was it just the way men looked at them that changed. Men that changed. Men that destroyed everything.

Finally, he drove off, his thoughts in ribbons, shifting uncontrollably inside him, a sickness. He sat in the car outside Rebecca Donnell's but couldn't bring himself to face the conversation with her parents. He sat there so long the windscreen fogged up from his breath. He wiped the screen with the forearm of his good tweed jacket, which he'd worn in case he had to go in. To make himself presentable. He thought he saw his daughter's shape in the bay-window of the living room. He desperately clawed at the handle to let air into the car, it came startling and cool towards him and he put his neck back on the headrest of the seat, drew in air, slowly steadied himself little by little, and when he was able turned the engine on and made for home.

It was late when he called Rebecca's house again, his clammy hand clutching the telephone.

Her mother answered curtly. She's here, yes, Patsy. She said you had a bit of a falling out.

He took his time to answer. Teenage drama, he said. You know yourself.

Rebecca's mother said nothing. The silence pierced him, forced him to talk, try to be good-natured. Will I come by and get her—

You know, Patsy, if it's all the same, I'll just drop her home in the morning. It's late, they're probably asleep already.

Oh. Right. Fair enough. Night, he said.

Night, she said coldly, and put the phone down first. He sat in the hall listening to the dial tone, mirroring the dead noise in his head, the sound of his failure.

PJ came in just then, all bright noise and a half-eaten box of popcorn shoved into Patsy's free arm, chatting animatedly about a trailer for a movie he hadn't seen, telling his da he had to go see it when it came out. *Speed*. About a bomb on a bus. Keanu Reeves—

Ke-an-u, what kind of name is that? Patsy said, as he hung the receiver back into the cradle. He knew PJ was covering. Probably had a drink on him, or been with a girl, but he didn't have the gumption to start a row with his son tonight. He knew he had sense. He wasn't polluted.

Ah, it looks class, PJ said, glancing at the clock.

Good, Patsy said, that's good, son. I'm away off to bed.

Sam up? PJ said.

She's at Rebecca's house, Patsy said.

He handed PJ back the popcorn and walked away, heavy-set with his sins.

You Are My Ice Cream but Fetch Felix First

Naoise, 1994

He couldn't control himself enough to make it last, make it go the way he needed to. She was gone when he woke up. He let everything come apart as he slammed his head against the wall, again and again.   Shit, shit, shit.

He felt rough.
house quiet and empty.
Eerie silence compared to the night before.

Belfast.
Met some mates.
                              Let the city   open itself up.
                    Bluffed pain. Purged feeling
Lost himself.   high, sky high.

Depraved   beauty   satisfied.
Betrayed just enough. To stop the thoughts
                              about her.   Refused her. Cuts her off.
                                        because he was afraid
                                    everything
                                        would come
                                                    tumbling
                                                    out

leaving again, couldn't be   left
all over again.
He needed her.   to
To make her stay.   survive

285

Fuck   fuck   fuck.

cracked knuckles, tender flesh. bored himself
he pushed
too far, too soon.   comeback
together   more than ever
                                more than he ever wanted

                                                    to stay.
He could wait.
He could.

She. Her. Them.   This closeness.

The heat of summer. Melting roads, tar pools.
The shine and swagger of the Twelfth. Lit with colour and
sound.

She didn't come over the next day. Or the next. She wasn't at work.

Then it was over.
She was gone.

She went away because of *him*.
Slipped herself into the mass exodus to escape from *him*.

Two whole weeks. Running into August without her.

Murph knew where.
Wouldn't tell at first.
Becca made him promise.
Murph.
Murph would give in.
Talk talk talk was all Murph wanted to do in the end. Make a
confession.

Naoise could listen, twist and release Murph, because Murph needed Naoise to love him.

Donegal.

He *borrowed* Chiz's car.

Left late at night.

Drove past the dying flames of pyres fuelled by what had been and what was yet to come.

The smell of smoke reminded him of her.

The idea that she could set fire to your heart.

That you'd let her willingly place your effigy upon her flickering need, and light up the sky with the black plumes of your love for her.

For them.

Boundaries

Sam, 1994

The rest of the summer is just more of everything and nothing, a calm body of water, the backdrop of a holiday postcard, which only becomes interesting when someone capsizes, goes under the surface, reveals the dangerous undercurrents. They all try to stay afloat, waiting for a day in August filled with brown envelopes – no one wants to go under yet. Some of Sam's friends will look back and remember every detail of the months before their lives would truly begin, and others, like Samantha, would cast aside everything in a haze, a whole summer wiped from her memory with dread and anticipation, a guillotine of a summer for Sam.

It's Becca's suggestion for Sam to join them. The row with Patsy seals the deal.

Do you want to come up to Donegal with us for a bit, Sam? Becca's mother says, casually, over breakfast the next morning. Becca would love it and so would we.

She hears Bec's mother on the phone later, polite, concise, firm. Handling her father. She wonders how she learnt that, keeps listening, trying to pick up knowledge that is just out of reach.

I'm so glad you agree, Patsy, I think a break is just what she needs, Becca's mother says. See you tomorrow morning, so she can grab some clothes.

They drive her home the next day and Patsy watches solemnly as she and Becca go into the house. She refuses to give him a second alone with her. Refuses to make it easy on him. He lingers in the hall as she rolls her eyes.

I feel kinda sorry for him, Becca says quietly. He looks upset.

It's all an act for you and your ma, Sam snaps.

Okay, Jesus, don't be such a cow.

Sorry, he's doing my head in.

You know, your da's not that bad—

I didn't mean him.

He's not gonna come looking for you.

He might.

Murph promised he wouldn't say anything, Becca says. Chiz is moving out, anyway. Belfast. Murph is bringing his stuff to his mum's this weekend. I don't know where Naoi—

Alright there, girls?

Great, thanks, Becca says, with a parent-friendly smile, while Sam keeps her head down, throwing things in her bag as Patsy lingers at the door. She won't look at him.

Right, so. Better let you get on with it, Patsy says. He closes the door ever so gently behind him.

Jesus, Sam.

What? Sam shrugs, points at a heap of clothes at the foot of the bed. Gimme that bra, will ye.

He drove around for hours looking for you the other night, Mum said.

Sam rolls her eyes again, continues packing.

He must'a felt really bad, like?

Whatever, let's go.

When they come out into the yard Patsy is stooped over, listening to Becca's mum. The adults stop talking abruptly and smile far too widely at the girls.

Becca's going to drive us all the way to Donegal, did I tell you that, Patsy? Becca's mum says. Passed her test first go!

What! Oh my god, Mum? Really? Becca is practically jumping up and down with excitement. Becca's mum gets out and Becca throws her arms around her, grabs the keys, and gets into the tiny bright red Ford Fiesta, moving her seat to find the most comfortable position.

Sam can see it's killing Patsy not to say something, some smart-alec comment brewing on his lips. He just folds his arms across his body, turns the corners of his mouth up weakly.

Sam didn't even know Becca was sitting her test. She was just as surprised as Becca when they saw the car with a huge white bow on it that morning. Left outside in the drive, by Becca's dad, an early eighteenth birthday present. Loud showy love on display makes Sam uneasy, but Becca positively basks in it.

Are you sure it's no trouble now?

None at all, Patsy. Sure, Sam's no trouble.

That's a fine motor you have there, Rebecca, Patsy says, changing the subject, patting the car with care.

Thanks, Mr Malin, Becca says, beaming. Sam slinks past her da and into the back seat before he gets the chance to mess up saying goodbye. She shoves the small bag in beside her. Clicks the belt in as Becca's mum gets in the front.

Behave yourself, won't ye, Samantha? Patsy says, leaning in the window, his words tailing off at the stoic faces of Sam and Becca's mother, Becca too engaged with her hands set at ten and two to notice.

Bye, Sam. Drive safe, Rebecca! he shouts, as he turns back to the house. Sam knows he'll be watching from the window, critiquing every move, but Becca breathes a sigh of relief, thinking she's escaped an audience.

Oh my god, Mum, I'm gonna run over a chicken.

Start the car, Becca, her mum says reassuringly.

Sam chimes in. They'll move once you start the car, Becca.

Becca turns on the engine and gently edges forward, the chickens play chicken, meandering in and out.

Mum! Becca squeals.

Becca, if you run one over, my da will just have it for tea anyway. Stop worrying. Becca's mum laughs and so does Becca. The pride on Becca's face reflected in the rear-view mirror as she finally swings the car out of the yard and onto the road.

Becca said you visited Donegal before.

When I was a kid, yeah. Once or twice. I was really little so I don't remember much.

Can't believe you girls are going off to college in a few months. Breaking my heart.

I'm only going up the road. I'll be back every weekend so you can do my washing, like Lucy's.

Eyes on the road. Eh, I don't think so, young lady. Becca's mother turns around to talk to Sam. Becca tells me you are thinking of going to Trinity or Bristol?

I applied, yeah, but I don't know. Sam shifts at the question.

What course?

Arts. Geography and English. If I get the points.

God, I loved university. I did law, like Becca. Best three years of your life, girls.

The conversation goes back and forth like that over the days that follow, Becca's mum gently ribbing her daughter about some little thing, chatting about the items Becca needs for college, duvets and covers, good winter coat, laundry bag. Normal mother/daughter conversations that Sam didn't know how to be part of.

Becca's parents seem to worship her. It isn't just the money, it is the trust, the faith they have in her, and she repays that trust, every single bit of it, by just being herself. They love Becca for who she is. That's the bit Sam covets most. They share that love around too – they make Sam light up inside when they talk about what she might do. Becca's dad says, Now Becca has the car, she can visit Sam whenever she wants.

Sam knows she'll never have what Becca has. Nothing that will happen in the future can insulate her from this life she's grown up with. The lack of care. She'll be trying to fix the imbalance for the rest of her life.

Partition

Sam, 1994

Sam tags along in Donegal, eats flake-topped pokes on long, sun-soaked beaches, as that stretch of the Atlantic coast pretends to be the Mediterranean – until they get out of the car and the wind blows their heads off. It's proper sunny, though, spotlight on them all and their little escape to softer accents and southern ways. A family holiday. She's never had a proper one of them, not that she can remember.

She hasn't explained to Becca what happened. She just tells her it is over. She has ended things and there is no going back this time.

A few days later she asks Becca can she have some time to herself, says it's to think about college. Becca's dad practically shoves the family in the car to go to Portsalon for some 'quality' time. An hour after they leave, she buys the cheapest pregnancy test in Letterkenny, despite the stares from the tight-faced woman in the chemist. The two minutes she waits in the pub toilets for the result are the longest of her life so far. She sobs afterwards; it's a waste of money for one thing, and he hadn't actually, he hadn't, he didn't.

She's so fucking stupid.

She cuts the words out of her head, promises herself it won't happen again. That is enough for now. All she can cope with. The memory of it put away, buried. She'll come back to it once a year, yank the images out, crush the flowery parts of the memory of him, hoping that eventually, all the good, all the bad, his body, his face, his voice, will decay and degrade and she'll be so good at forgetting, she will not know whether it was true or not.

She sits on the beach for hours afterwards, drinks some cheap cider, the good southern kind. Gets blocked enough to ring home from the phone box that smells vaguely of piss and weirdly of vinegar. Piss 'n' chips. She laughs at her own stupid joke, holds her nose.

PJ answers straight away, tells her her da is in a heap. When you coming home? he asks.

Does anyone care? she says, laughs, and hangs up.

It's Becca's eighteenth birthday the next morning. Sam lingers in bed, trying to give them space. Listens to Becca chatting to Lucy, who has rung from Greece to wish her a happy birthday. Later Becca drags her downstairs and Sam gives her black rosary beads and a tiny day-glo Virgin Mary for her car mirror, plus some Clinique blusher she nicked from the chemist, because it cost a fortune, and because the woman had been a right judgey cow when she bought the pregnancy test. If Becca knows it's nicked she doesn't seem to mind.

They celebrate Becca's birthday with a dinner with her parents. The restaurant owner greets Becca's da like a long-lost friend, slaps his back, leads them to the best table in the place, sends over pre-dinner drinks. Becca's parents get slightly jarred and indulge the girls with 'one' glass of fizz after their paltry vegetarian dinners – basically just veggie plates with the steak removed. A huge black forest gateau comes out, candle-laden, held high above diners' heads, the whole restaurant seems to be smiling, singing 'Happy Birthday', voices rising with memories of what it was to be young. Sam enjoys the glow of being included, being looked at with warmth, a bought joy but joy nonetheless, a family swell of happiness that wraps her up in its generous gaze.

Afterwards Becca takes Sam to the local disco, a once-weekly event that happens in the sort of huge country hotel bar which only exists in beach locations with massive car parks. During the day it is full of families, sea-swept and starving, but after a certain time they clear tables back and people arrive in droves to the only decent nightclub around. Becca flaunts her ID in the pub, not that she's ever needed it before, ordering vodka lime and tonics and pints for her cousins, flush with birthday money.

At midnight they are outside the disco talking to a group of Donegal lads for a while, that song by Yazz blaring out from the fogged-up windows above. The place is jammers. Becca and Sam wear paisley-patterned playsuits and tiny, silly cardigans. They look like twins. Sam wobbles in a pair of heels she borrowed from Becca as she tries to look vaguely cool while mildly flirting with a tall guy called Adam who turns out to be English. He's visiting family. His ma's from Derry. Studying Classics – whatever the fuck that is – at Bristol. He looks like a swimmer, his waist compact, shoulders fanning out to a V shape, but he's actually a rower.

He laughs when Sam says, Like, rowing what, boats?

Yes, boats. *Row* boats. He has a way about him that translates into easy conversation. He doesn't smoke. Listens. Tells her she is the perfect size for a cox, that he has a feeling she'd quite like to sit at the top of a boat and shout instructions to eight young men.

Adam's a mind reader. Watch this one, Becca, Sam quips.

She can tell he likes quick girls, bright minds and faces. He sets off something in her and she wants to impress him. They talk about books. It seems like everyone else falls away, the two of them sitting on the wobbly, damp picnic table, chatting. He excuses himself to go to the loo. She smokes and looks up at the dark sky. Music floats out from the bar. She watches as the few randomers link arms and try to Riverdance across the car park, legs flying, slipping into a parody jig, wheezing and laughing as they simultaneously mock and worship their homeland.

All alone waiting on me.

His voice knocks her out of her reverie. Naoise emerges out of the darkness. She can tell he is wired.

What are you doing h—? You shouldn't have come. How'd you even find me?

Chiz lent me his car.

Oh, you *borrowed* it, did you?

What a welcome. Almost think you didn't want to see me.

Fucksake, Naoise. I'm staying with Becca's parents.

Adam approaches then. Sits down beside her and hands her a drink. She sees Naoise bite the inside of his cheek, notes his disbelief.

Adam, Naoise. Naoise, Adam, Sam says.

Hallo, Adam says.

I need to talk to you, Naoise says, ignoring Adam. Alone.

I don't wanna talk to you. It's Becca's birthday and we're all going—

I don't give a shit if it's Becca's birthday, Sam. I drove all the way up here to see you.

So what? I didn't know you were coming. She is bold. Buoyed by freedom and Adam, his tall frame sheltering her.

Everything alright? Adam asks Sam.

I'm her boyfriend, Naoise says to him.

I thought you might have been her father, Adam says, deadpan.

Sam spits her drink out, laughing, high and free. Naoise grabs Adam, so fast it happens before the glasses shatter on the ground. Punching and kicking. Sam is on top of Naoise, screaming for help. Becca arrives and moments later others, her lardy cousins, some Riverdancers, pulling them apart like meat from a bone, trails of blood on their hands. Adam emerges with a swollen eye that will go black.

What the fuck is your problem, mate? Adam says.

My problem. You're all gonna let some English fella stand here and start on me? Naoise says, breathing ragged. He wipes his mouth. He has a bulging cut above his eye, blood weeping from it. The men hold him back.

You should go, Becca says. You're barred now, anyway. She nods her head at Adam. His uncle's the owner.

Fine. I will. When she comes with me.

She's not going anywhere with you, Becca says.

Are you okay? Sam whispers to Adam, touching his face as Naoise watches.

I will be, he says.

Just go home, Naoise, Sam says.

Go home. Who the fuck are you to tell me to go home? He shoots out the words at her.

C'mon, totally not worth it, Becca says, taking Sam's arm as they walk away from the fracas, back to the fire-door entrance of the nightclub. Adam joins them, takes Sam's other arm.

I'll see *you* later, Naoise shouts to Sam's back. You can count on that.

Sam turns to look. The mock Riverdancers are still holding Naoise, and she sees them get a few digs in before they let him go, shove him across the car park, towards the darkness. They call him scum, laugh as he staggers off into the night, and she feels bad, for him, and just for the briefest moment, she is torn; and in the next, she recognises she is blushing as Adam catches her, weirdly embarrassed for herself, for the fact that she had ever been with Naoise, that Adam saw her react like that.

She watches Naoise cross the car park, in and out of pools of light, imagines their shadows touching even if their bodies do not.

She is very very drunk when she wanders out later for a cigarette, wobbling until she leans up against the side of the building, the badly applied spiky whitewash nibbling against her skin through the cheap material of her flimsy clothes. No matter what way she positions herself, it seems to bite. One of the dancing fellas from earlier, the youngest of them, saunters over.

Got a light? he says.

She smiles. Sure. He has to hold her hand steady as she keeps missing the rollie dangling from his mouth. He smells of beer and cheap tobacco.

Sooryy, she says. I'm a bit pissed.

So who was that eejit earlier?

Ah, no one.

You a bitta a heartbreaker, are ye?

Er ... no. Nope.

Ach, I think you are? he says, still smiling. Sam notices he is leaning very close to her, his overworked arm tight against the building, his freckly farmer's tan lurid from the glow of the overhead lamps. The smell of Lynx radiating off him makes her feel like boaking; he's too close to her to be comfortable. She hears the music change inside, wind down for the slow set. She begins drunkenly humming softly along to The Cranberries, 'Linger', unable to help herself. He joins in. He waltzes out in front of her, takes a formal dance posture and beckons her out from the wall. She is laughing, shaking her head no, but gives in and joins him as he leads her in an old-time slow-dancey waltz at the chorus, like something her da would do at weddings if he were a man who liked dancing.

She notices this side of the car park is poorly lit, empty. She'd gone around to the back of the hotel to let the sea breeze work its cool magic, to get some space, clear her head. She is still giggling when they land back against the wall. He offers her a rollie.

No, thanks, I'm good, she declines, taking a cigarette from her own pack. She watches him make the rollie as she catches her breath. She lights it for him, then her own. They smoke for a few minutes in silence. He finishes his smoke quickly, the opaque paper burning down fast, the tip glowing amber.

Shit, I should go back in, she says.

She drops her half-smoked fag to the ground, stamps on it, but before she can move away he has his free arm around her waist, his mouth on hers. It happens so fast it overtakes her; she tries to pull away but he has her up against the wall, his hand groping her breast, the other reaching lower. She twists away from his grasp, but it's too late, his large body heavy on hers, the crust of the pebbledash throbbing through her skin, hot panic, then just as quickly he's gone, lifted off her, his hands reaching, desperate to hold on to her. She is off running, glances back, sees a dark figure knocking him to the ground, kicking him, dancing boy's yelps echoing as she scrambles up the sea grass-covered dunes and escapes onto the beach.

She abandons her shoes and skids, stumbling, down the sand bank. Wants to scream. She goes to the water's edge and steps in. It is cold enough to steady her, shock her into movement again, and she walks up the beach through the shallow water. She is shaken but the cold anchors her, so she stops, turns to go back, but pauses as she spots the outline of a person set against the sky, watching her.

Naoise.

It must have been him dragged that fella off her. He saunters down the path towards her and comes to a standstill on the sand. She starts to walk again, wades through the shallow water, putting distance between them. He follows her along the shore.

Sam. C'mere, he calls across the water to her.

When she hesitates, he turns and leaves her in the shallows, striking out towards the dune system, away from the wind's reach. He sits, quiet. Waiting. There is no one else around.

When she arrives she realises she must look wild, gathers her wind-blown hair at the nape of her neck in one hand, looks down at the wet sand freckled against her feet and ankles.

You alright? he asks.

She nods her head, a blurry yes.

You sure? he says. Sit down.

She pushes her hair out of her eyes then kneels down.

They sit in silence for what seems the longest time.

She feels him want to reach for her so badly, need radiating off him like sunburn.

Eventually he simply reaches out his hand to her and like clockwork, without even meaning to, she takes it. He pulls her down onto the sand beside him. Cups her face in his hands. Sam breathes heavily; even now, when she wants to run, she wants to stay, she wants things to be different between them. She wants him to look at her that way. Ashamed she feels anything for him at all. She wants to erase what happened, what he did to her, from her memory.

I love you, Naoise says.

They are still on the sand as he says this, grains shifting as he moves against her, his fingers pushing into her skin, intimate space between them closing.

He goes to kiss her but she rocks back, sand falling from her clothes and skin, moves away.

No, she blurts out.

No?

I can't. Do this. I don't know why you came up.

I'm here, aren't I?

It doesn't matter. We're done.

So that's it.

It is. Yeah. It's over.

You'll be begging me to take you back in a few weeks.

In a few weeks I'll be gone.

I can wait.

I'm not coming back.

Right. Trinity. He sneers. With all the posh gits.

It's not like that. I don't care where I go. As long as I go the *fuck* away from here.

You don't *get* to leave me behind. You don't get to stop this, he says. I'm in there. His finger stabbing her forehead, her chest bone. The jabbing of his fingers sets off a panic in her, an alarm that takes a moment to register. The need to run comes over her.

She holds her hands together tightly in front of her chest, shielding herself from him, from her memories.

She pushes herself up.

She is standing above him, brushing sand off her clothes. He's squinting up at her, the silver light picking out tiny wrinkles at the corners of his eyes. Dried blood smeared across his swollen eye. His face blotchy from too many drugs. She sees him in a way she has not before. Amazes herself, the way you can *see* someone, the change happening in her, the change in how she is seeing him, choosing to see herself, imperfect as she is. She feels herself letting go of him, a severing despite all the fear. Angry.

It's too late.

She watches him bury his face in his hands, battling to keep himself under control. As he stands up she can smell hurt on him.

We're done, Naoise.

He laughs loudly at her, and for a split second she feels like the stupid little girl she was when she first met him.

She isn't that girl, though, she's shifting into something else.

You're serious, he says, shaking off the laughter like a slap.

I am. Her words come out soft, quiet, trying to stifle the shake in her voice. She looks away.

It's about your ma, right? That fucking woman. Poisons everything.

She turns back to him. She has tears in her eyes. She is not crying for him. Some part of her knows Naoise is still the most beautiful creature she's ever seen, but he's ugly too, the ugliest person she's ever known and she can't let it go, what he's done to her. What he'd been to her mother. That was his fault. *Her* fault. Everything always came back to her. A woman she barely knew.

She walks away from him but he follows her, grabs her shoulder, turns her around.

What do you want me to say? You want me to admit it. Is that what you want? She can hear it now, something akin to pleading in his voice.

You want the truth? I love you. *You*, Sam. I love you.

Love me? You don't love me. You loved *her*. Maybe you still do. She wills herself to move away, to push through this numbness, but he catches her arm, traps her and she screams, This is *fucked up. We* are fucked up.

He grabs her face, makes her look at him. Soberness descends as her fear comes back, she can't control it. Can't move now, is stuck, every limb inert. She wants to be sick.

He is calm, takes a breath, draws himself up. I fucked your mother and you were there – watching us.

Tears roll down her face. Naoise is unrepentant.

I fucked her all the time before she left—

Fuck you! She screams out the words, pushes his hands off her face. You fucking prick! I fucking hate you! I hate her! She trembles as she finishes. He lets go of her.

We're sick, Naoise. She is sobbing now, takes a step back. This is wrong. We're disgusting. I can feel her when I touch you. Every time you touch me. You've taken everything from me, even her.

Everything from you? He comes back, consumes all the space between them, closes in on her again. Everything from you! Poor fucking Sam. Poor motherless fuck. And me? What about me? You have no fucking idea. No fucking clue what she—you think I wanted to feel like this? Is that what you fucking think? She realises he is holding on to her still. You are just like her, you know that? You wanted this.

I don't. Sam spat the words out. I don't love you. I don't think I ever did.

He instantly pushes his mouth against hers, tears at her clothes as she fights him. He is trying to kiss her as she struggles. He pulls back to look at her.

You don't get to fucking choose. He has her hair tight in his hand as he holds her head in place and forces his mouth against her again.

Sam is fighting him. Her hands scrabbling with his. You know. What you did. You know. Say you're sorry for what you did to me, she says, spit from her words landing on his face. Her voice shakes but she forces the words out. Say you're fucking sorry. I can't fix you. I'm not her.

He looks wild, ugly, hurt. Her face is wet with tears.

Naoise, I'm not her.

She is still shaking and her anger has morphed into fear. He might really hurt her; her rage has misjudged itself; she has been too honest; he is stronger than she is; there is no one around. She is just a girl and bad things happen to girls all the time and they become figures and facts and headlines. They become the past. They aren't people anymore, they aren't girls or women, no one knows the colour of their eyes or how they laughed, the idiosyncratic things that made them different to everyone else; they are hushed-over conversations, cautionary fairy tales and, eventually, they become nothing at all.

She feels his hands drop away from the nape of her neck, hair limp against her scalp.

Go, Sam, he says, and pushes her away. Leave.

She stumbles, moves, shocked. Inches away. She tries not to think that he might grab her, hurt her again, so she can keep moving; she is afraid she will not be able to go on, to get away, but he stays put, his arms hanging low against his frame, the wind dying down, a silent sudden calm descending as she finally turns away from him. Runs.

She can hear him calling her name over and over, getting lost in the wind that rises again. Then a faint call that sounds like Becca, casting out her name, Sam! Sam! Searching for her. Perhaps she just needs to pretend someone else is out there waiting on her, pleading with her to create a vast divide between them, between him and her, between what she needs and what she thinks she wants.

She races unsteadily towards the sound of other people. The lights in the distance. Forces her body to move, the sea grass lancing her skin, the sharp pain splicing with the quiet torment raging in her head.

She forces herself to keep going. Can't turn around. Everything telling her to run, every cell, until she can't hear him anymore, not looking back, just moving forward.

She's winded from running when she sees Becca, Adam a step behind, and she stops dead and lets them come to her.

Becca hugs her tight when she reaches her.

Jesus, you okay?

I'm fine, let's go, Sam says.

I had the whole place looking for you – well, the cousins, Becca says. Someone bate the head of that fella who was doing Riverdance earlier. The guards are here and St John's Ambulance. Where are your shoes? Becca asks.

They look down at her sandy feet, legs pink with cold.

I don't know, Sam says, shivering. I'm sorry.

Don't worry, just a cheap pair. I've loads at home, we'll find them tomorrow. Becca puts her cardigan around Sam's shoulders and wipes her face on the sleeve. They link arms. Adam walks quietly on the other side of Sam, sheltering her a little more from the wind. It's well past closing time and the nightclub is shut when they arrive back. Everyone is hanging around outside, waiting for lifts or snogging someone. Becca and Adam sweet-talk his uncle into letting them back into the downstairs bar and Becca takes Sam to the bathroom to get her cleaned up. Becca sits on the toilet peeing, listens as Sam relays almost everything that happened. Some things Sam will never talk about. Adam is there outside, chatting to one of Becca's pudgy cousins who hasn't pulled, waiting on them, his eye swollen tie-dye.

My mum's going to have a right go at me, Adam says sheepishly, as they wait for a taxi.

Sam keeps looking out to the horizon as they talk, expecting to see Naoise. She's relieved when the taxi drives away, for its warmth and the incessant chatter from the driver. Happens every year around this time, he tells them. Northerners can't keep their powder dry. Becca rolls her eyes as Adam laughs at the driver's refusal to understand a word he is saying. Sam snuggles into Becca's shoulder, rests her head and closes her eyes.

They drop Adam off first. Sam dozes in the back seat, wakes abruptly with Becca tugging on her arm to get out of the car. Becca wants to talk all night, but Sam can't keep her eyes open. She sleeps late the next day, remains uneasy, but no one comes looking for her.

In the afternoon they drive past the big hotel and onto the beach car park. Becca lets Sam practise driving, banging the dash every few minutes for emergency stops, leaving them both in hungover hysterics. They stay giddy while they look unsuccessfully for Sam's shoes, chat about results and boys and bands, even Adam, everything except *him*. That part of her life is over.

Corcule

Naoise, 1993

The kind of girl. He can't help notice. Only her. The wind forces her up into the air. Crow-black hair opening up like wings. She doesn't fight the rush of air that transports her, lets herself be lifted, welcomes it. He notes that. Everyone's bags empty across the road. He watches the crowd pay silent, solid attention to her. Not reaching for a thing. Letting books and cigarettes fly into the street, towards traffic. A hard pressure grows in his chest that he tries to ignore. Tries not to claim this. She *notices* him. Sees him. Recognises something. He knows she will be trouble, she will be hard, not easy, she is the echo of the drumming in his chest but he doesn't care. He wants her, that's what he pays attention to.

That kind of girl.

Gathers himself quickly, afraid someone might have seen this little blip in control. There is something in her face, the way she looks, like he feels he knows her. He's been away for a long time and a lot has changed. Hasn't ventured back there yet. Avoids the headland. All the places they used to go. Her tiny part of the world. Afraid of what that place might do to him again. The power of it. Even after all this time. Hates signing on. Having to live in a shithole. The life he fell into. The life *she* pushed him into. A future surges ahead of him like oncoming traffic, while he is stuck there, waiting for something to change.

When it is safe, after a while, he asks who she is.

I think the girls have got better looking in that school since I've been gone, Murph.

That's Sam, Samantha Malin. Chiz interrupts, lets this statement hang there. You know, Nuala Mal—

He interrupts Chiz then, brusquely sweeps the words away. I know who she was, yeah. Shit, that's her kid? Wow, she's the spit of her ma, isn't she?

He's not surprised when Chiz clams shut in front of him. Registers his pal is already remembering too much; all the long-dead rumours surface, and Chiz can't meet his stare. Naoise gets up to leave.

Where we heading? Murph asks.

Solo run, mate. Naoise smiles, pushes Murph's shoulder down. He might as well say *Stay*, because Murph is dog-bred obedient.

Knock yourself out, *mate*, Chiz shouts after him.

Fuck off, Chiz, he snaps back.

He follows the girl, Sam, at a distance, knows better than to crowd her out.

Fionnuala. Nuala Malin. Her name echoes inside his head. He sees her heart-shaped face made for love.

Samantha. Sam Malin. The same heart-shaped face. A quickening, a procession of hurt releases itself, draws the numbness away, matches the past and present together.

The girl glances back, barely a head turn.

And everything he has put in place willingly falls apart.

Mirror, Mirror, On the Wall,
Who is the Fairest of Them All?

Nuala, 1982

There is no spindle of love to tie me to this life.
I float away and dissolve.

There are no ways to say:

I didn't mean it

I'm coming back

I miss you   because it's too late

I wondered what we were made of and what traces of us were left
when we go.

I wondered would the universe notice if I disappeared, would
the sky crack open and cry out?
No.   Not in the dark heat, red dirt of here.
Nothing notices.
You are here and you are gone.
No matter what they say. No matter what they promise.

I *miss* you. The scent of you. Meadowsweet and perfect.

It's too late. To miss you.

Wait. Before it's too late. For me. Before it's far too late.

                              your fingers in mine
                    tactile comfort in saying goodbye
                        i've forsaken that for freedom

                    hold my hand and don't let go.

You have always been free. You have always mattered. You are
enough and you are nothing all at once. I miss me already. Isn't it
strange? Now that I am no longer. I am not.

You are still everything.
Always everything to me.

                                            But I couldn't stay.

Brown Envelopes

Sam, 1994

It is after sundown when Sam arrives home. She asks Becca to drop her at the top of the road. She hauls her bag over her shoulder, crossing the straps over her chest as she walks, then lights a cigarette, lets it catch, takes a long drag. There is the swathe of August heat, a ripe honeyed smell from the scent of cut fields that sit on either side of the lane full of golden stubble that hasn't been turned yet. The night air is as warm as it ever gets there. Harvest. It makes her feel contentedly giddy.

She hears him before she sees him. His sturdy, sure walk to meet her. She thinks about stubbing out the cigarette but decides, Fuck it.

Well, Patsy says, as he gets close enough for her to make out his features, cap on his head, that heavy tweed article that stayed there in all weathers, more Patsy than anything else about him. Him and that damn cap. The midges fly around his head; he takes the cap off and swats at them. How was it?

Sam is expecting a telling off, about smoking or the late hour, or any random thing he could find to give out to her about. She stays quiet in surprise more than anything else.

Cat got your tongue?

Sam haws, nearly chokes on her smoke.

Had a good time, yeah. Where's PJ?

Ah, he's … says he's away out to the pictures. But I think there's a girl. Some girl. There's the tea in the pot, he says as they cross the yard and he opens the back door.

I'm gonna have another smoke, Da, she says, waiting for the change to come.

Patsy sniffs, rubs his nose and goes inside.

Sam shrugs the bag off her shoulders, lights up another fag. Lets out a breath. Patsy appears a few minutes later with two mugs of tea in one hand and a saucer in the other. It's chipped and faded. Sam worries the thin, broken edge with her thumb, puts it down gently on top of her bag as she takes her cup from Patsy.

It takes a while but when she realises Patsy isn't going back in she sucks her smoke down in three sharp breaths, then stubs the butt onto the broken saucer.

He wrinkles his nose at the smell of nicotine in the air but the expected tuts don't materialise. She wonders how he manages it. His face doesn't betray an ounce of judgement, so she closes her fingers around the mug like she is praying to something. He made the tea dark and hot with two sugars. A drop of milk.

They stay outside, leaning against the wall. Sipping tea. Breathing awkward silences. Not talking, just settling in. Sighing. Coming to some sort of agreement. There is barely a breath of wind, stars at peace in the sky as she and her da stand in the dark till the chill of it threatens their bones. His old frame gives way first.

D'you not feel the cold? Patsy asks her.

Naw, I'm hot blooded.

You get that from your mother.

Neither of them say anything and it seems like an age as he hesitates, scratches his head. Night, pet, he says. Lock up. And he turns in.

Afterwards she washes up the saucer, trying to get the black mark out of it, rubbing the yellowish stain of nicotine till the water runs cold.

The next morning he offers to drive her up to school and she agrees as long as he doesn't come in. He has moved all the crap off the front seat, thrown it in the back, so she sits beside him.

Put on something, he says after a while, and she idly searches through the radio stations, pauses the dial on Radio Ulster but he says, Ah, no news the day, so she pulls a tape from her bag and puts it on. Tori Amos. 'Baker Baker' plays.

Not a bad singer, that one, Patsy says after the song finishes, and she laughs. She rolls down the window, leans out and they listen to her type of music all the way there.

Becca is already at the school, noticeably in a full face of make-up. Hurry the fuck up, Malin! she squeals from the top step.

Sam knows that all this time, Becca has been waiting for her to catch up and finally, when it matters most, she does. She does it for herself. Does it for Becca. So they can go on together.

Standing in the foyer of the school, Sam watches Becca get ready to accept her achievements, with no shade of doubt that she deserves top marks, perfect results. Sam studies her friend's face in the moment before they rip the envelope open and knows that, good or bad, everything will be different after. Everything will change. Change is all that Becca wanted for Sam.

Thought you weren't gonna turn up! Becca says smiling. Wanna get this over with?

Sam knows Becca will be fine – three A's, Law at Queen's – but all she wants for herself is to just get enough to leave this place and go as far away as possible.

Sam takes a deep breath, sighs. Becca hugs her.

It's alright, Sam. Whatever happens, it'll be alright. You ready?

Never.

Acknowledgements

Thank you for reading my book. So many people helped me get here. Thanks to: Becky Walsh, my editor. Graceful, funny, patient; you made this process an utter joy. Sara Marafini, for my gorgeous cover. My ace publicity team, Yassine Belkacemi, Charlotte Hutchinson and Elaine Egan. Eagle-eyed Belinda Jones and Howard Davies. Everyone at John Murray and Hachette that made my book happen.

My agent, Brian Langan, unfailingly kind and wise. You have made me a better writer.

Louise Farr, my literary sister, be lost without you. Michelle Walshe, the first conversation on the steps of the IWC, all the conversations since, journeys in the magic car. Anne O'Leary, our Cork Sundays, late night DMs and best writing advice.

Chekhov or Fuck off: Sheila, Elaine, Louise, Cassia, Katie and the two Stephens. Youse made me a better writer. Nothing would have happened without COFO's excellent feedback. Here's to embarrassing sentences and eventually ordering more than water in The Central Hotel.

I was very fortunate to find the *Stinging Fly* fiction course run by Declan Meade and Sean O'Reilly. Thank you for having faith in me when I did not.

The Irish Writers Centre provides essential access, opportunities and community. Deep gratitude to the IWC team, past and present, especially Valerie, Teerth, Betty, Hilary, Jess, Laura, Orla, Cassia, Mary and Paul. IWC Novel Fair 2020 changed my life. Thanks to the judges, Kevin Curran, Anthony Galvin and Niamh Boyce. Michelle Gallen, Sue Divin and Fiona O'Rourke for advice. The IWC Evolution Programme and participants. The warm welcome from NUIG during my semester as a teaching intern, from my students, fellow writers Melatu Uche Okorie and Liz Quirke, and Dr John Kenny and Mike McCormack. Huge thanks to Marian Keyes and the Arts Council for funding this internship.

During uncertain times funding is essential. Deep thanks for my Literature Bursary from the Arts Council of Ireland, so grateful to Sarah Bannan and her team. And likewise to the Arts Council of Northern Ireland, and Damian Smyth in particular, for my Individual Artists Award.

Thank you Jenny Sherwin and Wicklow County Council Arts Office, for support, funding and innovation. Arts Organisations are great, introduce yourself.

Tyrone Guthrie Centre is an artist's paradise. To director Eimear O'Connor, Mary, Ingrid, Martina, all the kitchen ladies, a heartfelt thank you. IWC and Noelle Campbell-Sharpe for Cill Rialaig Residency; the Cill Rialaig Seven – pure dotes. The John Hewitt Society Summer School. Peter Heathwood, CANI Digital Archive. Paul Maddern, The River Mill. Half Door Writers' Retreat. University of Limerick Creative Writing Winter School and the amazing Sarah Moore Fitzgerald, Eoin Devereux and the entire team. Alan Berrigan from Mactivate who literally saved this novel. BACK UP YOUR WORK.

My extraordinary mentors: Niamh Boyce, Words Ireland National Mentoring Programme; Danielle McLaughlin and Madeline D'Arcy Lane, Fiction at the Friary; Kit de Waal, Arts Council Professional Development Bursary.

Anja, Camilla and Matilde. Carole, Kelly, Allian, Caren, Suzi, Megan and Liz. Pat and Gill, Steve and Grainne. Misfit Pop-Up Gin Club. Poets; Emily, Nidhi, Mícheál. The almighty Dooligans. SMF Online Book Club. Susan Coughlan and Artist Connect Panel. Jan Carson, best literary auntie ever! Charlene Hurtubise; world needs your words. Greystones Library staff, especially Margaritte. Lauren (Uno Mas), Fíona S (flowers). Jane Francis. Forest Mums. Mary Fahy Bowes. GCNS. Debut 2022 Group. You kept me going.

To my lovely Dad, who never knew I would get published. We miss you. My mum, brothers and their wives. My niece Manu – a shining light, *obrigadíssima*! Much love to you all.

To my beautiful boys, Milo and Stellan. The best of me. And the worst. (Sorry about that). I love you the most. I love you forever. I'll love you when there are no words, no language, when I am dust.

To Brian, who never remembers anything but the good stuff. You inspire me every day. Love you. Here's to the good stuff always. x

Over three and a half thousand people died as a result of The Troubles. So many people still suffer from the loss of loved ones – like the families in Loughinisland. We owe them a huge debt and the very least they deserve is the truth.

I didn't grow up in a house full of books, but now writing is my great joy, obsession, terror. For everyone making art and to everyone who consumes it, supports the makers in emotional, practical, financial and other magical ways, thank you, for living, believing, and sustaining creative lives.